the Celebutantes

TO THE PENTHOUSE

ALSO BY ANTONIO PAGLIARULO

A Different Kind of Heat

The Celebutantes: On the Avenue

The Celebutantes: In the Club

Antonio Pagliarulo

the *Celebutantes*

TO THE PENTHOUSE

Delacorte Press

Published by Delacorte Press
an imprint of Random House Children's Books
a division of Random House, Inc.
New York

www.randomhouse.com/teens

Educators and librarians, for a variety of teaching tools, visit us at
www.randomhouse.com/teachers

Library of Congress Cataloging-in-Publication Data
Pagliarulo, Antonio.
The celebutantes : to the penthouse / Antonio Pagliarulo. — 1st ed.
p.   cm.
Summary: Unless wealthy teenage triplets Madison, Park, and Lexington Hamilton
solve the murder of a promising young sculptor during an Ambassadors for the Arts
Luncheon at the Waldorf-Astoria Hotel, their dear friend, Coco McCaid, may go to jail.
ISBN: 978-0-385-73474-5 (trade)
ISBN: 978-0-385-90473-5 (Gibraltar lib. bdg.)
[1. Murder—Fiction. 2. Wealth—Fiction. 3. Triplets—Fiction. 4. Sisters—Fiction. 5. New
York (N.Y.)—Fiction. 6. Mystery and detective stories.] I. Title.
PZ7.P148Cep 2008
[Fic]—dc22   2007043038

The text of this book is set in 12-point Filosofia.

Book design by Angela Carlino

Printed in the United States of America

10 9 8 7 6 5 4 3 2 1

First Edition

For Krista Marino,
Editor Extraordinaire

FOR IMMEDIATE RELEASE
TO: The Editors, *Social Scene* magazine
FROM: Park Hamilton (and on behalf of my sisters,
        Madison and Lexington)
RE: Jealousy, Lies . . . and a little bit of Truth

As you may (or may *not*) know, growing up in front of the world isn't easy. From being secretly photographed in the dressing rooms at Bergdorf Goodman—thank God I wasn't trying on anything sheer—to fending off reporters by the hundreds, my sisters and I have dealt with it all. We travel daily through the spotlight's dark underbelly and are usually prepared for whatever unpleasant surprises await us. But *nothing* is more irritating than opening up a magazine and reading outright and outlandish lies.

The first fib from your silly gossip column: "Now that celebutante Park Hamilton has made the jump into acting, she'll be able to keep an even closer eye on her man, top Hollywood stud Jeremy Bleu. Several sources working on the set of the big-budget action flick *Short Fuse* tell us that Park took the major role just so she could make certain bad boy Bleu doesn't end up in the cheaters' red zone."

This has to be the tackiest piece of slop ever written about me. Take note: I am not, nor will I ever be, one of those brainless, boy-obsessed girls who need a guy by their side in order to feel complete.

I'm too smart for that. Anyone who thinks I would sustain sixteen-hour days on a movie set just to keep my boyfriend on a leash is sorely mistaken. Acting is in my blood. Remember that gorgeous, incredibly talented woman who won an Oscar, a Tony, an Emmy, and a Golden Globe in the same year? My mother, thank you very much. And I just may follow in her footsteps.

The second lie: "Party princess Lexington Hamilton can get wilder than ever now that her fashion line, Triple Threat, has raked in an additional hundred million dollars for Daddy's empire. Rumor has it that Lex spent the past month jetting from New York to Capri and Paris to Prague with an extensive entourage on the Hamilton private jet. Do nightclubs and champagne inspire the young designer a little too much?"

My sister Lexington might love a party, but she's really only celebrating her success. One hundred million dollars is a good start. That whole business about our private jet crisscrossing the skies just for fun? Ridiculous. Lex happens to be a professional designer, and her frequent trips overseas have everything to do with the first Triple Threat boutique, which will be opening soon on Fifth Avenue. And, for the record, I can name at least ten exceptional artists who are inspired by a cold bottle of Dom Pérignon.

The last little faux pas: "The pretty and proper

Madison Hamilton, ruler of the triplet triangle, has shocked many people by carrying on a relationship with fellow celebutante and family foe Theo West, but the biggest shock of all? Sources tell us that Madison recently attended a meeting at the FBI's Manhattan field office, where she learned the newest techniques in fashionable crime fighting. Seems the Avenue girls know their way around the street."

Haven't you heard? Gold badges make great accessories.

As for now, we're going . . .
To the Penthouse

1

When Avenues Collide

The Ambassadors for the Arts Luncheon, held annually in the legendary Conrad Suite of the Waldorf-Astoria hotel, had officially begun.

Madison Hamilton rose from her place at the exclusive Michelangelo table and quickly scanned the room. She peered over the ornate floral arrangements that towered like skyscrapers. She glanced past the young violinist playing Bach beside the podium. She even pushed up on her tiptoes to get a clear picture of the L-shaped bar in the far left corner. The latter action made her thirst for a glass of cold champagne, but she immediately decided against it, not wanting to shift her thoughts from the problem at hand.

And it was a big problem.

Her sisters, Park and Lexington, were missing. Or, more specifically, they hadn't yet returned from their impromptu trip to the restroom a half hour ago. How long could it possibly take to reapply lip gloss and blush?

Madison was fuming. She had made it very clear to Park and Lex that there was a schedule to keep. The paparazzi were prancing around the hotel freely, and today's event was surely one of the most important of their lives. In a few short minutes, she, Park, and Lex would be called up to the front of the room by the mayor of New York City to receive their newest honor. The Hamilton triplets were being appointed ambassadors for the arts by the Royal Crown Society of the Americas. Composed of eminent artists, composers, actors, and philanthropists, the society rarely admitted new members; membership was a distinction reserved for only a select handful of people of "superior qualifications." As ambassadors, Madison, Park, and Lex would be sitting on a committee that had its hands in everything from museum acquisitions to the construction of art-deco hotels and the restoration of historical sites. They would have the chance to arrange exhibitions, support rising artists, and be among the first to view exceptional works of art.

The very idea of standing before a Renoir or Picasso made Madison's heart race. She had a passion for art history and the great master painters. In fact, she had spent many an hour fantasizing about one day being granted a seat at the society's roundtable. To her, there was no greater honor. She belonged there, in the midst of high-brow discussions of Caravaggio and Degas, Titian and Monet. Park and Lex weren't as psyched to be joining the society, but Madison wasn't about to let their lack of interest ruin the most exciting moment of her life.

And it wasn't just their induction into the society that had Madison jittery. It was the fact that she and her sisters would also be unveiling the newest painting by famed artist Tallula Kayson before a very eager crowd. Tallula was *the* artist of the moment, a genius who had already drawn comparisons to many of the modern masters; barely out of high school, she had rocketed to stardom nearly two years ago because of her jarring talent and signature style. Tallula Kayson's paintings weren't just an amalgam of color and delicate brushstrokes; they were mysterious, awe-inspiring creations that seduced the senses. Madison had been dying to meet her ever since two of Tallula's paintings sold for several million dollars. Tallula was brilliant and beautiful and worldly, and Madison wanted to gain her friendship.

But how was she going to accomplish that when her nerves were so on edge?

She stared to her left and saw Mayor Kevin Mayer schmoozing with a young waitress while guzzling from a champagne flute. The mayor was tall and handsome in his Ralph Lauren Black Label suit, but if the rumors were true, he liked women and booze a little too much. On the flip side, he had done an adequate job in public office, supporting many of the city's forgotten neighborhoods and doing away with all those silly parking restrictions on Fifth Avenue. Thanks to him, a girl could now hop out of her limo and run into Saks for a full ten minutes while her driver waited outside. Just off to Mayor Mayer's right was the Kahlo table; Madison spotted her best friend, Coco McKaid, staring aimlessly into space—a clear sign that Coco had guzzled her stolen martini too quickly. All the other tables were buzzing as waiters served cocktails and watercress salads. The majority of the guests were quite old: legendary socialites and philanthropists, a few well-known producers. It was a smattering of beyond-Botox wrinkles and shiny canes. Madison recognized a handful of her classmates from St. Cecilia's Prep, but there was still no sign of Park or Lex.

"Madison, dear, are you all right?"

The voice startled her. Madison glanced over at the older woman sitting at the Michelangelo table and sighed inwardly.

Poppy van Lulu was a character in every sense of the word. She was well into her sixties but looked at least ten years younger, courtesy of an excellent plastic surgeon and weekly visits to the Spa at Mandarin Oriental. Her red hair was cut in a blunt bob. Her oval face was caked with makeup. Her waiflike body was wrapped in a too-tight beige dress that made her look like a matchstick.

But it wasn't Poppy's eccentric appearance that instantly annoyed Madison. It was, rather, Poppy's penchant for otherworldly drama.

A well-known psychic to the stars, Poppy had a colorful reputation that stretched from New York to Hong Kong. She had given readings to just about every celebrity on the planet. She even appeared regularly in tabloid magazines, where she dished astrological advice and divined Hollywood's scandalous future. Having married into the powerful and socially elite van Lulu family at twenty-five, Poppy was now one of the wealthiest divorcées in the world—*and* one of the most theatrical. She couldn't appear in public without prophesying an actor's secret infidelity or a rock star's imminent journey into rehab.

It irked Madison. She'd met Poppy on several occasions but had always kept a cool distance from the woman. Didn't everyone know that infidelity and rehab were staples of the Hollywood life? There was nothing supernatural about foreseeing the inevitable. It was true that Poppy had accurately predicted the winners of *American Idol* and *America's Next Top Model* every season, but that didn't exactly make her a shaman. Madison didn't believe in psychic phenomena and had little patience for Poppy's behavior.

Madison gave the impish woman a curt nod. "I'm fine, Mrs. van Lulu."

"Are you . . . sure?" Poppy asked, the last word merely a whisper.

Madison met Poppy's cloudy, wide-eyed stare. "Yes. Are *you* okay?"

With a dramatic turn of her head, Poppy sat back in her chair and looked across the room at nothing in particular. "I suppose so," she replied quietly. "But there's such a . . . strange feeling in the air today."

Ignoring her, Madison glanced around at the other guests sitting at the Michelangelo table and smiled. She kept her shoulders squared and her head held high. "Please excuse me," she said softly, reaching for her purse.

Several of the old men pushed back their chairs and

stood up in a rare gesture of old-fashioned courtesy. Madison gave them each a graceful nod. Then she locked her eyes on the huge crystal chandelier at the very end of the room and strode toward it. She felt the customary sweep of stares following her. A photographer from the *New York Times* quickly snapped a picture, and Madison hoped he had managed to get a full-body shot. It would be a shame for anyone to miss seeing her in the stunning dress Alexander McQueen had designed especially for her; made from the finest silk, it was canary yellow, off the shoulder, and trimmed in lace. A rare black-diamond necklace from Cartier completed the dramatic but elegant look. Madison had never felt so appropriately graceful—and so dangerously enraged—in all her life.

She kept the smile plastered on her face until she exited the Conrad Suite. When she stepped into the empty corridor that led to the restrooms, her lips knitted together and her shoulders dropped. She forgot the ladylike sashay and broke into a clumsy jog. If Park and Lex weren't loitering in the vicinity of the toilets, they would end up swimming *in* a toilet when she got done with them.

Behind her, the violinist's last few notes rang on the air.

Crap! Our names will be called in a few minutes. The urgency hit Madison even harder. And so did the fear of what she might find. The last time she barged into a bathroom, she'd found Park getting a little too comfortable with Jeremy Bleu.

Reaching the restroom door, she curled her fingers around the knob and threw it open. The door slammed against the side wall like a clap of thunder.

"Oh!" The shocked voice belonged to Lex. She was standing against one of the sinks, her cell pressed to her ear. She shot Madison an irritated look, then ran to the opposite end of the room and slammed into a stall.

Madison felt a fresh wave of anger wash over her. "What the *hell* are you doing?" she screamed.

Park, applying a fresh coat of gloss to her lips, stared at Madison in the mirror. "Calm down," she said. "We're almost done." She capped the lip gloss and dropped it into her purse.

"Calm down?" Madison ranted. "It's been half an hour! Are you both insane? We're due at the podium in a few minutes!" Her high-pitched voice bounced off the walls, drowning out the echo of Lex's chatter from the last stall.

Park sighed and turned around. She was dressed in an exquisite white Triple Threat suit that matched her waifish fashion tastes. Lex had designed it, but Park had added the man's thick tie that tapered down to her waist. If not for her heels and flowing hair, she might have been mistaken for a skinny guy with expensive taste. "Now, listen to me," she said calmly. "Lex is on a very important call. She's really trying to hurry it up, but—"

"I *don't* want to hear it!" Madison snapped. "Nothing is more important than what's happening to us today!"

"That's not necessarily true," Park replied evenly. "Lex is having square footage issues with the interior designers who are putting together the Triple Threat store. And if these issues aren't resolved soon—"

Growling, Madison shoved Park to the side and stormed past her. She reached the stall where Lex was holding her conference call and pushed against the door.

It was locked.

"Open up!" Madison screamed, and banged on the door for dramatic effect. "Do you hear me? Get off that phone!"

Lex kept chattering. "Gimme a minute!" she called out.

But Madison was beyond hearing excuses. She took three steps back, carefully pulled her dress up to her thighs, and extended her right leg, black satin heel pointed out like a gun. She took aim and fired.

The kick rattled the door with a boom.

"Whoa!" Lex screamed.

"Get out!" Madison's voice rose to a new level of hysteria. "Get out *right now* or I'll knock the damn door down!"

Park sighed. "Madison, you're going to break out in a sweat, and you know how bad that can be for your complexion. If you don't wash your face right now, you'll clog your pores."

"I exfoliated this morning," Madison snapped.

"That might not make a difference." Park plucked a tissue from the box on the sink and began gently dabbing Madison's forehead, even as Madison gave the door another kick.

"Listen, I'll have to call you back," Lex said nervously to whomever she was talking to. "I've got a psycho on my hands!"

Five more seconds ticked by. Madison gave the door another karate kick, and this time the force of the blow nearly snapped the lock.

"Oh!" Lex cried. "You total nut!"

"Get out!"

The door swung open.

Madison's upper lip curled in a nasty snarl as she stared at Lex, who was pressed up against one side of the stall. "Ha!" Madison said. "Cornered like a rat!"

Suddenly, Lex bent down and grabbed a plunger from behind the toilet. She held it up like a sword. "Stand back! I'm not afraid to use this!"

"It's rubber," Park said, running the tissue along Madison's neck. "You're not really going to do any damage with that."

"I can make a round imprint on your dress!" Lex yelled, jabbing the plunger at Madison. "Seriously, I can! Stand back!"

Madison straightened herself against the sink and clutched her purse tightly. Then she pointed at the gleaming tiled floor. "Get. Out. Here. *Now!*"

Lex gulped. She dropped the plunger and quickly ran out of the stall, taking her place beside Park.

"If Dad were here I'd make him confiscate both of your AmEx cards!" Madison screeched. "A half an hour in here—when everyone is expecting us outside!"

"It was an important call!" Lex shot back. "I just found out the wall treatments for the boutique are too bright, and the flooring is—"

"I don't care!" Madison continued, her cheeks tomato red. "This is the most important day of our lives, the biggest honor we've ever received. And what do you two do? You ignore it!"

"Nobody's ignoring it," Park answered gently. "We're here, and we're happy to be here."

"But I wouldn't exactly call it the *biggest* honor," Lex added, then just as quickly bit her lip.

Madison gasped. "The Royal Crown Society of the Americas!" she snapped. "Priceless art! Brilliant people! Brilliant artists! There are only fifty ambassadors in the world! Do you *hear* me?"

Lex frowned and cast her eyes downward. "It's not as exciting for me as it is for you, okay? I mean, being appointed ambassadors by the society is very . . ."

"Nice," Park chimed in cheerily.

"Nice," Lex agreed. "But it doesn't rock my world. I'm glad it makes you happy, Madison, but you can't expect me and Park to pretend it's the realization of our biggest dream or anything like that. Because it's not."

Madison shook her head disapprovingly. "I should have *known* the two of you wouldn't be able to appreciate something like this. I guess being appointed ambassadors for the arts isn't as lofty as being invited to the Chanel spring collection."

"Hey!" Lex snapped angrily. "Fashion design happens to be art!"

Madison chuckled, her bad mood not budging. "You can't compare sketching cocktail dresses to painting or sculpting the way fine artists do."

Lex's jaw dropped. "The hell I can't! Look at your dress—you wouldn't call that art? Alexander would be horrified to hear you say that. And now that we're being brutally honest, let me tell you that I'd rather be at a Chanel show than at this society luncheon, sitting with a bunch of farting old geezers. Even a *resort* collection show."

Madison's hand flew to her chest. "How dare you!"

She had never heard anything so hurtful. "Those people happen to be responsible for building the greatest art collections in the world! They—"

"They wear dentures and can barely chew their boiled carrots," Lex shot back. "We're lucky the vodka isn't being spiked with Metamucil. It's a retirement home party in that room. You *so* know I'm right."

Madison clenched the ends of her purse, then gritted her teeth. She didn't have much of a rebuttal. The luncheon *did* resemble something of an upscale bingo game in Vegas. But that didn't minimize the very important mission of the society. It didn't minimize the brilliantly artistic atmosphere either. "What about Tallula Kayson?" she asked. "Aren't either of you the least bit curious to meet her? She's not old. She's only a few years older than us."

"I can't wait to meet Tallula," Park said evenly. "I loved the interview she did on MTV last month. She listens to Pink while she paints."

"Does she?" Lex sounded impressed. Her tone was suddenly excited. "Good taste."

"Tallula isn't going to be interested in talking about pop music," Madison said stubbornly. "After we're introduced and receive our honorary society brooches, we're going to unveil her latest painting. That's going to be the topic of conversation, got it?"

Lex made a sour face at her sister. "You don't have to be so aggressive. Is acting like a wolf suddenly in vogue?"

"I'm not acting like a wolf," Madison countered. "I just get *very* annoyed when the two of you go out of your way to embarrass me."

Park held up her hand, and silence instantly descended over the bathroom. She kept her expression calm and soft as she looked at her sisters. "Both of you, cut it out. I can't stand this. It's stupid fighting, and that's not what we do. I mean, when's the last time we actually had a fight?"

Madison and Lex stared at the floor.

"Answer me," Park said, gently but firmly.

"I can't remember the last time." Madison's voice was low, her tone regretful. She raised her head and looked at Lex.

"Neither can I," Lex agreed.

"That's exactly right," Park said. "All of this negative energy is making me sick, and it happens to be bad for our makeup." She trained her gaze on Madison and gave her shoulders a comforting squeeze. "Listen, honey . . . we know why you're a little wired up, but it's not *our* fault that you're upset with your boyfriend. Now, if you want to talk about it . . ."

Madison's eyes flashed with pain. She turned around and stared at herself in the mirror and made a pretense of inspecting her complexion. But it was impossible to hide the sadness on her face. Sadness, and a wee bit of anger. Her boyfriend, fellow celebutante Theo West, had left on Sunday for Antigua, where his father had just completed building a new hotel. Initially, Theo had wanted Madison to join him on the trip—a romantic few days under the sun, away from the chaos of Manhattan—but last week, Theo changed his tune completely and told Madison that he would be spending the entire time working alongside his father. There were financial plans to reexamine, last-minute construction details that probably needed attention, and a whole marketing campaign to review. The West family was banking on the new hotel to bring them out of a business slump.

That, at least, had been Theo's side of the story. Madison chose to believe him because believing anything else was just too painful. She didn't want to consider the possibility that Theo had reverted to his playboy ways, or that he was having a fling with his horse-faced ex-girlfriend, Annabelle Christensen. After a lifetime of being social rivals—the Hamiltons and the Wests did *not* get along— she and Theo had finally found a common ground on which to build a relationship. They talked. They went shopping together and spent up a storm in Bergdorf's. They took Sunday strolls through Central Park. Everything had been going perfectly.

Until now.

She hated being away from Theo. Even though it was already Wednesday and he was scheduled to return Saturday morning, Madison couldn't help feeling like a bride who'd been left at the altar. She missed Theo. She was confused by his actions. And if she had to admit it, she was a little suspicious too. All those emotions made for an edgy disposition. She felt a sudden prickle of guilt in her stomach. This was the first time in a very long time that she'd gotten so angry at Park and Lex. They never fought, and they had never been able to stand seeing one another upset.

Sighing, she turned around again and faced her sisters. "I'm sorry," she said quietly. "I didn't mean to be a bitch, but it's just that I . . . well . . ."

"You miss Theo," Park said matter-of-factly. "You shouldn't be ashamed of that."

"But I *am* ashamed of it." Madison frowned. "Not because it's wrong to miss him, but because I'm worried about what people might be thinking. And what they might be saying."

"That's silly. It's nobody's business." Park shrugged and gave Madison's shoulder another squeeze. Then she reached into her purse, pulled out her compact, and flipped it open. She began dotting at Madison's makeup. "There's a little too much moisture under your eyes," she said. "If we don't fix that, your mascara will run and you'll look like you're headed for a heavy metal concert."

"God, Park, now I'm going to have nightmares!" Lex exclaimed, quickly following suit. She squatted down and began smoothing her hands over Madison's dress, trying to flatten the wrinkles that had cut into the delicate fabric.

"I mean, I trust Theo," Madison said, looking up as Park worked around her eyes. "I don't think he's doing anything bad, but it's just weird. Back in June, he asked me to go with him on this trip, and then all of a sudden he came up with excuses." She stretched her arms out as Lex fussed with the top half of the dress.

"Well, if it's any consolation, we're glad you didn't go," Park said. "And anyway, if you *had* gone, you wouldn't be able to be here today."

Lex nodded. "It's totally dumb to be worrying about this. Theo's crazy about you. And if he *does* try to pull off anything stupid, I'll personally kick his ass."

Madison didn't feel like delving into the roller-coaster

state of her emotions, even if they did need some buffing. Why on earth would Theo cheat on her? She was, after all, one of the most famous and beautiful girls on the planet. It was flat-out silly to think Theo had suddenly fallen out of love with her. "Maybe you're both right," she said. "I'm letting this get to me, and it's totally screwing up my brain. I'm just going to forget it." She lifted her arms over her head. "Lex, did I tear the dress anywhere when I kicked in the door?"

Lex circled Madison, carefully inspecting the dress. "No, you're clear." She gestured her head at the door and smirked. "But I think you did some damage to that lock."

"Not a big deal," Park said with a fluttery wave of her hand. She closed her compact, then stepped back to inspect Madison. "Beautiful. Your makeup is perfect."

"Thanks," Madison answered. She took a deep breath and smiled wearily.

Park was quick to identify the half-strong, half-sad look. She had seen it on Madison's face only a handful of times, but it was upsetting. Thankfully, however, there was a surefire cure. She reached under her shirt collar and pulled out the necklace hanging around her neck; at the end of the chain was a thick, stunning, glittering emerald. She unclasped the necklace and held it up so that the jewel caught the light and glittered like a disco ball.

Madison gasped and stared at the rock with glazing eyes. The angst she had been feeling vanished and was replaced by a surge of warm, buttery happiness. "Stunning," she whispered. "Just . . . stunning."

Park nodded. "From my private collection. I knew it

would do the trick." And it always did. She knew better than anyone that jewelry possessed otherworldly power: you couldn't set eyes on a rare rock without completely losing yourself.

"That'll chase away any girl's blues," Lex commented.

"Tell me how much it's worth," Madison said quietly, swooning. "How many carats?"

"Not so expensive—only seven hundred thousand," Park replied. "But it's six carats."

Madison gasped with pleasure.

"Go ahead, honey," Park said. "Hold it. Feel the weight. Precious gems are our best friends."

Madison took the emerald and cradled it in the palm of her right hand. She let the sparkles of light eclipse everything else. It was true: jewelry had a magical effect on the body and the mind. She ran her thumb over one smooth edge and literally shivered with pleasure. "I feel a million times better," she said, handing the necklace back to Park.

"*Six* million times better," Lex chimed in.

Madison took another deep breath, then squared her shoulders confidently. "I'm just going to think about that emerald for the rest of the afternoon. Come on. Let's head back out there."

They walked single file out of the bathroom and down the long hallway. A photographer coming up the wide staircase offered them a courteous nod and raised his camera. Quick on cue, Madison froze. She waited for Park and Lex to assume their familiar positions beside her. They plastered smiles on their faces as the picture was snapped.

"Now, remember," Madison whispered over her

shoulder as they stepped into the Conrad Suite, "steer clear of Mayor Mayer—he's already drunk and you know how touchy-feely he gets when he's drunk."

Park shrugged. "I can handle him. And from the way he looks right now, I don't think we're being called up to that podium anytime soon."

"Totally right," Lex agreed, noting that Mayor Mayer had just reached for another drink as he began chatting with an attractive female guest. "But I swear to God, if he even so much as squeezes my shoulder, I'll knee him right in his Picassos."

Madison shook her head firmly. "It's bad enough that he's already drunk, and I don't want to create any kind of scene. So keep your knees to yourself, okay?"

Lex was about to nod, but then she caught a glimpse of the odd and scrawny Poppy van Lulu charging across the room toward them, waving both her arms.

"Oh, great," Madison said under her breath. "Just what we need. A report from the ghost world."

"That's not nice," Park whispered. "Poppy has never said anything mean about us, and she happens to be a member of the society and a fellow lover of art."

"She also happens to be three dresses short of a sample sale," Madison said. "She can't be seen in public without causing a scene, and it's annoying. Remember two years ago at the Academy Awards? She told Johnny Depp he was a pirate in a previous life—and I think he believed her."

"Let's not say anything bad about Johnny." Lex's tone was fierce. "He's the only one who can wear pirate-inspired fashion outside of a movie set and still look damn hot."

Madison nodded. "True, but I don't like it when men wear feathers in their hair."

"Heads up," Park whispered. "Here comes drama."

Poppy van Lulu's eyes were wide, the look on her face customarily frantic. She put a hand on Park's shoulder and shook her head vigorously.

"Mrs. van Lulu," Park said politely. "Are you okay?"

"No, I'm not," Poppy replied dramatically. "I'm *certainly* not."

Park kept a smile plastered on her face. "What's wrong?"

Poppy rested a hand on her forehead, then swayed to one side as if she were about to faint. "Girls, you *have* to listen to me," she said weakly. "What I'm going to say might sound strange, but I'm very serious. You have to get out of here *now*."

"What?" Madison snapped.

"Now!" Poppy cried. "I've just had a frightening premonition. We're all in danger. There isn't a moment to spare. *Something terrible is about to happen!*"

2

A Little Bit of Coco

The words were said with such urgency, such breathless desperation, Park actually felt a chill scale her spine. She gently touched Poppy van Lulu's hand. "Why would you say a thing like that?" she asked in her best soothing voice. "This is a very small event. There's nothing dangerous here."

Poppy shook her head again. "Because it's true. And it's awful. I've just seen . . ."

Park waited patiently for a description.

"I've just seen . . ." Poppy put a hand to her forehead and closed her eyes.

"Seen what?" Lex snapped. "A vinyl handbag? Where is it? Or worse—vinyl shoes? What did you see?"

"I think I've seen the shadow of death pass over this room," Poppy stated quietly, seriously. "A dark cloak of peril."

"A *what*?" Madison's voice was sharp and impatient.

"A dark cloak of peril," Poppy repeated.

"Maybe it was a shawl," Lex said offhandedly. "Purple is back in fashion, and with this lighting, a purple shawl could easily look like a dark cloak."

"Or a cape," Park added. "I think I saw one in Dior's last collection."

"I happen to like capes." Lex made a pretense of throwing one over her shoulders. "Easy to put on, and easy to take off."

"No, you're not understanding me!" Poppy suddenly cried. Her voice drew several stares from around the room. "I know what I'm talking about. I've seen the shadow before, and I'm never wrong when I see it. We have to get out of here now."

Park put both her hands on Poppy's shoulders. "Mrs. van Lulu, I think you just need to relax. Why don't you let me get you a drink?"

"No, Park. You aren't listening to me, and you *must* listen to me." Poppy's eyes grew watery, and her lips tightened into a grimace. "The danger in this room is immense. Someone here is going to die!"

At that, Park and Lex both jumped back and looked at each other.

"That's enough!" Madison said through gritted teeth. She gave Poppy her coldest stare and then quickly led her just outside the room, Park and Lex in tow. "Now, you listen to me, Mrs. van Lulu. We're here for an important event, and no one is interested in hearing your psychic rants."

"But—"

"There's no need to continue," Madison interjected. "My sisters and I aren't listening to any nonsense, so I suggest you go back to your table and keep it zipped."

Poppy's jaw dropped. "You don't have to be so rude, dear," she said. "I'm just trying to save someone's life."

The look on Madison's face was clearly unsympathetic. "I apologize if I've offended you, Mrs. van Lulu, but to be perfectly frank, I don't believe in psychics or any kind of supernatural stuff, so your warning is just the result of an overactive imagination."

"Have I ever been wrong about *American Idol* and *Top Model*?" Poppy shot back. "Was I wrong about Britney?"

"You weren't," Lex said quickly. "By the way, do you think she'll ever make another album?"

"The point I'm trying to make," Madison said firmly, "is that there isn't time for this. I want you to go back to your table, Mrs. van Lulu, and I want you to sit there for the remainder of the luncheon."

Poppy's face once again registered panic. She looked at Park and Lex, obviously seeking help, but they merely stared down at the floor and waited for the embarrassing moment to pass.

Madison pointed in the direction of the Michelangelo table. "Right now."

"Fine," Poppy said. "But I can't stay here. I'm too frightened! I know what I saw, and my visions are never wrong!" And with that, she turned around and marched away.

"I just can't believe the nerve of that woman," Madison said. "Doesn't she ever give it a rest?"

Park shrugged. "You know how Poppy is. She's been doing that for ages, and she'll keep on doing it till she slips into a designer toe tag. It's just her way."

"But what if she was right?" Lex blurted out suddenly.

The question was followed by dead silence.

Madison blinked twice. "You didn't really just say that."

"Well . . . I mean . . . she sounded really upset," Lex said. "And you know, whether or not you think she's a flake, you have to admit that some of her predictions have come true."

"Coincidence, honey." Park waved her hand dismissively.

"All of it?" Lex asked. "What if she had a premonition about one of us? Like, what if there's a psycho stalker in the room, watching us?"

"Oh, God," Madison moaned. "Lex, you really have to stop reading those silly New Age books about crystals and love spells and sex magic."

"Sex magic?" Park squinted. "Is there really such a thing?"

"Never mind." Lex shook her arms and legs, as if trying to rid the sudden onslaught of fear from her bones. "Let's just forget about it and get a move on, because now I'm creeped out."

"Whatever you do, don't mention any of this craziness to Tallula Kayson or her boyfriend, Elijah Traymore,"

Madison said. "It'll make us *all* look dumb, and I want to make a really good impression. Tallula and Elijah are artists of the first rank."

Lex giggled. "The first rank? Sometimes you sound like such an old lady when it comes to these artists. I mean, Tallula paints and Elijah sculpts. They're both twenty-two and college dropouts. I don't know if I'd call them artists of the first rank."

Madison ran a hand through her long dark hair. "They aren't college dropouts," she said dramatically. "It just so happens that their talent transcends the need for four years of dorm living."

"Speak of the devil," Park suddenly chimed in. "There's transcendent Elijah talking to Coco, who looks pretty drunk from here."

"What?" Lex said.

Park gestured her head to the right. "Over there. It's Elijah. I recognize him from that whole spread he and Tallula got in *Vanity Fair.*"

Madison and Lex stared across the room. It was true. Huddled in a corner just to the right of the bar were Coco and Elijah Traymore, seemingly rapt in conversation. But it didn't take a genius—or an artist of the transcendent variety—to deduce that Coco was trying her best to play the role of seductress: she was staring up at Elijah with wide eyes and pouting lips, and one of her spaghetti straps had slipped off her shoulder. The martini glass in her right hand was nearly empty.

Elijah didn't seem to mind. Tall, lean, and definitely the artist in the room, he was dressed in paint-splattered jeans, a wrinkled black blazer, and scuffed black biker boots. His pale complexion was accentuated by messy jet-black hair and an assortment of silver chains dangling from his neck. If the girls weren't mistaken, there was even a wee bit of black eyeliner around his blue eyes.

"Damn," Madison whispered, instantly panicked. "We have to get over there. You know what happens when Coco drinks too much. I don't want her on Page Six again."

Lex and Park nodded. Coco McKaid was a dear friend, but booze played a wicked number on her. Two weeks ago, at a Jackie Collins book-release party in Beverly Hills, Coco had guzzled three too many drinks and ended up skinny-dipping in the pool with a former member of a popular boy band. Thankfully, there hadn't been any photographers hanging around to capture the chaotic scene.

If Madison, Park, and Lex didn't move fast, Coco would probably end up undressing right here in front of everyone.

"Look at her," Lex said quietly. "She's drunker than Lindsay out of rehab."

Park tucked her purse under her left arm. "Come on. Let's do this quickly."

Madison led the way. In her typically staid fashion, she held her head high and smiled at the other, much older guests who turned to stare at her. In ten seconds flat, she, Park, and Lex made it to Coco's side.

"Oh!" Coco said loudly when she felt Madison's fingers curl around her arm. "Hi there!"

"Hello, dear." In one smooth gesture, Madison whisked the martini glass out of Coco's hand and gently bumped her friend against the bar. Then Madison looked up at Elijah. She smiled brightly. She extended her hand. And, in an incredibly dramatic tone, she said, "Elijah, it's such an *honor* to meet you. I absolutely *adore* your work."

Lex rolled her eyes.

Elijah Traymore, visibly flattered, set his drink on the bar and fixed Madison with an equally admiring stare. "Well, the Hamilton triplets," he said. "I was hoping to meet you." He took Madison's hand and kissed it. And held it. "You look absolutely stunning. I noticed you when you first came into the room."

Madison blushed instantly. "Well . . . thank you."

"No, thank *you*," Elijah said, a bit too seductively.

Madison cleared her throat as his eyes swept over the length of her body. She felt his hot stare everywhere. It was obvious that he came on strong and fast, and she had to actually yank her hand free of his.

Elijah quickly turned and stared at Lex, studying her with the same unabashed gaze. "You're quickly becoming one of my favorite designers," he said quietly. "And you're even more beautiful in person than I expected."

The spicy comment didn't make Lex the least bit un-comfortable. "Aren't I, though?" She tossed her head back and nudged him with her shoulder. If not for Park's hand pulling her back, Lex would have taken Coco's place close to Elijah.

"Hi," Park said, stepping in between them. "It's a pleasure to meet you, Elijah."

"No, Park. The pleasure is all *mine*." He reached out and clasped her hand. His eyes locked on hers, and he grinned suggestively. "I just can't wait to see you make your big-screen debut. I'll bet your director can't stop staring at you. Let me tell you—that Jeremy Bleu is one hell of a lucky guy."

"Thank you," Park replied coolly. She extracted her hand from Elijah's, but she didn't allow herself to appear rattled by his overt pass. That, after all, was exactly what he wanted.

Elijah Traymore wasn't the kind of guy who dropped subtle hints. He genuinely thought he was beyond it all. Sudden fame could do that to people. Especially men. Public adulation and good looks coupled with one spread in *Vanity Fair* and a guy could easily lose his grasp on reality. Park didn't have to get to know Elijah to make that assessment. It was obvious. And it was an instant turnoff.

She wasn't flattered by his compliments either. Everyone was waiting to see her screen debut. For the past six weeks, she'd been working tirelessly on the set of *Short Fuse,* the big-budget action thriller starring her boyfriend, Jeremy Bleu. Not a day went by without a celebrity reporter sneaking past her trailer and snapping a pic of her in wardrobe. Park was enjoying herself, but talking about this new chapter of her life was somewhat scary. She had never intended to become an actor. She hadn't really wanted to follow in the footsteps of her mother. She knew that most people—especially critics and celebutante haters—would be eager to completely trash her performance once the movie was released, and that very annoying fact was what forced her to push herself harder than ever. She didn't see *Short Fuse* as a way to expand her fame; she saw it as a job for which she was being paid, a serious business venture that required the highest levels of professionalism and determination. She was going to make one hell of an excellent impression on-screen.

Though Jeremy always encouraged her to talk about the movie, Park preferred letting the mystery of her acting career thicken. If there was one thing she'd learned about growing up in the public eye, it was the Rule of Silence: the less you said, the more people talked about you.

"Tell me," Elijah continued, locking his eyes on hers, "are there any parts of the movie that have made you feel . . . uncomfortable?"

What an arrogant horn-dog, Park thought. But she shook her head and said, "None at all. My role doesn't require nudity. And I'm sure that's what you're referring to."

He smirked. "I hope the thought of nudity doesn't make a girl as beautiful as you uncomfortable. I'd love to sculpt you one day."

"Sculpt me?" Park asked, sounding purposefully whimsical. "Why, I've never thought of that."

"It takes a special kind of person to be an artist's muse," Elijah said, and winked. "And I think sculpting your body would be an incredible experience."

Park chuckled. "I have a personal trainer for that, so you might have to find someone else to buff your clay."

Lex, who had been watching the exchange intently, burst out laughing.

Madison cleared her throat and quickly regained control of the situation. "Speaking of sculpting," she said, "can you tell us anything about your newest project, Elijah?"

"My latest sculpture will be unveiled in a few weeks," he replied, reaching again for his drink. "Then it'll go up for sale. Sotheby's is handling that, of course."

"Sotheby's!" Madison's voice hit a high note. She was shocked. "That's so rare. Sotheby's doesn't usually work with such young artists. But it's great news. I've acquired a lot of my art through Sotheby's. I also enjoy the smaller galleries, though."

"I saw you talking to Poppy van Lulu," Elijah said suddenly. "Are you clients of hers?"

"Clients?" Madison laughed—she couldn't help herself. "For God's sake, no. She's a total . . . a great patroness of the arts, but still a little . . . ya know . . . *eccentric.*"

"Is there anything to eat?" Lex asked, completely shattering the art-snobbiness of the conversation. "I'm starving."

Madison shot her a disapproving look.

"Hey!" Coco suddenly said. She bumped past Park and Lex, her head wobbling drunkenly. "I'd like to be sculpted. In fact, Elijah and I were talking about that before you guys interrupted us." She hiccupped. "I mean, we were sort of discussing that. Or something like that. Or . . ." She glanced at her empty hands. "Hey, where's my drink?"

"It's gone, honey." Lex took Coco's limp hand and gave it a sympathetic squeeze. "Just bottled water for you from this point on. The last thing you want to do is puke on that dress."

"Anyway," Madison said loudly, still fighting to salvage what was left of their introduction to Elijah Traymore, "I'm thrilled to hear that your fans have a new

sculpture to look forward to. Can you give us a little hint about what inspired you?"

Elijah smiled—a gleaming, fake smile. "It's dedicated to my girlfriend—Tallula certainly has it coming to her."

"Absolutely," Madison answered. "Her paintings are just extraordinary. She must be your muse every minute of every day."

"You could say that," Elijah said. "Tallula's a unique person. I've known her for a few years and I can honestly say that she's more mysterious than anyone I've ever met. She's still upstairs getting ready. You'll meet her in just a few minutes."

"I can't wait." Madison gave her head another dramatic toss.

Elijah glanced at his watch. "I should go and give her a call. She's always late. It was a pleasure meeting all of you." He dropped his steamy stare to Coco. "See you soon, I hope."

"Thank you." Madison touched his arm, hoping to distract him from her very drunk friend. "I'm looking so forward to seeing your piece, Elijah."

"And I'm sure Elijah would love showing it to you," Park said, managing to keep a straight face.

Madison's face flushed a vibrant shade of red.

Elijah Traymore turned and hurried out of the room.

"What a little creep," Park said quietly. "The nerve of him, talking to us like that."

"Totally," Lex agreed. "At first I thought he was just coming on a little too strong, but if that was his way of introducing himself, I don't want to see what comes next."

"I hate to say it, but I agree." Madison gave the room a

quick scan to make sure no one else could hear them. "After that introduction, I don't know what Tallula Kayson sees in him. How in the world did he manage to score her? He seems like the kind of guy who'll sleep with anything."

"Thanks a lot!" Coco snapped.

"I didn't mean it like that," Madison assured her. "I'm just saying that Elijah isn't the right guy for you."

"He's cute," Coco said. "And he's smart and funny and . . . a great artist. And we were getting along *fine* until you barged in on us." She pointed down to her shoes. "And I even wore my Akiko Bergstroms. Five thousand dollars a pair, thank you very much."

Madison made a sour face. "Please! As if he even noticed your feet. He practically jumped down Park's dress right in front of you. Not to mention the fact that he's very publicly involved in a very serious relationship. Did he mention that during your meet and greet?"

"Well . . . no." Coco folded her arms over her chest and looked away. "But he *did* say that I have a nice body." She hiccupped again. "And . . . I think he's smart and mature and very worldly."

"That's just the alcohol talking," Park said. "Sober, I can tell you that he's an immature twenty-two. And he likes himself too much. Trust me, Coco—I know his type. And besides, he's way too old."

"But you said he's immature, right?" Coco quipped. The words should have sounded angry, but they came out slurred and thick, as if she were chewing a big wad of gum. She leaned against the bar as the last punch of vodka chugged through her blood. "That should even out the age difference, right?"

Not for the first time, Madison studied her best friend and felt a stab of pity. Coco had everything going for her—an adorable body, a beautiful face, a great personality—but she never recognized any of it. When she looked in the mirror, she saw a scrawny girl with a flat chest and big feet. The really hot guys never went for her. In the society pages, she was always photographed beside someone else. It was always *Hayden Panettiere with celebutante Coco McKaid, Emma Roberts with celebutante Coco McKaid, Princes William and Harry with celebutante Coco McKaid.* It was never just *Celebutante Coco McKaid in Zac Posen.* Even at St. Cecilia's Prep, Coco often found herself reminding classmates that *she* had just as much money as *they* did. The McKaid family owned the most successful wineries in the world, thank you very much. And so the result was a dangerously insecure sixteen-year-old who drank too much and gave herself over to the first guy who paid her enough attention.

Madison had tried talking sense into her on countless occasions. She'd sit her down and go through a list of things Coco had to be grateful for—her dress size, her flawless complexion, her parents' summer home on the French Riviera—but the confidence induced by these nuggets would only last a week or two. Before long, Coco would be back to her old self, searching for acceptance in all the wrong places.

Now, as the drunken spell took a tighter hold, Coco looked like a little girl who had just lost her bid for emerald earrings at a Cartier fund-raiser. Her lips curled into a frown. Her eyes grew watery. And, in the most unlady-like of gestures, she grabbed a cloth napkin from the bar and blew her nose into it; the accompanying sound was reminiscent of a gunshot. "I shwear," she slurred. "Elijah liked *me.*"

Madison felt the last hour's tension drain from her body. How could she go on worrying about this damn luncheon when her best friend was looking lower than the ratings on the CW? It was silly to put so much importance on matters that were ultimately trivial. Ambassadors for the arts. Yeah, she loved the sound of it. She loved being on the art world's A-list. But in the end, Madison knew she was too smart to let superficiality overshadow her compassion. And she was already on enough A-lists to really care too much about one more.

She threw an arm around Coco and said, "You're just feeling down because you drank too much. And you didn't know Elijah Traymore long enough to actually like him. He's a sleaze, and you deserve someone with way more class."

"You also look way too good in that dress for a guy like Elijah," Park chimed in. "He was dressed like a goth kid from the East Village. But not even in a cool way—in a stuck-in-the-nineties way. Your wardrobe completely outranks his."

"And you're going to inherit seventy percent of the world's wine-producing grapes," Lex added thoughtfully.

When the moments of commiserating were over, Coco looked up and nodded slowly. She blew her nose again. "Thanks," she mumbled. "I guess you're right. Maybe . . . maybe I did have a little too much to drink. I'm just going to go fix myself up in the bathroom."

"I'll come," Madison said, genuinely wanting to accompany her friend in her time of need.

"No, it's okay." Coco stood up rigidly, balancing herself on those expensive heels. "Besides, I think Mayor Mayer is looking for you guys." She gave her friends a weary smile, then trotted, a little crookedly, out of the room.

Madison was about to follow her drunk friend, just to make sure she got where she was going in one piece. But when Madison turned around, she saw Mayor Mayer wave a hand at her, then indicate the podium at the very front of the room.

"Well, it's about time," Lex complained. "How long does it take the geriatric community to get a show like this on the road?"

Park couldn't help laughing at the comment. Looking at Madison, she said, "That was nice of you—offering to go with Coco. She really shouldn't have gone alone."

"I know." Madison drew a compact out of her purse and checked her complexion. "Thank God we came when we did. That oversexed biker was probably trying to convince her to join him for a roll across the red carpet."

"So what's the plan, Madison?" Lex asked. "Once we're called up to the podium, do we each have to give some sort of speech?"

"No, just me. Follow my lead and smile a lot. It'll be in the Style section of the *Times* for sure."

Ten minutes later, as Mayor Mayer was introducing them to the eager, albeit ancient, crowd, Madison did a quick scan of the room. She had everyone's admiration and her place in the art world's high society. Then it hit her.

Coco hadn't returned from the bathroom.

3

Painting the Town

In penthouse four of the Waldorf-Astoria tower, twenty-two-year-old Tallula Kayson was readying herself for yet another public appearance. Her fourth in just as many days. She was exhausted. The frenzied publicity schedule had left her feeling less than adequate. Despite the crowd waiting for her downstairs in the Conrad Suite, despite the fact that her newest masterpiece would at last be unveiled to a rapt audience, she wanted nothing more than to grab a pillow and fall asleep. She always loved a party, but for some reason, this luncheon felt more like a chore.

It was early afternoon. Sunlight filtered into the bedroom in muted shades of red and blue, creating a stained-glass mosaic on the hardwood floors. The delicate colors accentuated the room's ornate furnishings: a canopied bed with silk cream-colored sheets, a plush duvet, and half a dozen striped pillows; a mahogany desk; and a gilt-framed mirror that hung over the fireplace mantel. Just off to the left was a small nook occupied by an oversized chair. It was Tallula's favorite piece in the room. Trimmed in red and gold fringe, an exquisite patterned throw draped across one arm, the chair resembled something out of King Arthur's court. She had reclined on it several times since checking into the Waldorf four days ago. For some reason or other, it seemed to give her inspiration. When she rested her head against the soft upper pillow and closed her eyes, she imagined a blank canvas, big and square and empty. Then she imagined her hand guiding the paintbrush as she made the first delicate stroke on that field of whiteness. Soon, an image formed before her. Vivid blues and greens and yellows. The kind of painting that had made Tallula famous virtually overnight.

But there was no time now to relax in the wonderful and stately chair. The clock was ticking, and she had a packed day ahead of her.

Crossing the bedroom to the walk-in closet, Tallula ran a hand through her mane of blond curls. Her hair was still damp from the hasty shower she had taken twenty minutes ago. In fact, she hadn't even completely dried off underneath the terry cloth robe. The air-conditioning was too low. Sighing loudly—loudly enough that her assistant, Ina, would hear—Tallula quickly began toweling herself dry.

"Tallula? Is something wrong?"

Tallula smiled as she studied her assistant, who had appeared on the threshold.

Ina Debrovitch was petite and pretty with delicate features. She was twenty-four but still looked like a teenager. Her red hair tumbled past her shoulders in curls. Her milk white skin was smooth and unblemished, save for the remarkable star-shaped birthmark on her chin. She had been born and raised in Romania, then immigrated to the United States at nineteen. She had worked first as Tallula's housekeeper, but a quick eye and a sharp mind had earned her the assistant position. Ina was organized. She was discreet. She had good fashion sense. What was more, she had learned to decipher Tallula's moods and didn't ask insignificant questions. Wherever Tallula went, Ina went. It was Ina's responsibility to run just about every facet of Tallula's life, and she had done an excellent job of that so far.

You wouldn't have known Ina was handicapped unless you listened to her very closely; then, you might notice the way she slurred certain words, as hearing-impaired people often do. The word *what* often came out sounding like *whaah,* but overall, she had mastered the art of lipreading. She was never without her trusty hearing aid, and when she removed it before showering or going to sleep, she made certain to say so, because neither Tallula nor Elijah liked feeling as though they were being ignored.

"It's very stuffy in here," Tallula said. "You know how I hate the heat—it makes me feel icky. Would you be a kitten and fix that?"

"I'll see that it gets cooler," Ina replied. "I'm sorry. I

didn't realize the air-conditioning wasn't turned up as high as you like it."

"I already feel out of sorts because of it." Tallula sighed again. "Anyway, I don't know what to wear, and I assume these Society of the Americas people will talk if I don't meet their approval." The thought annoyed her. She had never looked for anyone's approval when it came to her fashion tastes. She had a wild sense of style, and on more than one occasion she'd appeared in public wearing completely over-the-top outfits: torn and tattered dresses with paint-splattered cowboy boots; skirts with mismatched blouses; men's oversized suits that made her look ten pounds thinner. At a gallery opening in Santa Barbara last month, she had showed up in a black dress to which she had sloppily pinned several brightly colored bows. At an event before that, she'd worn a huge pink velvet top hat that made her look like a character from a Dr. Seuss book. Once, at a private gala at the Guggenheim, she'd dressed in a gold kimono and slipped a paintbrush through her hair. She hadn't paid attention to what the tabloids said about her. She hadn't given mind to the shocked stares either. She was an artist, and sometimes she felt the need to express herself beyond the canvas. And besides, her outfits always got attention, and Tallula liked attention.

"The society is very conservative," Ina said, having done her research. "Mostly older people. I think you should probably wear something professional, maybe a little understated."

"Oh, how fun."

Ina frowned. She put down the small notepad she'd been holding. "Should I look through your closet?"

"Yes. And let's do it quickly. I'm so tired. I swear, if I sit down on that bed, I'll fall asleep."

"We don't want that to happen," Ina said gravely. "Everyone is waiting to see your newest painting. Lots of press downstairs."

"Anyone interesting?" Tallula asked.

Ina was standing in the closet, shuffling through the few outfits she had packed for her boss. "Well, editors from *Vogue* and *Cosmo* will be present. The *New York Times* will be covering the event for the Sunday Styles section. Oh, yes—and the Hamilton triplets are here. They'll be introducing you and unveiling the painting."

Tallula perked right up and smiled. "Really? Ha! That's great! I didn't know I'd be meeting the Hamiltons today." But the smile faded quickly from her lips and was replaced by a look of worry. "Ina, why didn't you tell me they were coming? I would have asked you to buy me a few Triple Threat pieces. You *know* how I like to be prepared, and those girls practically eat and breathe fashion!"

Ina came scurrying out of the closet, a pensive expression on her face. "It's all on your itinerary. I left it on your desk at home weeks ago."

"How often do I sit at that desk?" Tallula snapped. "When I'm going to be in the company of special guests, I *need* to know beforehand, Ina. You should have just told me in person."

"But you were working in your studio—you've been in there for weeks," Ina replied quietly. "And I'm not allowed into your studio. I'm sorry, Tallula. Truly, I am. It won't happen again."

With a theatrical toss of her head, Tallula stared up at the ceiling. "As an artist, I have a tendency to lose myself in my work. Next time, just find me when I walk out of my studio."

"I'll do that." Ina cleared her throat. "But if it's any consolation, you're looking beautiful today, and I think I've found the perfect outfit." She disappeared into the closet again, then came out holding a strapless vermilion silk dress; it was cool and summery, yet sophisticated. "Catherine Malandrino. One of your favorites."

"But I don't have a tan," Tallula remarked, studying the dress. "I'll look so pale in that."

"You'll look beautiful. Here, at least try it on." Ina laid the dress down on the bed.

Tallula threw off the last towel and stood naked before the mirror. She was pleased with her reflection. The past few days of stress had undoubtedly burned two or three pounds from her already thin frame, but she didn't mind that at all. Growing up, she had been told repeatedly that she'd inherited "the fat gene" from her father's side of the family, which meant the arrival of a huge butt and meaty thighs the day she turned thirty. She had every intention of fighting that dire prediction, so being underweight suited her just fine. Besides, thin always looked better in photographs. And lately, her life had become an encyclopedia of photographs. From New York and Los Angeles to Tokyo and Johannesburg, Tallula's face had appeared just about everywhere. She'd been invited to several movie premieres in Los Angeles and London, countless art shows in Paris and Vienna, and a number of universities all over the country. In the middle of all that, she'd granted hundreds of interviews and sat for countless photo shoots. It seemed as if everyone wanted a piece of her.

Tallula wasn't a recluse. She didn't seek seclusion

from the world like most artists. She didn't feel the need to weave a web of silence around herself in order to create. Her house in the upscale suburb of Greenwich, Connecticut, was large and drafty and set back from the main road, but she had plenty of company. She had Elijah. She had Ina. She had a handful of friends who lived nearby and visited every so often—a small, select group of people from high school. In truth, Tallula didn't always enjoy seeing them because they inevitably reminded her of a time she wanted to forget. Her days at Alban Country Prep didn't comprise happy memories. She hadn't been beautiful then. She hadn't been popular or particularly confident. She certainly hadn't been famous. For the most part, she'd been the proverbial girl in the shadows, spending her free periods in the library and skipping out on extracurricular activities. Even art. She had wanted more than anything to join the school's highly regarded painting club; there, at least twice a week, she would have been able to relish in the one act that gave her complete bliss. But Tallula hadn't bothered asking her parents to sign the requisite admission form provided by the art department's chairperson. She'd known better than to ask.

All those hours painting things that may or may not be appropriate? her father would have said sternly. *Why, when you can dedicate that time to more important subjects?* And of course, her mother would have agreed. End of story. It had happened like that nearly all her life. Strict parents. Harsh rules.

When she thought back on those tough years, Tallula was often overcome by a sense of amazement. She still didn't know how she'd managed to develop her artistic skills. She didn't know how she'd accomplished the feat of sneaking under her parents' radar. Climbing up to the attic in the middle of the night with a flashlight and a sketch pad would have earned her a punishment of some sort, but she'd done it anyway. Time and again, she'd done it. Crouched under the garret's slanted ceiling, drawing whatever came to mind. Pages and pages of sketches. Dozens of small canvases that she later hid under the floorboards in her bedroom closet. It was her escape, her therapy. In the mysterious act of creating, she lost and found herself completely. For a long time, she'd thought her art would be relegated to her own eyes—her parents would never have understood it, and she knew she couldn't risk showing her work to a single soul with all those household rules on her shoulders.

But then life took a dramatic and unexpected turn, and her entire universe changed.

Tallula was nineteen when her parents died, courtesy of a drunk driver who smashed into their car on a rainy stretch of Connecticut roadway. It had been a stormy August night. Tallula had stayed home, readying herself for the trip back to St. Stephen's College in Maine, where she was set to begin her second year as an undergrad. The phone call came just after eight p.m.

In a matter of hours, Tallula went from being the daughter of restrictive, overbearing parents to being alone. Scared. Cut off from the cloistered world she had always known. She inherited a house and money and a thousand memories she wanted to forget. She returned to college, but it became immediately apparent to her that she wouldn't be staying. Instead of going to class and paying attention to her assignments, she channeled all her energy into her art. One painting after another. Long nights spent perfecting her skills. She was mourning one loss and at the same time celebrating all she had found: freedom, confidence, friendships. There was no more hiding, no more worrying. She felt inordinately energized.

And it was that surge of self-esteem that ultimately led her to Elijah Traymore. Like her, he was a student at St. Stephen's College. Unlike her, however, Elijah had been raised in a liberal, highly educated family that encouraged artistic endeavors. He had a brooding and somewhat mysterious presence on campus. Everyone knew him as the Sculptor. *That guy with the black hair and painted black fingernails? He's strange. Spends all day in the woods with a bunch of clay and makes these statues that crowd his dorm room. He hates being here. He doesn't speak to anyone.* But he spoke to Tallula when she approached him one night in the cafeteria. The attraction between them had been instant and intense. Kismet. What followed was a whirlwind romance: days spent examining each other's unique works of art, nights spent in heated conversation. Tallula felt as though she'd found her true soul mate.

It was Elijah who encouraged Tallula to exhibit her paintings. She hadn't expected much from her first showing—a small rented space in SoHo and only ten small paintings with ambiguous titles—but it had impressed the right people. In fact, it had utterly stunned a number of high-powered art critics and collectors. *Who are you?* they asked her over and over. *How long have you been painting? Where did you study? Have you exhibited before?* Tallula had been flattered by their collective enthusiasm. And she'd answered them with a little speech, the same speech she used today when addressing the press.

I began painting when I was very young. Art is my passion, my lifeline. I had to hide it from my parents, who were very strict and private. They knew I was interested in art, but they never understood what it was all about. They never suspected that I'd been working in private throughout my teenage years. Dozens and dozens of sketches and canvases. Painting became an escape for me. I always thought I'd have to hide it, but eventually, the need to share my particular vision of the world eclipsed everything else. I take my inspiration from the great master painters. Sometimes I feel them speaking through me. . . .

A suitably dramatic monologue, but a sincere one. And the critics and buyers and public agreed: Tallula Kayson was a wunderkind. Her works drew comparisons to most of the modern masters. There was an internal vision to her abstractness, a mystery that both seduced and shocked. A unique use of color and light and shadow. She might have seemed too young to possess such talent, but the proof was there. A flurry of publicity followed that first showing; there were magazine and newspaper articles and brief televised clips. Headlines read *Where Has She Been All These Years?* and *Twenty-Year-Old Artist and College Dropout a Genius* and *The Mystery of Tallula.* Her first show in the little gallery in SoHo sold out, and the amount she walked away with was more than most people made in a year. She became an overnight sensation in the art world—and a bona fide celebrity.

But fame wasn't exactly a gift. She was learning that

lesson more and more every day. Although being recognized and idolized made life fun and flashy, it also created roadblocks and changed the way things unfolded around you. There were petty little jealousies. There were egos. Try as she might, Tallula simply couldn't keep a handle on everything. She couldn't control certain forces . . . or certain people.

Elijah was proving to be her toughest battle yet.

Reaching for the dress Ina had picked out, Tallula slipped into it and looked at the full-length mirror again. Yes. She did look good. No mistaking that. She stepped into a pair of strappy sandals.

"Well?" Ina asked. "Do you love it?"

"I do," Tallula admitted. "You were right. But it needs something. It needs a little splash." She turned, went to her suitcase, and riffled through it. She found her favorite bright red silk scarf—which totally clashed with the outfit—and carefully smoothed it out. Then she wrapped it around her head and knotted it just over her left ear, fashioning a wacky-looking bandana. "There," she said, glancing into the mirror again. "That makes more of a statement. Now, Ina, would you be a dove and tell me how much time I have left?"

"Just a few minutes." A pause. "Um, Tallula? Do I . . . do I have to come with you today? To the luncheon, I mean."

Tallula stared at her assistant. "Of course you have to come. Why would you ask a question like that?"

"I'm just not feeling too good," Ina said quietly.

"What's wrong?" Tallula walked toward her, a look of concern on her face.

Ina cast her eyes downward. "I think I have a stomach flu or something like that," she replied.

"But you look fine, and I need you, Ina. And I promise, we won't stay long." Her tone was firm, and that ended the possibility of Ina staying in the penthouse while the luncheon unfolded. Tallula walked back to the mirror and studied herself again. "Now, Ina, would you be a cookie and tell me what the rest of my day looks like? I'd like to go shopping while I'm in Manhattan."

Ina reached for her notepad and flipped through it. "You have an interview with *Art in America* at four-thirty, a telephone interview with the *Chicago Tribune* at five-thirty, and dinner with your agent at eight."

Tallula blinked, confused. "Dinner? Is that tonight? I wanted to eat in tonight."

"I can call and cancel. . . ."

"No, don't do that." Tallula reached for her purse. "I don't want to upset anyone. Besides, I don't plan on coming back into Manhattan for several weeks, so I guess I should keep the dinner appointment."

Ina smirked. "Everyone wants to meet you, Madam Famous Artist."

"I just wish *I* felt like meeting everyone." She gave herself another quick once-over in the mirror. Then she shuffled through her purse for lip gloss and applied some. Trying to sound offhanded, she said, "I haven't heard Elijah, and he's usually so noisy. Where is he?"

"He left while you were in the shower," Ina replied. "He said he was going downstairs."

"To the luncheon?"

"I suppose so."

"Well . . ." Tallula gulped over her rising anger. "I wonder why he'd go without me? He knows I like making an entrance together."

Ina stayed quiet. She had learned long ago that silence was the best option when Tallula got mad.

But in truth, Tallula was more hurt than mad. She knew it was visible in her eyes. She had never been able to hide her emotions, and this was especially true when it came to Elijah. No, he wasn't perfect. He wasn't even always nice to her. He was, however, all she had. Lately they had been arguing more, and Tallula found herself having to stay quiet, to step out of his path when the threats came and her fear level spiked.

Now she stared at Ina. "Let's go, then," she said quietly. "I guess we'll meet him there."

"Of course."

Two minutes later, they were strolling through the huge suite, both clasping their purses, Ina cradling an appointment book and several press kits. Then they reached the foyer and a loud knock sounded at the door.

"Who could that be?" Tallula asked no one in particular.

Ina turned the knob, expecting to shoo away a reporter or photographer. But when her eyes met Elijah's face, she stepped back and quickly let him inside.

"Oh!" Tallula smiled. "There you are, darling. Why didn't you use your key?"

"I forgot it." Elijah stormed past her, his expression dark, his movements impatient. He didn't look at either of them as he headed for the bedroom.

"Where are you going?" Tallula called back into the room. "It's time for the luncheon."

"Forget it," Elijah snapped. "You go ahead without me."

"What?" She stared at him, trying to sound amused. But her voice cracked and belied the little smile creasing her lips. "Why wouldn't you want to come? You know how important—"

Elijah spun around. His eyes were as sharp as daggers. "Did you hear me? I told you to go without me. I'm not in the mood for any stupid luncheon. Just leave me alone." He went into the bedroom and slammed the door.

Ina had kept her gaze cast downward. She slowly turned the knob again. And, not for the first time, she bit her tongue as Tallula stormed past her in tears.

4

Taking the Plunge

Lex stared down at the green brooch pinned to her dress and tried not to barf. It was a garish color, shaped like a paintbrush, and way too big. From a distance, it probably looked like something obscene.

She was standing beside the podium with Park. Madison, of course, was still giving her acceptance speech—a long, rambling monologue about what art meant to her and how honored she was to be a member of the Society of the Americas. Every geezer in the audience was staring up at her with wide eyes. Nice, yes. But Lex couldn't wait for the afternoon to be over. She wished she had some of

Park's ability to look interested or, at the very least, polite. But she didn't. Lex knew that boredom was showing on her face like a fat pimple.

Inwardly, she sighed. It was better to use this time wisely, so she glanced up at the beautiful chandeliers and started reviewing all the work she had to do in the next couple of weeks. Her biggest project right now was the opening of the first Triple Threat store at the Hotel Gansevoort. An Upper East Side girl by birth and by choice, she had a special place in her heart for the Meatpacking District; it was trendy and chic and always pulsing with life. She preferred the nightclubs there to any of the ones in the East Village. The area's unique architecture almost made it feel as though you were stepping back in time to a different, older Manhattan. Not that she actually wanted to visit that turn-of-the-century era: horse poop–covered streets, no cell phones, and a severe shortage of cosmetics counters made for a very unfashionable city. But the current mix of cobblestone streets and sleek clubs made the Meatpacking District a perfect place to open the first Triple Threat store.

Shopping would be a new and exhilarating experience. There would be an on-site restaurant, and a resident masseuse would relieve the aches and pains that sometimes accompanied the trying on of clothes. Bending to pull pants over your legs. Lifting your arms to get a shirt over your head. It wasn't all fun and games. A girl could easily break a sweat selecting a new wardrobe. Above the main floor, a DJ would spin beats and get shoppers into a partying mood.

The announcement of the store had been huge news.

It had also been a complete surprise to Park. Busy with filming, Lex and Madison had decided to arrange the details quietly so that none of Park's attention would be drawn away from her script. But the *real* news was that the store's opening would coincide with the premiere of *Short Fuse* in late fall; a star-studded cast party was already in the works, and Jeremy Bleu had agreed to make an inaugural appearance once the front doors opened. What was more, Lex had used her connections—actually, her father's personal little phone book—to clinch a special deal with Paramount Pictures that would make the New York boutique a celebrity landmark: the studio had agreed to hold four premiere parties a year in the fashionable space, so the media blitz surrounding the store would be constant.

She had never been so excited. The Triple Threat line was selling phenomenally well around the world, and her newest collection was coming along nicely. Thank God school was out—homework had a tendency to get in the way of designing. But there was still a lot of work to be done. Tonight, Lex knew, she had to hit her desk and put the final touches on a new dress she'd dreamed up. After that, she'd have to revisit the sketches of the shoe line she had made two weeks ago. The line would be small—only three to four pairs of women's shoes—but they would be gorgeous. It was all time-consuming and exhausting. But it was also the most fun she'd ever had. She couldn't imagine doing anything else with her free time. Except maybe going out on a date every now and then. But she hadn't had one of those in ages. With her crazed schedule, how could she? People had gotten into the habit of pegging Madison as the future workaholic, but now Lex seemed to have taken over that role. Lex wanted to meet a nice guy with a brain and looks. That combination, however, seemed to have gone extinct. Some of the guys who walked in her social circle were hot, including several at St. Cecilia's Prep. In the end, though, they wanted nothing more than to hop under the sheets and then forget you, and Lex just wasn't in the mood for that kind of fling-thing anymore. Better to be single than to be with a moron running on cigarettes and testosterone.

". . . and my sister Lexington," Madison said, her voice booming across the room.

The moment Lex heard her name, she broke out of her reverie. She lifted her eyes and focused and saw that every gaze was on her. *Oh, shit.* Was she supposed to say something? Do something? She hadn't heard a word of Madison's speech. A few tense seconds ticked by. Swallowing hard, Lex finally brought her right hand up and gave the crowd a fake windshield-wiper wave. It seemed to do the trick.

A round of applause echoed on the air.

The speech was finished, and Lex smiled at no one in particular as she followed Madison and Park off the stage and back to the Michelangelo table. "Can we go now?" she asked flatly.

"Of course not," Madison said. "We still have to meet Tallula Kayson and introduce her new painting." She looked around. "Hey, have either of you noticed that Coco didn't come back from the bathroom?"

"You're right," Park confirmed. "She didn't. Maybe she went home."

"She wouldn't do that." Madison sat down. "She wanted to go shopping after this. We had it all planned out. I just hope she didn't run back into that sleazy Elijah somewhere out there. It took all three of us to call him off last time."

It was the cue Lex needed. "I tell you what," she said. "I'll run out and look for Coco and make sure she's okay. She really was pretty drunk."

"That would make me feel a lot better," Madison said, relieved. She gave Lex's arm a thankful pat. "And make sure she isn't with Poppy van Lulu either. Coco can't resist a Hollywood divorce bet."

Park chuckled. "Do we really need a psychic for that? We all *know* who's getting divorced next."

Lex swung her bag—otherwise known as the magic purse—around her shoulder and bolted from the room. The moment she stepped into the empty hallway, she breathed a sigh of relief. She was thrilled to be away from the confines of the luncheon. If she heard one more person make some snooty highbrow remark about Pollock or Rosenquist she'd positively lose it. She had an appreciation for art, but after a while, discussions of that nature tended to bore her. She ripped the ugly brooch from her dress and dropped it into her purse. Then she hung a right and headed for the bathroom. Peeking her head through the door, she called out Coco's name. When she got no response, she pushed all the way in and did a quick scan of the stalls: empty. Great. Where could the drunken Miss McKaid have gone? That question had about a dozen answers, and Lex didn't even want to consider most of them. Coco completely lost her brain after a couple of drinks. It wouldn't surprise Lex to find her standing behind the front desk of the hotel checking in guests.

She left the bathroom and decided to head for the main lobby. On her way down the wide staircase, she ran into a group of Japanese tourists, cameras hung around their necks. Several of them recognized her immediately and began nodding and pointing and chattering. An older man dressed in a bright green shirt, pale blue shorts, and flip-flops blocked Lex's path; he held out a map of Manhattan and, speaking excitedly in Japanese, pointed to the words *Lexington Avenue.*

"On TV," he said in broken English. "I see you!"

Lex smiled warmly. "Yes," she said. "I'm Lexington." When one of the women in the group held up a camera, Lex struck a pose and waited patiently while several pics were snapped. Her vision blurred with flashing white spots. She gave the tourists a final wave and then dashed the rest of the way down the staircase.

The lobby was crowded. As inconspicuously as possible, Lex scanned the large area. Lots of people with suitcases and several businessmen heading to the Peacock Alley bar. But still no sign of Coco. Lex didn't want to admit it, but she was starting to get a little nervous. She flipped out her cell and speed-dialed Coco; the line went directly to voice mail. That was weird. Coco never turned off her phone.

Where the hell could she be?

Lex took a few more steps into the lobby so that she could peer into the bar. She didn't want to be recognized again. Though flattering and sweet and perfectly lovely, having to give autographs would slow her down, and going back to the luncheon without Coco meant facing Madison's wrath.

She moved swiftly and quietly across the floor. She peeked over a tall plant and stared into the bar. Nothing. She took shelter beside the plant's long fronds as she pondered her options. Madison was right—Coco wouldn't have left without saying anything. Had she wandered into an open elevator by mistake? Had she tripped coming up the stairs? Or, worse, had she been nabbed by Poppy van Lulu and forced into an impromptu séance? Just a conversation with the woman was enough to ruin your day—a séance would probably have lasting effects on your personality.

Another minute passed, and Lex decided to check the gift shop. Drunk people got hungry, right? Maybe Coco was eating her way out of a bag of potato chips and drinking a Coke. That was it. That had to be it. All this time wasted when all Lex had to do was head for the one corner of the hotel that sold fast food. Totally annoying. She didn't want to risk being recognized again, so she tore off one of the large fronds and held it up in front of her face like a fan. A pointed edge poked her in the nose, and a sneeze itched its way across her face. She pinched her nostrils. She held the big leaf up higher so that it covered her cheeks. If anyone stared at her suspiciously, she'd have to convince them that she had just come out of a botanical spa treatment. She ripped off an edge of one leaf and slipped the thin piece behind her ear for effect. That was better. Made it appear as though she'd gotten a hair treatment too.

She stepped out of her hiding spot and turned around quickly.

And slammed head-on into another body.

A tall body with long arms, arms that were holding a stack of thick telephone books.

"Whoa!" Lex shrieked before falling to her knees.

But her voice was muffled by the massive bang of the other body hitting the floor, and by the telephone books raining through the air.

"Watch out!" one of the hotel clerks at the front desk screamed.

Everyone in the lobby whirled around.

Lex looked up from her place on the ground just as a phone book hit a vase, tipped it over, and spilled two dozen tulips smack-dab on the head of an elderly man sitting in one of the leather chairs.

Assailed by a shock of cold water and about two hundred dollars' worth of flowers, the man let out a yelp. Then the vase crashed and shattered into a hundred pieces. People scurried toward the man quickly, their arms outstretched. He stood up and immediately began wiping down the front of his blazer.

Well, Lex thought, *so much for not getting noticed.* She pushed away her leafy mask and yanked the piece of leaf from behind her ear. Mortified, she considered crawling her way out of the lobby, using her purse as a shield, but the idea vanished when she felt a big, warm hand lock around her wrist. She glanced up and caught her breath. She realized suddenly that the tall boy standing over her was the body she had slammed into a moment ago.

And, in the next instant, she realized that slamming into him hadn't been such a bad thing.

"Holy Jeez!" he said. "Are you okay? Let me help you up."

Lex nodded dumbly. "I'm . . . I'm fine." She heard the words but didn't actually hear herself say them. She was too busy checking out the hottie whose hand was now wrapped around hers.

He was well over six feet. He was thin but looked strong. All smooth lines and pumped-up muscles. His eyes were brown. His hair was black and buzzed close to the scalp. Nice full lips too.

"Hey, I'm really sorry about that," he was saying. "I know I shouldn't carry the phone books like that, but I really didn't see you. I—"

"It's okay," Lex said gently, staring up at him. "Really, I'm fine." *Totally fine,* she thought.

"Are you sure? I mean, maybe you need to sit down. Maybe . . ." He froze. His voice trailed away and he cleared his throat nervously.

Lex knew what the look on his face meant: he had recognized her. She had seen that very look thousands of times. Usually, when someone made the connection between her and the word *celebrity,* she was quick to offer a smile or a courteous wave. But now she simply stood there, content to stare up at him and let the moment play out.

"Oh, wow," he said. "Hey, you're Lexington Hamilton."

"Yes. I am."

"Holy Jeez. Well . . . wow."

Lex chuckled. She also found herself blushing. Which, of course, was completely out of character. She waited a few seconds for him to say something else, but he remained frozen, staring down at her with starstruck eyes. She realized then that his hand was still holding hers. "Since we've already shaken hands, I guess I should say it's nice to meet you," she remarked lightly.

"Oh, damn. I'm sorry. I . . . I didn't even realize that." He tightened his fingers around hers. "Nice to meet you too. You sure you're okay?"

"Yeah, I'm fine." She gestured her head at the old man, and at the people patting him dry. "I'm glad he's okay too."

"Yeah. That was actually really funny. Not in a mean way or anything. Just . . . funny."

"It *was* funny," Lex said. She wanted to do the right thing and walk over to the older man, but she couldn't take her eyes off the stud standing in front of her.

He flashed a quick smile, then nervously slipped his hand out of hers. "Um . . . well . . . is there anything I can help you with? Like, I mean, maybe you need a brush or something."

"A brush?" she repeated.

He pointed to the top of her head, where a remnant of leaf was sticking out of her hair.

Embarrassed, Lex quickly batted it away and smiled self-consciously. *The one time I run into a totally hot guy and my hair looks like it was styled by a florist,* she thought angrily. "I was finishing a spa treatment," she said quickly. She patted her cheeks. "Big plant leaves are good for exfoliating, and they help smooth out split ends."

"That's cool. You sure you don't need anything?"

And then she realized that he was dressed in the black pants and light blue shirt of hotel employees. The uniform wasn't particularly cool, but it looked great on him.

"I work here," he said, responding to the look on her face.

"You look so young to be working here," Lex commented. "You look, like, my age."

He nodded. "I'm seventeen. My dad is the assistant director of security here, and I work in his office during the summer and on weekends throughout the year. Nothing important. Just stupid paperwork and stuff like that."

Lex found herself smiling again. She liked the way he talked—a sexy mix of preppy and native New York. "What's your name?"

"Brooklyn."

"Seriously?"

He sighed and made a sour face. Then a smile broke over his lips. "Yeah. Brooklyn DiMarco. But everybody calls me Brock for short."

She felt like she'd been hit in the butt by one of Cupid's diamond-studded arrows. Brooklyn? How cool was that? How *coincidental* was it? His name wasn't Bob or Mike or Steve. It wasn't even Dakota or Tennessee. It was Brooklyn. You couldn't exactly take Lexington Avenue to the Brooklyn Bridge, but it was close enough. "That has to be the cutest name I've ever heard," she said. "It totally fits you." She gave his shoulder a playful and hopelessly girlish tap.

"Well, thanks," he replied sheepishly. "But sometimes it can be pretty embarrassing. You can't imagine what I went through as a kid."

"I totally get you," Lex told him. "But you should be proud of your name now. After Manhattan, Brooklyn happens to be my favorite borough. It's so *hot* there this time of year. Way hotter than Manhattan, anyway."

That totally did it. Brooklyn DiMarco blushed brighter than a jar of tomato sauce. But before he could say anything else, his cell beeped. He wrenched it from his pocket and stared at it. "Oh, damn," he snapped, clearly disappointed. "That's my dad looking for me."

"I hope I haven't gotten you into trouble," Lex said flirtatiously. "Not that a guy as big and strong as you should be scared of anything."

He smiled an incandescent smile. "Well, I have to get going. It was really nice meeting you, Lex Hamilton."

"You too, Brooklyn DiMarco. Maybe I'll see you again sometime."

"Maybe. But I don't walk in your circles. I'm just a plain old Brooklyn boy."

"My circles can be overrated." Lex felt a whole freakin' school of butterflies scurry through her stomach. She *so* didn't want this moment to end.

"I'm always here on the weekends," he said. "If you're ever around, ask for me." Then he gave her a quick wink and turned to go.

"Will do." Lex fanned herself with her purse as she watched Brooklyn DiMarco jog across the lobby and disappear through a door behind the front desk. Talk about hot. She was a Manhattan girl, but she totally knew which borough she wanted to visit next.

◇   ◇   ◇

It was official: Madison had found a new BFF in Tallula Kayson.

They had been inseparable for the better part of an hour. The moment Tallula walked into the room, Madison approached her, put out her hand, and started tossing out compliments. Flattery always worked. But it was more than just that. Tallula had seemingly warmed up to Madison quickly, because within a matter of minutes, they were sitting down at the Michelangelo table and chatting up a storm.

Park observed the new little friendship from a distance. She was happy for Madison, and not altogether surprised: Madison and Tallula shared a voracious passion for art. But that, in Park's opinion, was where the similarities ended. Tallula was elegant and beautiful and radiated a certain kind of mystery. She wasn't the type of girl who just smiled and nodded and made small talk; she was the type of girl who studied you with her eyes and took mental notes on your character, your demeanor, your choice of dress. Park liked that—it showed a certain level of depth and intelligence—but there was also another, less flattering side to Tallula. The famous pop artist was hopelessly dramatic and downright bitchy. Park had spoken to her for a few minutes, and in that short span of time, Tallula had snapped at her assistant twice and blatantly stared down three of the waiters. She had also given a rather chubby female guest one of those cold you-don't-belong-here stares. What was that all about? Park didn't like it at all, which was why she had extricated herself from the conversation quickly.

Now Park leaned against the bar and listened as Beethoven played on the air. She observed Madison and Tallula, taking note of how touchy-feely Tallula was— tapping Madison's shoulder, holding on to Madison's hand, launching into a quick and giddy hug. They looked like long-lost sorority sisters. The spectacle disturbed Park as much as it intrigued her. Why was Madison so blinded by art fame? Couldn't she see past the façade? All in all, Park pretty much felt like Tallula Kayson was full of shit, the kind of girl who chose to be your friend only after she calculated the diameter of your spotlight. Totally disappointing.

She was about to reach for her cell when she saw Lex walk into the room and head her way. "Well," Park said, "that took you long enough. Did you find Coco?"

"No, I didn't." Lex shrugged. "I looked everywhere—the bathroom up here, the bathroom downstairs, the lobby, the gift shop. And her phone is turned off. She must've gone home."

Home? That idea didn't sit well with Park, and she knew Lex wasn't buying it either. Coco had never ditched them. "That's really weird," she said quietly. "Why the hell would she turn off her cell?"

"Beats me." Lex frowned. "But I know Madison won't be happy about this failed mission."

"Madison's as happy as a fifty-year-old woman at a Botox party." Park pointed to the Michelangelo table. "She and Tallula are now BFFs. And that girl sitting beside them, the one who isn't talking to anyone—"

"Is Tallula's assistant," Lex guessed.

"Right. Her name is Ina. Very professional."

"And very invisible. I don't know how these personal assistants do it." Lex shuddered. She had witnessed too many times the abuse that befell personal assistants. They got screamed at and things thrown at them; they were bullied and threatened on a regular basis. And then, after being fired, they usually violated their confidentiality agreements and sold ugly stories about their former bosses to the tabloids. That was precisely why she, Park, and Madison had opted not to have personal assistants: the cycle was just too vicious. She scanned the room, looking past Ina. "Where's Elijah?" she asked.

"Not here."

"Figures. How's Tallula?"

"Eh." Park made a sour face.

Lex knew what that meant. "Bad, huh?"

"You know the type," Park said. "All girly and happy as long as she's around other famous people. I know I just met her, but I think she's kind of fake."

Lex crinkled her nose. "Eeeww. But Madison doesn't see it, right?"

"Nope. Not yet, at least."

"Being blinded by art fame is totally rank," Lex said quietly. "And can I just ask an important question? What's with that ugly thing around Tallula's head? She completely ruined that dress."

"You know these modern-art types," Park answered, her tone sarcastic. "They have to look a little crazy in order to be happy. But don't tell that to Madison—she thinks Tallula's a goddess."

"In that getup?" Lex sighed. "Maybe Madison'll snap out of it once I tell her I didn't find Coco."

"Did you try looking for her in the bar off the lobby?"

"Of course. All I saw were a bunch of businesspeople drinking, which completely amazes me. How do these older men get drunk so early in the afternoon?"

"They probably work in advertising," Park said

offhandedly. "Anyway, let's get over to the table. They're about to unveil the painting, and Madison will have our heads if we aren't there."

After the introductions—Lex complimented Tallula on her dress, Tallula complimented Lex on her shoes—Madison pranced happily across the room and to the podium. She clapped twice to get everyone's attention. "Ladies and gentlemen," she said, "it's the time we've all been waiting for. In just a few moments, we will feast our eyes on Tallula Kayson's newest masterwork."

There was a round of applause as two men walked to the front of the room; one was holding a steel-framed easel, which he set down next to the podium, and the other carefully lowered a large draped canvas onto the easel's edge.

The lights dimmed.

"Ladies and gentlemen," Madison announced proudly. "I give you Tallula Kayson's newest work, *Blue Love*." She struck a pose, thrusting both her arms out like a hostess on *The Price Is Right*.

One of the men whisked the white drape off the canvas.

A flurry of gasps echoed through the room, followed by a round of spontaneous, sustained applause.

"Oh!" Madison cried. "Oh, how *spectacular*."

"It's extraoooooordinary," a well-dressed elderly woman said.

"Truly remarkable!"

"Oh—look at the colors!"

Blue Love was, indeed, an interesting work. Brilliant, vivid colors. Wide strokes of black that blended into the edges of the canvas. A flurry of small dots that looked like blue snowflakes. But that was all. Typically abstract, the painting was a true example of pop art: there wasn't anything visibly obvious about it, no landscape or figures or faces. No scene. But the painting had all the trademarks of a genuine Tallula Kayson: the pointillism, the shadowing, and the two oval-shaped orbs hidden strategically in the background that represented God's eyes staring down at the majesty of it all. The somewhat eerie supernatural element was a staple of Tallula's. "God's eyes" could be found in every one of her paintings, but you had to study the canvas for several minutes to spot them. And once you did, there was no escaping their originality.

The second round of applause thundered through the air. Tallula nodded and smiled and waved as she walked to the podium. She hugged Madison. Then she assumed a graceful posture and let the photographers do their thing. The barrage of flashes lasted for nearly two minutes.

Lex leaned into Park. "Is it me, or does that painting look like a big, stained dish towel?"

Park bit her tongue to keep from laughing. "It's called *abstract* art."

"Well, then call me an abstract artist," Lex whispered. "Because I could totally splash a bunch of things on a canvas and give it a silly name."

Another round of flashes followed.

"Please," Madison said over the din of voices and applause, "give us a speech."

Tallula positioned herself in front of the podium. "Thank you all very much," she began. "It's a pleasure to be here, and an honor to unveil *Blue Love* in the presence of the Royal Crown Society of the Americas. Thank you, truly, for your support." She stepped away from the microphone. "Ina, would you be a mouse and help me down?"

Ina Debrovitch scrambled toward Tallula, both arms outstretched.

Tallula followed Madison back to the table. Another wave of clapping broke across the room. People crowded around the painting and began chattering amongst themselves.

"Looks like you're a hit again, Tallula," Lex said, trying to sound genuinely interested. "I'm sure that beauty of a painting will create a frenzy at auction."

"All the money will be going to an orphanage in Connecticut," Tallula explained. "The society will be handling everything, and now that you girls have been appointed ambassadors, you'll be involved in that."

"I can hardly wait." Madison was still beaming. She looked as though she were about to move the tables and do a series of cartwheels.

Ina Debrovitch came to Tallula's side. "I'm sorry to interrupt, but you told me to tell you when it hit two-thirty. You have lots of phone calls and e-mails to attend to."

"Yeah, I know." Tallula sighed and turned back to the girls. "Sorry to cut this short, but I have to get back upstairs. See you later, okay? Call me and let's have lunch soon." She turned around, locked her arm inside Ina's, and together they strode out of the room.

"Isn't she amazing?" Madison breathed happily. "She's even cooler and more interesting than I thought she'd be."

"What were you two talking about for the last hour?"

Park asked. "You looked like a couple of prep-school girls who hadn't seen each other for a whole summer."

Madison reached for her purse. "It was just an instant friendship. I tend to get along right away with artists and people who have a high intellect." She gave her head another airy toss, then looked at Lex. "Where's Coco? Did you find her?"

"No, I didn't. And I looked everywhere." Lex did another quick scan of the room as guests continued mingling. "I have a feeling she met Poppy somewhere along the way and got too spooked to come back and join the fun."

"Oh, God," Madison moaned, her expression turning serious. "You really think that's what happened?"

"It's totally possible," Park said.

Madison sighed. "Then we have to save her. Come on. Let's go."

It took another half hour to make an exit. A proper exit. They couldn't simply walk out of the room. They had to say good-bye to every member of the society, thank the appropriate guests, pose for more pictures. As Madison had expected, polyester-for-brains Mayor Mayer was nowhere to be found; like Coco, he had apparently made a quiet departure. Those kinds of disrespectful infractions irked Madison tremendously—and she didn't forget them. Next time she granted *New York* magazine an interview, she'd let an unfavorable comment about Mayor Mayer slip out. *Oh, I didn't get much of a chance to speak with him at the luncheon because he spent most of the afternoon at the bar.* A nonchalant and seemingly innocent remark like that would have him fending off reporters for at least three days.

And as for Coco . . . well, Madison would have to take more drastic action. But finding her and making sure she was okay was the first order of business.

She, Park, and Lex did a second sweep of the hotel's first two floors. They split up and each took a section. Forty-five minutes later, they met in the lobby, each of them empty-handed. Coco's cell was still turned off, and a call to her parents' apartment went unanswered. By that time, the luncheon had ended and nearly every guest had left.

"We've done what we could," Lex said. "I'm sure Coco will call soon and apologize."

They left the hotel through the main doors and scanned the busy stretch of Park Avenue. Donnie Halstrom, medical school dropout-turned-chauffeur, was nowhere to be found. Lex dialed him without having to be asked to do so.

It was a muggy afternoon. Smog cloaked skyscrapers and the air was heavy with exhaust fumes. Finally, they spotted their limo at the corner and began walking toward it.

But before they even made it to the curb, a scream rent the air, cutting through the cacophony of traffic like a clap of thunder. A woman getting out of a cab pointed frantically at the sky as several cars ground to screeching halts.

Madison, Park, and Lex looked up. And froze.

They didn't know what was plummeting through the air until the body slammed into the pavement five feet from them with a resounding *thud*.

5

An Artful Corpse

Elijah Traymore had never looked so dead.

He had landed on his back. His skull was spouting blood across the pavement in torrents. His arms were outstretched and his eyes stared unseeingly at the sky. To make matters worse, he'd taken the plunge in a white T-shirt and shorts, and bright speckles of red created a ghastly polka-dot pattern across the front of his body.

The whole picture was unspeakably ugly. So much so that Madison, Park, and Lex remained frozen for several seconds, too stunned to breathe. All around them, chaos had erupted: the woman who had screamed was still screaming as she leaned against the cab in front of the Waldorf; people had emerged from their cars and gathered on the sidewalk; and two doormen were shouting commands from their posts at the revolving doors.

It was Park who took control of the situation. She grabbed Madison and Lex by their arms and pulled them back. She turned them around so that they wouldn't have to stare in shock at the broken corpse. Then she inhaled deeply and said, "Madison, whatever you do, don't look at the front of your dress."

But the order went unheeded.

Madison looked down at the front of her dress. And there, in a messy zigzag pattern, was a series of ugly crimson flecks staining her one-of-a-kind McQueen. Upon impact, blood had sprayed from Elijah's body and followed a very weird trajectory. When Madison realized that her dress looked as if it had broken out in chicken pox, she screamed.

"I told you not to look!" Park snapped.

"This is horrible!" Madison wailed. "I'm covered in blood! Ugh! This will *never* come out! Blood is worse than soy sauce!"

"Calm down," Park urged her. "We're surrounded."

"I don't care," Madison carried on. "Lex, open the magic purse! Do you have any club soda? Oh! I can't even stand here and look at myself!"

Instead of reaching into the magic purse, Lex laced her fingers around Madison's shoulders and gave her a good, steady shake. "Stop it!" she barked. "First of all, there happens to be a dead body behind us. Second of all, people are starting to stare at you. And *third* of all, that dress is made from the finest silk, and club soda would be too abrasive to use on it. Now take a deep breath and maintain."

Madison swallowed hard. She nodded and wiped a line of sweat from her forehead. "You're right," she said breathlessly. "I don't know what I was thinking. Club soda is a dumb idea."

"Damn right it is," Lex said sharply.

"Everybody, please stay *away* from the body!" Park called out, cupping her hands over her mouth. "Remain at the curb and do *not* come forward until the police get here!" She made clear gestures with her arms, instructing the men who had run out of their cars to take several steps back. "For those of you who may be feeling faint, please lean forward and breathe deeply. Do not be afraid to sit down on the street. I will pay for your dry cleaning bills personally. Please note that this ugly scene is an obvious tragedy and has nothing to do with any *live* person here."

"And Hamilton Holdings is an equal opportunity employer," Lex said to the gathering crowd, noting the strict professionalism of Park's tone.

"What the hell happened?" Madison asked. There were tears in her eyes. "Did . . . did Elijah jump? Commit suicide? Oh, God—it's just so horrible!"

"I don't know if he jumped or what," Lex answered. "But I guess we have to check."

"Check?" Madison's voice rose. "Do we have to? I totally don't feel like scoping out a corpse today!"

"We have to move in and inspect the scene," Lex shot back. "What if . . . what if by some strange twist of fate he's still *slightly* alive?"

"Look at him!" Madison pointed to the body. "He may as well be a mannequin in a Macy's storefront window. He's practically headless! There's blood everywhere!"

"Right now," Park said evenly, "we're going to handle this calmly and have a look-see. And because I know a Krispy Kreme shop opened yesterday on Third Avenue, it'll take at least three more minutes for the cops to get here. Besides, we're good when it comes to homicides."

"Homicide?" Madison blinked furiously.

Park nodded.

"What . . . how do you know it's a . . ." Madison closed her eyes, shook her head, and took a deep breath. "Maybe he fell . . . or jumped on purpose! We don't know that it's a homicide!"

"I think I saw something on Elijah's body I don't like," Park said. "And I'm pretty sure we're looking at a homicide."

"Oh, *great*," Lex whispered. "I guess I'm not going to get any work done tonight."

"Ignore the crowds and follow me," Park instructed them. She led the way to the body. She mentally blocked out the people who had gathered all over the avenue and sidestepped three separate pools of blood. From this vantage point, she could see the blue-tinged pallor of Elijah Traymore's neck, as well as the way the back of his head had literally flattened against the concrete. "Well, it's obvious that he changed clothes after meeting us and leaving the luncheon," she said. "He's not in the biker outfit."

Madison cupped a hand over her mouth. Tears streamed along her fingers. "The poor guy," she whispered. "He probably died of fear before he even hit the ground. The adrenaline must've shot through him and totally wrecked his heart."

Lex nodded. "I know. He might've been sleazy, but this is a horrible way to go. But I don't think he died in midair, Madison. The fall was too quick. He died instantly from the blunt trauma of hitting concrete at a million miles an hour."

"Right," Park said. "But the cause of death is from internal hemorrhaging. Every organ in his body is oozing right now, not just his brain."

"And look at his right ankle," Madison said. "It's all blue and broken. Isn't that multiple combustion?"

"Multiple *contusions*," Park corrected her. She pointed down to the front of the body. "But look very closely. Do you see what I'm seeing?"

"All I see is white T-shirt and blood," Madison said.

"Me too," Lex agreed.

"Look closer," Park urged them. "Pretend the bloodstains aren't there. Look right in the middle of the shirt. Do you see it?"

Lex leaned forward, cradling the magic purse against her chest. She squinted and cupped her hand over her eyes. "Oh, shit!" she said a few seconds later. "It's a handprint."

Park smiled. "Bingo."

"Move over," Madison said. She pushed Lex to the side and assumed the same position. Then she righted herself, and her eyes went wide.

The faint outline was there, darker in certain spots than others. At first glance it looked like a simple, light water stain pressed into the white fabric. But on closer examination, it totally resembled a handprint. Or the first three fingers of a handprint.

"I see it," Madison said quietly. "But . . . couldn't *he* have made that himself? What if it's *his* handprint we're staring at?"

Park shot her a suspicious look. "What if it isn't?"

"It's definitely not a simple stain," Lex said. "Look at how dark the upper tip of the imprint is. If it was water, it would have dried by now."

"I have to agree with you there." Park reached for her cell, flipped it open, and snapped three pics.

"So you're saying that he was pushed just because of that little mark?" Madison asked incredulously. "That handprint could be anything. Maybe it's not water, but what if it's something that just dried there?"

"Like what?" Park asked in return.

"Like . . ." Madison's voice trailed off.

"Like an oil-based moisturizer?" Lex said suddenly. "I hate them—they always leave stains."

"Both of you are taking this too far," Madison countered. "You can't make that kind of assessment until his shirt has been examined forensically."

Park dropped the cell into her purse. She examined the body more closely. She noted its position, its slackness. Then her eyes caught something suspicious, and she felt her pulse quicken. "Look at his hands."

Madison blinked. "His hands?"

"Yep," Park said firmly. "I don't like what I'm seeing here."

Lex squatted down beside the body, her heels just missing pools of blood. She looked at Elijah's right hand, then his left. She gasped. "His palms are *scraped*," she said fiercely. "And two of the fingernails on his left hand are broken."

"Evidence that he tried desperately to hold on to the ledge after he was pushed," Park deduced.

"Or evidence that he got scared and tried to hang on to the ledge in the last moments before he committed suicide." Madison folded her arms across her chest. "Like maybe he changed his mind."

Park walked around to examine the other side of the body. "We saw him less than two hours ago, Madison. He didn't strike me as the suicidal type."

"Maybe not outwardly," Madison replied. "But who knows what was going on in his head?"

"That's true." Lex stood up. "We really didn't know him at all." She cupped a hand over her eyes and stared up. "But if he plunged from that penthouse balcony, he knew it would do the trick. That's totally high. I think it's forty-two stories."

"Tallula," Madison whispered suddenly. "Oh my God. What happened to her? What's going on up in that penthouse suite?"

Lex slipped an arm around her sister's shoulder. "Just stay strong. Everything will be fine. I'm sure Tallula is . . ."

"Is what?"

Lex gulped uncomfortably as she looked up at the tower. "I'm sure she's just . . . hanging out somewhere."

"*Hanging?*" Madison's voice broke. "Oh my God! Oh—no!"

Lex bit down on her lip. She probably shouldn't have used that word.

In the distance, sirens wailed.

Park circled the body completely. She stopped when she was directly beside Elijah's waist. She swept her eyes across the ground and trained her gaze in an outward circular motion, scanning the concrete for clues. The spatter of blood spiraled off to the left; several drops had sprayed Madison, so that was the trajectory that followed the impact. She had read all about body splats in one of her forensic textbooks. The cause of death would ultimately be hemorrhaging of the internal organs caused by blunt trauma, but when a body hit hard ground after a lengthy fall, what it left in its wake was an ugly, Spin Art mess.

Splat.

Without standing exactly where Elijah had been standing just before he took the plunge, Park couldn't deduce all that much. There wasn't anything too telling about the rivers of blood—except that they were plentiful. Crimson stained the sidewalk in ugly, jagged slats.

She raised her gaze and scanned the crowds. Too much commotion for her and Madison and Lex to *really* be noticed. A monkey wearing Victoria's Secret could have been hopping around out here, but all eyes would *still* be locked on the blood and gore.

She was about to walk away when something caught her eye.

Right there against the wall of the hotel, a good ten feet from the street and maybe four feet from the body, sunlight glinted off a metal object.

Park walked over to it as casually as possible and bent down. Her lips parted in surprise when she saw a skeleton key lying beside the wall. It was silver and scratched . . . as if it had bounced off the ground and skidded across the concrete.

A key; its stem was silver, its square top blue. *WTF?*

She knew leaving it there would be the right thing to do, but she gave in to impulse and picked it up, closing her fingers around it. She stood and threw a glance over her shoulder just as a long line of uniformed men poured out of the front doors of the hotel. Security.

And careening down the avenue, the cops. Lights and sirens flashed everywhere as several cruisers screeched to a halt.

"Get over here!" Madison ordered her, instinctively backing up, wanting to join the crowd of onlookers.

Standing close together, they watched as security guards tried to fend off photographers, as uniformed cops dropped blue barricades into place, sealing off the street. A white sheet was immediately draped over Elijah Traymore's body.

"Hey!" one of the onlookers said. "Isn't that the famous sculptor kid? The one who was on *Entertainment Tonight* last week?"

"I read about him in *Vanity Fair*," another person said. "Oh, God—did he kill himself?"

"You see?" Madison whispered. "There's no reason to suspect Elijah was pushed."

The word *pushed* grated against Park's brain again. That was when she remembered something else she had read in one of her forensic books, and the mathematical equation of suicide by jumping didn't compute here. "People who jump from high floors usually land facedown," she said. "Elijah landed on his back."

Madison swallowed hard again. "Well, maybe he decided to do a few flips on the way down? Like maybe he wanted to go out feeling like an acrobat?"

"Hey, Brooklyn!" Lex's voice suddenly echoed above the din of the crowd.

Madison, shocked and horrified, grabbed Lex's arm and gave it a tug. "What the hell are you screaming about? We're in Manhattan, you birdbrain."

"Brooklyn!" she called out again.

"Is your dress cutting off the blood to your head?" Madison snapped. "People are staring at us."

"Don't people generally stare at us?" Park tossed that out nonchalantly as she studied the skeleton key in her hand.

Then all eyes fell on the tall, incredibly good-looking guy racing toward Lex. There was a hint of a smile on his face.

"Holy Jeez!" he yelled, running up to her. "Are you okay? We heard about a body landing on the pavement and we were all like, *What? No way!*"

"We saw it happen!" Lex said. She rested her right hand on his arm as she stared up at him. "The body fell like a few feet from us! It totally almost flattened us!"

"They're saying it's Elijah Traymore!" Brooklyn looked to them like he wanted details. "That he jumped from the penthouse balcony."

Lex nodded gravely. "It is Elijah. We saw him . . . and all the blood."

"Damn." Brooklyn turned and stared in the direction of the body. Dark stains had begun seeping through the sheet. "He seemed like a cool guy too."

"Did he?" Lex sounded as though she didn't believe him.

"Yeah. I mean, I only met him once. Saw him and his girlfriend when they checked in with their assistant. They all seemed pretty cool."

Madison cleared her throat loudly—so loud, in fact, that Park jumped.

"Oh," Lex said, smiling and shrugging. "Sorry. Brooklyn, these are my sisters, Madison and Park. Girls, this is Brooklyn DiMarco."

"Pleasure to meet you," Park said, shaking his hand.

"Hello." Madison shot him a long stare before smiling politely, if a bit uncertainly. Then she turned the stare on Lex.

And Lex knew what that meant. An explanation was in order. "Brooklyn and I met earlier today, when I went searching for Coco. He and I kind of . . ." She smirked. "Bumped into each other."

"We kind of *keep* bumping into each other." Brooklyn laughed.

"Oh," Madison said, confused. She cleared her throat, unsure what to say. She smiled again and held her hand out to Brooklyn. "Nice to meet you. Where . . . um . . . where do you go to school?"

His eyebrows knitted together. "Huh?"

"School," Madison repeated. "You look about our age."

"Oh. Right." He nodded. "I'm a senior at LaGuardia. You know, Performing Arts. Over on Sixty-fourth and Amsterdam."

"No kidding!" Lex said. "That's where Jennifer Aniston went. We were just at her birthday party!"

"*I* didn't go to that party," Madison said. "*I* was at the UNICEF dinner." She stared up at Brooklyn again and couldn't help feeling suddenly hot. One more blink and she would officially be flirting with him. "Is Brooklyn your real name, or is that just a nickname?"

"It's my real name. But everyone calls me Brock."

"Except me," Lex said. "*I* call you Brooklyn."

Park, who quickly recognized the attraction between Lex and Brock, smiled broadly. "A few of the production assistants on the set of *Short Fuse* went to LaGuardia," she said. "Are you an acting student?"

"Nah," Brooklyn replied. "I play violin."

Lex squeezed his forearm again. "That's my favorite instrument. It's so romantic."

"I'd love to play for you sometime," he said, and took a step closer to her.

"Hey, Brock?" Madison looked him squarely in the eyes. "Do you know anything about what happened here? Do you know if Tallula Kayson is okay? Where is she?"

"The cops are swarming the hotel," he said. "Right before my father—he's one of the security directors here—ran out, I thought I heard him say that they located Tallula."

"Oh my God," Madison whispered. "So they've told her. They've—"

And for the second time that afternoon, a high-pitched scream pierced the air.

Madison spun around and saw Tallula standing just outside the hotel doors. She was being contained by a doorman as she wailed and fought to break free from his hold. "No!" she cried. "Elijah! He can't be dead! He can't be dead!"

People everywhere were cupping their hands over their mouths and whispering to each other.

Madison rushed forward, ignoring a number of security guards who screamed for her to stop. "Tallula!" she called, opening her arms wide. "Oh, honey. I'm so sorry!"

Tallula tore herself from the doorman's hold and hugged Madison fiercely. "I don't believe it's him!" she sobbed. "They won't let me see his face, but I have to see his face! I don't believe it's him!"

Madison wrapped her hands around Tallula's shoulders. "It's him," she said gently. "I saw him."

"No! No!"

Park and Lex joined Madison's side. Brooklyn stood a few feet behind them. They remained silent as Tallula cried and cried on Madison's shoulder.

"I loved him," Tallula sobbed. "Why would he do this to me? How could he? We . . . were going to get married in the spring. . . . Not my Elijah. Not my Elijah . . ."

Park had been looking down at the ground. Now she raised her eyes to get a glimpse of the police activity.

Two detectives were kneeling beside the body, pointing to the trails of blood. One of them stood up and, his gaze locked on Tallula, began walking toward her.

"Excuse me, Ms. Kayson? I'm Detective Roan." He was short and bald with a ruddy complexion and small blue eyes. Probably fifty, but too many years of being a cop in New York City had added puffy dark bags under his eyes. "This is a terrible tragedy. I'm very sorry, but I'm afraid I'm going to have to ask you a few questions."

Tallula lifted her head from Madison's shoulder. "I don't know what happened!" she cried. "I wasn't up in the penthouse! I don't know why Elijah's dead!"

"Had he been having any suicidal thoughts recently?" Detective Roan asked her flatly. "Did he say anything like that to you?"

Tallula wailed louder.

"Maybe now isn't the right time, Detective," Madison said gently.

Park tugged at the sleeve of Detective Roan's shirt. "Hi," she said quietly, pulling him off to the side. "I was just wondering . . . didn't you happen to take a look at the deceased's fingers?"

"Excuse me?"

Park brought her face close to his. "Scrapes in and around his palms. And two broken fingernails. They could be defensive wounds, but they could also mean he tried to hold on to something. . . ."

Detective Roan's face registered confusion and outrage. "You're Park Hamilton, right?"

"Right."

"I'm a fan, and so are my daughters," Roan said. "But I think you should leave the police work to us."

"Just look into it," Lex urged him quietly, if a bit impatiently. "We're rarely wrong when it comes to murder."

The detective's eyes nearly popped from their sockets.

That was the precise moment Park stared over his shoulder and saw Coco McKaid running out of the hotel's front doors, looking mussed and harried and disheveled. "Coco!" she called out. "Over here!"

Brooklyn tapped Lex's shoulder. "Who's Coco?"

"One of our friends," Lex explained. "I was looking for her when I bumped into you."

Coco eased her way past the security guards and the police. She was more sober than before, but she still looked like hell. She nearly stumbled into Park. "Hey," she said breathlessly. "What's going on? What's with all the cops?"

"Where have you been?" Madison asked. "We were looking for you!" She stared Coco down, noting her disheveled appearance and the pallor of her skin. "Are you okay?"

"I'm sorry. I just . . . I . . . well . . ." Coco swallowed hard and shot the detective a curious glance. "Hey, that's Tallula. . . . Why is she crying?"

Park cocked her head to the right.

Confused, Coco turned around. Her eyes widened. She drew in breath to speak, but no words came out.

As the body was being lifted onto a gurney, the sheet fell away for a split second and revealed Elijah's blood-stained face.

"Oh my God!" Coco screamed. She stared in disbelief. She brought her hands up to her mouth, and her purse tumbled from her fingers and crashed to the ground, spilling its contents over Park's shoes.

Everyone looked down.

Tallula gasped, her jaw dropping. She lowered herself to the ground and, pushing aside a lipstick and compact and a bottle of custom-mix perfume, twined her fingers around one item in particular: a gold rope chain. She held it up and let it dangle from her forefinger; at its end was a five-pointed star.

"What is it, honey?" Madison asked.

Tallula stood up and fixed her eyes on Coco. The grief evident on her face only moments ago was replaced by rage. "This is Elijah's," she whispered. "He never took it off. Never. *What the hell is it doing in your purse?*"

6

My BFF, the Killer

"I found it on the floor on my way to the bathroom," Coco explained quickly, trying to keep her voice steady. "I picked it up because I knew it looked important. Expensive. I meant to turn it in to the front desk, but I never got the chance."

"Liar!" Tallula screamed.

Detective Roan had moved the party into the lobby, which had been cleared several minutes earlier by hotel personnel. Now they were all standing in a nook beside the empty bar. Madison, Park, Lex. Coco and Tallula. Brooklyn had been called away by his father promptly—

the entire security team would be working late—but before leaving, he had managed to slip Lex his cell number.

That, however, was the furthest thing from Lex's mind now. Her stomach was in knots as she watched the surreal scene unfold in front of her. She couldn't believe any of it. She felt as though she were walking through a nightmare that had just taken another ruthless turn.

Tallula's accusatory eyes. Coco's frightened voice. Detective Roan's mounting suspicion. Those ghastly red dots on Madison's dress that clashed terribly with her shoes. It was almost too much to bear.

"I'm not lying!" Coco screamed back. "You don't even know me! How can you accuse me of anything?" Her voice broke and her eyes welled with tears. Her fear was painfully obvious.

"I think we should all calm down," Park said, not for the first time. "Things will get better faster if we all just take a deep breath."

"And maybe do a quick yoga stretch," Madison chimed in.

Tallula rolled her neck. "Oh, I'd love to be able to stretch right now."

"Excuse me!" Detective Roan shouted. "Nobody is doing anything except answering my questions!" He glared at Madison, Park, and Lex. "And *you* three are just getting in the way! You'll have to wait outside!"

"Absolutely not!" Tallula screeched. She clutched Madison's hand firmly. "I won't answer any questions without my new BFFs here!"

"Neither will I!" Coco said quickly. And just as

quickly, she whirled in Madison's direction. "I thought *I* was your BFF!"

"You are," Madison answered shakily. "Both of you are my friends. Really, you are. But right now, just stay cool and answer the detective's questions."

Detective Roan's face took on the expression of a pit bull. "I'm only going to say it once, got it? The only people I want here with me are Tallula Kayson and Coco McKaid. That means anyone named after an avenue has to leave!"

Lex clucked her tongue. "Can't you be more original than that?" she snapped.

"I agree," Madison said firmly. "There's no reason to resort to clichés. I mean, *really.*"

"Detective, may I ask you a question?" Park took a step in his direction. "Are you conducting an official police interrogation here? Because if you are, I believe Coco and Tallula have the right to have an attorney present."

His lips curled in a little snarl. He stayed quiet.

"That's right!" Coco snapped. "And a publicist! I'm being made to feel like a criminal!"

"And you can't expect *me* to answer any questions!" Tallula wailed. "I'm in shock!" She stumbled toward a chair and plopped into it, covering her face with her hands.

It was a clear defeat for Detective Roan, and he knew it.

But Park didn't give him a smug expression. Instead, she smiled brightly, dug into her purse, and pulled out a roll of Life Savers. She popped one into her mouth and then gingerly offered him one.

The snarl still in place, he grabbed a piece and crunched down on it.

"Now," Park said firmly. "We need some questions answered, right? Let's start with you, Coco. Tell us exactly what happened, please."

"It happened just like I said," Coco explained. "When I left the luncheon I went to the bathroom, and I . . . I saw the chain on the floor and I picked it up. End of story."

Madison looked at Lex, who looked at Park.

"Where'd you go after the bathroom?" Park asked.

"Madison, you told me that Lex went to the bathroom when I first arrived at the luncheon," Tallula said.

"So the two of you went to the bathroom together," Detective Roan stated. "Is that right?"

"No, it's not." Lex sighed. *Damn.* She didn't want to have to speak up about Coco's whereabouts just yet. But she knew she had no choice. "I went looking for Coco because Coco never came back from the bathroom. I looked for her for nearly an hour."

Coco blushed.

"So then where did you go during that time, Miss McKaid?" Detective Roan asked.

"I . . . I was just wandering around." Coco cleared her throat nervously. "I had a little too much to drink at the luncheon and I was annoyed and I—"

"Elijah went to the luncheon before I did," Tallula interjected. "Did any of you see him?"

Madison bit down on her lip.

Lex played with the strap of her purse.

Park didn't bat an eye. She stood as calm and unshakable as ever. "Yes. In fact, we met him. And Coco was with us."

Coco shot Park a *how-could-you-do-this-to-me?* look.

"Park, did you or your sisters see Coco leave the room with Elijah?" Detective Roan asked.

"No," Park replied. "Elijah left a few minutes before she did."

"But then Elijah came back up to the penthouse just as Ina and I were leaving to come to the lunch—" Tallula started as if she'd been pricked with a needle. She shot out of the chair. "Oh my God! Ina! I completely forgot about Ina! She was up in the penthouse! She had to have been there when Elijah fell! Oh my God! Where is she?"

"I'm sure she's fine," Madison said soothingly. "The police are probably up there right now talking to her."

"But what if she's been hurt?" Tallula cried. "I have to get upstairs!"

Madison grabbed Tallula's hand and held her back.

Detective Roan was already rattling orders off on his cell.

"Tallula, what happened after you and Ina left the luncheon together?" Park asked coolly. "I know you don't feel like answering questions, but please try."

"We walked down the hall to the elevator," Tallula began, wringing her hands. "Ina hadn't felt so good this morning, and then it just got worse—she must've eaten something at the luncheon that didn't agree with her. We rode upstairs and went into the suite. Ina went right to her room and told me she wanted to take a shower and lie down."

"And where was Elijah?" Lex asked.

"He was in the bedroom." Tallula paused, as though trying to recall every detail of those critical moments. "He was on the Internet, sitting at the desk. He asked me if I'd go back downstairs and buy him a pack of cigarettes, and that's exactly what I did. I left the penthouse and got back into the elevator—but the elevator got stuck on its way down. I was in there for at least ten minutes before it started moving again. I made it to the lobby, and that's when I saw all the commotion. That's when I . . ."

When I came outside and saw Elijah dead on the pavement, Park thought. She smoothed a hand over Tallula's arm. "And is there any possibility that Elijah . . . took his own life?" she asked gently.

Tallula shook her head. "No, never. Someone had to have . . . pushed him." Tears spilled over her cheeks again.

"Well then, I guess it's Ina we should be speaking to," Madison said quietly, insinuating the obvious.

"That can't be," Tallula whispered. "It just . . . can't be."

Detective Roan snapped his cell shut. "Ms. Debrovitch is being questioned in the penthouse by my partner. She's okay, but very shaken up."

"I have to see her!" Tallula cried.

"Not yet." Detective Roan trained his eyes on Coco. "Tell me something, Miss McKaid—where were you for all that time after you left the luncheon? Lex said she searched for you for about an hour."

"I was . . . just walking around," Coco said, and not very convincingly.

"Is that right?" Detective Roan sounded purposely skeptical. "No chance you met up with Elijah while Tallula and Ina and your friends were all at the luncheon, is there?"

"Of course not!" Coco shot back. "Are you crazy?"

Madison stood up. "Detective, why would you ask a question like that?"

"I was drunk!" Coco ranted, sounding more and more panicked. "I . . . My head was spinning and I even felt like throwing up. I was probably in that bathroom when Lex came looking for me—she just didn't know it."

"I thought you said you were walking around." Detective Roan smirked. "I'm pretty sure that's what you said."

"No . . . yes. I mean . . ." Coco raked a hand through her hair. She had begun sweating. She stared beseechingly at Madison, at Park, at Lex. Her breaths came sharply.

"Think, Miss McKaid," Detective Roan pressed. "Maybe there's something you're just not telling us."

"I've told you everything!" Coco snapped. "And I'm tired of answering your stupid questions. I want to get out of here."

Detective Roan held up the gold chain that had fallen out of Coco's purse. The chain that had belonged to Elijah Traymore. "You see this?" he said. "The latch on the back of this chain is completely bent, and it looks to me like there're a few specks of dried blood on it. As if it was yanked off Elijah's neck. By force."

Park leaned forward and tried to get a good look at the chain without upsetting Detective Roan. "Oh, yes," she whispered. "I see that. But—wait. Then you're saying Elijah was involved in some sort of physical confrontation. You're saying he was pushed."

Detective Roan smiled and gave Park an exaggerated wink. "You might make a good cop one day, little lady."

"Only if they change the uniform," Madison commented.

Under normal circumstances, Coco would have

laughed at the comment. Or added something to it. But now she was frozen, staring at the floor like a kid who's just been caught going through her mother's jewelry safe.

"A whole hour," Detective Roan continued, circling her as he held out the chain. "Unless you have an alibi, I could probably place you just about anywhere. A lot can happen in an hour."

Madison reached out and tapped Coco's shoulder. "Why aren't you saying anything?" she asked frantically. "What's wrong with you? Don't you understand what he's trying to imply? Tell him where you were so you're not a part of this whole mess."

Coco remained silent.

Just then, the elevator behind them yawned open and a uniformed officer stepped out of it. He walked up to Detective Roan, held up a small plastic bag, and said, "We found this in the penthouse, just outside the terrace. Looks like evidence of a struggle."

Detective Roan held up the plastic bag; in it was a gold cell phone. "This look familiar, Miss McKaid?"

Madison gasped. Lex grabbed Park's hand.

"It's mine," Coco answered, her voice barely audible. Then her eyes glassed with tears. "It's . . . mine."

Tallula lunged forward, but the shock of the moment got her, and she stumbled back into the chair. "Murderer!" she shrieked, pointing at Coco. *"Murderer!"*

◇   ◇   ◇

"Ina, are you okay?"

Park kept her voice gentle and soothing, not wanting to add to the chaos happening all over the hotel suite. She,

Madison, and Lex were standing in the small study just off the main foyer. They were clutching their purses as they stared down at Ina—a trembling, pathetic figure of a girl slumped on the couch. They each had the instinct to reach out and comfort her, but Park knew playing that card wouldn't be a good idea. There was a lot of work to do, and they had to maintain a low profile.

It had been a feat to get in here in the first place. Detective Roan had protested all the way. Madison and Lex—both in shock from watching Coco be escorted to a police cruiser in handcuffs—had nearly fallen apart. Park had assumed the role of leader and muscled their way into the hotel suite. Thankfully, Tallula had agreed that extra company would be good for her and Ina.

But getting in was only half the battle. Now Park had to find a way around all the crime-scene technicians. Not to mention Detective Roan, who had gotten a lot meaner in the last half hour.

"Ina?" Park said again. She tapped the girl's shoulder. "Are you okay?"

Ina Debrovitch trembled and played with the edges of the quilt that had been draped around her shoulders. She didn't touch the cup of tea on the table before her, nor did she look up at Madison, Park, or Lex.

"You're just in shock," Madison said, kneeling down beside her. "But you don't have to be afraid to talk to us. We're Tallula's friends."

"That's right," Lex chimed in. "You just need to relax. Here, let me help you." She opened the magic purse and pulled out her small bottle of custom-mix perfume. She reached down and gently took hold of Ina's left wrist.

"This is one of the rarest and most expensive perfumes on the planet. Some of the botanicals come straight from the Amazon. Trust me—once you get a whiff, you'll feel a lot better."

Ina stared up at her. Dark circles rimmed her eyes. There were blotches on her forehead. "But I don't like perfume," she said quietly. "I—"

Lex aimed the nozzle at Ina's wrist and spritzed. "Mmmmmmm!" she said immediately, sniffing the air. "Spectacular."

"Glorious," Madison agreed, raising her nose.

Park waved the scent over to her. "Like standing in a Parisian garden in springtime."

"But I—" Ina caught a whiff of the perfume and cracked a smile. She sniffed her wrist. The look on her face went from disinterested to immensely pleased in a matter of seconds. "That's amazing. It's so . . . so beautiful! Oh, wow!"

"See?" Lex nodded. "I told you—it's impossible to smell this custom mix and not feel better." She sprayed the air again for effect.

Ina tried to keep the brave expression in place, but it collapsed quickly and she began sobbing. Heavy, choking sobs that racked her body. She felt as if she were floating out on the open ocean in the middle of a storm—it was all dark skies and dangerous waves, with no chance of ever being rescued. And she heard the lonely whisper of the wind too, like a voice that kept saying *Elijah is dead, Elijah is dead, Elijah is dead.* She pulled the quilt tighter around her shoulders. Almost ninety degrees outside, and yet she was trying to stay warm.

Madison and Lex patted her shoulders.

But then Park pulled them both away and shook her head, indicating that they were taking the wrong actions. She sighed inwardly. Madison and Lex were dumb with shock. Though Madison had managed to fix her tearstained face with a quick flash of her compact, she was still operating in slow motion. Park knew that much. If Madison had her brains together, she wouldn't be commiserating with Ina. Same went for Lex. Technically speaking, they were standing in the vicinity of the crime scene—the balcony from which Elijah had been pushed was only a few rooms away—and getting a good look at it was crucial to their investigation. And that meant keeping a distance from any potential suspects.

At the moment, all they knew was that Ina had been showering when someone—or, according to the cops, Coco—shoved Elijah to his death. Ina had removed her hearing aid and left it on her nightstand. She hadn't been able to hear any fighting or screaming. When she emerged from the shower several minutes later, the hearing aid was broken on the floor. She walked out of her room and saw that the balcony doors were open. The suite, of course, was empty. She hadn't known anything was wrong until hotel security burst through the door.

That little configuration of events made sense to Park, but when it came to crime, there was always more than met the eye.

The way it looked now, Coco had been in the suite with Elijah while Ina was showering. There'd been some sort of struggle. Coco had done the deed and then split, all before Ina made it out of her bedroom. Possible, yes. But

Park couldn't bring herself to believe that it had happened that way. And neither could Madison and Lex. Coco, a killer? No way. It was easier to believe J.Lo had actually designed her own clothing line.

Park was about to begin one of her interrogations when Tallula came striding into the study. She was still wearing the vermilion dress, but the head scarf had been replaced by a black hat to which she had pinned a long piece of black lace. The lace acted as a veil, obscuring her face so she looked like a widow in mourning.

"Ina!" she cried, sitting down on the couch and throwing her arms out wide. "Oh, honey—I know!"

Ina heaved a sigh. Another cry escaped her lips. "I'm . . . so . . . scared," she said, her speech more slurred than usual.

"Don't be," Tallula replied. She wiped the tears from Ina's cheeks, despite the fact that her own tears were flowing past her chin. "Everything will be okay. You'll see." A piece of the lace caught in the side of her mouth, and she flicked it away with her tongue.

"I wish I could have helped," Ina whispered. "But I didn't know. I couldn't hear. . . ."

Tallula began sobbing again. "It's okay. It wasn't your fault." She looked up at Madison, Park, and Lex. "I just can't believe this is happening. I don't know what I would do if you girls weren't here."

Madison gave Tallula's shoulder a squeeze as she held back her own tears.

It was, according to Park, another bad move. *Duh,* she thought, looking at Madison. *Tallula thinks your best friend is a killer. You have to stand back from this.* But even as the words pranced through her brain, she knew it was hopeless. And she really couldn't blame Madison for being confused: it wasn't every day that one of your closest friends was accused of cold-blooded murder.

"Um, Tallula?" Park asked gently. "Where did it happen? I mean, where's the balcony?"

"Down at the other end of the suite," Tallula answered, flicking another piece of lace away from her mouth. "In the east wing. Oh—it's a mess! Broken glass, two vases trampled like little ants. The phone's been knocked off the hook too. It looks like a disaster area!" She sniffled. "And those *CSI* people—they have no respect for Queen Anne—period furniture! You should see them—throwing white powder everywhere, spraying chemicals on the floor! You'd think they've never been in a penthouse suite before."

"Most of them haven't," Lex muttered. Then she bit her lip. It had been a stupid thing to say, but *someone* had to defend the forensic techs just a little bit. Lex had a lot of respect for people who worked crime scenes—they had to wear plastic bags over their shoes and slip their hands into uncomfortable latex gloves. Not exactly glamorous.

"You have to stay calm, Tallula," Madison said evenly. "For all of us."

Tallula nodded weakly. "I know. I just don't think I can stand any more of it." She had answered only a handful of questions so far. She told the detectives that she didn't want to imagine how it had happened, and submitting to their heartless demands did just that. Even now, sitting quietly beside Ina, the vivid scenario flashed in her mind like slides from a horror movie—how Elijah had probably slammed against the concrete railing after being pushed, how he had obviously struggled to stop his weight from pitching over the side, how his palms and fingernails had scraped helplessly in those final seconds before he plunged through the air. The images made her throat close.

She held Ina tightly against her chest. In the nine months since she'd become Tallula's assistant, Ina had never once cried. She had a stalwart demeanor. She acted like a little soldier, getting the job done and getting it done efficiently. She never said more than was expected of her. She didn't dish her personal opinions.

Tallula. Elijah. Ina. They had become something of a family, albeit an untraditional, odd family. And Tallula had known it would be that way from the moment Ina walked into her life. Like her and Elijah, Ina was alone in the world: her parents were gone and the cousins she had back home weren't really close. Ina had been orphaned at a young age, and living with Tallula and Elijah had given her a true sense of security. Of friendship and love.

"Heads up," Park said, indicating the man who had just walked into the study.

Tallula looked at Detective Roan as he approached the couch.

"I'm sorry to have to do this again," he said, "but I need to speak to Ina." He shot Madison, Park, and Lex disapproving stares.

"Of course," Tallula replied quietly. "But we're both in shock, Detective. Please remember that. So would you be a pancake and try to keep it short?" She gave Ina an encouraging hand-squeeze.

Ina wiped the tears from beneath her eyes and coughed. She pulled the quilt around her lower body. "All right," she said. "I can speak to you."

Detective Roan flipped open his small notepad. "Now, Ms. Debrovitch, you said that when you came back from the luncheon, you went right to your room and took a shower, correct?"

Ina nodded. "Yes. I was sweating a lot. I didn't feel so good."

"Why not?" he asked.

She shrugged. She didn't say anything.

"Were you nervous about something?" Detective Roan pressed.

"No," she answered right away. "I just had . . . stomach problems."

He scribbled onto the pad. "When did that start?"

"Why does any of this matter?" Ina shot back, her voice rising. "I wasn't feeling well—that's my answer!"

Before Detective Roan could open his mouth to speak, Park took a small step forward. This was her chance to put her plan in motion. She needed to exit the room inconspicuously, even if it meant doing so at Ina's expense. "Excuse me for interrupting," she said politely. "But maybe Ina's just talking about gas."

Madison started as though she'd been pricked with a pin.

Lex mouthed the word *gas?* as she stared uncertainly at Park.

"Gas?" Detective Roan repeated.

"Oh," Tallula said quietly. "Oh, dear." She looked at Ina. "Honey, is it that problem again? Is that why you were feeling sick all day? It's okay—you don't have to be embarrassed."

Ina turned beet red.

"They served watercress this afternoon," Lex said, deciding to follow Park's lead. "Very gassy."

"Y-yes," Madison stammered, catching on. "I . . . I had to drink some peppermint tea earlier because I had so much . . . well . . . uh . . ."

"Gas," Park said matter-of-factly. "It happens. Ina, is that why you were feeling sick?"

She nodded, clearly mortified.

"Next time, just be a butterfly and tell me," Tallula said. "That way I can give you something for it."

"I hear chewing celery works," Madison added.

Park looked skeptical. "But that's a vegetable. It's gassy on its own."

"Is it?" Tallula asked.

"Excuse me!" Detective Roan shouted. He banged the notepad against the small coffee table. "*I'm* the one conducting this interrogation here, and I don't need any help!"

"Detective," Tallula said sternly. "I asked you to be a lollipop and speak calmly. You don't have to be so uptight!"

He took a deep breath and wiped a line of sweat from his brow.

Lex knew a stressed-out person when she saw one. She raised her arm and quickly sprayed the custom-mix perfume at him.

"Hey!" he screamed, waving his arms in protest. "Stop that!"

"It'll help you," Lex said. "Just inhale. And besides, it'll cover up any gaseous odors."

"I didn't do anything!" Ina protested.

Detective Roan caught a stream of the sweet perfume and immediately inhaled deeply. A look of pleasure washed over his face. "Oh, wow . . ."

It was the moment Park needed. "We've been talking about gas," she said quickly. "And I think there might be something to the power of suggestion." She clutched a hand over her stomach and feigned pain. "Tallula, can you point me to the little girls' room?"

Tallula gestured at the door. "Make a left at the end of the hall." She coughed, the lace veil sticking to her mouth again.

As Park exited the room, she shot Madison and Lex a look that said: *Stay here and cover me. I'm goin' in!*

In the Bedroom

She dashed down the hall.

Park held her breath and hoped to God that she'd done the right thing. The chances of interrogating Ina with Detective Roan present were virtually nil, and she knew Madison and Lex would fill her in later on Ina's story. Right now, she needed to search the premises.

She heard voices coming from the left and knew the forensic techs and cops were still swarming over the scene. The huge living room was just around the bend, and that was where Coco's cell had been found. Where she had allegedly torn the chain from Elijah's neck in a struggle. And, of course, where Elijah had taken his fatal plunge. But there was no way to make it inside. She couldn't just waltz into the living room and start snooping around. She couldn't psych out the cops either.

Damn.

She froze, wondering where to go. She didn't have gas, so there was no need to visit the bathroom. But she couldn't go back into the study yet either. She turned right and scanned yet another corridor. No one around. She tiptoed down it, her shoulders pressed to the wall. She reached a door that was partially ajar, long fingers of light spilling from inside. She held her breath again and pushed it open gently. Then she walked over the threshold.

It was a bedroom. But not just any bedroom. She could tell from the open suitcase and the elegant, expensive clothes peeking out of it that this was the bedroom Tallula and Elijah had shared. A master suite, it was huge and airy, the windows affording a spectacular view of the skyline. The walk-in closet was open; Park saw several dresses on hangers and a few pairs of shoes. Everything was Tallula's. Where the hell was Elijah's stuff? She walked around to the other side of the king-sized bed, and there, in one corner, she found a second suitcase overflowing with black T-shirts, socks, boxer shorts. There was also a small travel case, which Park scooped up and quickly unzipped. Inside were several razors, a tube of Kiehl's shaving cream, and a black eyeliner pencil. Nothing all that interesting.

She dropped the case and turned around. On the bureau was a laptop, its screen dark. Tallula had said that

Elijah had been surfing the Internet when she last saw him. What had he been looking at? Park wondered. Had he sent Tallula downstairs because he hadn't wanted her to see something? She walked over to the bureau, then paused. It would take too long to boot up the laptop and try to wade through all the cookies. She didn't have much time. Another minute or so and Tallula would come looking for her. Or, worse, one of the crime-scene techs might walk in and find her snooping around.

She stepped back, hands on her waist, and scanned the room thoroughly. The most important person in a homicide investigation was the victim, and at this point she knew very little about Elijah—other than the fact that he'd been kind of sleazy. Why had Coco met him up here? Was there more to it than the quick hookup Detective Roan had insinuated? Park scowled inwardly and forced herself to stay focused. This wasn't the time to ask so many questions. This was the time to narrow in on Elijah. She would deal with Coco a little later.

And then she saw it.

Right there on the nightstand, not more than five feet away.

Elijah's wallet.

Her heart racing, Park clasped her fingers around the thick leather wallet and flipped it open. Four hundred and thirty-two dollars in cash, an AmEx card, his own personal business card . . . and a condom. She rolled her eyes. *Typical.* She stuck her forefinger into the lowermost compartment and scraped it along the edge.

A small folded piece of paper popped out, its edges dog-eared, as if it had been torn hastily from a notebook.

Park unfolded it. Today's date was scrawled at the top, and beneath it was written: *Dakota, tonight, 6:45.*

Park scratched her head as she studied the little note. Dakota? Probably some girl Elijah had been planning to hook up with. Was that it? She turned the piece of paper over and scanned yet another cryptic note: *To the Penthouse RCS00491.*

The penthouse? She glanced around. Well . . . duh. Hadn't Elijah just plunged from a penthouse? Was this some sort of crazy joke?

She knew she should have deposited the piece of paper back into the wallet, but impulse got the best of her again, and she dropped it into her purse beside the skeleton key she'd discovered earlier. She walked over to the bureau; ignoring the laptop, she opened the first drawer and found more clothing. She recognized the black jeans and shirt Elijah had been wearing when she, Madison, and Lex had met him only hours before. She yanked out the jeans and dipped her hands into the pockets. Nothing in the front two ones. But in a back one, she found a small business card inscribed with a single Web site address: www.otherworldpeeps.com.

Huh?

It was the strangest URL she had ever come across. She dropped the card into her purse as well, then set her eyes on the master bathroom.

"Uh . . . excuse me?"

Park jumped at the sound of the voice. She spun around and locked eyes with a tall middle-aged man dressed in an NYPD Crime Scene jacket. His hands were gloved. She knew better than to let her shock show, so instead of stammering out something stupid, she relaxed her shoulders and smiled brightly. "Hello there," she said, her tone cheerful.

The man gave her a perfunctory nod. "Yeah, hi. Can I ask what you're . . ." His voice trailed away as he recognized her, then his eyes lit up. "Hey, you're Park Hamilton, right?"

"I sure am!" She strode across the room as calmly and confidently as if she were walking down a red carpet. She extended her arm.

He took her hand in his and nodded. "I just read about you and that movie you're doing. I can't wait to see it." He cleared his throat. "But . . . um . . . I have to ask you what you're doing in here—we're collecting evidence."

"Such a tragedy," Park whispered gravely. She shook her head, then casually opened her purse and pulled out her own makeup bag. "I came in here to get this for Tallula. My sisters are keeping her company in the study. Oh—I hope I didn't do anything wrong by coming in here." She bit down on her lip, trying to look like an apologetic little girl.

The trick seemed to work. The man shrugged and waved her toward the door. "Don't worry about it. I'm sure it won't be a problem."

"Thank you." She stepped into the corridor. She hesitated, turning to face him again. "Is that the way to the living room area? Where Elijah fell off the balcony?" She pointed straight ahead.

The man nodded. "Yeah, it is. But don't go in there. Lots of cops are still working the scene. It's best if you just head back to the study."

Park nodded politely. *Shit,* she thought, totally annoyed. How was she going to inspect the scene? She got to the next corridor and swung the left that would bring her back to the study, all the while trying to figure out a way into the living room. But she knew it was a pointless plan. She wouldn't be able to do anything useful unless she had free rein of the area.

Voices suddenly burst through her reverie—loud, panicked, angry. They were coming from the study.

Park ran up the corridor and walked into the room. What she saw astonished her: Tallula was standing up, her veil pulled up and face pinched with rage as she glared at Detective Roan, shouting obscenities. Lex was chasing Ina around the couch, spraying her with the bottle of custom-mix perfume. "Just inhale deeply!" Lex kept saying. "It'll relax you!" Ina looked exhausted and irritated. Standing off to the left was Madison; she was riffling frantically through Lex's magic purse, shaking her head, whispering to herself. She finally found what she'd been looking for and pulled it out. She brought the whistle to her lips and blew.

The shrill sound cut through the noise and everyone froze.

"Everyone be quiet!" Madison shouted. A few seconds later, silence having descended over the room, she looked at Park.

"Can someone please tell me what's going on here?" Park asked gently.

"I'll tell you what's going on!" Tallula shouted. She pointed down at Detective Roan, who was sniffing his wrists. "This man is making ridiculous accusations, and I won't stand here and listen to him hurl a bunch of crap at me!"

"What is he saying?" Park took a small step toward them.

"He's trying to insinuate that Elijah invited your little slut of a friend up here for a roll in the hay!" Tallula ranted. "He's trying to make me believe that Elijah was some sort of sleazeball who cheated on me left and right."

And sideways, Park thought. But she didn't say anything. Instead, she shot a glance at Madison, who was obviously weighing the fact that Coco had been called a slut and once again been implicated in the crime.

Detective Roan sighed loudly as he continued to sample the lovely scent on his wrist. "That's not what I'm saying—not exactly," he said. "I'm just explaining to Ms. Kayson what the evidence suggests."

"And what exactly *does* the evidence suggest?" Park asked him sharply. "We know there was a struggle, and that Coco McKaid's cell phone was found at the scene and that she had Elijah's necklace in her purse. But what *else* might the evidence suggest?"

"Whaddya mean?" Detective Roan stared at her, confused.

It was an excellent question, the very question Park needed. But she knew she had to be careful here—she didn't want to make an enemy of Tallula. So she walked over to him and said gently, "I mean, has Ina told you anything useful? She was the *only other person* here in the suite when the crime occurred."

The underlying accusation in the statement didn't slip past Ina. "I didn't do anything!" she wailed. She batted her arms at her sides impatiently.

Beside her, Lex spritzed the bottle of perfume again.

"Stop that!" Ina screamed, whirling around and giving her a nasty look.

Detective Roan stood up and flipped his notepad closed. "Look," he said flatly, "Ms. Debrovitch has given us sufficient information. She didn't hear anything because her hearing aid was deliberately broken. And personally, I think Elijah Traymore broke it because he knew he wanted to have a little fling with Coco McKaid, and he didn't want Ms. Debrovitch hearing anything. But something went wrong, there was a struggle, and Miss McKaid lost control. She shoved him, and that's that. End of story."

Tallula gasped. She held in her breath, her cheeks puffing out and turning bright red. "You . . . you . . . little pig!" she screeched, pointing at Detective Roan. "Get out! Get out of here right now!"

"Please calm down," Madison whispered. She went to Tallula's side and patted her arm.

Tallula began sobbing. She lowered herself onto the couch and wiped the tears from her eyes. "It just isn't fair! Elijah's dead and now I'm supposed to believe that I never meant anything to him!"

"It's not true," Madison whispered, trying to sound encouraging. She looked at Lex.

Lex merely shrugged.

"It's a sick and heartless thing to say!" Tallula continued. "I won't answer any more questions, and neither will Ina. We're done! Do you hear me, Detective? Done! It's not enough that my boyfriend's been *murdered*! You have your killer, so stop bothering me!" She illustrated this last point by giving her head a firm toss; as she did so, the black hat tumbled forward over her face, dragging the lace mesh down with it. She yanked it away impatiently, then sniffled. "Madison, would you be a candy apple and find me a tissue?"

◇ ◇ ◇

A news chopper was circling overhead. On the street, reporters and spectators created a nearly impenetrable wall across the front of the hotel. Madison, Park, and Lex had managed to leave via a narrow side exit, but it hadn't been an easy escape.

"No matter what, she's still my best friend," Madison said as she sat staring out the window in the back of the limo. "Coco may be a lot of things, but she isn't a heartless killer." She dragged a crumpled tissue across her nose. The full weight of the situation had finally hit her.

It was late afternoon, and the overcast sky had cleared. She didn't want to go home. She certainly didn't want to go back to the Waldorf. What she wanted was to slip into the ground and disappear and forget that any of this had happened.

Coco. Her oldest and dearest friend. The girl who had ridden ponies with her for years, who had spent holidays in Europe with her, who had shopped for diamonds with her at Tiffany's the year they'd turned fourteen. And then there were the hopes and dreams and little secrets they had shared. The intimate wishes that, at this point, might not ever come true—for Coco, at least.

There would be an avalanche of media reports about her. There would be front-page headlines and dozens of stupid pseudo-news broadcasts on those entertainment channels. Coco would be depicted as some sort of spoiled boozer who liked throwing men off terraces. A trial would likely follow. Maybe one of those garish paperback true-crime books with her mascara-stained face on the cover. And even in six or seven months—after making appearances on *The View* and *Larry King Live*—Coco would be reduced to a single heartbreaking image: a spoiled little rich girl who deserved to spend her days behind bars.

What was it with celebutantes ending up in jail these days?

What saddened Madison most was that few people would ever know the real Coco McKaid. Beneath the bubbly and giddy persona was a sweet, smart, warmhearted girl who loved animals and kids and old people. She volunteered at Roosevelt Hospital on a fairly frequent basis. She'd spent a whole four weeks working for Meals on Wheels. Her unspoken dreams—the ones she'd shared with Madison—had nothing to do with fame or fortune. Instead, Coco fantasized about moving to Montana or Wyoming and living on a farm, where she could watch the horses being exercised and supervise the team of beautiful stablemen. More than once, she had expressed a desire to leave their elite social scene for something more meaningful.

Coco wasn't a killer. She wasn't a heartless Lolita. And if, by some very rare stroke of fate, she *had* killed Elijah Traymore, her guilt was a complex matter. Nothing about it was open-and-shut. Madison knew the reasons for Coco's possible guilt, and those reasons had everything to do with insecurity, self-deprecation . . . and vodka. Coco had never felt good about herself. She had always looked to other people for acceptance, had always measured her self-worth according to which boys liked her. And Madison was sure that she had fallen prey to Elijah Traymore's seductive powers.

He had probably told Coco that she was beautiful and wonderful and sexy, that he wanted to sculpt her and immortalize her in a timeless work of art. He might've gone as far as to tell her he felt their meeting was love at first sight. Or something of that dramatic variety. And Coco, of course, hadn't been able to see through his sleazy act. All he'd wanted was a cheap, one-time fling with her. Pretty ironic that the one-time thing had ended up being his last-time thing.

"I can't believe it either," Park whispered. "We know Coco better than that. The really crappy thing is that the evidence places her right there at the scene of the crime."

"True, but we've seen that a lot with innocent people." Lex looked hopeful.

"What about that almost-handprint you two saw on Elijah's shirt?" Madison said. "Lex, you said it was probably the result of an oil-based moisturizer. Coco would never use something oil-based. She only uses serums."

Lex frowned. "I said it *could* be the result of oil-based moisturizer. But it could also be a bunch of other things. And in any case, that'll probably be a minor thing. Right now, we have to consider the facts."

Madison sniffled. "The facts don't all make sense."

"Coco left the luncheon a few minutes after Elijah," Park said. "We saw the two of them getting a little close. Coco was drunk and Elijah probably took advantage of that. He probably told her to meet him up at the penthouse for a little alone time, and obviously that's where Coco went."

"There's no way she was in any of the bathrooms on the first two floors," Lex added. "I checked them, and they were totally empty. She was up in the penthouse while Tallula and Ina were at the luncheon with us."

"And something ugly obviously happened up there," Park said quietly.

"Ugly?" Lex raised an eyebrow. "It doesn't get any uglier. For whatever reasons, we're supposed to believe Coco shoved Elijah off a balcony. He hit the ground and splattered like a water balloon."

"We know there were signs of a struggle," Park whispered. "So I guess that means . . ."

Silence.

"It means what?" Lex was sitting on the edge of her seat, waiting for one of Park's customarily accurate crime reenactments.

A hard, pensive look clouded her face, but Park simply shook her head. "Nothing. I just can't piece it together. Not without being there in that living room."

"Where did you go when you left us all in the study?" Lex asked. "I totally thought you'd scoped out the living room and the balcony."

"I couldn't." Park shrugged helplessly. "There were all those crime techs around. I went into the bedroom and—"

"It's my fault," Madison said suddenly.

"What?" Lex stared at her.

"It's my fault," Madison repeated. "I should've known

Coco would fall under Elijah's cheap little spell. And she was so drunk. I let her leave the luncheon by herself and I should have gone with her. I would've been able to stop her from following him upstairs."

"Madison, that's insane!" Lex snapped. "You were busy. You had other stuff on your mind. And besides, Coco's been drunk and alone before."

"Yeah, and look at all the dumb things she's done in the past!" Another tissue and another honk of her nose. Madison knew her makeup was a mess, but she didn't really care.

"The fact of the matter is that Coco wanted to hook up with Elijah," Park said. "If you had been able to stop her today, who's to say she wouldn't have gone and done it tomorrow? Or any other day? You've always been a good friend to her, Madison, and I don't want to hear any more crap about this being your fault."

Madison let the words sink in. "I just don't understand how it happened," she whispered. "I mean, Coco wouldn't hurt a fly. How do you go from *that* to being accused of shoving someone off a penthouse balcony?"

"Self-defense." Park folded her arms across her chest and leaned back in her seat.

"What?"

"Self-defense," she repeated. "I'm not saying I think Coco did it. I'm just saying what'll happen once she's formally charged and arraigned."

Madison crinkled her nose. "I don't get it."

"Look, we all know what kind of guy Elijah was," Park began. "On the outside, at least. God knows how many times he cheated on Tallula. He was probably the youngest guy on the planet with a Viagra prescription. The point is, I think he got a little rough with Coco when she met him in the penthouse. Maybe he forced himself on her. Maybe he said things to really upset her and she wanted to leave. But he wouldn't let her, and that's why there were signs of a struggle. There's no other reason why Coco would suddenly become a killer."

"Homicidal impulse," Lex said, snapping her fingers. "I've read about that. It happens a lot. It's like a short circuit of the mind. Like, the plug in your brain gets overloaded and just explodes."

Madison's eyes were wide. She looked at Park. "I know we've solved two murders in the past, but is this impulse info true?"

"In a manner of speaking," Park replied. "The psychology of homicidal impulse goes deeper than that, and it's a little different than plain old self-defense. People who claim homicidal impulse aren't always in a life-threatening situation. People who claim self-defense *are*."

"So then, you're saying people are going to think Coco went temporarily psycho?" Madison sounded uncertain, and just a wee bit spooked. "You're saying a psychiatrist would tell a jury that she was insane?"

Park wagged her finger. "*Insanity* is a legal term, not a psychiatric one. People who plead guilty by reason of insanity have a hell of a tough time trying to convince a jury of that. I don't think psychiatry is going to enter into this. If we want to solve this case fast, self-defense is going to be Coco's only option. She's going to have to prove that she did what she did because she felt threatened, because she defended herself. She wasn't temporarily insane—we stood with her and Detective Roan right after Elijah's body hit the sidewalk, and she didn't appear to be insane."

"True," Lex said.

"But what about Ina?" Madison cried. "Don't you think she's a suspect? She was in the damn room when it happened!"

"But her story pieces together nicely," Park said, disappointed by the fact that it did. "At least, for now it does."

Madison closed her eyes and heaved another sob.

Park leaned over and gave her sister's hand a squeeze. "Honey, *we* don't think she's guilty. But right now, everyone else does."

"And the only two people who *could* have been suspects have alibis," Lex chimed in. "Well, sort of. I mean, Ina was in the shower and her hearing aid got trashed. And Detective Roan said that it's been confirmed that Tallula got stuck in the elevator for like ten minutes after she left Elijah in the suite. So who the hell else could've gone up there?"

"Anyone," Park said. "And no one. That's what sucks about this. It's impossible to believe Coco did it, but it's just as impossible to think someone else could've done it. That leaves us in a big pile of investigative poop. The way it stands now, Coco's headed for the slammer."

Madison covered her face with her hands. "Oh, God! I can't listen to this anymore! I can't!"

"You're going to have to get used to it, sunshine," Park said firmly. "Each one of us is going to have to give a formal statement to the cops, and if Coco pleads not guilty and the case goes to trial, we'll be called as witnesses."

"You think the trial will be televised?" Lex asked.

Park shrugged. "Depends on the judge. It would totally be a ratings sweep."

"What do you wear when you're going to testify in court?" Lex reached into the limo bar and grabbed a bottle of water. "I mean, think about it—you can't be too flashy because that would obviously turn off the jury. You can't wear black all the time because that would imply mourning, and maybe even guilt. It's a tough one."

"I guess a smart suit would work," Park mused. "But nothing with a plunging neckline. Maybe you should start a line of clothing for celebrities who are about to go on trial. There're a lot of those these days."

Lex guzzled the water and seemed to be considering the possibility. "We could call it Innocence."

"Ha!" Park laughed out loud. "I like that! Too bad they're not necessarily all that."

"Will you two please stop it!" Madison screeched. "We're supposed to be figuring a way out of this for Coco, and you're both cracking jokes!"

"You're right," Park said. "But we're stumped. Coco has no alibi. I want more than anything to come up with a different scenario and solve this. You know nothing excites me more than a homicide."

"Poor Coco," Madison whispered, staring out the window. "She'll never live this one down."

"Listen," Park said calmly, "we're going to go home and sit down and try to piece this together. Coco will be arraigned tomorrow, and hopefully she'll be released on bail. Then we'll be able to talk to her. And stop blaming yourself—no one could have known this was going to happen."

"You're wrong about that," Lex chimed in briskly. She stared at Madison, then at Park. "Poppy van Lulu knew it was going to happen. She told us someone was going to die."

"Holy shit!" Madison screamed. She sat up so fast, her purse flew off her knees. "You're right! She *did* say that! I completely forgot!"

Lex nodded. "Remember the dark cloak of whatever she saw hanging in the air? I guess it wasn't a shawl after all."

"That rhymes," Park said. "Very cute."

"I'm covered with goose bumps!" Madison said. "How could Poppy have known something so horrible was going to happen? How?"

"She's a psychic," Lex answered flatly. "That's kind of her job."

"*I* don't believe in psychics, so as far as I'm concerned, Poppy has some serious explaining to do." Madison leaned forward, stretched her arm through the partition, and tapped Donnie Halstrom's shoulder. "Donnie? Forget about taking us home. Take us to the Dakota on Central Park West, where the little shaman lives."

"Okay," Donnie answered.

Park perked right up. "Wait a minute. Did you say the *Dakota*?"

"Yes. That's where Poppy landed herself an apartment after her last divorce." Madison made a sour face. "Right next door to Yoko."

"Huh," Park said. "I might've just added someone to the suspect list." She opened her purse and pulled out the skeleton key and the crumpled piece of paper. She held them up. "I found the key a few feet from the body," Park explained. "I think it might've bounced out of one of Elijah's pockets—but I don't know what it's for. And this little sheet of paper you see here? I found it in his wallet when I went snooping around the bedroom. Look what it says on it." She unfolded it and held it up for Madison and Lex to see.

Dakota, tonight, 6:45.

Madison gasped. "Oh my God! But wait. Park—you just stole that from his wallet? And you took the key from the sidewalk? What if someone finds out?"

"You know I have a little problem when it comes to collecting evidence from a crime scene," Park replied lightly.

"Hot damn!" Lex shouted. "You think Elijah meant Poppy's apartment?"

"Could be." Park carefully placed the evidence in her purse again, then stopped and yanked out the black business card with the weird Web address on it. "I also found this," she said, handing it to Lex. "I don't know what it means either, but it looks interesting."

"Looks weird," Lex said. "But it sounds like something paranormal."

Park nodded. "That's what I thought."

"Is this everything?" Madison asked. "You didn't spot anything else interesting in that bedroom?"

"There wasn't any time to," Park answered. "And I almost got caught. A crime-scene tech came in while I was there. I had to come up with an excuse. Thank God he believed me."

"Well, I don't like this little connection one bit," Madison said. "It's too much of a coincidence that Poppy predicted something terrible and that Elijah had the word *Dakota* written on a piece of paper."

Park nodded, feeling her pulse quicken. "Remember how Elijah made that comment about Poppy when we first met him? He asked us if we were clients of hers."

"You're right," Lex said. "He seemed a little too interested in her. And now that I'm thinking about it—Poppy left the luncheon after Madison yelled at her, and she never came back. Where did she go? What did she do? She could have gone *anywhere* in that hotel."

Madison made no attempt to hide the anger contorting her face. "Anywhere," she repeated in a whisper. "Even to the penthouse."

8

The Psychic and the Celebs

Poppy van Lulu opened her apartment door with a whoosh. She cut Madison, Park, and Lex her coldest stare and said, "When the doorman told me it was *you three,* I almost asked him to send you away."

Madison opened her mouth to speak. Or, more precisely, to say something harsh.

Park knew this, so she immediately stepped in front of Madison and smiled at Poppy. "We didn't mean to offend you today at the luncheon," she said brightly. "And if we did, we apologize."

Poppy regarded her with suspicion. "Well, it's nice to know that, dear. But I'm not sure I believe you."

Park kept the smile in place. "Mrs. van Lulu, you've known our father for years. My sisters and I have never been disrespectful toward you. We're all just very upset, and we'd like to speak with you. May we please come in?"

With a defiant little shrug, Poppy waved them inside. She was dressed in a bloodred nightdress that draped down to her ankles and accentuated the pale boniness of her frame. Matching high-heeled slippers encased her feet. It was still early, but it looked as though she had readied herself for bed.

The duplex apartment overlooked Central Park. Light spilled through the living room windows, illuminating the gleaming hardwood floors and the tall bookcases. The chintz sofa was plush. Several original paintings hung on the walls behind protective glass casings. Marble statues of Greek goddesses stood on pedestals like guards. The apartment was eccentric and opulent. Just like Poppy.

"This place is totally sweet!" Lex commented, letting her eyes sweep across the expansive room.

"Thank you," Poppy said quietly. "I decorated it myself."

"That's a Chagall." Madison pointed to one of the paintings. Her jaw nearly dropped. "He's one of my favorite artists, but his originals are nearly impossible to get. I've . . . I've never seen one so close up." She walked to it and studied it, her eyes glazing over. Then she studied the next painting on the wall. "That's a Stefan Luchian! Oh—it's such an amazing landscape! How did you find that?"

"It's nice to know you have good taste when it comes to art, dear." Poppy walked to the bar and poured herself a glass of pomegranate juice. "I've traveled all around the world buying exceptional art. I'm impressed that you noticed the Luchian—most people don't. I knew there were brains behind that rather rude and testy attitude of yours."

Madison blanched. She hadn't expected such outright hostility, but thinking about it now, she couldn't blame Poppy for completely disliking her. She *had* been a wee bit rough on the old woman.

"I love the statue of Persephone," Park said. "She's my favorite Greek goddess."

"And a powerful goddess, at that." Poppy sipped from her glass. "I often summon her when I'm meditating. She tells me things, you know."

"Speaking of you being told things . . ." Madison cleared her throat and assumed her no-nonsense posture. She was still angry, and she wanted to say something like *How the hell did a psycho like you know about what was going to happen today?* But instead of letting the words shoot out, she pursed her lips and stared at Park, giving her the green light to work her investigatory magic.

Park understood the look perfectly. She was a master when it came to interrogating people. There wasn't an FBI agent or cop out there who could do it better, and any good detective knew that information was the most important thing when it came to solving a case. Even a case as seemingly open-and-shut as this one. She dropped her purse onto a nearby chair and sat down on the couch, crossing her legs and leaning back to impart a relaxed demeanor.

"I know why you girls are here," Poppy said coldly. "I'm not stupid. I'm not some crazy old lady. You all want to know how I knew someone was going to die at that hotel today."

"Well . . . yeah," Lex answered bluntly.

Poppy stared down at the floor. "I don't blame you for wanting to know, but I can tell you right now that there isn't an easy explanation. And the last thing I want is more publicity—cops asking me questions, reporters at my door. I didn't know Elijah Traymore, and I'm very sorry he's been killed, but I can't tell you anything else."

"My best friend has been charged with killing Elijah," Madison said. "And I know she couldn't have done it. If you know anything that could help us, Mrs. van Lulu, we'd appreciate it. Or maybe you could just explain . . ."

Poppy shot her another cold stare. "Psychic phenomena can't be explained—they can only be experienced."

"I couldn't agree more," Park replied evenly. She hadn't expected to say those words, but she knew there would be only one way to get around Poppy. They would have to psych her out. "You know, Mrs. van Lulu, that young women like us have to be very careful when we speak about certain things or go to certain places. People are always following us, snapping our pictures and stuff like that. A simple act like buying a book can end up in the gossip columns for us. And that's exactly why we don't talk about our own personal beliefs when it comes to psychic phenomena. You know how mean people can be."

Poppy nodded. "Of course, dear. I've dealt with that all my life. When I divorced my husband, everyone said I'd only get one hundred and fifty million, but I knew better. I had already seen my settlement in a vision, and when I said publicly that I'd be receiving *two* hundred and fifty million, people said such awful things about me."

"And that must have been terribly difficult." Park folded her hands in her lap. "But believe it or not, my sisters and I know exactly what that feels like. That's why we know we can trust you."

"Trust me?" Poppy set down her drink. "With what?"

"With a little confession," Park replied. "We believe completely in psychic phenomena. In fact, we've had several otherworldly experiences ourselves."

"Do you . . . do you mean that?" Poppy asked in a whisper. "You're not just saying that to fool me, are you?"

Park smiled even though she felt a pang of guilt in her stomach. It wasn't nice to take advantage of old people. It was even meaner when an old person exhibited early signs of dementia. She was sure Poppy van Lulu didn't get psychic vibrations from anywhere but the new fillings in her teeth, but playing along seemed easier than having to explain another side of the story. "Of course we're not trying to fool you," she said. "Madison and Lex and I don't like talking about it, but we know how gifted you are. And we know all about visions and energy and premonitions."

Poppy gasped. "I *knew* there was something different about you girls. I've always known it. Since the day you were born. I can feel it now too. Right now. Your collective energy is . . . different. Stronger than most people's."

Lex walked to Madison's side. She had to bite her tongue to keep from laughing.

"That's very true," Park said. "In fact, Lex has very strong psychic powers. She doesn't like talking about them, but she's simply amazing. She happens to be a fashion psychic, and she's got it down to a science."

Poppy whirled around, her mouth open. "Really?" she asked excitedly. "Tell me, Lex—what is it you can do? A fashion psychic? I promise I won't spill the diamonds."

Lex's eyes went wide with shock and she swallowed hard. The spotlight had fallen on her unexpectedly, but she knew she had to play along. She didn't want her uncertainty showing, so she nodded quickly and said, "Oh, yeah. Totally. I'm like . . . extremely psychic."

"How?" Poppy asked, her excitement growing. "Oh, please tell me. I'm so glad to hear that you girls don't think I'm a complete nut."

"Yes," Madison said with a smirk, "tell Poppy about your otherworldly adventures, dear."

Lex cleared her throat nervously. She *hated* being put in this position. She was good at faking excuses for not doing her homework, but the nuns at St. Cecilia's Prep were easy to handle. This was new territory. "Well," she began, "it's . . . I . . . It came to me suddenly when I was designing one day a couple of years ago. It all has to do with certain . . ." Her voice trailed off as she opened the magic purse and started rummaging through it. She spotted her trusty tape measure and held it up. "Measurements!" she said. "It all has to do with measurements. You see, when I'm measuring someone for an original piece, I get very intense psychic vibrations. The numbers tell me things I wouldn't know otherwise." She held the tape measure up and gave it a wiggle.

"Fascinating," Poppy whispered. "Do you astral-travel?"

"I only travel by private jet," Lex answered automatically.

Only when she felt Madison jab her in the side did she realize her faux pas. "Oh! You mean . . . *astral* travel. Like, leaving my body while in meditation. Yes, sometimes I do. I've . . . I've uncovered some of the best sample sales an ocean away while astral traveling."

Poppy was nodding as she absorbed that bit of information. She didn't look as though she disbelieved the strange claims. In fact, she looked more relaxed than she had a few minutes ago. More trusting. Less defensive.

It was exactly what Park wanted to see. She inched her way to the edge of her seat. "Tell me, Mrs. van Lulu . . . was that how you knew Elijah Traymore was going to die today—through astral travel?"

Poppy turned around. "I . . . I'm sorry," she said quietly. "But I don't want to talk about that. It's still much too shocking to me. I *knew* I should have just gone to the police when I had my premonition—but the police don't bother with me anymore."

Park knew from experience to stay quiet.

Nearly a minute later, Poppy walked to one of the windows and stared down at the treetops of Central Park. "I saw a body plunging through the air," she said gravely, wringing her hands. "I knew death was in that room today. And I *can't* talk about it. Not now. I'm sorry. I—"

"I understand," Park cut in gently. Then she motioned with her thumb for Lex and Madison to join the mission.

Taking a deep breath, Lex pranced across the room to Poppy's side. "Here," she said, "let me show you what I can do. It'll relax you." She pulled one end of the tape measure out, striking an over-the-top pose as she did so:

both arms outstretched, her right hip jutting out. "I'm already feeling your energy."

Poppy gasped. She froze and quickly forgot her train of thought.

Playing along, Madison opened the magic purse and pulled from it a long white silk scarf. She wrapped it around Lex's head three times, creating a fashionable little turban. "Is it me?" she asked dramatically. "Or did the room just get colder?"

"A temperature drop," Poppy said. "The first sign of a spirit presence."

Lex snapped out of the pose and circled Poppy twice. Then she flicked the tape measure like a whip, the sound reverberating through the living room.

"The spirits are churning," Park commented from her place on the couch.

Lex pressed one end of the tape measure against Poppy's forehead and then drew it down along the length of her body. "Seventy-three inches," she whispered. "In fashion numerology, seventy-three is the number of power and knowledge. That means you know intuitively how to choose your battles *and* your outfits."

Poppy nodded and closed her eyes.

"Tell me," Park said, "when you had that vision of the body plunging through the air, did you know it was Elijah?"

"No," Poppy answered right away. "I only saw a figure . . . a form. Nothing else."

"What did you think of Elijah Traymore?"

"A nice young man," Poppy said quietly, distractedly.

Lex flicked the tape measure again; this time, she

wrapped it around Poppy's waist. "Twenty-four," she said. "The number of steps it takes to get to the middle of a standard runway at Bryant Park. You know the path you're walking on right now is very dangerous. You also had a secret desire to be a model many years ago."

"Oh, yes! I did!" Poppy smiled. "When I was younger, I used to practice walking as if I were in a show."

Park stood up. She liked what she was seeing. Poppy was loosening up, letting her guard down. Now it was time to up the ante. "What else do you think about Elijah? His personality."

"Smart, intuitive. He believed in ghosts," Poppy murmured.

"He did?" Park kept her voice even. "How do you know that?"

Poppy's lips twitched. "I . . . I'm feeling light-headed. I think I need to sit down."

Madison quickly placed her hands on Poppy's shoulders to keep her in place. She knew better than to let the act disintegrate. After all, how many chances would they get to psych out a crazy psychic?

"Did you know you have very circular shoulders?" Lex continued. "They measure sixteen inches across. Sixteen is the number of secrets. I can tell you have a few secrets floating around."

"No," Poppy said. "I . . . don't. . . ."

"Maybe Elijah told you he believed in ghosts?" Park offered. "It wouldn't surprise me to hear that. Did you know he wore a pentacle around his neck? A five-pointed star held in a circle."

"The symbol of modern-day Wicca," Madison added,

prying for more information. "You must know all about that, Mrs. van Lulu."

Poppy gulped. "I . . . no. He didn't say anything to me."

Impossible, Lex thought. She couldn't imagine the self-important and dramatic Elijah not talking about his connections to the occult. She wrapped the tape measure around Poppy's head. "A perfect twelve. That's the number of truth. There's something important you really want to say."

"What did he tell you?" Park asked pointedly. "Why did he believe in ghosts?"

"He was . . ."

"He was what, Poppy?"

She didn't answer. Instead, she gasped as Lex yanked her arms high above her head, zipping the tape down along one side of her.

"Thirty-four," Lex said. "That's the number of fear, of worry. Dresses or gowns with this measurement always find their way to women who are afraid of getting caught wearing something from Macy's."

"I would *never* shop there," Poppy replied in a strained whisper. "Just . . . just that one time back in 1991, when I was desperate . . ."

"There's no excuse," Madison said firmly.

"My head hurts," Poppy murmured. "I think your energy is draining me of strength. I can't—"

"Did Elijah drain you of energy?" Park asked quickly. "Did he ask you about ghosts?"

"He asked me to—" The words came out too quickly. Poppy bit down on her lip and, immediately recognizing the slip, opened her eyes.

Madison, Park, and Lex were staring at her.

"So you *did* know Elijah Traymore," Park stated firmly. She had both hands on her waist, and her eyes narrowed. She felt a strange combination of anger and excitement surge through her. "What did he ask you to do?"

"I don't know what you're talking about!" Poppy snapped. She stumbled back, a hand on her forehead. "You see what you've done? My energy is completely thrown off now!"

"And *my* energy is telling me that you're hiding something," Lex said. She flicked the tape measure one more time for effect.

Poppy tossed her head back dramatically. "I don't have to stand here and allow you three to intimidate me. I can very easily point you to the door!"

"And after you do that, we'll very easily point the police and a few reporters to this very apartment," Park said sweetly. She pulled the torn sheet of paper from her purse and held it up and out. "This was in Elijah Traymore's wallet."

Poppy studied the writing on the little sheet of paper. Her mouth twitched. Her hands went still. She might've been good at being eccentric, but she wasn't nearly as good at masking fear. "So what," she answered, a bit too quickly. "That could mean anything. He could've been writing someone's name." The look in her eyes belied the firmness of her voice.

"Maybe." Park gave a little offhanded shrug. "But why don't you take us to your appointment calendar and show us what it says in the six-forty-five time slot? I'm guessing it says you had an appointment with Elijah Traymore."

The color drained from Poppy's face. She remained silent.

Park knew she was completely in control of the situation, and she liked the feeling a lot. This was what cops felt in an interrogation room. Watching suspects break down under the weight of their lies was downright fun. "Basically, Mrs. van Lulu," she said calmly, "you have two choices. You can speak to us, or you can speak to the cops."

"Well?" Madison asked. "Which is it going to be?"

Wringing her hands again, Poppy stared down at the floor and started pacing. "I didn't know Elijah Traymore well," she said quietly. "He contacted me several weeks ago and said he wanted to meet me."

"And did you meet Elijah?" Park asked quickly.

"No," Poppy answered. "We only had at the most three phone conversations. We were going to meet for the first time tonight. He knew I was going to be at the luncheon today, but he told me he didn't want to talk to me there. He wanted to keep our association quiet."

"What did he want from you? What did you two talk about?"

Poppy stared at Park. "I can't go into details about that, young lady. It's a private matter. Elijah was very, very private."

"And now he's very, very dead," Lex said. "We're only trying to help here, Poppy."

"By threatening me?"

"By trying to piece together a very ugly puzzle," Park said.

"Well, you just may be wasting your time, because there's nothing left to piece together." Poppy stormed across the room and picked up her glass of pomegranate juice. She drank, then pointed to the flat-screen. "It's all over the news. Everyone knows Coco McKaid pushed Elijah off that balcony. Everyone knows she's guilty."

"She is not!" Madison shot back. Tears sprang to her eyes unexpectedly, and she covered her face with her hands as she wept. She hated herself for falling apart like this. It wasn't in her character to lose control quite so easily. Sure, she had shoved people up against walls and tackled guys during a chase, but that was different. *Those* people had annoyed her. Here, she was letting her guard down out of pure sadness, and she hated it. "I'm sorry. I didn't mean to . . . It's just that . . ."

Lex slipped her arm around Madison's shoulders. "It's a lot to handle. We don't all have best friends who end up killing people."

"Thanks a lot, Lex!"

"What I think she meant to say," Park interjected, "is that seeing your best friend being accused of something so horrible is tough. Especially when you know she's innocent."

"I do know she's innocent," Madison said. "Something else went on in that penthouse. It wasn't Coco's fault."

Park turned around and faced Poppy again. A little spike of anger had risen in her blood. There was the messy matter of Coco's life to consider, but seeing Madison crumble like freeze-dried caviar threatened to send her over the edge. "Okay then," she said firmly. "You don't have to tell us why Elijah came to see you, but we *will* get to the bottom of this, and when we do, we'll remember that you totally withheld information from us."

"And *that*, by the way, is a dangerous thing to do." Lex poked her head in between them and put on a mean face. "People who withhold info always end up needing us later on."

"But I have nothing to do with this!" Poppy protested. "I don't want to be attached to a murder!"

Lex sighed. "You already are attached to it . . . in a way. *We* know you were acquainted with Elijah, and a few hours before he's scheduled to meet with you, he ends up dead. The way I see it, we're being pretty nice here, Poppy. The cops would have already torn you to pieces."

Poppy lowered herself onto the sofa. The nervous twitching of her mouth had dissipated. Now she looked downright defeated. "Elijah Traymore was a brilliant young man," she said quietly. "I gathered that much from the first time I spoke to him. He was an artist, yes, but he was also involved heavily in the occult. He wore that pentacle around his neck because he practiced Wicca, just as you all suspected. He didn't do it for show or for power. He practiced his faith honestly. He believed what I've always known—that there's a lot more to this world we're living in than just flesh and blood."

Inwardly, Park sighed with relief. She recognized the weak tone of Poppy's voice for what it was: the beginning of a confession.

"Did he say anything about Tallula being Wiccan?" Madison asked.

"No, dear. He never mentioned her to me." Poppy

cleared her throat. "Anyway, we warmed up to each other right away. We talked about parapsychology and the experiences he'd had. He was a big believer in channeling and séances. And that's why he contacted me. He wanted me to channel a spirit for him."

Park's eyes went wide. "A spirit," she said. "You mean, he wanted you to hold a séance."

"Yes."

"For what reason? Who's this spirit?"

Poppy shook her head slowly. "He didn't tell me *why* he wanted to hold the séance. All he told me was that it was incredibly important. He told me the spirit he wanted me to contact was named Corky."

"Corky?" Lex chuckled unconsciously. "Not exactly a spooky name."

"The names don't have to be spooky, dear," Poppy said. "Elijah was going to come here tonight, and he and I were going to try and stir up the spirit of this person. I don't even know if it was a man or a woman. Elijah wouldn't tell me. He said he'd explain more when we met in person. But that's not going to happen . . . obviously."

A tense silence descended over the room. Madison sighed loudly, then walked over to the window and stared outside. "I just find all of this hard to believe," she stated flatly, looking directly at Park and Lex. "I mean, for God's sake, we're talking about ghosts here."

Poppy stood up, her eyes locked on Madison. "I know you think I'm some sort of nut. You don't believe I have the abilities to see glimpses of the future and communicate with the dead. That's fine. Sad, but fine. I don't need your approval, young lady. But I've told you everything I know at this point."

"Where did you go when you left the luncheon this afternoon?" Madison asked pointedly.

Poppy shook her head. "Right out the front doors of the hotel, thank you very much."

"And then where to?" Lex asked.

"Home!" Poppy answered defensively. "I walked here!"

"That's a really long walk," Park observed, keeping her tone neutral. She knew it was important not to sound accusatory. At the same time, however, she needed to let Poppy know that there was something suspicious about her explanation.

Poppy caught the hint. "Yes, well . . . a woman of my years doesn't keep a trim body without exercising," she replied. She ran her hands down her sides. "Not an ounce of fat on me. Don't you girls know that staying fit is important to a woman in her forties?"

Lex didn't hide her shock. *Forties?* she thought. *Poppy, you're freakin' closer to eighty than you are to forty.* "I've really never thought about it," she said quickly. "But if there were a woman in her forties standing in this room, I'd ask her about it."

Madison reached out and gave Lex's hair a tug of warning.

Poppy scowled.

"Look," Park said gently, "it's been a really stressful day for all of us, but we just want you to understand something." She walked over to Poppy and touched her arm. "A horrible crime has been committed, and we know our friend isn't a killer. All we want is your cooperation. Now, are you sure you don't remember anything else about your conversations with Elijah?"

"No, dear. Nothing else. As I've said, he was intuitive and intelligent. I'm sorry he's gone. I wish I could have stopped it from happening, but death is a very strong man, a lot stronger than any of us. When he asks you out, there's nothing to do but accept the date."

Park couldn't help laughing. "I hear you."

"So wait a minute," Lex jumped in. "Let's just say I happen to believe you, Poppy. Like, let's say I think you really can talk to the dead, okay? Why can't you talk to Elijah right now?"

"A very good question," Poppy said. "A soul cannot be reached until at least twenty-four hours after death. This is especially true with those who've left this world violently. I can't reach out to him just yet."

It was a typically hollow response, and Madison didn't try to hide her disapproval. She clucked her tongue as she looked at her sisters. "Well, if you can't reach out to him yet, can we leave him some sort of message? I mean, don't the dead have voice mail?"

Poppy regarded her coldly. "I'm afraid they don't."

"Voice mail?" Lex turned around and faced Madison. "That doesn't sound right to me. It makes more sense that they'd have something like a heavenly Instant Messenger. You know—like a message box popping up in the clouds somewhere."

"I was being sarcastic," Madison said. "But just for the record, I think it makes more sense for them to have voice mail. How would they be able to see Instant Messages if they're floating around everywhere?"

The impromptu—and unusual—interrogation had gone as far as it could go. Park knew Poppy had put up her guard again. It would take more than a Ouija board to get her to spill whatever else she knew at this point. "Well, I think we've asked you enough questions today," she said, her voice polite but firm. "We hope we haven't bothered you too much."

Poppy took Park's hand and folded it in her own. She closed her eyes. "You have such steady energy," she said. "This is a very golden time in your life, Park. You'll find a lot of success in your acting career. But be prepared for an awakening—you're getting stronger in lots of ways, and you'll be shocked at your own decisions."

"Thank you," Park said quietly. "I appreciate that."

Poppy reached out and took Lex's hand in her own. Again she closed her eyes. "Ah, yes. So much excitement. So much *enthusiasm*. Your love life is about to take a dramatic and wonderful turn, young lady. An unexpected prince has already bumped into you."

Lex shivered. "Whoa," she whispered. "That's totally bizarre."

Poppy smiled. She turned and stared at the resistant force otherwise known as Madison. "Come here. Give me your hand. Don't be afraid, dear."

With a reluctant sigh, Madison walked over to Poppy and extended her arm.

Poppy closed her fingers over Madison's. She was silent for several seconds. "A true heart of gold you have," she said slowly. "You always mean well, and you have a deep fear of being betrayed. But right now you must be strong—stronger than ever. Someone close to you will reveal himself as a liar."

Startled, Madison yanked her hand out of Poppy's.

"I'd like to leave now," she said quietly. She started for the door, Park and Lex behind her.

"Girls," Poppy called after them.

They turned around in unison.

"Be here tomorrow night at ten o'clock sharp," Poppy said.

Madison's eyes flashed with curiosity. "Why?"

"I'll give you the benefit of a séance," Poppy answered, her tone purposefully dark. "I'll summon Elijah and ask him to tell us what *really* happened to him on that balcony. Believe me, girls. Believe in my abilities. Tomorrow night, the dead will speak."

9

The Deceptive Code

Midnight. Madison tossed and turned, her eyes cutting through the shadows in her bedroom and landing on the closed window, the paper-strewn desk, the Picasso hanging just to the right of the door. She was wide awake. Every muscle in her body was tense, every hair on the back of her neck sticking up. Not even two glasses of her favorite champagne-and-chocolate-milk concoction had managed to soothe her anxiety, nor had a twenty-minute dunk in the Jacuzzi.

Someone close to you will reveal himself as a liar.

She threw back the sheet roughly. Poppy van Lulu's

voice—her dire little prediction—grated against Madison's nerves like a razor-sharp knife. It shouldn't have, because she didn't believe in psychics or premonitions or any of that crap. But for some strange reason, it did.

No, she told herself sternly, *not a strange reason. I know the reason.*

She hadn't heard from Theo at all today. Not a phone call or a text message or an e-mail. Nothing. Madison had left him two voice mails, and now she was beginning to wonder and worry. She was beginning to doubt herself *and* Theo. What if he was lying? What if he was frolicking on a beach right now with some other girl? The very thought of it sent a rush of heat through her blood. She had been honest with him about everything from the moment they decided to make their relationship official—and public. In typical Madisonesque fashion, she had given one hundred percent of herself to the cause, believing he had changed, telling herself again and again that he had outgrown his playboy ways.

She had given and worked and *believed*. Now she wasn't sure she believed anymore.

Someone close to you will reveal himself as a liar.

"Oh, shut up," she muttered, climbing out of bed and storming across the bedroom. That was when another thought occurred to her. What if Poppy had been referring to Coco? Was it Coco who was lying? Was that it? What if her gut feeling about Coco's innocence was somehow . . . wrong?

She pulled open the door. The hallway was quiet and dark, and she padded into the kitchen as softly as possible. Opening the fridge, she stared straight past the champagne and spotted the small glass bowl covered in plastic wrap. Inside were several slices of the expensive organic cucumbers Lupe used when whipping up one of her famous salads. Madison reached for the bowl, tore off the plastic, and took a slice out. She pressed it to the center of her forehead. The cool moisture seeped into her skin, making her sigh. She hadn't any doubts that the stress of the day had wreaked havoc on her skin. The little cucumber slices were like dermatological miracles. Even better was the fact that they relaxed her completely. The only problem was that they were generally off-limits: Lupe positively hated it when Madison used food to give herself impromptu spa treatments.

She carried the bowl into the living room, her head tilted back as the lone slice dripped water over her temples. She moved as if she were walking on a tightrope. But she stopped dead in her tracks when she caught the jagged slats of light cutting across the hardwood floor. She stared straight ahead and saw that the double doors to the terrace were wide open. Her heart slammed in her chest.

What the hell?

She quickly set the bowl on the coffee table and was about to turn around and start screaming when she spotted Park's hair blowing in the breeze. Then she saw Park's thin silhouette in the moonlight.

"Hey!" Madison called to her sister. "What the hell are you doing out there?"

Park whirled around and came forward into the room. She was dressed in shorts and a tank top, her feet bare. "I hope I didn't wake you," she answered. "I was trying to be really quiet."

"You didn't wake me, but you scared the hell out of

me." Madison picked up the bowl and grabbed another cucumber slice. She tilted her head back again, then applied the slice to her chin. "What are you doing?"

"Trying to reenact the crime," Park stated flatly. "I figured I'd try it from our terrace, since we can't get into the suite at the Waldorf."

Madison shook her head in response. The two slices flew off her face. She sighed and replaced them, rubbing a new one across her cheeks. "What's to reenact? You give somebody a shove and they just fall over. And then *wham.*"

"Maybe, but it's not exactly that simple."

"It's not?"

Park shook her head. "Come on out here."

"You know I hate it out there," Madison said. "If I look down, I'll hurl my dinner onto Fifth Avenue. And I'll be dropping pieces of cucumber all over the place."

"And now that you brought it up, *why* are you using those slices?" Park narrowed her eyes. "You *know* how crazy Lupe gets when you use her produce to help your skin."

Madison shrugged. "Well . . . I'm stressed! And my skin's been through hell today. I *need* these cucumber slices to help reduce the swelling around my eyes."

"You could just as easily use moisturizer."

"Moisturizer reminds me of that handprint we saw on Elijah's shirt!"

"Put the bowl down," Park said simply. "You've already wasted like five slices. And from the looks of them, they've already been marinated in olive oil."

"Of course they have," Madison replied. "That's even

better for the skin." She took another slice and placed it over her left eye, tilting her head back. "Ahhh. That feels so good."

Park muffled the urge to laugh. Madison was standing with one arm stretched out and several slices of cucumber plastered to her face. Despite the humorous picture, it *did* look relaxing. "If Lupe wakes up, she'll freak out. She'll threaten to make us salads from frozen vegetables."

"This is an extenuating circumstance, Park. How are we going to concentrate on solving a crime if our faces are tight and swollen?"

Park considered the point. She didn't want to end up looking like every overworked cop in New York City, so she grabbed two slices from the bowl, put her head back, and covered her eyes. The instant cooling sensation made her sigh with pleasure.

"I told you," Madison whispered.

"This has to be extra-virgin olive oil," Park said quietly, balancing herself beside Madison. "I can literally feel it seeping in. It's almost as good as pressing a cold gem to your skin."

Madison stretched her arms out. "Hold your head back all the way. Makes it feel like you're floating, and that helps the blood get back under your eyes."

Park tilted her head back farther. "Maybe we should talk about *falling,* not floating. The news reports are going crazy. Coco's totally being painted as a psycho."

"I know," Madison said gravely. "I've been trying to think a way out of this for her, but nothing's coming. There has to be something we're not seeing!"

Like a blind man groping at solid objects, Park

reached out and grasped the edge of the bowl. She plucked another slice from it and pressed it to her cheek. "There's a lot we aren't seeing. But according to the cops it's open-and-shut. They have everything spelled out already."

"All that evidence is circumstantial! They'll never get a murder conviction—not with the attorneys good money can buy."

A slice of cucumber slipped off Park's cheek and plopped onto the floor. "Come to think of it, I doubt they'll be going for a murder conviction. It's more like manslaughter. This wasn't a premeditated act."

"Whoa!" Madison suddenly screamed.

Park jumped, the cucumbers flying off her eyes. She looked down and saw what had spooked Madison.

Champagne, Lex's Chihuahua, had slipped into the room unnoticed. He was busy munching at the slice just beside Madison's bare foot.

In her ensuing panic, Madison had managed to hold on to the bowl, but not its contents: the remaining slices of cucumber had apparently taken flight and were now sitting on top of her head in a wet, dripping mess.

Park muffled her laughter.

Trying her best to appear unaffected and customarily composed, Madison feigned pleasure and daintily patted the messiness dripping through her hair. "Like a balm," she said easily. "I won't have flyaways for months."

Champagne hopped onto his hind legs and waited for another slice to come his way.

Madison plucked one from the top of her head and dropped it onto the floor.

"Maybe you should follow me," Park said, turning and leading the way back out onto the terrace.

Madison only stepped over the threshold, and not an inch farther. She pressed herself back against the door as her eyes scanned the stunning view of Central Park in the moonlight, the skyscrapers of Midtown, and the distant vista of the Hudson River. It was breathtaking. It was also painfully timely, given the fact that Elijah Traymore had plunged from a similar balcony only a few hours earlier.

Park faced Madison, pressing her back against the high stone-and-concrete railing. "Now," she said, "this is just about where Elijah must've been, right here along the edge when he and Coco were arguing—"

"When he and *his killer* were arguing," Madison corrected her.

"Fine," Park replied. "When he and his killer were arguing. Anyway, things got rough before they even came out here, right? Signs of a struggle. So they're arguing or whatever and then he comes out here, or maybe she comes out here and he follows her, and then . . ."

"And then what?"

"Well, let's just pretend we're building Coco's defense, okay?" Park held her arms out and made a small square TV screen with her hands. "Coco comes out onto the terrace, Elijah's getting rough with her. Maybe he grabs her or even threatens to push *her* over the edge, right? So she turns around and tries to make a run for it. But he grabs her, spins her around. His back is to the railing, just like mine right now, right? They struggle. She totally feels like he's gonna kill her so she gives him a hard shove—not because she wants to throw him off the terrace, but because she wants to break free of him. But he hits the railing and loses his balance, and then—"

"And then he turns the sidewalk into a red carpet," Madison cut in.

Park nodded. "Pretty much."

"It sounds like it's plausible, but we still don't know what the hell's going on with Coco." Madison folded her arms across her chest. "I called her parents on their cell, and they're in Italy, of course. They sounded freaked out when they saw everything on the news. They sent their attorneys to Central Booking, but I haven't heard anything in hours."

"They're grilling her," Park said. "Trust me, they want to tie this up and try to get a full confession out of her right away."

Madison stared out into the night, her gaze troubled. "You said a minute ago that reenacting the crime wasn't easy. But it looked way easy to me. And that's what scares me. It could totally be true."

"I'm just posing theories here," Park said. "What I just reenacted could have absolutely happened, but there're still a lot of weird things I don't get."

"Like what?"

"Like that handprint on Elijah's T-shirt. Like why Ina Debrovitch didn't hear anything if she was in that suite. I mean, I know she's deaf, but there has to be more than what she's saying. And *this,*" Park said, reaching into her pocket and pulling out the sheet of paper she had stolen from Elijah's wallet. She held it open to where the words *To the Penthouse* had been scrawled, followed by the strange numerical line.

"What is it?" Madison asked.

"I only showed you the front of this note in the limo today—we were all so fixated on getting to the Dakota, to Poppy." Park handed the piece of paper to her. "But look at what it says. How strange is that?"

Madison gasped as her eyes swept over the writing. "This is *freaky*. I mean, the fact that he would write *To the Penthouse* and then plunge from one is . . . it's . . ."

"Too much of a coincidence?"

"Maybe. I mean, it's just crazy. I totally got the chills."

"You think that number is a code of some sort?" Park sounded hopeful.

Madison brought the piece of paper closer to her face. *RCS00491*. Why did the little code look so . . . familiar? She studied it closely—repeated it in her head—and then walked back into the living room and turned on a lamp.

RCS . . .

"Hey," Park called after her. "What is it?"

Madison traced her eyes over the code a second time. Then a third. Then a fourth. She didn't blink. She didn't move a single muscle as everything came crashing into place.

RCS . . .

"This is an art code!" she said excitedly. "I *knew* I'd seen it before!"

"An art code?" Park shrugged. "What's that?"

"RCS. It stands for *Royal Crown Society*. It's how any piece of art the society has acquired is labeled. Kind of like an inventory code. Every one of their pieces begins with these three letters." Madison hopped up and down excitedly.

"Are you sure?"

"Positive. I even saw numbers like this in the society's private catalog when I went there for that dinner three weeks ago!"

"So then . . . *To the Penthouse* refers to a painting?" Park asked.

Madison nodded, still thrilled with her investigative discovery. "It must. I've never heard of it, but that doesn't necessarily mean anything. There's so much art out there that we never hear about." She lost herself for a moment in the truth of that statement, picturing colorful canvases and big, gleaming sculptures. She let out a dreamy sigh.

"Yeah, okay. Fine. But why would Elijah have a private art code if he wasn't a member of the society? How did he get it?"

The question hung in the air like a pair of used gym socks. Madison crinkled her nose, and the happy expression left her face; it was replaced a moment later by a look of complete confusion. "I . . . I have no idea," she finally said. "There are only fifty members in the Royal Crown Society, and I know all their names. He's sure as hell not one of them."

"Then how did he get this code?"

"I already told you, I don't know."

They both fell silent as they stared back down at the crinkled piece of paper. The first part of the puzzle— *Dakota, tonight, 6:45*—had been solved. The second part, however, was a much bigger mystery.

Madison had visited the turn-of-the-century brownstone in Gramercy Park that served as the Royal Crown Society of the Americas' international headquarters three times. She had toured the beautiful, expansive rooms, filled as they were with art from every corner of the globe. She knew Tallula Kayson and Elijah Traymore were both regarded as the most talented young artists of the day and that the society respected them tremendously, but neither Tallula nor Elijah was a member. And they *certainly* hadn't been appointed ambassadors. The society operated on a very private, if not completely elitist, level. You couldn't just ring the doorbell and prance into the brownstone. You couldn't ask to be a part of the society either. You had to be invited indoors, even if only to sit for tea in the front parlor.

Madison was certain Elijah hadn't been one of the privileged few. So how had he managed to score one of the society's art label numbers? She pictured a little lightbulb blinking on over her head. Was there something she didn't know about the society? She had never heard of a painting titled *To the Penthouse,* and that only made her want to know more about it.

"You're going to pay the society a little visit," Park said suddenly. "Now that we're ambassadors, we can't be denied entrance."

"We can't be denied anything," Madison replied curtly. "But tomorrow's Thursday. The society is closed. I'll have to pay them a visit on Friday and—"

"And what? You can't just tell them that Elijah was in possession of this code. That'll totally make them scream for the cops. And we can't have that."

Madison nodded. "You're right. I'll have to come up with something else."

Footsteps echoed on the hardwood floor. They turned

and saw Lex walking toward them, dressed in her usual work clothes: jeans, a men's oversized shirt, and her favorite pair of Louboutin flats. Her Dior glasses were perched on top of her head. She came into the living room holding a small stack of papers.

Park immediately told her about the code.

"How's that possible?" Lex asked, her tone edgy. "Who gave Elijah that code?"

"We don't know," Madison said quietly, worriedly. "But the codes definitely aren't easy to come by."

"Huh." Lex shook her head incredulously. "If the code refers to a painting or a work of art, then I guess that means he was trying to track it down for some reason."

"Yeah, but *why*?" Park threw her hands in the air.

"Maybe . . ." Lex's voice trailed off as she stared at Madison. Her eyes widened in confusion. "There's cucumber in your hair."

"Oh, you mean this?" Madison kept her tone nonchalant as she plucked a sticky slice from the top of her head and held it up. "It's . . . part of my beauty treatment. You should try it sometime." She rubbed the slice against a tuft of her hair.

"That's totally bizarre," Lex said. "Throw in a few carrots and some onion and you'd have a nice salad."

Madison shrugged, feigning absolute confidence.

"Anyway," Lex said, "I found a bunch of interesting info here." She waved the sheets of paper in the air. "That Web site address you found in the hotel suite? Weird. It's all about the supernatural and stuff like that. There's a whole message board where people post comments and questions and other links. Elijah Traymore *must* have been heavily involved in the occult scene. I found about thirty postings from him——replies to certain articles or comments about Wicca, ghost hunting, vampirism, and *channeling.*"

"Go figure," Park said. "I guess Poppy really was telling the truth."

Madison clucked her tongue. "Oh, please. I don't believe a word she said. It struck me as a little too far-fetched."

"Not really." Lex flipped to another page. "Elijah was involved in the art scene, yes, but he was totally immersed in the supernatural aspect of it. It says right here that last year he participated in a public séance in Paris, where he and a bunch of other people tried to raise the spirit of Claude Monet. Two weeks later he did the same thing in Rome, only this time his group tried to get da Vinci to hang out with them."

"So then it's obviously no secret that he was into this stuff," Park said with certainty. "Poppy was right—Elijah was a Wiccan priest."

"Yes," Lex said. "And he wore the pentacle around his neck to prove it."

"What does *any* of this have to do with what we're investigating?" Madison asked. She stormed across the room and dropped onto the couch. "I mean, it's freaky and all, but why should we care about *that* aspect of Elijah's life?"

"Because it proves that Elijah believed in channeling," Lex explained. "He obviously believed that spirits can be summoned or called up or whatever. It wasn't a joke to him. It's how he lived his life—spiritually. Which means that Poppy really might have been telling us the truth about why he contacted her."

"To summon a spirit named *Corky*," Madison said, laughing. "How silly. I've never heard of a master artist named *Corky* before."

"Lex is right." Park started pacing the living room floor. "Someone who believes in the paranormal doesn't have to think twice about whether psychics like Poppy van Lulu can communicate with the dead. People who practice Wicca believe in things like psychic ability and ghosts. It actually makes sense that he contacted Poppy for that reason."

"But she's the biggest flake on the planet!" Madison screamed. "Everyone knows that!"

"Not really," Park countered. "Half of Hollywood swears by her."

"And doesn't that prove my point exactly?" Madison stared at her sisters. "Since when has Hollywood ever been the voice of reason?"

"Okay," Park said, "I hear you. But whenever Poppy's written up in the tabloids, the stories are favorable. That's all I'm saying. She acts like a nut sometimes, but there *are* people out there who believe in her."

Lex frowned and shook her head slowly. She waved the pages in the air again. "There are, but only on a superficial level. I spent the last two hours searching for stuff about Poppy online, and when I finally got past the tabloid crap and her predictions about *American Idol,* I found a few interesting things."

Park sat down. "Like?"

"Like that in 1999, Poppy appeared on a talk show in Australia and totally embarrassed herself. She tried to give a bunch of psychic readings on the air but failed miserably at it. Like, hysterically funny. People down under think she should work for the circus or something. She totally came off as a quack."

Madison looked at Park. "Ha," she said, sounding purposefully superior.

"Yeah," Lex answered. "And Poppy's drawn a lot of criticism from parapsychologists—most of them claim she's nothing but a fraud in nice shoes."

"Ha-*ha*," Madison said.

Lex scanned her pages again. "Oh! And wait till you hear this! According to three different newspapers in Kentucky, Poppy van Lulu tried to aid FBI agents in a 2002 missing persons case in Louisville. A man named Joel Denner disappeared on a hunting trip early one Saturday morning. Poppy apparently dreamed something up and called the FBI. She led a bunch of agents to a wooded area over a hundred miles from where the guy had last been seen alive. And guess what?"

"They didn't find a body," Park said.

Lex giggled. "No such luck. But they *did* find sticks of beef jerky that were apparently ninety years old. The beef is now hanging in some sort of agricultural museum in Kentucky."

"So much for talking to the dead," Madison muttered.

Park stood up. "I just don't get it. Poppy told us at the luncheon that something horrible was going to happen, and something horrible happened. I mean, I never believed she was a genuine psychic, but if you found this info about her from a simple online search, couldn't Elijah have also found it?"

"Totally," Lex said. "Maybe he knew all about Poppy."

"But then, why would he want to see her and ask her to channel a spirit?" Park scratched her head and started pacing.

"Something about this whole thing smells cheaper than a dinner on Second Avenue," Madison said. "But what bothers me most is what Poppy told us about her walking home from the Waldorf. I'm not sure I buy it. She's *always* driven to events and then back home. She has a chauffeur at her disposal. What if she never left the hotel at all?"

"You think she could've gone upstairs to the suite and pushed Elijah off the balcony?" Park asked quietly. "What motive would she have?"

Madison stood up. "I'm not sure just yet, but I *am* sure that Poppy has some more explaining to do. Her stories aren't adding up. As far as I'm concerned, she's somehow connected to Elijah's murder."

"Then we're *totally* going to that séance tomorrow night," Park said. "And if the dead don't speak, *she* will!"

10

Ghost Ranch

Shadows danced in the moonlight. Ina watched them from her bedroom window on the second floor of the rambling main house. Situated on ten wooded acres in Greenwich, Connecticut, the Kayson estate was known around town as Ghost Ranch, in honor of the great artist Georgia O'Keeffe. Tallula had christened the grounds with that name the very day she and Elijah had moved in. Or so the story went. Ina had always liked the name, but now it seemed far too ominous. She felt like the namesake ghosts were everywhere.

She turned away from the window and stared at the

digital clock on her nightstand: 5:16 a.m. She should have been exhausted. Instead, she was wired and fidgety and trembling. Chills snaked along her spine like tiny pinpricks. She looked around the bedroom and tried to find in the delicate French country furnishings something that would make her feel relieved to be back. At home. In her bedroom. The place she had loved for the past year and a half, with its high ceilings and tall rectangular windows that overlooked—in daylight, at least—a circular patch of land colored intermittently by yellow and red tulips. The high four-poster bed was like something out of a fairy tale. The walls had been painted her favorite shade of red. Framed pictures of her little village in Romania sat on the nightstand. The room even smelled good—of the country, of grass and earth and fresh linen. Clean and crisp. She had no reason not to feel at ease here. Safe and protected. But fear paralyzed her. Adrenaline coursed through her blood in an angry gush.

Elijah, she thought gravely. *Where are you?*

A knock sounded on one of the walls, and Ina jumped. It was something she had heard hundreds of times, the noise of a big house settling, and yet the echo of that single hard rap caused her to jump in fright.

Elijah?

No, no. Of course not. That was a silly thought. There weren't any ghosts here. She couldn't allow herself to believe in the dark tales and superstitions with which she had been raised. She couldn't allow herself to remember all those eerie conversations she and Elijah had lost themselves in, sitting by the fire in the downstairs library, sharing shots of bourbon and smoking cigarettes. If she let herself go down that haunted road, she would never sleep again. The tarot cards and the Ouija boards, the candles and the herbs and the little altar Elijah had set up in the basement—she wished she had never seen any of it.

Her heart thudded as she walked to the bed and sat down. She was clothed in shorts and a flimsy T-shirt. Her hair was swept up in a bun. She had scrubbed the makeup from her face and showered as soon as she and Tallula walked through the front doors just past midnight. Her skin was still raw and dry from the scrubbing, from the force she'd used when dragging the bar of soap across her arms and legs and chest. She had spent nearly an hour under the hot jets. The water had washed away her tears, and for the first time she'd been glad for her handicap— glad that when the hearing aid came off, she heard nothing but blessed silence.

Elijah, you're really gone.

Ina buried her face in her hands. Where had it all gone wrong? How had she allowed her life to crumble so completely? It was so hard to believe that only one year ago she'd been perfectly happy. A new job as Tallula's assistant. A feeling of sisterhood between them despite Tallula's frequent outbursts and artistic temperament. Back when she had made the precarious journey to the United States as a girl of nineteen, she'd envisioned a future filled with the backbreaking work and the poor status that befalls so many immigrants. But a stroke of luck had put her on a path to unbelievable success. Through a series of housekeeping jobs she eventually found her way to Ghost Ranch, to a young couple that treated her—mostly—with respect and kindness.

From the very first, Ina had been paid well. She'd

been given a room in a beautiful home and had settled comfortably into her job. She found that she was good at juggling Tallula's hectic schedule and dealing with the media. She enjoyed piecing together the puzzle that was a young artist's life. What was more, Ina found that she loved being immersed in the thick of such beauty—not merely her surroundings here in Greenwich, but the beauty of art, of watching paintings and sculptures come to life so vividly. And then there were the giddy, girlish little shopping sprees that Tallula took her on, trips to Bergdorf's and Saks and Bendel's, where Ina learned to hone her innate fashion sense.

Now she shot a glance at the closed closet door and felt her heart sink. All those stunning clothes. The racks and racks of shoes and handbags and belts. Gifts from Tallula. Gifts from Elijah. Tokens of their appreciation. Signs that she really was a member of their odd and un-traditional family.

How could she ever leave it all?

Leaving wasn't something Ina wanted to do. It was something she *had* to do. The same stroke of fate that had delivered her into her own version of the American dream had now spun around and tossed her into a night-mare. She couldn't deal with it. She wasn't prepared to handle the repercussions. After the secrets emerged— and they surely would emerge—Ina knew she'd find her-self behind bars.

I can't let that happen, she thought frantically. *I made it across an ocean all by myself and survived in a new country. Now I'll run away again. I have no choice.*

She stood up. She glanced out the window again. A

faint line of light was just beginning to rise in the eastern portion of the sky. She had to escape as quickly as possible.

Before the police and the reporters found out. Before Tallula found out.

Swallowing her tears, Ina crossed the room and pulled open the closet door. She reached for the small suitcase on the top shelf. She unzipped it, tossed it onto the bed. Her hands shook as she began collecting the few items she would need to make the journey—where? It didn't matter. Maybe a new state. Maybe back home. She ignored the cheap pants and underwear and packed her pair of Manolos, her Habitual jeans, three TSE cashmere scarves. Only what was necessary. Nothing else. She sobbed quietly as she dropped the suitcase onto the floor and pushed it under the bed.

I'm sorry, Tallula. I'm sorry, Elijah. One day you'll forgive me.

She repeated the words over and over again as she considered her next move. And behind those words was another mantra, the one that would haunt her for the rest of her life: *I didn't mean to do it, I didn't mean to do it, I didn't mean to do it. . . .*

❖   ❖   ❖

The white clapboard guesthouse had been converted into a proverbial artist's studio early last year. Once upon a time, it was composed of two bedrooms, a small kitchen, a circular eating area, and a den. Now it looked like a Chelsea gallery, replete with stark white walls, skylights, and an open floor plan that soaked up the day-light.

Tallula was sitting on her stool before a messy canvas. It was dawn. The sun's rays illuminated the space, casting long yellow lines across the rows of paintings she had carried up from the basement the week before. She was dressed in her work clothes—paint-splattered jeans, sandals, and a blue tank top that hugged her thin frame—but she had no intention of working. After leaving Manhattan late last night, she had come home, showered, and drunk several cups of coffee. Then she had gone roaming about the house like a mad, grief-stricken widow, walking from room to room cradling a box of tissues in the crook of her arm and a small framed picture of Elijah in her right hand.

She still felt as though she were moving through a fog. Her body was sluggish and her mind couldn't absorb what had happened. She was afraid to fall asleep because whenever she shut her eyes, even for a few seconds, a ghastly image appeared on the insides of her eyelids. What she saw was a snapshot of Elijah's long, lean body plunging through the air. It was imagined, of course, but in it, Elijah's arms were outstretched and his lips were frozen in a terrified grimace. She knew she would be haunted by that single image for years to come.

She swiveled around in the chair and reached for the bottle of water on the floor. She uncapped it, took a long sip. She stood up and walked to the window at the very end of the studio, the one that afforded a perfect view of the rambling front lawn and the two tall gates at the very front of the property. She could make out the little crowd waiting behind the wrought-iron bars. Reporters. They had been gathering there all night like ants in a sugar bowl, hoping against hope that she would come outside and give some sort of statement. But Tallula had no intention of speaking to the press right now. She didn't feel like reliving the horror of yesterday, nor did she look particularly attractive. She hadn't bothered with makeup or her hairbrush. If a picture of her ended up in a newspaper now, the public would have a field day pointing out her flawed skin and recent breakout.

She drew back the curtains and stepped away. She scanned the studio for the hundredth time, noting the dozens of paintings set against the walls, ready to be shipped off to the auction house. Her favorite, *Brunch in Paris*, was a small canvas done in oil. It would take a lot to part with it. The blue and pink pastels weren't her usual style, but the painting was magnificent, a hodgepodge of shapes and strokes reminiscent of a perfect sunrise in Paris. It didn't look like brunch or Paris, but that was the beauty of modern art: everything was in the eye of the beholder. Beside it was *The Italian*, a striking painting of a long black line that was meant to represent a human figure; around it were small flecks of purple, and in one corner sat a small gray bird.

Tallula loved all of them. She knew they would sell, and her agent had already left her two messages—one was a condolence, the other was a polite reminder that last night's missed dinner would have to be rescheduled sometime in the near future.

Like maybe in a year or two, Tallula thought bitterly. The last thing she felt like doing was sitting around a table making small talk. Whenever she unveiled new works to her agent or gallery, she had to go through all the usual explanations, pointing out that the paintings didn't look particularly "new" because she'd completed most of them several years ago when she'd been a teenager. Just talking about that dark period of her life made her weak. She tried to avoid it at all costs, but sometimes it was necessary. A number of the paintings had to be retouched because the small space under the floorboards of the house where she'd been raised had been damp and musty. She'd hated dropping her paintings and sketches into that godforsaken little hole. Shortly after selling the house, she had cleared everything out and kicked in the floorboards, never wanting to see them again.

Tallula closed her eyes and leaned back against the wall. She listened as the birds chirped outside in the oak trees. It was usually such a pleasant sound, but today it grated on her nerves. In fact, being here in her studio was proving less peaceful than she'd thought it would be. The studio had always been her sanctuary, a private realm that no one else dared enter. Ina wasn't allowed in here. And Elijah—when he'd been alive—had known the rule as well.

An artist's studio wasn't merely a place in which to create; it was a place in which creation itself lived.

Through the long hours of painting—of refining the image she wanted to project onto the canvas, of making the measurements and mixing the colors to get the perfect hues—Tallula made the studio her home. The very air in here was different—charged and infused with a wild energy. A personal energy. She felt it whenever she stepped over the threshold and crossed the floor to her workstation. She felt it whenever she lifted a brush and swirled it against the palette. In the throes of the creative process, she let herself go completely—paint under her nails and in her hair, bristles sticking to her shirt, splats of color on her hands and arms and face. But that was totally fine because in her studio, *she* didn't matter. Only the work at hand mattered. She could look like a perfect horror, but no one was going to barge in on her and stare her down and say something like: *Are you okay, honey? You're a mess!* She got in touch with her art by any means possible. If that meant walking through the studio resembling a creature from a J.R.R. Tolkien novel, then so be it.

A few hours ago, Tallula had thought that retreating into this space would do the trick. That it would help her forget, at least for a short while, the nightmare raging just outside the doors. But it hadn't happened. Elijah's death was still too new for any kind of escape.

She went back to the stool and sat down. At her feet was a pile of brushes and several clean palettes. A dirty hand rag was bunched in between the bottle of water and the easel's left leg. She stared at the painting in front of her; it was a work in progress titled *Where Lovers Meet*. For the first time in a very long time, she was trying her hand at a realistic painting. She had spent the past three weeks outlining the gentle silhouettes of the young couple: the girl with her long blond hair and delicate fingers, the boy with his dark eyes and brooding stare. They were sitting on a bench in what she hoped would look like a wild garden. Tallula had wanted to inject a lot of realism into the painting. It was, after all, modeled after her and Elijah and their unique romance. Or what she had previously believed to be a unique romance.

Studying the painting now, however, she saw only the

faint touches of a refined talent. *Where Lovers Meet* was incomplete, but it didn't possess the arresting air that the art world often referred to as "Kaysonesque." She hadn't put her trademark God's eyes up above, hidden in the swirls and indentations of the paint. She hadn't captured the visceral energy present in all the previous works that had made her famous. That burning realization sliced through her like a sword.

She stood up and walked over to the far right corner of the room. She stared at the locked door to the basement and fought the impulse to break it down. What good would it do? Everything downstairs was just another reminder of how much she had been betrayed by the one person she'd loved most.

Maybe we were just too young, she thought. *Maybe I should have stayed in college. I'd be a senior right now. I'd be partying in a dorm instead of worrying about what the whole damn world is going to think of me. Instead of watching my life fall apart.*

"Damn you, Elijah," she whispered.

She stormed across the room again and angrily knocked over the stool. Then, in one swift gesture, she lifted *Where Lovers Meet* off the easel and punched a hole straight through the canvas.

11

Confession

Snap. Flash. Pop. It was raining paparazzi.

At just after ten o'clock the next morning, Coco McKaid was released from police custody. She had been processed, fingerprinted, booked. She had spent a night in jail and then been arraigned on a charge of first-degree murder. Bail, set at four million dollars, was posted quickly, courtesy of her parents' attorneys, who had stepped in while Robert and Monica McKaid were making their way back from a vacation in Tuscany.

But Coco hadn't left Central Booking on the arm of her daddy's lawyer; instead, she'd called the one person in the world she trusted most.

Now she was sitting in the back of the limo beside Madison. And, perhaps more significantly, beside Lupe Ramirez, the Hamilton family housekeeper.

Coco stared out the window at the crowd of reporters blocking the entrance of 974 Fifth Avenue. A virtual pack of wolves. Flashes sparked the air like lightning.

"Unbelievable!" Madison screamed. "I knew we were being followed! Someone tipped off these monsters, and now they're going to stop us from getting inside!"

"I didn't see anyone following us," Donnie said from the driver's seat.

"I don't think I can do this." Coco looked at Madison. "It's too crazy out there. I mean, look at them. They'll kill us with those cameras!"

"We've seen worse," Madison replied. "What I don't understand is why my building's security team hasn't cleared a path for us. We're going to have to punch our way through there."

"Don' worry 'bout nothing," Lupe said suddenly, her voice low and guttural. She leaned over the seat and pressed her shoulder against the door. Her lips curled into a sneer as she looked outside. She made a fist with her right hand and then slammed it into the palm of her left. "I take care of them."

Coco gasped. "Um, Madison?" she whispered. "Why does your housekeeper look like she's about to turn one of those reporters into a strip steak?"

"Because she watches *Scarface* and *Gladiator* every single day," Madison said flatly. "She likes to think of herself as a cross between Russell Crowe and Tony Montana."

"I mean, seriously," Coco snapped. "I'm totally scared of her."

"You should be—she's worse than I am." Madison didn't want to get into her own anger-management problems, but the truth of the matter was that Lupe's rage far outdid her own. "Now, Lupe, I want you to stay calm. Don't hit any reporters or photographers. At least, not in their faces. Remember back in May when you gave that guy from ABC a black eye? Daddy's still trying to settle that one out of court."

Keeping the sneer in place, Lupe scraped the front of her right shoe against the floor of the limo as if she were a bullfighter in Pamplona. "If they mess with bull, they get horns," she grunted.

"Just give us a minute," Madison said. She opened her purse and pulled out her makeup case. She stared at Coco. "Look at me. Oh, God—your face is way too pale. You don't even have lip gloss on."

"A night in jail will totally neutralize any makeup!" Coco cried.

"Oh, honey, I know." Madison went to work quickly, grabbing eyeliner, cream blush, lip gloss, concealer. She managed to cover up the black circles under Coco's eyes. The fresh coat of gloss perked up her complexion a little bit, but her cheeks still looked sunken.

"What about my hair?" Coco asked.

"It's fine. It has that sexy windblown look," Madison said. She took a deep breath and nodded at Lupe. "Okay. I think we can move now."

Lupe lifted one end of her gray all-purpose maid's dress and slowly circled her fingers around the door handle. "Let's roll, *chiquitas*. I'm ready to kill."

Coco gulped.

"Oh, heavens to Saks," Madison murmured.

The limo door flew open. A barrage of flashes and voices overtook Madison and Coco as they clasped hands and followed Lupe out onto the sidewalk. They tried to keep their eyes open and focused, but the whole scene exploded in a flurry of activity.

"Coco!" one reporter screamed, charging toward them. "Why did you kill Elijah?"

"Coco! You pleaded not guilty! What's your defense?"

"Coco!"

"Coco!"

A gasp of fear escaped Coco's lips. "Madison!" she screamed. "Oh my God! I can't even breathe!"

"Just stay calm!" Madison screamed back, holding her arm up to shield them from the cameras' flashing bulbs.

But the crowd had closed in on them, jostling them like tourists at Times Square. Madison tripped and pitched forward. Coco caught her and pulled her back. Then they both pitched to one side as a camera flashed in their faces.

"Coco!"

"Why'd you kill him?"

Through a sea of sparkling white dots, Madison suddenly saw their salvation. Straight ahead of her, a short, squat body erupted like a volcano, arms shooting out and head bobbing back and forth. Lupe shoved three reporters back with her elbows. Then she swung her big hips to the left, slamming a photographer with her butt.

"*Hohh!*" she screamed. "*Outta my way!*"

A microphone flew into the air. A camera skittered to the sidewalk.

"Ouch!" a female reporter shouted. "That hurt!"

"It's the crazy maid!" another said. "Everybody stand back!"

The crowd began dispersing.

Lupe broke into a second round of animalistic force, pulling a dish towel from one of her uniform pockets and flicking it like a whip to clear a path to the front door. A fearless male reporter ignored her and stuck his microphone in Madison's face. But he didn't get the chance to ask his question: the dish towel whacked him clear across the cheek, bouncing the glasses right off his nose. "Say hello to my little friend!" Lupe screamed, spinning the dish towel in the air.

Madison grabbed Coco's hand and ran forward. She saw the building's front doors open. Ten feet. Five. Three . . .

They leaped into the lobby and immediately hid behind the doorman, Steven Hillby.

"Holy God," Coco said breathlessly. She ran a hand through her sweaty, limp hair. "I feel like we just survived a Macy's sale."

Madison fanned herself with her purse. "Don't even joke about that. Thank God I'm wearing my Torys. I don't know how you're doing it in those heels—I don't think they're meant to be worn for longer than three hours. You're being so brave, honey."

Coco stared down at herself. She was still dressed in yesterday's outfit, but now everything was wrinkled and worn against her pale skin. She hadn't looked this bad since FedEx lost her Goyard trunk in Egypt.

The front door opened again and Lupe stepped inside, wiping the beads of perspiration from her face.

"You were amazing!" Coco cheered. "You, like, saved our lives!"

Lupe nodded. Then she looked at Madison and said, "Tomorrow I ask your father for raise."

"And you totally deserve it." Madison patted her shoulder as they headed for the elevator bank.

It took a full minute to ride up to the Hamilton penthouse. When the doors yawned open, they stepped into the stately foyer and saw Lex waiting for them, holding a tray of champagne flutes.

"Surprise!" she said. "I figured you all needed a little pick-me-up."

Madison, Coco, and Lupe each grabbed a flute as they walked into the living room. Champagne, Lex's teacup Chihuahua, came bursting out from under a sofa, barking and yipping at Coco's heels.

"Oh, my sweet little munchkin," Coco cooed, bending down to pat his head. "You'll never guess what Aunt Coco's been through."

"He's used to scandal," Lex told her. "He's been watching *The View* since he was a baby."

Coco sipped from the champagne flute, then made a disagreeable face. "Ugh! This is just orange juice! There's no booze in it!"

"And there *won't* be any booze in it, ever again," Madison said sternly. She took Coco by the arm and pushed her down onto a chair. "Alcohol is a big part of why you're in this whole mess."

"I don't need a lecture! Not after the night I've been through." Coco set the flute on the coffee table and held up her hands, splaying out her fingers. "Look! I'm

174

covered with ink. And let me tell you—those cops are rough! They treated me like a criminal!"

"That's what usually happens when you're charged with murder," Lex said.

"But they didn't even offer me something to drink," Coco shot back. "Or a pillow for those horrible vinyl-back chairs they make you sit in. I mean, whatever happened to courtesy?"

"Have you lost your mind?" Madison asked, her tone incredulous. "Everyone in the whole world thinks you shoved Elijah Traymore off a penthouse balcony."

"But I didn't kill him," Coco said firmly. "And if you thought I was guilty, I wouldn't be sitting in your living room right now."

"Well, you sure as hell got yourself into a horrible place." Madison crossed her arms over her chest. "Our father's in London on business, and he told us this morning that it's the lead story over there. He doesn't exactly buy that you're innocent, and he's not alone. So sit back and start talking."

"Not again!" Coco cried. "Don't make me explain it all over again! I was talking more than half the night!"

"Start talking again." Madison sat down in the chair opposite her. She motioned for Lex to assume the stenographical position.

Lex grabbed a notebook and pen from the bar, ready and eager to start an investigative log.

"Okay, fine. Here goes." Coco sighed. "Yesterday, when I met Elijah, I was drunk. He came on to me—told me I was beautiful and that he wanted to sculpt me. Told me I had beautiful, kissable lips. The whole spiel. And I really thought he was being sincere. Before you girls came to break it all up, he asked me if I wanted to go back up to the penthouse for a little fun."

"And you said yes?" Madison asked incredulously.

"Well . . . I liked him!" Coco snapped.

"But that's so not like you at all."

"Exactly. It's *not* like me. I'm always the Goody Two-shoes, and where has that gotten me?" Coco picked up her champagne flute and drank down the rest of the orange juice. "So I just figured I'd take a chance and be a little wild for once. Have fun."

"And catch herpes in the process?" Madison cut in.

Coco rolled her eyes. "Do you want me to tell you what happened or what? If you do, try being quiet, okay?"

Lex waved her pen in the air. "How do you spell *herpes*?"

"Never mind that," Coco said. "Anyway, he asked me to meet him in the penthouse suite and he told me he was going to head back upstairs in a few minutes and that I should follow right after that, because Tallula and her assistant would be coming down to the luncheon. So after he left and you and Lex and Park totally embarrassed me in front of him, I went to the bathroom and then . . ."

Madison waited quietly.

Lex, scribbling down as fast as she could, looked up. "And then what?"

"And then I saw Tallula and her assistant get off the elevator and head for the luncheon," Coco answered. "And I got into the elevator and went up to the suite, okay?"

"No, it's not okay." Madison gave her a hard, disapproving stare. "What the hell is wrong with you? Since when do we hook up with boys we've just met? Especially sleazy ones."

"Respect for the dead," Lex said quietly. "Elijah's colder than cheap, prepackaged caviar right now, remember?"

"Dead or not, he was still sleazy." Madison sipped her orange juice as she shook her head.

"Well, I was drunk!" Coco cried. "Isn't sleaze-radar the first thing to go? Can you please stop looking at me like I just boffed half of Hollywood?"

"There are worse things," Lex said, trying to sound comforting. "You could've been caught driving drunk, with a suspended license. That's way worse than boffing half of Hollywood, if you ask me."

"Thanks, Lex. I'm glad *someone* isn't judging me so terribly." Coco waved her hand at Madison.

"Get on with it," Madison snapped. "What happened when you got up to the room?"

"Elijah was a total creep, okay? A sleaze, just like you said." Coco cupped a hand over her mouth as tears welled in her eyes. "We kissed a little, but then he got rough with me. Really rough."

Madison started, as if she'd been pricked with a pin. "Rough? What's that mean? How did he get rough with you?"

Coco stared at the floor again. "He . . . he tried to force himself on me."

Madison looked at Lex, who had stopped jotting notes to listen. They were both speechless and fearing what Coco might say next.

But she didn't say anything. She kept her eyes cast downward and folded her arms across her chest, as if seeking warmth from a chill only she could feel.

Madison leaned forward and put her hand on Coco's knee. "Hey," she said. "What did he do?"

"He got rough. Like I said."

"How?"

Coco stood up slowly, then lifted her dress almost up to her waist and turned around. There, on the back of her right thigh, were two long purplish bruises that looked vaguely like fingers.

"Holy sleazeball," Lex gasped. She dropped the pen and notepad.

Madison stared, unable to break away. She was beginning to feel her stomach clench up.

"He kept grabbing at me," Coco said. "And I kept telling him to stop. He totally scared me. So I kept pushing him away, and he kept grabbing at me like some scary tropical crab."

"You must've been petrified," Lex said.

"I was! But he was so much bigger than me—every time I pushed him away, he came at me again. First I hit him with my purse—socked him right across his head. Well, that didn't work, and my purse popped open and my cell phone fell right out. That's why the cops found it there."

"And what about the chain—the pentacle—that was in your purse?" Madison asked. "How'd that get there?"

Coco sat down again. "Right after I hit him with my purse, he came at me again. I shoved him away, and my fingers caught the chain and I pulled and the chain snapped right off his neck. He screamed and called me a bitch, but by that time, I had already started running for the door. I was totally panicking. I just held on to the chain—I didn't even realize I had it until I got into the elevator."

"What a little shit!" Madison seethed. "Park was right—it *was* self-defense!"

"It wasn't anything!" Coco cried. "Because I didn't kill him. I left him in that penthouse totally alive! And I was only in there for, like, twenty minutes at the most."

Lex was scribbling furiously again.

Madison, on the other hand, remained rigid in her chair, taking in both Coco's story and her last claim—that she hadn't killed Elijah Traymore. And of course Madison believed it. She had believed it in her heart from the very start, but there'd been a tiny voice piping up in the back of her brain, saying: *If Coco's side of the story doesn't make sense, you'll have to consider that maybe you don't know your best friend that well after all.* Now that voice was completely gone.

More than anything in the world, Madison wanted to throw her arms around Coco and tell her that everything would be okay. But she couldn't. Not just yet. The equation of Coco's guilt still added up too neatly. Twenty minutes was the time frame Coco had given them, which left a whole lot of other unanswered questions. And now Madison heard Park's voice resounding in her head: *When you question Coco, keep an open mind. You have to doubt a suspect before you can totally believe a suspect. Guilt before innocence. Every cop knows that.*

And Madison knew it too. She got up and started pacing. "Okay, then. Explain to us what happened after you left the penthouse," she said, keeping her tone flat and unemotional.

"I got in the elevator," Coco answered. "And let me tell you, that damn elevator was nuts! It stalled once on the way down. It shook like an amusement park ride. I started crying because I was so scared! Then all of a sudden the doors opened on the twenty-ninth floor and I jumped right out. I was *freaked*. My heart was racing. I was too scared to get back into another elevator, so I ran into the stairway and started walking down. Not easy in these shoes, okay?"

"And you walked down all those stairs?" Lex asked incredulously. "Drunk and pissed-off and scared?"

"Yes, I did! What other choice did I have? I mean, the adrenaline was pumping through my blood, but I was still a mess. At one point, when I was feeling a little calmer, I tried to get out of the staircase, but the doors on floors twelve and thirteen were totally locked—there was no reentry into the hallways. So I just kept walking."

"But that couldn't have taken you an hour," Madison said. "I mean, you could've taken off your shoes and made it down in half an hour." She kept her tone sounding disappointed, much the way a cop would. Disappointed and a little suspicious. It was a hard role to play—she felt awful doing it—but it had to be done. In the days and weeks to come, Coco would be under intense scrutiny. The public certainly wouldn't have pity, and neither would the district attorney.

"I *could* have," Coco told her. "But I didn't. And when I got to the seventh floor, I felt sick. Disgustingly sick. I thought I was gonna puke all over the place. So I sat down on the stairs and just put my head in my hands and waited. And cried. I was so embarrassed, so upset. Everything had gone wrong—I was drunk, Elijah had turned out to be a psycho, I'd made a fool of myself, and I looked like hell. I just wanted to sit there and wait for the whole luncheon to be over. I didn't want any of you to see me because I didn't want anyone knowing what had happened. And my feet were killing me."

"But he practically tried to rape you!" Madison yelled. "Why wouldn't you want to go to the cops and tell them that?"

"Who the hell would've believed me?" Coco yelled back. "I went up there by myself, intending to . . . I don't know . . . hook up with Elijah. No one ever believes the girl. And even when I told it all to the cops last night and showed them the bruise on my leg, they didn't believe me. *Obviously.*" She wiped tears from her eyes and took a deep breath. "It's the worst thing in the world to be charged with murder!"

Lex chucked the pen and notepad onto the coffee table. "I don't get it," she said. "Why would you be charged with murder? A manslaughter charge I can understand, but why murder? This wasn't a *premeditated* act."

"It wasn't any kind of act!" Coco spat. "But according to the cops, I went up to the penthouse with *intent.* Like, I went up there planning to seduce him and kill him from the beginning. How stupid is that?"

"Tallula said that after the luncheon, she and Ina went back up to the penthouse," Madison said slowly, counting off the points of information on her fingers. "According to how it's all been sketched right now, you would have been there, hiding. Which was why Elijah asked Tallula to go back downstairs and get him a pack of cigarettes. She goes into the elevator and it stalls—almost exactly what happened to you, except that she's trapped in there for more than ten minutes."

"Right," Lex said. "And according to the newspapers this morning, that's all been confirmed by the hotel security, so we know Tallula couldn't have killed Elijah."

"Of course she didn't kill him," Madison said dismissively. "That doesn't make any sense. The newspapers also claim that Ina took a shower in her bedroom on the other side of the suite, and that when she came out, her hearing aid was broken. She didn't hear a damn thing, the poor girl."

"Well . . ." Coco sighed, irritated. "Maybe she didn't *need* to hear anything."

Madison shook her head. "Meaning what?"

"Meaning that she knew she and Elijah were alone in the suite, and that *she* shoved him off that balcony," Coco stated firmly, vehemently.

"And don't you think the cops would have figured that one out by now?" Madison asked. "I mean . . . *duh.*"

Coco shot to her feet again. "Well then, *someone* had to be in that penthouse while Tallula was in the elevator and Ina was showering. Someone other than me! Elijah and I didn't even argue near that stupid balcony."

"But there were signs of a struggle," Lex said. "Didn't you knock stuff over? Throw things down on the floor? Your cell was found in the living room."

"No," Coco replied. "None of that. If the cops found any sign of a struggle—like, broken things on the floor— Elijah must've fought with someone else after I left. It wasn't me!"

Madison was silent.

Lex was silent.

The room itself was too silent, and Coco felt the tension in the air. "Don't you believe me?" she asked, looking at them both.

"Did Elijah mention anything to you about someone named Corky?" Lex tapped the pen against her chin. "Or did he say anything, like, spooky?"

"No," Coco said. "What the hell is that all about? You believe me, don't you? You believe I didn't kill him, right?"

Madison ran her hands over her face. She couldn't go on acting like the tough cop anymore. It was taking too much out of her. She felt the stress wearing away at her. "Of course *we* believe you," she said. "But no one else does. Right now it makes more sense for everyone to believe that you killed him in self-defense, and that's the big problem. You were being attacked. Once your side of the story hits the papers, people will see it that way. They'll say it wasn't your fault—"

"Ugh!" Coco grunted. "How could you even say that? How? I'm telling you the truth!" She curled her fingers into fists and batted them against her waist in frustration, and in rage. "Or maybe it's just that you found yourself another best friend!"

"What the hell is that supposed to mean?" Madison asked.

"Oh, come on! Face it—I'm not a glamorous, famous artist. I'm not Tallula Kayson."

"That's ridiculous," Madison shot back. "And you know it is. So don't even *try* to play that card on me. I've been a good friend to you my whole life."

Coco stayed quiet. She knew she didn't have much of a rebuttal—Madison *had* been the ultimate best friend. And with nothing to do or say, Coco dropped her head into her hands and started sobbing.

It took Madison less than five seconds to walk across the room and wrap her arms around Coco. "We have to get back into that penthouse," she whispered. "We *have* to. There are clues that someone's just not seeing."

"Then we'll get in." Lex flipped open her cell, scrolled through her address book, and selected her newest—and hottest—entry. When the person on the other end of the line answered, she said, "Hey, Brooklyn? It's Lex Hamilton. You doing anything special tonight?"

12

Clues

"That's a wrap!"

The director's voice boomed across the set, and Park
heaved a sigh of relief. It was nearly one o'clock. It was
also hot and muggy and terribly sticky. She had been
working steadily for five hours under the blazing midday
sun and the searing lights that were everywhere on a
movie set. *Short Fuse* was a true location shoot, with
nearly ninety percent of the movie being shot outdoors,
which meant more takes and a greater number of distur-
bances from people on the street and equipment mal-
functioning. Basically, more work.

Thankfully, today had been relatively tame. The cameras had operated perfectly, the sound technicians hadn't experienced any big problems, and the onlookers packing the pavement had stayed behind the blue barricades. All five shots went smoothly. Nonetheless, Park felt totally worn down. Now, as she waited to be lowered back onto the sidewalk, she realized that she hadn't slept well last night. Thinking about Coco and Elijah and Poppy had kept her awake, tossing and turning. And seeing Madison so distraught over the whole mess made matters doubly difficult. They had quite a situation on their hands and very little time to get to the bottom of it.

The last time she, Madison, and Lex found themselves embroiled in a murder scandal, their close friend and fellow St. Cecilia's Prep student Concetta Canoli had been two feet from the slammer. That had been incredibly tough to see. But seeing it happening to Coco hit even closer to home.

The ten-by-twelve-inch steel platform on which Park was standing started to move. She was twenty-four feet aboveground. As she descended ever so slowly, she forced herself to study the busy stretch of First Avenue below. Fans waved. Cabs honked as they zipped by. Being this high up didn't really scare her, but it did make her cognizant of just how dangerous moviemaking could be. One wrong move and she'd strain herself against the harness locking her in place. She was wearing torn jeans, a torn shirt, and high-heeled boots. Not the best outfit in which to roll around and fend off a potential nuclear attack, but the flimsy getup was her official wardrobe. *Short Fuse* was about a young couple hired by the government to basically stop the world from ending. Park's character, Lily Zane, was feminine and smart and high-spirited—a perfect sidekick to Jeremy Bleu's rough-and-tumble action-star persona. Together, they had already dangled from the Williamsburg Bridge and shot down an elevator shaft at breakneck speed. Today's shoot had everything to do with Park trying to scale the side of the United Nations building on Fortieth Street in order to stop a terrorist from killing a diplomat. She—or rather, Lily Zane—had succeeded.

The platform made a grinding sound as it locked into place one foot above the sidewalk, and a production assistant came running over to help Park down. "Thank you," she said, smiling at the young man who always brought her coffee and water in the morning. She felt a great wave of relief as she stepped onto solid ground. She tore off the harness, then wiped the sweat from her brow. As she did so, a line of crimson droplets gathered on her fingertips. Fake blood. There was a perfect zigzag cut arcing above her left eye, courtesy of the makeup team. The rest of her face was matted with Hollywood dirt and grime. Lily Zane was petite and girlish, but she didn't mind wearing her battle scars, thank you very much.

"Hey, Park!" a young girl screamed from across the street.

"Hi there!" Park waved back. In fact, she stopped walking for a few seconds and waved to just about everyone staring at her. It felt so damn good to see people getting excited about the movie. There were only two weeks left of shooting, but the publicity campaign had already started. Paramount Pictures was rushing *Short Fuse* through its production schedule so that it could land in theaters for the big Thanksgiving Day weekend. Park had already granted Mary Hart an interview on *Entertainment Tonight,* and last week she'd secured a September slot on *Live with Regis and Kelly.* She also knew Diane Sawyer was vying for a pre-release appearance on *Good Morning America.* Park was happy to do all of it. The only problem was school when it started back up again. St. Cecilia's Prep was tough when it came to academics, and Park wouldn't be able to miss too many consecutive days of class at a time.

But she couldn't worry about school right now. It was no use, and she was too tired and too damn hot. She gave a final wave to her fans and jogged to her trailer. What she needed was a cold glass of Pellegrino and a hot kiss from the guy who'd be pouring it. Pulling open the trailer door, she smiled. "Well," she said, "if I'd known *you* were going to be in here, I'd have tidied myself up a bit."

Jeremy Bleu was sitting on one of the plush chairs in a far corner. His hair was longish and tousled, a few wiry strands hanging over his forehead. He was wearing battered blue jeans, scuffed black shoes . . . and nothing else. Walking around shirtless wasn't a habit, but most of his scenes in *Short Fuse* required him to show off those thick pecs and washboard abs. He stood up, sauntered across the floor, and wrapped his arms around Park's waist. "You're looking plenty fine to me, Lily," he said, his voice gravelly and deep.

"Yeah, I can say the same about you."

Jeremy leaned down and planted a kiss on her lips, holding it until he nearly had to gasp for air.

"You're going to zap the rest of my energy," Park said, pulling away from him reluctantly. She smoothed her hands over the bare pathway of his shoulders. She wanted to smooth them just about everywhere else too, but you never knew when a paparazzo might shove a camera lens through a window. She walked past him and opened the small fridge, grabbed a bottle of Pellegrino, and happily guzzled it down.

"You did great today," Jeremy said. He bit into an apple and sank back down into the chair. "You totally rocked those stunts. You're getting dangerously good at that."

"Not as good as you," Park answered. "I still can't quite make myself dangle from a building ledge twelve stories in the air."

Jeremy shrugged. "By the time you make your next movie, you'll be diving out of helicopters. And maybe Lex can design some sweet jumpsuits for both of us."

Park looked at the marble countertop and saw her tattered copy of the *Short Fuse* script. She had earmarked the pages she wanted to rehearse with her acting coach later on today, but something else caught her eye.

The stack of newspapers.

The *New York Times*, the *Daily News*, the *Post*.

She felt her stomach drop as she reached for them and scanned the front pages.

Body Plunges from Penthouse, Young Artist Dead one headline read. And the next: *Killed at the Waldorf*. And the last: *Young Celebutante Charged with Murder*.

"Shit," Park muttered. "I can't stand this." She flipped open the pages. She saw the garish pictures of Coco being led out of the hotel in handcuffs and of Elijah

Traymore's body being wheeled into the medical examiner's van. There was even a shot of Tallula Kayson standing in the lobby of the hotel, her hands covering her face.

"Totally sick about Elijah," Jeremy said, chomping on the apple. "I mean, talk about *splat*. I can't believe it happened right in front of you, babe."

"It was pretty gross." Park picked up the *Post* and walked to the chair opposite him as she read. The article didn't cover any new ground.

"You must be really worried about your friend," Jeremy said. "I mean, being charged with murdering the guy and all. That's totally twisted."

"Yeah, but whether or not it's twisted, the evidence happens to point to her."

"That sucks."

"It more than sucks, Jeremy. It means we might have to see one of our best friends sent to prison."

He swiveled around in the chair. "Whaddya mean?"

"I mean that Coco is really the only suspect right now. Which is bad. There are a few other questions, a few things I don't understand about this case, but Coco is at the top of the criminal list."

"But you don't really think she did it, do you? I mean, like, you don't think she up and shoved Elijah over the balcony?"

Park stared at him. She tried to follow the investigatory rules and keep her expression pensive, but the truth burned through the guise. "Of course I don't. But I haven't really had a chance to investigate the way I'd like to," she said. "Madison and Lex are with Coco now, but I haven't heard from them yet. I know in my heart that Coco's innocent, but I have to keep my mind open to every possibility."

Jeremy chucked the apple into a nearby garbage can. "What do you think happened?"

The question struck Park as funny—not that Jeremy had asked it, but that she found herself so eager to answer it. She hadn't thought it would happen that way. Confused by the evidence, angered by the circumstances, she had spent most of the night in a state of mental limbo, too scared to truly delve into the heart of the mystery. Now, however, she felt the urge to plunge right in and start hammering away at it. The uncertainty had made her restless.

She met his curious gaze. "Seriously? I think someone else shoved Elijah off that balcony."

Jeremy thought about that for a long moment. Then he shook his head. "I don't get it."

"I'm not sure I get it either," she murmured. "But I know I'm on the right track." An image of Poppy van Lulu popped into Park's mind, and the image was as intriguing as it was incongruous. An old little toothpick of a woman like Poppy shoving Elijah off that balcony? Park couldn't picture it, but stranger crimes had certainly been committed.

"Wasn't Tallula's assistant—what's her name, Dina?— in the suite when it happened?" Jeremy asked.

"*Ina.* Yeah, but she was taking a shower, and she's deaf and wasn't wearing her hearing aid. And the cops believe her."

A sly smile spread across Jeremy's face. He had caught

the familiar glint of suspicion in his girlfriend's eyes. "Aha!" he said. "But *you* don't believe her, right?"

Park considered the question. "It's more like I don't want to believe her, but the crappy thing is that I don't really have a concrete reason to think she's lying." *And that's because I haven't had the chance to interrogate her yet.*

Jeremy squinted and stroked the sides of his mouth, trying to look like a detective in one of those old black-and-white movies. "You want to know what I don't get? I don't get how a girl who's, like, five foot one and weighs a hundred and ten pounds pushes a six-foot guy who probably weighs one-sixty off a terrace."

"Those aren't exactly the right weight and height measurements."

"Whatever. But you get what I'm saying, don't you? I just don't think it makes sense."

It didn't make sense to Park either—not from the outset. But she knew of cases in the annals of criminal justice where the strange combination of adrenaline and alcohol had created superhuman strength in people. The mind stayed foggy but the body reacted. And that was the theory the cops were going with right now. They needed at least that much to turn Coco into a killer. Park took another chug of the Pellegrino, then decided to change the subject. "Do you know anything about skeleton keys?"

"Skeleton keys?"

"Yeah." Park reached for her purse and pulled out the key she had found close to Elijah's body yesterday afternoon. She held it up. "Like this one."

Jeremy stared at it. "My mom still has doors in her

house in Iowa that you need those kinds of keys for. They're in, like, old houses."

"That's it?"

"Does it say *locksmith* on my forehead?" He smirked. "Why the sudden interest in skeleton keys?"

I have no idea, Park thought. She put the key away and shrugged. "It's nothing," she said offhandedly. "You never met Elijah or Tallula, right?"

"Never." Jeremy put his feet up on the counter. "But I hear she's totally talented. And that he was a great sculptor. Shame he's dead."

"You know what's crazy about the art world?" Park said. "Now that Elijah's dead, his sculptures will be worth double what they were when he was alive."

"That's kinda creepy, when you think about it." He reached for the bottle of Pellegrino and took a sip. He stifled a yawn. A look of disinterest melted onto his face. "Anyway, babe, what are we doing tonight? Hayden called me this morning—she's in town and wants to have dinner. Or maybe we can swing by Cleopatra and hit the dance floor?"

"No," Park said with a brusque shake of her head. "Tonight, we're going to a séance."

Jeremy's response to the completely strange news was typical of him: he shrugged, nodded, and smiled. "Cool."

Park dropped her attention back to the newspaper. *Damn,* she thought, *there has to be something I'm not seeing, something that nobody's caught yet.* She stopped reading and simply stared at the grainy pictures. One in particular caught her eye: it was the one of Coco being hauled out of the hotel in handcuffs, her face a mask of mascara-laden tears. Park ran her finger over the image. Coco really was tiny—petite to a fault, in fact; she must have been possessed of superhuman strength when she gave Elijah that final, fatal shove off the balcony. Park tried to reconstruct those dark moments in her mind's eye again, sensing the panic, hearing the cries, feeling the weight of Elijah's body against the palms of her hands—

She gasped out loud. Her heart racing, she lifted the newspaper as close to her face as possible and stared at the grainy image of Coco, giving special attention to the shoes she'd worn yesterday. The shoes that were very obviously in the picture.

"Of course!" she said, slamming her hand down on the counter. "Now I see it!"

"See what?" Jeremy asked.

But Park hadn't heard him. She was too busy scrambling for her cell.

❖   ❖   ❖

At four-thirty that afternoon, the Hamilton limo pulled off the Merritt Parkway in Greenwich, Connecticut, and turned down Round Hill Road. Stately mansions flanked either side of the manicured green. Gardeners were outside, trimming hedges and replanting rosebushes. Madison peered through the window and felt her anxiety climb a notch. Hidden behind her trademark Oliver Peoples sunglasses and a silk scarf that covered most of her head, she uttered a silent prayer that no stray reporters would snap a pic of the limo's license plate. She didn't need the media finding out that she was visiting

Tallula Kayson a mere twenty-four hours after Elijah Traymore had died. But Madison knew the chances of her little trip to Connecticut not leaking out were minuscule.

"I think the house is up there," Donnie Halstrom said in his usual monotone.

Madison leaned forward, hanging over the front partition. At the end of the road were two news vans, and beyond them, a crowd. "Shit," she muttered. "That has to be it. I can't believe this mess!"

Traffic on the two-lane road was heavy. As the limo inched forward, Donnie honked the horn and turned on the blinker.

The reporters and cameras surged in. A flash cut through the tinted windows of the limo, and Madison pulled the scarf tighter around the edges of her face.

"Okay," Donnie said a few seconds later. "We're in the clear."

Madison looked up just as the two tall front gates stretched wide open. The gravel road wound to the right, the land hidden by a canopy of trees and bushes. Then it opened up, and Ghost Ranch came into view.

The Tudor-style mansion was set far back on the property and flanked by beautiful green acreage. Evergreens shadowed the side of the house. Far to the left, nearly obscured by an army of oaks, was a small white clapboard house with blue shutters and a bird fountain beside it. Madison was sure it was Tallula's studio.

She felt her stomach knot as the limo came to a stop a few feet from the tall front door. "Just wait here, Donnie," she said quietly. "I shouldn't be that long."

"Okay."

Not until she began walking up the front steps did she pull the scarf down around her neck and remove the sunglasses. She reached the front door, then hesitated a moment, her hands balled into fists. She stared at the doorbell with a heavy heart and just a little bit of fear. She wasn't scared in the traditional sense. She was just nervous about the task at hand. It was going to take a lot of guts to get through it smoothly without her sisters.

She pushed the button and waited.

A few seconds later, Tallula Kayson appeared on the threshold, a weary smile already in place. She waved Madison inside and said, "I'm so glad you called. Thank you for coming."

"Thank you for agreeing to see me," Madison replied. She stepped into the bright, spacious foyer and gave Tallula a quick once-over.

She looked bad. There was no other word to describe her. Tallula's blond hair was pulled back in a messy ponytail, her eyes red-rimmed and swollen, her face completely devoid of makeup. She had the appearance of a widow in mourning—and of a young woman who hadn't slept in the last twenty-four hours. Her jeans were paint-splattered, her tank top caked with particles of food. But she hadn't completely forgotten her artsy self: a huge brown satin ribbon was tied around her waist, making her look like a hastily wrapped present.

Madison wanted to offer her some blush and lip gloss but resisted the urge to do so. She doubted a prettier face would make Tallula feel better.

"I can only offer you water," Tallula said apologetically. "I haven't gone shopping in ages, and the fridge is totally empty."

"I'm fine," Madison said. She set her purse down on the foyer table and followed Tallula into the living room. It was large and airy, the skylights taking in the sunlight, the furniture an eclectic mix of art deco and old English. Dark wood pieces stood next to lacquered white ones. The paisley sofa was adorned with a pink cashmere throw. Inwardly, Madison smiled. Only an artist like Tallula could pull off such a feat of interior design.

"I was so glad when you called," Tallula said. "God knows, I don't want to be alone right now." She lowered herself onto the sofa and indicated the chair across from her. "I couldn't even think about staying in Manhattan for another minute. I wanted out of that hotel, out of the craziness. Every time I looked outside I saw . . ." She heaved a sigh. A tear trickled down her cheek. "I can't talk about it. I'm just so glad you're here. I feel so alone."

"Where's Ina?" Madison asked.

"Up in her room."

Madison cleared her throat. "Well, in that case, I'm glad we're alone. There's some stuff I'd like to talk to you about." She sat down on the couch, clutching her purse in her lap. The coffee table before her was barely visible under the mess of papers, crumpled tissues, and small boxes. It was the boxes that held her attention: it appeared as though they were filled with men's clothes. Elijah's clothes—and lots of other stuff that had probably belonged to him.

"Oh, it's such a mess," Tallula said when she caught Madison staring. "Can you believe this is how the hotel people help you clean up after one of their guests has been *murdered*? Everything of Elijah's got tossed into boxes. I haven't even looked inside them yet."

Madison was surprised by her own internal reaction. Her pulse started racing at the thought of scouring those two boxes and examining every item that had belonged to Elijah Traymore. Maybe Park had missed something yesterday.

"I knew when I met you yesterday at the luncheon that we'd become fast friends," Tallula said sweetly. "Truth is, I don't have many friends—just a few kids from high school, but we're not really that close. And plus, to be perfectly honest, they don't know about art the way you do. We totally have that in common. Would you be a cookie and grab me a tissue?"

"We have so much in common," Madison agreed, handing her the tissue. "I . . . I pretty much feel like I can talk to you about anything already. That might sound a little strange, but I swear it's true."

"I feel the same way. It's kismet. We were meant to be friends. I just can't believe we didn't run into each other at Fashion Week last year."

"It's so crazy," Madison said. "All those crowds and cameras. You know how it is."

"Well, no cameras in here! Those beasts won't leave my front gate, but I'll shoot them if they step onto my lawn!" She sniffled and blew her nose.

"Is everything else okay, Tallula? Have you sorted things out with your publicist?"

"Yes. She's going to start releasing statements over the weekend."

"Why so late?"

Tallula shook her head and stared into her lap. "Elijah's family—they're a bunch of pigs! They've always hated me. They say I'm the one who made him drop out of college, that I pulled him away from his parents. And now they're blaming me for what happened in their own way. They're not even letting me go to the funeral! His body is being released from the medical examiner's office today and then it's being flown to Massachusetts."

Madison heard herself gasp. "That's awful!"

"I know! I called Elijah's father this morning, and I know he hates me. But I said to him, 'Mr. Traymore, would you just please be a double-fudge cupcake and let me come and mourn Elijah properly?' But he wouldn't hear it! He called me a black widow!"

Madison shook her head. Then she cracked a nervous smile and looked down. "I know talking about Elijah and what happened is tough, Tallula, but that's part of the reason I came here."

"I know why you came here," Tallula replied quietly. "Because Coco McKaid is your best friend and you think she's innocent."

Well, that was easy, Madison thought. But she knew the conversation had only just begun. She also heard the slight edge of coldness in Tallula's voice and saw the angry gleam in her eyes. Which, of course, was entirely understandable. The only problem was that Madison felt lost right now. She wasn't sitting at her desk at home tackling a term paper. She wasn't on the phone discussing business for the first Triple Threat store. Either of those tasks would have been easy for her—all work and no emotion. Here, it was different. She had to manage the nearly impossible feat of discussing Coco while not offending Tallula. She had to keep her voice even-keeled and choose her words carefully. In truth, it was a job more suited for Park.

"I understand where you're coming from," Tallula said. "Really, I do. You've known Coco your whole life and you can't picture her doing what everyone thinks she did. Everyone including me."

"No," Madison said, "I can't."

"It's shocking to me too. But what else am I supposed to believe, Madison? The cops explained everything to me."

Madison met her stare. "Then you know Coco's side of the story?" she asked bluntly. "You know about . . . about how Elijah . . ." *How Elijah attacked Coco.* She wanted to say it, but couldn't.

Tallula rose from her place on the sofa and began pacing. Her face crumpled into an angry mask. "I have no choice but to believe that Elijah invited Coco up to the penthouse, and that he planned on cheating on me," she said tightly. "I'm angry about that. I hate Elijah for it. But that doesn't mean he deserved to die. It just doesn't."

"Of course it doesn't," Madison agreed.

"And that whole bit about Coco shoving him off the balcony in self-defense?" Tallula went on. "I don't know if I buy that. I think she just lost control . . . or . . . or . . . maybe *he* rejected *her*. Did you think of that possibility?"

Madison stared down at her hands again. "Tallula, I never believed that Coco was guilty, not even in self-defense. I mean, I made myself consider that possibility, but I know her, and it's just . . . impossible." A pause. "To tell you the total truth, I don't even think Coco was in the room when you and Ina went up there after the luncheon."

"What?" Tallula asked sharply.

Madison swallowed hard. The knife-edged tone of Tallula's voice worried her.

"I don't understand," Tallula said. "What are you talking about?"

"My sisters and I think we can prove that Coco wasn't in the room when you and Ina got there, and so we think we can prove that she didn't kill Elijah," Madison stated very matter-of-factly.

Tallula sat back down again. *"How?"*

Ignoring the question, Madison looked up at her. "Did you know Elijah had been speaking to Poppy van Lulu? That last night he had an appointment to meet with her at her apartment on Central Park West?"

Tallula's eyes widened in clear shock. "That old crazy psychic?" She chuckled. "I mean, I know Poppy is a patroness of the arts, but she's cuckoo for Cocoa Puffs. And Elijah knew that."

"He did?"

"Yes." Tallula rolled her eyes. "Elijah practiced Wicca and spent all his spare time collecting information on books and ghosts and spirits and haunted sites. Some stuff he believed. Some he didn't. But he was always up for talking about it. It wasn't one of our similarities. Is that why he was going to meet with Poppy van Lulu again? Does she practice Wicca too?"

Madison flinched. "Again? You mean, he met her before?"

"Of course. When we were students at St. Stephen's College. The school has a really big psych department, and back in 2004, I think it was, they held some sort of scientific experiment about psychic phenomena and ESP. Stuff like that. Anyway, Poppy van Lulu was one of the psychics who participated. Elijah met her back then."

Holy shit, Madison thought. "You're sure about that?"

"Yes. Why?"

"Did he ever say anything about Poppy?" Madison asked, trying to conceal her mounting excitement. "Like what happened when he met her? What he thought of her?"

Tallula sniffled. "He said she was a total fraud. She was the laughingstock of the experiment—I think it was called the Borely experiment. Elijah worked with two of the professors on it. Anyway, none of that information about the experiment was ever released because Poppy was smart—she made a huge financial donation to the college, but it was really hush money. She didn't want that getting out to the public."

"Of course she didn't," Madison whispered, more to herself than to Tallula. "But Elijah knew about it." Her heart pounding, she let this new delicious nugget of information sink in. It proved that Poppy had lied to her, Park, and Lex yesterday—but did it also give Poppy a reason to want Elijah dead? And if he knew Poppy was a fraud, why had he made an appointment to meet with her?

"And when I saw Poppy yesterday, I almost laughed right in her face," Tallula said. "I can tell a fraud a mile away."

"Wait," Madison said. "Poppy left the luncheon—she left the hotel—before you and Ina arrived. When did you see her?"

"When Ina and I left the luncheon and walked back to the elevators," Tallula said. "I saw Poppy coming out of that little gift shop."

Madison's heart slammed in her chest. Could it be? She blinked rapidly. "Are you sure?" she asked. "I mean, are you *absolutely* sure?"

"Of course." Tallula was staring at her blankly. "Madison, would you please be a coconut and tell me what this is all about?"

Madison smiled, trying her best to appear in control and collected. She knew she couldn't spill the beans. Not here. Not yet. There were still too many unanswered questions. "Listen . . . you think Elijah believed in things like . . . channeling, right?" she asked.

"I guess so," Tallula replied. "Why?"

"Did he know anyone named Corky?" Madison pressed, again ignoring the question.

Tallula blinked several times. She shook her head. "I . . . I don't understand any of this. What's with all these questions? No—I've never heard him talk about someone named Corky. Why? Corky? What kind of name is that?"

"Elijah asked Poppy van Lulu to channel someone named Corky," Madison said. "As in, call up a spirit. Literally. I know it sounds totally lame, but it's true."

Tallula stood up. She stared around the room unseeingly, her eyes darting here and there, her face growing longer. Tears spilled over her cheeks again. She took a step, but then stumbled and fell back onto the sofa as if about to faint.

"Oh my God!" Madison shrieked, reaching out to her. "Are you okay?"

"I'm . . . fine." Tallula wiped a hand over her face. She took several deep breaths.

"Should I call someone?" Madison asked worriedly.

"No, no. Really. I'm fine. Would you be a rabbit and get me another tissue?" She grabbed Madison's hand and gave it a squeeze. "It's just that hearing all this . . . weird news . . . it's just so shocking."

"I know, and I'm sorry. But I'm trying to help." Madison sat down beside her and handed her yet another tissue. "Listen, Tallula. What I'm going to say isn't easy, and it won't be easy for you to hear. But the thing is . . . well . . . I think we need to start thinking about other things. Like maybe Elijah had more secrets. Maybe he was trying to hide something, or expose something. Maybe he angered someone—"

"But . . . who? And what does any of this have to do with him being pushed off the balcony?"

"I'm just trying to figure out if maybe there was someone else in the hotel yesterday who could have done it," Madison said patiently, cautiously. *Like a fake psychic who doesn't want certain information made public.*

Tallula shook her head. Impatiently. Not so cautiously. "None of this is making any sense! Channeling? Someone named Corky? I mean, who do I look like— Nancy Drew?"

Madison glanced in the direction of the window. She felt like a total polyester-for-brains. She wasn't making any sense. She was irritating Tallula. But she still had questions, and there was no chance of stopping now. *Here goes,* she thought, quickly running a hand through her hair. "Did Elijah ever visit the Royal Crown Society?"

"He hated the society," Tallula said quickly.

"He did? Why?"

"He said they were a bunch of snooty fools. Oh—I'm sorry to say that to you. You're an ambassador. It's not what *I* think. It's what *he* thought."

To the Penthouse, Madison thought. *How did he get that code?*

Tallula coughed loudly. "Oh, my throat. Would you be a mouse and grab me that bottle of water on the mantel?"

Madison crossed the room, got the bottle, and handed it over.

Tallula took a long drink. Then she stared at Madison, her eyes bright. "Do you think a member of the society could have killed him? Is that what you're saying?"

"No, it isn't. I was just curious." *And you're sounding dumber as the minutes tick by,* a little voice in her brain said. *Dumber and dumber.* She had only *one* other possibility to toss onto the table, and the very thought of doing so sent her stomach roiling.

She got up and walked over to the window. She pretended to stare outside but was in fact taking a few deep breaths. "Tallula," she said, keeping her voice steady, "is there any way that maybe . . . *Ina* isn't telling us everything?" She heard the sentence float out onto the air and waited for a reaction—a gasp, a scream, an angry grunt. When several seconds passed in silence, Madison turned around.

Tallula was staring at the floor, rapt in thought. She didn't appear disturbed or enraged or even the least bit flustered. She actually seemed to be considering the question.

That, at least, was Madison's assessment. But when another minute ticked by in silence, she figured it was just her own wishful thinking. "Tallula? Did I totally upset you? Did I—"

"No, totally not." She looked up. "It's just that I . . ."

"That you what?"

"This morning," Tallula said, "Ina and I had a little . . . argument. And I'm not sure what to make of it. I know she's just as upset as I am, but still . . ."

"What was the argument about?" Madison asked.

Tallula's eyes went glassy again. "Ina told me that she doesn't want to stay here with me. She said she wants to go back to the city for a while, rent a cheap hotel room in some Howard Johnson's on Houston Street, and sort things out."

"You mean she quit being your assistant?"

"No. She didn't say that. She just said that she needs time to be alone. She's very shaken by what happened. But I still thought it was strange." Tallula wiped tears from her cheeks. "It was really hard for me to hear that, because I don't have anyone without her. She and Elijah were my family. So I yelled at her. Called her an ungrateful little bitch. It was just my nerves talking—I hope she knows that. I didn't mean it."

"I'm sure she knows," Madison said. "But this whole thing about her wanting to leave—had she ever mentioned anything like that before?"

"Never. She was always so happy to be working for me. I treat her well. And she's great. Once a month I take her on a shopping spree—Saks, Barneys. I buy up a storm." She sniffled. "I even bought her a John Galliano."

"Couture?" Madison asked, shocked.

Tallula nodded. "It was the cutest little dress. Wild

and outrageous but impeccably designed. You know, typical John."

"I've only met him twice," Madison said. "Lex would probably know exactly the piece you're talking about. She had dinner with him a couple of weeks ago."

"Well, whatever the case . . . I don't know why Ina would want to leave and be away from me. I just hope she isn't planning on going back home to Romania."

Madison flinched. "What makes you say that?"

"I heard her on the phone this morning," Tallula said sadly. "And I could have sworn I heard her ask for the number to some airline." She reached for the box of tissues on the coffee table and whisked three out, drawing them across her nose. "Maybe I got it wrong, but what if I didn't? How cruel can someone be? I treat her like a sister. Why would Ina want to leave me? Why would she want to run away?"

Madison stood up. "To escape from something," she said pointedly.

Just then, footsteps sounded on a staircase in another part of the house. Ina Debrovitch came into the living room carrying a suitcase and cradling a small leather datebook against her chest. She paused when she saw Madison standing by the fireplace. "Oh," she said quietly. "I'm sorry. I hope I didn't interrupt anything."

"Hi," Madison said, her voice shaky. "Um . . . Ina . . . we were just talking about you. We—"

Tallula shot off the sofa, sobbing openly. "Ina! Why are you doing this? Why are you leaving me when I need you most? Haven't I been a good friend to you?"

Ina heaved a sigh. A pained expression formed on her

face. She put the suitcase down and dropped the datebook onto the coffee table.

Madison stood stock-still, her gaze boring into Ina. There was something different about her today, something that hadn't been present in her demeanor yesterday. After a few seconds, Madison realized what it was—an edgy coldness, an arrogance that she exuded with her squared shoulders and tight lips.

"Answer me," Tallula continued. "Ina, just tell me why you're leaving like this! Why won't you just be a panda bear and stay here with me?"

Ina remained silent.

"Well, Ina?" Madison said softly. "Why *won't* you be a . . . a panda bear?" She felt like an idiot uttering such a dumb term of endearment. She was about to ask another question, but then her eyes shifted and she glanced at the leather datebook, at the silver seal emblazoned on the right-hand corner. It was the image of a small picture frame over which the letters *CIG* were superimposed. It took less than five seconds for her to identify what she was staring at. *Chateau Innis Gallery,* she thought. *One of the most famous and highly regarded art galleries in France.*

"Answer me, Ina," Tallula pressed.

Madison momentarily forgot the drama unfolding before her. She was struck by the realization that Ina owned something so rare. The leather datebooks could be purchased only if you visited the Chateau Innis Gallery. That in itself wasn't such a big deal, but the link forming in Madison's brain was making her pulse quicken. She walked over to the coffee table and picked up the datebook. She looked at Ina. "When were you at the Chateau Innis?" she asked.

"I—I worked there briefly," Ina stammered. She had been caught off guard, and now she was staring at Madison strangely.

"Ha!" Tallula yelled. "And you think *that* little receptionist job you had six years ago is going to help you in the art world? You're acting like an idiot, Ina! An idiot!"

Ina's eyes welled with tears. She shook her head quickly, then ran from the room.

But she didn't run quickly enough.

Madison had caught the look on Ina's face, and it was the look of pure, unarguable guilt.

13

Lex's New Favorite Borough

Lex had two goals to achieve before midnight: the first was to gain entrance into the penthouse suite from which Elijah Traymore had taken his fatal plunge; the second was to get kissed by Brooklyn DiMarco. And she didn't have any doubts that she would be able to accomplish both successfully.

Providing, of course, that her outfit did what she wanted it to do. She was wearing a new piece from Proenza Schouler: a waist-hugging black dress with a plunging neckline. It was a total scene-stealer.

At six o'clock, she walked into Nello, her favorite

restaurant in Midtown. Every table was occupied. And, almost immediately, she felt eyes zooming in on her as diners froze to gawk. Whispers crackled on the air—— *Look! It's Lex Hamilton, the youngest of the triplets*—and she gave the admiring crowd one of her perfunctory nod-and-smile acknowledgments. A waiter carrying two dishes of pasta came to a dead stop in the middle of the floor and looked at her. Weeknights weren't generally good for celebrity-spotting, but she had just shattered that little rule.

She scanned the very back of the restaurant.

There, sitting at her usual corner table, was Brooklyn. He spotted her and waved.

Lex walked over to him smoothly, swinging the strap of her magic purse over one shoulder. "Hey there!" she said cheerfully.

Brooklyn pushed back his chair and stood up. "Hey yourself," he said quietly. He picked up the single rose lying on one side of the table and held it out to her.

Lex felt herself begin to melt. It was too early in the date to melt, but there was no stopping the feeling of warmth that rushed through her. She accepted the rose and held it up to smell. "Thank you so much," she said gratefully. "You didn't have to do that."

Brooklyn smiled. "Holy Jeez," he whispered. "You look really beautiful."

"You're not looking so bad yourself." Lex settled herself into the chair, sweeping her eyes over his tall, toned body. He was dressed in jeans and a tight black T-shirt, but his cut-up physique practically screamed through the simple clothing. She was seeing him up close for the first time—or, more precisely, without any distractions. No telephone books flying over her head, no dead body within eyeshot. He was even better-looking than she'd initially noticed.

"I was pretty surprised when you called me this morning," he said.

"You were? Why?"

He shrugged sheepishly. "You're famous. I'm not."

"Oh, please." She shook her head as she reached for her glass of water. "That's just silly. Sure, my sisters and I grew up in the spotlight and all that, but we were raised to see beyond it. And like I said when I first met you, the circles we walk in can be totally overrated."

"And totally scary!" He laughed. "I've only been working with my dad at the hotel for a few months, but I've dealt with a few celebrity types already, and let me tell you—they aren't always easy."

"I know." She put down the glass and leaned in closer to him flirtatiously. "But *I'm* not like that, so you don't have to worry."

"Yeah, I already figured that out." He smirked as he looked at her.

Not just a simple look, Lex noted quickly, but a deep, fearless stare. His eyes were expressive, and right now they were expressing a lot of sexiness. She fanned herself with the menu. "Um . . . so . . . you're going to be a senior in September, right?"

"Yeah. And you want to know the truth? I'm actually pretty bummed about it."

"No way. Why's that?"

He shrugged. "Because I like high school. Sounds

weird, right? But it's fun for me. I like being able to focus a lot of my time on playing violin and doing concerts. Plus I have a lot of close friends, and it's hard to hold on to them when you all go away to college."

"Have you started looking at colleges?"

"Yeah. I think I want to stay here in the city. Either NYU or Columbia. I'm pretty nervous about those applications. The SATs totally sucked."

"Tell me about it." Lex made a sour face. "At my school, St. Cecilia's, we had to do a whole term of that pre-SAT stuff, and I think it confused me more. My sister Madison—she's the one who'll score ten million on her SATs."

"You think you'll major in fashion design?"

It was a good question, and Lex really didn't know how to answer it. College, for her and Madison and Park, wasn't about earning a degree that would start you off on a career. It was about earning a degree that would enrich your life intellectually. Whatever they decided to do in the future was already planned out for them in great and meticulous detail: Lex could easily go on designing, Madison could choose to help run Hamilton Holdings, Park could make more movies or take on Broadway. They had the connections that would further their dreams. And if those dreams changed? That would be fine too.

Lex knew that much. She had always known it. She wasn't the type of celebutante who could sit in front of Barbara Walters and say something like: *Oh, nobody gave me an ounce of help, I made it all on my own.* It was absolutely true that she worked hard at designing. But it was also true that she had a powerful last name and the media empire to prove it.

"I'm not so sure," she replied. "I mean, I'll always love fashion, but in college I might want to take up something else."

"That's totally sweet. Maybe in college you'll end up majoring in business—because you've done such an amazing job with your fashion line."

"Eh, business means a lot of math, and I'm not too good at that. How about you? I bet you'll always play violin."

"Definitely," Brooklyn said. "My goal is to make it to the Philharmonic. So I figure in college I'll get a BFA in music. You like classical music?"

"I do," Lex said. "We grew up listening to it—Mozart, Chopin, Bach. I think you'd have to be twisted not to like it—it's so romantic."

"Yeah, it is. But that's the thing about classical music—it can be anything. Romantic, sad, scary. When you listen to a Mozart requiem, you can totally feel the darkness. And with Bach—some of his pieces, you can feel the passion."

She resisted the urge to fan herself with the menu again. Instead, she kept her eyes locked on his heart-shaped lips and broad, muscular shoulders.

"Maybe one day I can play for you," he said with yet another smile. "We can walk to Central Park and find a nice secluded spot. I'll sneak some champagne out of my house. We can have, like, a picnic. Maybe that'll be our second date."

"Definitely." Lex felt her heart beating faster. She had

never experienced such sincere and unabashed sweetness. The moment was so damn *perfect*. Hell, she felt like kicking off her heels and running through a field of daisies. She loved that she could sit here, look at the gorgeousness of Brooklyn DiMarco, and just talk to him about simple, everyday matters. He wasn't going to bring up the subjects that most people brought up when she joined a dinner table. No chitchat about celebrities or trendy nightclubs. No name-dropping. His world was a galaxy away from hers, and yet the light-years between the two seemed impossibly close.

"So," she said, steering the conversation in another, but equally significant, direction. "How long have you been single?"

"About a year. I broke up with my ex-girlfriend at the beginning of last summer."

"Sorry to hear that."

He shook his head. "Don't be. We weren't right for each other. She was obsessed with keeping a leash on me, calling me every hour on the hour. She never believed me when I told her I was going to work, or that I had to help my dad with stuff around the house. She, like, wanted to be together *all the time*. But that's not how I am. I think it's good to have space when you're in a relationship."

My kind of guy, Lex thought.

"How 'bout you?" he asked. "I can't believe a girl as beautiful as you is single."

"Oh, stop," she said with a fluttery wave of her hand.

"No, seriously." Brooklyn gave her an open, honest stare. "I'm not trying to score points here. I'm just telling it like it is."

"Thank you." She cleared her throat nervously, and the action shocked her. Was it possible? Was the no-guy-can-make-me-feel-weak-in-the-knees Lex Hamilton getting . . . weak in the knees? "I've been single forever," she finally said. "A really long time."

He shot her another wink. "Well then, I guess today's my lucky day."

"You know, Brooklyn, I'm beginning to think it's *my* lucky day too." She leaned in closer to him, her chin resting in her palm, her eyes cloudy with the look of hotness-at-first-sight.

The rose. The talk of playing his violin for her. The mention of their second date in a quiet place away from the glare of the public. It all appealed to Lex a lot. It made her feel like a different person—not in any way ashamed of her wealth and fame, but at ease with the thought of leaving it behind for a little while. Of not being dominated by it.

She had been on plenty of dates with hot guys, but in the end, they always proved too shallow for her taste, and too obsessed with the details of the high-society world. They talked about getting into the newest clubs and buying another Ferrari and getting stoned at whoever's mansion in L.A. They certainly didn't mention growing up in a middle-class New York City neighborhood and working part-time at a hotel for extra cash.

But Brooklyn DiMarco did. Over the course of the next hour, over appetizers and sodas, he told Lex all about his "crazy Italian family" and how he had played Little League as a kid. His mother ran a bakery in Bensonhurst. His father had worked security at the Waldorf for nearly twenty years. He had three uncles who were cops and two aunts who were nurses. He had spent every Christmas of his life in Brooklyn and every summer working some odd job or another. He had never been to Paris or London or Monaco. He hadn't even been to Aspen. But he *had* gone on a school trip to Florence last year.

Lex listened to him intently, entranced by his good looks and at the same time attracted to his intelligence. He spoke about the great composers and their master-pieces. He spoke about the performances he'd seen at Carnegie Hall and Lincoln Center in the past two months. And then he mentioned his other passion—his dog, Tequila.

"Wait a minute," Lex said, holding up her hand. "You have a dog named *Tequila*?"

Brooklyn nodded. "A Lab," he said. "I swear, she doesn't have a mean bone in her body."

An image of Champagne, her teacup Chihuahua, popped into Lex's mind. How could you go wrong with two dogs named after booze? "Brooklyn," she said with a laugh, "I think we have a hell of a whole lot in common."

At eight o'clock, Brooklyn paid the bill—he insisted—and they walked out onto Madison Avenue. Lex linked her arm in his, but she kept their pace deliberately slow, wanting to enjoy as much time with him as she could. Before a photographer showed up and ruined the moment.

When they got to the corner a few minutes later, she finally stared up at him and said, "So, listen. I have a favor to ask of you."

The wry expression on Brooklyn's face said it all. "You want me to bust you into the penthouse, right?"

Lex frowned. "Yeah, I do. But I hope you don't think that's why I called you."

"I don't think that." He slipped his hands into the pockets of his jeans, and his triceps flexed deliciously. "But for me, it's always pleasure before business." And he leaned down and pressed his lips firmly against hers.

◇　◇　◇

"It's a definite link," Madison said excitedly, looking at her sisters.

She, Park, and Lex were standing in one of the first-floor bathrooms of the Waldorf-Astoria, changing into their requisite disguises. Lex and Park had the good fortune to be slipping into gray maids' uniforms. Madison, on the other hand, had been given an oversized green jumpsuit and a matching cap reserved for maintenance workers.

"Explain it one more time," Lex said.

Madison nodded. She had spent most of the afternoon piecing together the strange little puzzle that had formed in her mind, and now it was a clear picture. "Yesterday, when we were in Poppy's apartment, remember how I commented that she had a Stefan Luchian painting on her wall? Well, he happens to be one of the greatest Romanian painters. Been dead for a long time, but his works are amazing. Anyway, when I was at Tallula's house today, I noticed that Ina had a datebook from Château Innis Gallery in Paris. Turns out Ina interned there six years ago for a couple of months as a receptionist. And I remembered something really interesting: six years ago, Chateau Innis held a huge auction for a number of Stefan Luchian's works—it was written up in the *Times, Art in America,* the *New Yorker.* A pretty big deal in the art world. And *that* was when Poppy van Lulu bought the painting."

"I don't know if I'm following you," Park said. "What's so important about that?"

"I called the gallery in Paris today," Madison said quickly. "And I was able to confirm that Ina worked there while they were holding the auction for Luchian's paintings. Don't you see? Ina Debrovitch and Poppy van Lulu met six years ago at that gallery. They've known each other all this time!"

Park and Lex stopped putting on their outfits and stared at each other.

"No way!" Lex finally screamed.

"Amazing," Park said calmly, impressed. "A direct link between two suspects that no one's made yet. How did you manage to get that info from the gallery?"

Madison tossed her head back as she slipped further into the ugly green jumpsuit. "You *know* my French is as flawless as my Italian. I pretended Ina was applying for a job in my gallery, and I asked for a reference. They didn't tell me much about her, but they confirmed that she worked there."

"Huh," Park said. "It's a big link, but it doesn't mean Ina and Poppy were in on killing Elijah."

"No, it doesn't," Madison agreed. "But I told you guys about that scientific study that Poppy totally failed? Well, she knew Elijah from back then also, and she didn't want that info being leaked to the public. Elijah knew all about it. So that could very easily be Poppy's motive—she wanted to keep him silent."

"But if that's her motive, where does Ina fit into it?" Lex asked. "And what about the art code, and the key Park found? What about *To the Penthouse*?"

"I don't know yet," Madison answered. "But that's what we're going to find out." She struggled with the rest of the jumpsuit, then sighed. "This is insane!"

"It's the only way to do this safely," Park said. She fastened the buttons of her stained white shirt and then fitted the gray vest over her upper body. She clamped a hairnet over her messy bun. "The last thing we want is to get caught. Don't forget, we're visiting a crime scene."

"A *former* crime scene," Madison corrected her. "And maybe I wouldn't be so pissed off if I didn't have to walk around in this stinky jumpsuit." She pointed down at it. "It smells like a sumo wrestler wore it."

"Just put it on." Lex wrapped her long hair into a bun and secured it with two bobby pins. She checked her reflection in the mirror. Gray wasn't her color, but the uniform fell over her trim figure nicely. She tied the accompanying apron around her waist.

"So just to review," Park said. "Poppy apparently didn't leave the hotel like she told us she did. Tallula saw her coming out of the gift shop, which will have to be proven. Ina was in the shower and she allegedly didn't hear anything. And she found her hearing aid broken on the floor when she came out of the bathroom." She slipped on the apron and stood up straight. "And maybe, just maybe, Poppy and Ina killed him together." Park knew she sounded overly confident, but she *also* knew that when it came to crime, the level of coincidence was staggering.

Beside her, Madison nodded thoughtfully. "Together they could have totally chucked him overboard."

"Well then . . ." Lex froze and swallowed hard. "What does that say about the séance we're attending tonight? If Poppy and Ina are in on something, then—"

"Then it means we'll probably be in mortal danger," Park said matter-of-factly but still offhandedly. "Anyway, Lex, how was your date with the borough beefcake?"

Lex felt herself blush. "Very nice. He's a sweetheart."

"And he's got the hottest bod this side of the Atlantic." Park gave her a thumbs-up. "He must bench-press his freakin' weight every day."

"I didn't ask him about his workout routine," Lex said. Then she smiled devilishly. "But I'm hoping to see him minus the T-shirt soon."

Madison yanked the pant legs of her mannish uniform up to her waist. "I think it's great that you like him and all, but shouldn't you be concerned with another very important matter?"

"Which one?" Lex asked.

Madison sighed as she pulled the uniform over her arms and zipped it up. "You told us he lives in Brooklyn," she said, a little disappointedly. "That absolutely qualifies as a long-distance relationship. Don't you have to take a train there or something?"

"I've actually thought about that already," Lex told them. "And here's how I see it: if this relationship really does turn into something long-term, Brooklyn and I will just have to do the bulk of our dating in SoHo. That's a nice meeting-up midpoint for both of us. And for our six-month anniversary, I'll buy him a car or something."

Madison nodded. "Not such a bad idea. I guess it could work if you look at it that way. But at *some* point, you're going to have to go to Brooklyn to meet his family or his friends, and for that . . ." Her voice trailed away gravely.

"What?" Lex said. "Finish what you were going to say."

Park put a hand on Lex's shoulder. "For that, honey, we're going to have to tease your hair up high and paint your fingernails red, otherwise you'll stick out like costume jewelry at Cartier."

For a split second, Lex lost her balance and leaned into Park as if she were going to faint. "My God," she whispered, "I never thought of that. You mean you'd have to use actual hair spray?"

"Straight from the drugstore," Park said flatly. "I know it sounds awful, but it's the truth. There's no point in sugar coating it."

"But I wouldn't worry about that yet," Madison said, trying to sound encouraging. She slipped the ugly green baseball cap over her head. "If the two of you hit it off, maybe you'll be able to get away with just wearing spandex pants with white sneakers."

"Or one of those black sequined dresses from Loehmann's," Park added. "You know, the ones that you can spot at every Italian wedding. They're not *so* bad if you add the right accessories."

Madison crinkled her nose. "I hate those things. She'd be better off wearing something from Lord and Taylor."

"Stop!" Lex cried. "You're both really scaring me!"

Madison reached out and hugged her protectively. "Don't be scared. If it comes to that, Park and I will tease our hair up too just to give you some company."

The fear in Lex's eyes softened. "You promise?"

"Promise," Park said.

"Me too," Madison added. "But right now, let's go. I think we're ready."

Still cringing, Lex reached for her magic purse.

"That looks kind of silly," Madison observed. "A maid sporting a two-thousand-dollar bag?"

"I got that covered." Lex stepped into one of the bathroom stalls and pulled from it a housekeeping cart: the first row was stacked with dusters and paper towels and cans of Lysol; the wide bottom portion was covered on both sides by miniature drapes. She pulled back one of them and clapped twice.

Coco's head popped out. "It stinks in here!" she said. "I can barely breathe!"

"Deal with it." Lex handed her the magic purse, and a second later Coco disappeared behind the concealing drape again.

Madison nodded weakly. "I forgot about your little assistant hiding down there. Now, what's the plan?"

"Park and I will take one elevator, and you take another," Lex explained. "We'll all meet by the banks on the thirtieth floor, and from there we'll take another elevator to the penthouse."

"Where's Brooklyn in all this?" Madison asked.

"He's meeting us halfway up." Lex patted her bun so that the few unsecured strands wouldn't fall over her eyes. "And if we're lucky, we'll find something that proves

Ina could've killed Elijah, or that she and Poppy were in on it together. I just hope Ina doesn't board a plane home tomorrow."

"I told you Tallula said she only *thought* she overheard Ina saying that," Madison whispered. "But I have to admit, something's not right with that whole Ina story."

"Then we'll just have to meet her tomorrow," Park said, picking up a duster and batting it playfully at Madison.

Lex pushed the cart toward the bathroom door and gestured her head at Madison. "See you thirty stories up. Any problems, just text me."

Madison nodded, then ducked out of the bathroom and hung a sharp left.

Lex and Park, clad in their maids' uniforms, turned right, pushing the cart gingerly down the hall. An elderly couple passed them, and Lex made certain to smile curtly. "This uniform is totally itchy," she said quietly over her shoulder.

"Just forget it," Park answered. "We can't stop to scratch now."

The elevator bank was just ahead.

"Hurry," Park whispered. She reached out and grabbed a duster from the top of the cart; she fluffed it over the window displays and the walls, making a pretense to look busy.

Lex gave the cart a hard push; it hit a bump on the floor and shook.

"Ouch!" Coco yelped, her disembodied voice echoing through the hall.

Lex plastered a nervous smile on her face. The cart hit another bump.

"Hey!" Coco snapped from inside the cart. "Can you please take it easy?"

Park stepped in front of Lex, going around to the side of the cart. She lifted her left leg and jabbed it into the curtains, hitting Coco in either the shoulder or the arm. "Keep your mouth shut!" she warned her. "Don't say a word!"

Instead of responding, Coco made a low, growling sound.

Park fell back in step with Lex. "Hey, did you remember to bring the shoes?"

"In my purse," Lex replied. "But you still haven't told me what they're for."

"You'll find out once we get upstairs. Here, let me help you." Park laced her fingers around the bar of the cart and applied extra weight to it so that it coasted down the long hall faster.

She and Lex looked up just as a man in a business suit came out of one of the bathrooms.

He glanced at them as he walked away. Then he came to a dead stop and glanced at them again. "Excuse me," he said. "Can I ask—"

"We have cleaning emergency!" Park called out in her best Swedish accent. "Questions to front desk."

They rushed past him, the cart jiggling from side to side, the cans of Lysol rolling back and forth in the upper bin.

Her heart pounding, Lex stared down at the floor. That was when she noticed what the man had obviously seen—the fingers of Coco's left hand poking out from one end of the cart.

"Forget it," Park said. "Keep moving."

And together, they did just that, swinging the cart around the bend at the end of the hall and racing into the first open elevator. Park hit the button for the thirtieth floor, then they both leaned back against the walls and exhaled.

But the doors didn't close; instead, they yawned back open as the elevator welcomed another passenger.

It was Ina Debrovitch.

14

To the Penthouse

She was in her own little disguise—black turban, wire-rimmed glasses, an ankle-length blue skirt—but her face was instantly recognizable. Ina Debrovitch would always be recognizable, courtesy of the star-shaped birthmark on her chin. She had done a poor job of trying to conceal it with cheap, drugstore-bought foundation.

Park and Lex stared at each other. The words *holy shit* were etched in their eyes. Suddenly the elevator seemed far too small.

Park quickly set the example by casting her gaze downward and assuming a rigid posture.

Lex followed suit. But just as she turned her head away, she caught a glimpse of Coco's hand peeking out of the cart again. She couldn't tap the hand with her foot because Coco would make another sound—or, worse, she might even stick her head out and say something. The girl wouldn't know stealth if it bit her in the butt.

Ina was standing with her back to them, staring up at the numbers as the doors closed and the elevator ascended. She was visibly tense: shoulders squared, head bent. She reached out and pushed the number-twelve button.

Park counted off the seconds on her fingers. One, two, three . . . the damn elevator just wasn't moving fast enough. But even more worrisome was the fact that the steel doors acted like a mirror, reflecting everything back so that Ina could see her and Lex even without turning around. Through the corner of her right eye Park tried to make out what she could, any little detail. All she saw was the outline of Ina's turban, and how it covered her ears.

Only a few more seconds, she thought, the panic rising in her blood. *Please don't look at us. Don't recognize us.*

Lex was unconsciously shifting her weight from one foot to the other. She didn't so much as blink.

But she started when a sneeze echoed through the elevator. A loud, wet sneeze that had come from the housekeeping cart.

Aaaahhhhhhh-chooooooooooooooo!

Park make a quick pretense of lifting her hand to her nose and shaking her head. If Ina turned around or stared at the doors to see who was behind her, she would see that little move and, with any luck, think nothing of the sneeze.

Lex turned beet red.

The elevator came to a stop with a loud *ding* and the doors opened. Ina stepped out onto the twelfth floor and made a sharp right.

It wasn't until the doors closed and the elevator started moving again that Park let out a mammoth sigh. "Holy shit!" she said. "I can't believe it!"

"Do you think she recognized us?" Lex asked worriedly.

"I'm not sure. I couldn't tell. What the hell is she doing here? Madison said she and Tallula checked out last night."

"And why did she get off at the twelfth floor?"

Park fanned herself with her hand. "I have no idea. But that was too close. I totally thought she was going to turn around and say something. Did you see her getup?"

"Awful!" Lex said. "That turban looked like a tablecloth."

"Who are you talking about?" Coco's head popped out from the bottom of the cart again.

"Get back in there and *don't move* until I tell you to!" Lex snapped. "Got it?"

Coco grunted. "It's not easy being down here! And I'm totally freaked about being in these elevators again—they scare the hell out of me."

"Get in!" Lex hissed, shoving at Coco with her shin.

Coco retreated into her little cubbyhole again just as the elevator stopped, dinged, and opened on the thirtieth floor. Lex and Park shoved the cart out into the hallway.

Madison was waiting at the last elevator. Beside her was Brooklyn DiMarco, dressed in his simple uniform.

"What the hell took you two so long?" Madison gave a worried look.

"We just saw Ina Debrovitch in our elevator!" Lex said, a bit too loudly.

Brooklyn waved his hands. "Shhhhhhhh! You've gotta keep it down, okay?"

"Sorry." Lex gave him a quick wink.

Madison reached out and grabbed her arm; the movement was so sudden, the cap on her head tipped over onto her forehead. "Are you serious? What the hell is she doing here? Where is she now?"

"Twelfth floor," Park said. "She hung a right out of the elevator."

"The twelfth floor?" Brooklyn sounded skeptical. "You sure?"

Park nodded. "Positive. Why?"

"Most of the twelfth floor is undergoing renovation right now," he said. "I don't even think anyone's down there."

"Someone has to be there," Lex told him.

Brooklyn turned his attention to the elevator that had just opened to his left. He motioned them inside.

Madison and Lex took hold of the cart, pushing it into the elevator.

It took less than thirty seconds to reach the forty-second-floor tower suites.

Once they were standing in the long, lavish foyer that led to penthouse four, Madison tapped on the cart. "Come on, Coco. You can get out of there now."

With a long, weary sigh, Coco climbed out from her cubbyhole on all fours, moaning and stretching like a cat. Lex's magic purse dropped to the floor.

Lex bent down to pick it up. "Jeez, it really is tiny in there. Thank God you're so small."

"Small or not, I feel like a pretzel," Coco snapped. She shivered as she looked around at the all-too-familiar surroundings. "I hate being here. I never wanted to see this place again."

"Well, I need you to show me exactly what happened," Park said gently. "So try to keep your head clear." She turned around. "Hey, Brock. Bust open the door."

Brooklyn scanned the long hallway. It was clear. "Shit," he whispered. "My dad finds out about this, I'll get totally sacked."

"If anyone finds out, just blame us," Park said calmly.

Brooklyn smirked. "You girls must have really sweet lawyers."

"We do," Madison said. "But we have even better publicists."

In one smooth gesture, Brooklyn slipped the key into place and turned the lock. He threw open the door and waved them all inside.

It was dark in the suite. Slats of light filtered in through the windows, but shadows loomed in every corner. There was a scraping sound from one of the walls as Brooklyn searched for a switch; he found it a few seconds later and flipped it.

They were standing in the wide foyer. The sheer elegance of the furnishings was instantly evident, but as they tiptoed into the large living room, Madison, Park, and

Lex recognized the telltale signs of police presence: the yellow tape scattered across the floor, the remnants of fingerprint powder. The suite, still in the stages of evidence collection, had not been cleaned by the maintenance staff.

"Be careful where you walk," Park warned everyone. "And don't touch anything."

"Shit. The cops really tore this place apart," Brooklyn whispered.

Madison found herself marveling at the interior again. "I just love this old English décor. These antiques are incredible!"

Park stared in the direction of the two closed doors at the far end of the room—the doors that led out onto the balcony. She circled the two sofas and the Queen Anne chairs. The seating area was a good distance away, but if her suspicions were correct, none of that would really matter. "Okay," she said. "Let's do this." She looked at Lex. "Did you bring the goods?"

Lex nodded and opened the magic purse. She pulled out the pair of stunning Akiko Bergstrom heels Coco had worn the day before and held them out.

"You didn't even tell me why you needed those," Coco suddenly said. "You're not gonna make me put them on again, are you?"

"Yep, I am." Park took them from Lex and handed them over to Coco.

With a grimace, Coco kicked off her flats and slipped into the pair of silver heels. "They are beautiful," Coco mumbled thoughtfully. But her expression changed to a wince of pain the second the shoes were on her feet.

"I hate to have to point this out to everyone," Park said firmly. "But those shoes are *not* real."

"*What?*" Coco shrieked. Her face flushed.

"They're fakes," Park continued. She pointed down at Coco's feet. "Akiko Bergstrom heels are expensive and incredibly well made. But, I can tell you right now that the ones you're wearing are fakes, Coco. The straps that go across the top of the foot—"

"These have straps!" Coco cut in, clearly offended.

"Yes, they do," Park said. "But if you look at those straps, you'll notice that they go from inside to outside, meaning that the clasp is outside of each shoe."

Coco grunted. "So?"

"A signature of these shoes is the straps—on real pairs, they only go from outside to inside." Park made a genuinely apologetic face. "That's an absolute fact. I didn't notice it yesterday at the luncheon because I really didn't look at your feet. But when I saw that full-body shot of you in the paper this morning, it hit me. I'm sorry to have to tell you that those little numbers on your feet are *fashion contraband.*"

Madison gasped. "At five thousand dollars a pair?"

Lex, unable to accept the news, lost her balance and stumbled straight into Brooklyn's arms. She was horrified, but the move had been purely strategic: she wanted those arms around her.

"Hey!" Brooklyn said, holding her tightly. "Lex, are you okay?"

"I'll be . . . fine," she said faintly. "I . . . I just need a minute." With a sudden burst of energy, she spun around and, pressing herself hard against Brooklyn's chest, wrapped her arms around his neck.

"Jeez," he said. "That shoe thing is pretty bad, huh?"

"It's *awful*," Lex whispered, purposefully letting her weight hang.

Brooklyn scooped her up, holding her sideways like a newly married groom about to carry his bride into a honeymoon suite. "That feel better?" he asked, smirking.

Lex smiled. *"Much."* She kept her arms linked around his neck.

"I can't believe it!" Coco cried. "My mom said she got these directly from an exclusive boutique in Hong Kong!"

"They're obviously a copycat pair," Madison said gravely. "That's why they hurt so much. As soon as you get home, throw them out."

Park held up a hand. "Don't throw them out yet—I have a feeling they're going to come in handy as evidence. Lex, could you please lend me Brock for a minute? I need his . . . outstanding physique."

Brooklyn flushed as Lex hopped out of his arms.

"Fine," Lex whispered in Park's ear. "But be quick—he's on loan."

Park bit her tongue to keep from laughing. "Okay," she said. "Coco, tell us exactly where you and Elijah were standing when you started arguing."

"Right there." Coco pointed to the wide area between the sofas. "We started out by sharing . . . a little kiss on the couch. But then when he started getting rough, I pushed him away from me, and then we were standing up, facing each other."

"Let's pretend Brock is Elijah," Park said. She went around to his side and moved him into position. Then she took Coco by the arm and placed her into position as well, so that they were facing each other. "Does that feel familiar?"

Coco nodded. She heaved a sigh as tears sprang to her eyes.

"No crying!" Madison warned. "There's no time to fix your makeup."

Coco swallowed hard over the lump in her throat. "Okay."

"Now," Park continued, "let's just pretend that you wanted to shove Elijah clear across the room toward the balcony doors."

"But the balcony doors were closed," Coco said.

"It doesn't matter." Park waved her hands. "Let's just pretend. Go ahead and start pushing at Brock. Pretend he's Elijah. Go. Start pushing him."

"What are you doing?" Madison asked quietly.

"Never mind," Park said. "Coco, start pushing him. Shove him hard. As hard as you can. Brock is a little bigger than Elijah was, but not by much. It'll still prove my point. Coco—*shove him.*"

Taking a deep breath, Coco began batting her hands against Brooklyn's chest and stomach. She looked like a mouse going up against a lion. She pushed him twice, then stopped.

"Again," Park instructed her. "Do it hard. Just like you would have when Elijah was getting rough with you. Defend yourself, Coco. You're fighting for your own safety, right?"

Coco repeated the shoving motion.

"Harder!" Lex snapped. "That sleazy dweeb tried to hurt you."

"But this isn't what happened!" Coco said desperately. "I didn't shove Elijah like this."

"That's what I'm trying to prove," Park answered. "Just keep pushing."

Grunting, her forehead breaking out in a line of sweat, Coco began ramming her weight against Brooklyn with all her might, fingers splayed.

Brooklyn didn't seem to be feeling anything. His body inched back slowly, but Coco's petite frame was nothing against his own.

With a final, raging grunt, Coco shoved into him; as she did so, she stumbled back and to the right. The heel of her right shoe snapped off, and she went sailing toward the floor.

Lex's arms shot out and caught her.

"Oh!" Coco said, slamming into Lex. "Oh my God!"

Park bent down and picked up the broken heel. She held it up. "Now, an authentic Akiko Bergstrom heel would never snap under your weight," she explained. "Those shoes are designed with a steel support that is actually anchored within the body of the shoe. These are fakes, but that's not what's important. If you had really shoved Elijah with all your weight—hard enough to send him over the balcony—this heel would've broken yesterday, not right now."

"That's totally right!" Coco said, her eyes wide and suddenly hopeful. "Park, you proved it!" She kicked off both shoes and jumped back into her flats.

"Wait a minute." Madison stepped into the circle. She stared down, then back up. She shook her head pensively. "Okay, you proved a point here, Park. But it's still pretty circumstantial. You think the cops are going to buy that?"

"They'll have to," Park said. "When you come right down to it, it's science. Coco's way too small to have shoved Elijah off the balcony, but no one's looking at that point because her phone was found here at the scene, and because she had Elijah's necklace in her purse."

Madison squatted and picked up both shoes. She turned to Coco. "You told us that after the elevator spooked you, you got out on the twenty-ninth floor and started walking down the stairs."

"I did." Coco nodded. "That's what happened."

"But you tried to get out of the stairwell on floors thirteen and twelve—"

"—and the doors were locked," Coco said.

Madison looked at Brooklyn. "Why would those doors be locked? Is that normal?"

"No," he replied. "Yesterday morning, the stairs between floors thirteen and twelve were painted. That's why the doors were locked."

"Then that means . . ." Holding her breath, Madison turned both the shoes over slowly. And there, right against the black sole of the left shoe, was a gray smear.

Tiny flecks of paint.

"Ha!" Lex said. She went to Madison's side. "Look at that! It's staring us right in the face!"

"It really is." Madison's voice was low, the shock on her face obvious but laced with excitement.

"You're right," Brooklyn said. "The paint in the stairwell is gray. I bet that's it, on the shoe."

Park smiled broadly. "I think the DA will agree that

this proves you were in the stairwell when you said you were—*and* that if you had used all the weight and force needed to shove Elijah off that balcony, your shoe would've broken, and if it had broken, the cops would have seen that yesterday."

A tear streaked down Coco's face. She looked dazed and overwhelmed and starry-eyed, as if she had just witnessed a premonition of the Marc Jacobs spring collection.

Madison handed the shoes over to Lex, who wrapped them carefully in a scarf and dropped them back into the magic purse.

"Pretty amazing," Park said. "But at the same time, pretty scary."

"Why scary?" Lex asked.

"Because it's obvious that the real killer is still out there," Madison answered. "The case is anything but solved."

Lex swung the purse over her shoulder. "The only other person who could've done it is Ina. Poppy's as small as Coco and a million years older—how could she have pushed him? Ina was here at the right time. Taking a shower with or without her hearing aid, but whatever. Maybe *she* broke her own hearing aid in order to make it look like she couldn't have heard anything."

"Ina's already showing signs of her own guilt," Madison said. "She's probably planning to leave the country any day now. *And* we just saw her very obviously in a disguise right here in the hotel where the crime took place. *And* isn't it a fact that most criminals come back to the scene of the crime?"

"It is," Park said. "Most killers feel a need to revisit a crime scene because it gives them a sense of power, and because most people are killed by friends, relatives, or familiar faces, revisiting the crime scene reinforces a feeling of intimacy, of closeness. It's totally bizarre."

Lex shivered. "Oh, God. That's so creepy."

Park started pacing the floor as she reviewed the facts in her head. It was obvious from her expression that something valuable had clicked into place. "You know, the fact that Ina came to the hotel tonight might seem circumstantial, but it's actually the strongest piece of evidence against her. She didn't only revisit the place where Elijah died—she went out of the way and disguised herself to do it. That's a clear indication of a psychopathic personality. It fits right in there with victimology and with the psychology of criminal behavior. It's just the kind of thing that leads to recidivism." She paused and looked up.

Everyone was staring at her silently.

"Huh?" Lex said.

Park shook her head. "The point I'm trying to make is that Ina exposed a lot about herself by coming here tonight. The only problem is that we don't know her motive. And we don't know her well enough to even begin guessing it." She turned and started walking across the suite, through the living and dining areas and past the kitchen.

"Hey," Lex called out. "Wait up!"

They trailed Park until she reached the third bedroom. "This must've been Ina's," she said. The door was open. The room was large and ornately furnished; the bed was made up and everything looked like it was in place.

"And there's the door to the bathroom," Lex pointed out. She, Madison, and Park stepped over the threshold and onto the immaculate tile floor.

"So this is where Ina claims she was when it all happened," Madison said. She nodded. "It's pretty far away from the balcony. No wonder the police believed her. She wouldn't have ever been able to hear anything in the shower."

"*Especially* without her hearing aid," Lex said.

"But that's the old story," Park reminded them. "If Tallula left the suite, then only Ina and Elijah were here, and if she killed him, she couldn't have been in *here*."

"And how the hell do we prove that?" Lex asked. She clenched her hands in frustration. Not seeing anything, she walked back out to the bedroom area and quickly began opening and closing the bureau and nightstand drawers. *Open, shut. Open, slam.*

"What are you doing?" Madison asked, walking around the queen-sized bed.

"Looking for something. Looking for *anything*," Lex replied.

Madison shot a glance at Coco and Brooklyn, who were standing on the threshold like helpless statues. "This will only take a sec," she said, trying to sound offhanded. She didn't know what she was supposed to be looking for, but she started searching the perimeter of the room, glancing behind the bed, around the bed, under the bed. It was when she was on her knees with the comforter draped over her shoulders that she spotted something half hidden in the shadows just beside the headboard: a small, circular thing that, when she grabbed it, reminded her of a cosmetics jar. She held it in the palm of her right hand as she stood up, bringing it out fully into the light.

It was, in fact, something cosmetic. Made of glass. Smooth. There was a blue cap on it, but no label.

"What's that?" Lex asked from across the room.

"I'm not sure." Madison unscrewed the cap and opened the little jar. The smell that wafted out was at first familiar—moisturizer—but something else had been mixed into it, something heavy and cloying. The odor made Madison wrinkle her nose. "Eewww," she said, holding the jar out. "I don't know what this is, but I guess Ina forgot to pack it when she and Tallula left last night."

Lex came over and placed the little jar in her own hand. She studied it carefully. "This isn't a store-bought product," she said with certainty. "No sign of a label, and I think they stopped making packaging like this back in the nineties." She took one whiff of it, then drew her head away, then repeated the movement.

"What's that smell?" Madison asked.

Lex held the glass jar up and out. "This is definitely moisturizer, but not the usual kind. This is cocoa butter mixed with extra-virgin olive oil and vitamin-E cream."

Madison let that sink in. And when her brain made the link, she gasped. "Oh, shit! An oil-based moisturizer! And the handprint on Elijah's shirt—or what we think was a handprint!"

Park came strolling out of the bathroom.

"This could easily explain the stain on Elijah's shirt," Lex said coolly. "But it also tells me something else."

"What's that?" Coco took a step toward them.

"Cocoa butter and extra-virgin olive oil is a home-made preventative measure for stretch marks," Lex explained. "And ninety-nine percent of the time, it's used by *pregnant women.*"

A thick silence settled over the room as they all stared at one another.

Then Park sighed and said, "Well, that explains a lot."

"It does?" Madison asked.

Park nodded. "Of course. It tells us why Ina's in such a rush to get away from everything. She doesn't want anyone knowing that she's pregnant with Elijah's baby."

15

Psyching the Psychic

"You really think that's it?" Madison asked as their limo pulled up in front of the Dakota on Central Park West. "I mean, how can you be so sure? What's if she's pregnant by someone else? What if she's not pregnant at all?"

"Remember what Tallula said?" Park answered. "She said that yesterday, after the luncheon, she and Ina hurried back to the penthouse because she wasn't feeling well. She also said that Ina had vomited yesterday morning."

"Yeah, I know," Madison agreed. "But I thought it was because she had gas. How does any of that prove she's pregnant—and, if she is, how does it prove that the baby is Elijah's?"

Lex tightened her grasp on the magic purse. "If it's *not* Elijah's baby, then why would she be in such a hurry to run away? It would make more sense for her to stay here with Tallula in that condition. Ina doesn't have much money. She wants to run away because she can't let Tallula know the truth."

"At least Ina has a brain," Park said flatly. "Can you imagine how much fuel this would add to the fire? Tallula already knows Elijah was a skank, but now she'll have to face the fact that Ina betrayed her too."

Madison closed her eyes. "I just can't imagine it. How much horrible luck can one girl have? Tallula will never get through this."

"The thing is," Lex said, perched on the edge of her seat, "we're pretty much sure Ina's pregnant with Elijah's baby, but that doesn't spell out a motive."

"No, it doesn't," Park agreed. "But there has to be something else connected to the little fact of Ina being pregnant. It could be as simple as a lovers' quarrel. Maybe Ina wanted Elijah to break up with Tallula. Maybe Ina tried to blackmail him. Who knows? But I'll bet anything that Ina shoved him off that balcony. She was the only other person in there."

"That we know of," Lex added.

"So we still think Poppy has something to do with this?" Madison asked quietly.

"I think she totally knows more than she's saying," Lex answered. "That's why we have to use this séance to flush out more info. We have to follow the plan."

Park nodded firmly.

Madison bit down on her lip. The "plan" Lex was referring to was something they had hatched a few minutes ago—a dangerous, slightly insane blueprint to trap Poppy van Lulu in her own lies. The very thought of going through with it made Madison edgy. She looked at her watch. "Come on, it's almost ten. Oh, man. My stomach feels like it's in knots. I'm totally nervous about doing this."

"Don't be nervous," Lex said nonchalantly. "Think of it as entertainment."

"Do we really have to do this?" Madison asked in a strained whisper.

"Yes, we do." Park popped the door open. "It's the only way to find out what Poppy really knows. She won't give us a straight answer without putting on some sort of show. That's just how she is."

"But what if she has some sort of other plan for us tonight?" Madison asked worriedly. "Like what if she's aiming to chuck us off a balcony too?"

"There's safety in numbers," Park said. "And besides, I do most of my own stunts now, so I'd be able to hang on or walk along the ledge."

Lex nodded. "Donnie, just stay put. We'll only be a little while."

"Okay," Donnie said. "Call if you need me."

They exited the limo and walked up to the building's elaborate entrance. The doorman confirmed their appointment with Poppy and pointed them to the elevator bank.

That was where Jeremy was waiting. His eyes lit up

when he saw Park coming toward him. "Hey!" he said. "I was just about to call you, babe. It's, like, ten o'clock."

"I know." Park gave him a quick peck on the lips. "We got a little . . . caught up."

Jeremy kissed Madison and Lex on the cheek. He was dressed simply in jeans and a white Dior shirt. "So, um . . . were you serious about what you said when you called me fifteen minutes ago?"

"You bet," Park confirmed, leading the way to the elevator. "Just follow our lead, okay?"

The elevator opened. They stepped inside and rode up in silence. From the beginning of the long, narrow corridor, they could see that Poppy van Lulu's apartment door was already ajar.

Lex checked her magic purse to make sure everything was in readiness. Then she knocked and poked her head inside. "Hello?" she called out, giving the door a shove. It slid open with a creak.

At first glance, the apartment was dark. But as Lex stepped inside, she saw candlelight flickering against the walls and the glass-encased paintings. She smelled the pungent aroma of incense. "Poppy? Hello? Are you here?"

"Maybe she's not coming," Madison whispered nervously. She stared at the Stefan Luchian painting and felt a pang in her stomach.

"It's *her* apartment, you titmouse," Lex answered. "She's probably—"

"I'm right here."

They all jumped. Lex's magic purse hit her chin. Madison nearly lost her balance and stumbled. Park bumped into Jeremy so hard, he fell back against the door, closing it.

Poppy van Lulu came striding out of the shadows. She was wearing a black dress that swept straight down to the floor, several silver bracelets, and a glittering pendant. On her head was a diamond encrusted tiara that caught the glint of the flickering flames. She looked at Madison, at Park, at Lex. Then her gaze locked on Jeremy. "Hello there, young man," she said quietly.

Jeremy smiled his thousand-watt smile. "Hi, Poopy. Nice to meet you."

"It's *Poppy*," she snapped. She raised her head to look him squarely in the eyes. "Haven't you heard of me?"

"Uh, yes. Of course I have." He cleared his throat nervously and shot a glance at Park. "I'm totally psyched to be here."

Poppy reached out and took his hand in hers. She closed her eyes. "A good heart, but a restless mind, you have. Good luck follows you—sometimes too much. You have an unexpected bend in the road ahead."

Jeremy didn't quite know what to say, so he just nodded.

"Mrs. van Lulu, we'd like to begin," Park said gently. "I have lots of questions for Elijah."

Poppy nodded. "I can already sense him in the atmosphere. I know he's waiting to speak."

Park looked at the pendant around Poppy's neck. "That's a ruby. From the cut, I'd bet anything it's from South Africa. There's a legend attached to rubies—they can act as a person's third eye."

"You *are* perceptive, dear," Poppy replied with a

smile. "I guess all those rumors about your jewelry are true." She turned around and led them through the apartment, past the kitchen and dining room, past three bedrooms en suite and past the den. Just when it looked like the corridor would end, it wound sharply to the right. The door just ahead seemed . . . odd.

"We're having a séance in the closet?" Lex asked, irritated.

"No, dear." Poppy pushed open the door. "Just step inside. It's the spirit room."

The room was large and rectangular and illuminated softly by candlelight. A round wood table sat in the middle of the floor, and on it was an empty champagne flute, a stack of paper, and a thick crayon. Long velvet drapes covered the two windows.

Madison gulped over the lump that had sprouted in her throat. This was totally eerie. Like, haunted house eerie. Like, graveyard eerie. In an attempt to calm herself, she studied the paintings on the walls and tried to find in at least one of them something that would reassure her she wasn't in some horror theme park. But her nerves were wound too tightly. She tore her eyes away from the walls and sat down in one of the chairs.

Lex and Jeremy sat on either side of her.

Park chose the seat directly beside Poppy.

They stared at one another as candle flames danced around them.

"I'm going to begin the séance by asking you to join me in a few seconds of meditation," Poppy said quietly. "Close your eyes and relax. Imagine a place filled with extraordinary white light and lots of positive energy."

"Saks at Christmastime!" Lex called out.

Madison nudged her shoulder.

Poppy shot her a disapproving stare. "Something a bit more spiritual, dear. A bit more like heaven. Does everybody understand?"

"Of course," Madison replied. "Not Saks at Christmastime—the Spa at Mandarin Oriental at Christmastime."

Poppy nodded. "Precisely."

Lex closed her eyes after everyone else did. A minute later she let out a long, luscious sigh. "That feels so good. I'm totally relaxed."

"The mud bath and the full-body massage," Park whispered, lost in her own spa-induced meditation.

"The cucumber-and-chamomile facial," Madison muttered.

"Yes," Poppy said in a barely audible voice. "And the aloe pedicure. Don't forget the aloe pedicure."

"And the shoulder and back waxing." Jeremy tossed that out as if everyone visited the Mandarin and underwent extensive hair-removal procedures. When several seconds passed in complete silence, he opened his eyes and saw that Madison, Park, Lex, and Poppy were all staring at him, wide-eyed and slightly disturbed. "What?" he snapped. "It was for a role, okay?"

"Relax and breathe," Poppy said. "Breathe deeply. Deeply . . ."

Park let out a sudden gasp.

Madison and Lex looked at each other.

Showtime.

"Park, are you okay, dear?" Poppy asked.

Park pushed back her chair and stood up. "I'm sorry, but I'm not okay," she said, feigning disappointment. "This is all wrong. The whole setup is out of sync, and I can feel the energy in the room shifting."

"So can I," Lex agreed. As if on cue, she opened her magic purse and pulled out her all-purpose silk scarf. She tied it around her head turban-style. "Our psychic energy is telling us that something isn't right."

Madison pressed her fingers to her temples. "Awful!" she screamed. "These spirits are killing me!"

Jeremy's eyes widened.

"They . . . they are?" Poppy said quietly, worry etched on her face.

"There's only one way to do this, Mrs. van Lulu," Park said. "Our way."

"*Your* way? I'm the psychic, dear!" Poppy snapped.

"But don't forget that my sisters and I have psychic ability too," Park said firmly. "We know what we're doing." She stepped into the middle of the room and took several deep breaths. She followed the same procedure she used to get into character on the set of *Short Fuse,* mentally preparing herself to cross that sketchy line between fact and fiction. After several seconds, she stretched her arms out and started to grasp at the empty air. "This is a strong vortex, and it isn't going to work properly unless we manipulate it."

"Manipulate it?" Poppy repeated.

"Yes," Madison said. "My sisters and I studied with Native American shamans, and we know that the only way to rouse the spirits properly and effectively is through dance."

Jeremy mouthed, *Dance?*

"Dance?" Poppy asked, sounding more and more confused.

Madison stood up. She fished her iPhone out of her purse, pressed two buttons, and set it down on the table.

Tango music started playing; the sexy beats echoed through the room.

Madison walked over to Park, doing her best to sashay seductively. She knew from the disagreeable look on Jeremy's face that it wasn't working, so at the last possible second, she stumbled back into her old gait. She put her left hand on Park's shoulder and gave her head a toss.

"Now the spirits will churn," Park said. She looked at Poppy. She looked up at the shadow-webbed ceiling. Then, in sync with the music, she stomped her foot and launched into a dance.

The tango was Park's favorite. She had studied it for the past two years—gym class at St. Cecilia's Prep required dance shoes, not sneakers—and she knew how to swirl and dip and shake her body across any floor.

Madison was a slightly different case. She also loved the tango, but when it came to dancing, she got a little . . . well . . . clumsy. She certainly didn't mean to trip or step on anyone's feet; it just *happened*. At the moment, however, she was gliding along perfectly, following Park's lead as they turned Poppy van Lulu's spirit room into an Argentine fiesta.

"Oh, my!" Poppy said, staring at them wide-eyed and stunned.

Jeremy bit his lip to keep from laughing.

Lex watched the dance carefully. She counted the spins—there had been two so far—and slowly slipped her hand under the table, splaying her palm against the thick smooth wood.

"Bravo!" Poppy cheered as Madison and Park danced straight past her.

They spun a third time. Lex caught her cue and gave the table a hard shake, assuming a happily shocked expression as she did so.

The champagne flute spun.

"Oh, look!" Lex cried. "The spirits really are here!"

Poppy van Lulu stared at the trembling table in front of her and nearly jumped out of her chair. She pulled her hands up and back. She gulped in what was very obviously fear.

Not the look of a true psychic, Lex thought.

"Olé!" Madison shouted suddenly as she lost her balance on a spin and nearly crashed into a bookshelf.

Lex quickly reached into her magic purse and retrieved a plastic red rose. She put the stem between her teeth. She stood up, gesturing at Jeremy to join her. Then, flinging one end of her scarf-turban, she started prancing around the room in circles. She stopped every five beats to give her hips a shake.

Well aware of what he was supposed to do, Jeremy grabbed Poppy's hand and yanked her out of the chair. She slammed against him with a yip. But the shocked look vanished from her face the moment he stared down at her and squinted seductively. "We must contribute our energy to the dance," he whispered.

Poppy nodded, half dreamily and half uncomprehendingly. She didn't protest as Jeremy began gliding and shaking her across the floor. The gust created by their bodies snuffed out several candles.

"Olé!" Madison screamed again, stumbling back as she lost her footing.

Park caught her. She held her up and continued on with the dance.

Lex, still running around them in circles, thrust her hips out and made a series of strange, otherworldly noises. "The spirits are here!" she cried out, her voice guttural. When no one was looking, she grabbed a book off one of the shelves and quickly hurled it across the room.

Poppy screamed. "Everybody stop! Oh! Stop!" Her voice was filled with raw fear—but why would a psychic allegedly accustomed to communicating with the dead be scared of a little unexplained phenomena?

Holding tight to that question, Lex surreptitiously grabbed another book from the shelf and sent it sailing through the air.

Poppy wailed louder.

Jeremy clasped her hands tightly, pulled her against his chest, and leaned her back in an impromptu dip.

The tiara pinned to Poppy's hair flipped to one side.

It was the moment Park needed. She forced Madison into a series of violent spins, twirling her like a top as she inched her steadily across the floor.

Lex ran to the door and pulled it open.

Madison whirled out of the room at breakneck speed, her hair flapping in the air, her arms held high and rigid. She felt as though she were being sucked into a tornado. She didn't stop until she slammed into a wall with a thud. Breath shot from her lungs. She saw a smattering of stars in her field of vision. She pulled herself together just as Lex shut the door to the spirit room again. It had been a successful escape. Madison knew Poppy hadn't seen her make an exit. She also knew that she didn't have much time to snoop around, so she gave her head a hard shake, forced the dizziness from her brain, and started down the corridor.

She muffled a laugh as the tango music stopped suddenly and was replaced by the opening bars of the Italian tarantella dance. "Everybody circle to the left!" Park yelled from behind the door.

Madison dashed to the very end of the corridor and flicked on a light. She was standing in the master bedroom. It was clearly Poppy's personal space, because the bedsheets were slightly wrinkled and there was a TV remote control on the nightstand. The air smelled of perfume and moisturizer. For a few seconds, Madison felt overwhelmed: there was a huge bureau, a small antique desk, a vanity, and a large walk-in closet. She didn't have enough time to scour through everything. She knew that in just a few minutes, Poppy would either demand an end to the theatrics or come running out of her spirit room in fear.

She took a deep breath and scurried across the room to the bureau. She yanked open the first drawer. She spotted lace underwear, stockings, lavender eye pillows, and several silk camisoles.

Strike one.

The second drawer held equally useless stuff: a jogging suit, a ski cap, gloves. It was no good. Madison felt a line of sweat breaking out on her forehead. She ran to the antique desk and pulled open the drawer. Her eyes were moving so rapidly, she almost missed an interesting—and vital—clue: a worn paperback titled *How to Be Psychic: Awaken Your Secret Spirits!* Several pages were creased, several passages underlined. Madison shook her head, both irritated and incensed. A guidebook? It was further evidence that Poppy van Lulu didn't kick back and drink vintage wine with the dead as so many people thought.

Madison dropped the book into the drawer and slammed it closed. She ran across the room to the closet and stepped through the French doors. The overhead track lights were already on. Rows and rows of clothing, racks and racks of shoes. One corner was reserved for hats alone, a four-foot tower of oval boxes. Her eyes flew from left to right, up and down. She swept her gaze along the floor. In her mind's eye she kept the image of what Poppy had been wearing at the luncheon—where the hell was that brown Fendi purse?

She froze when a sound echoed down the corridor. A thud. Had Poppy run out of the spirit room? Madison waited for several seconds, her back pressed to the wall. Then she heard the familiar notes of the tarantella and several hands clapping in rhythm. Lex had probably chucked another book against the wall.

Madison squatted down and began crawling across the carpeted floor of the closet. She shoved away several boxes. She threw fallen blouses over her head. Nothing. She was about to stand up again when she spotted the familiar dark brown lining of the purse peeking out of a small marble bin. Her heart pounding, she reached for it and quickly popped the latch. It wasn't big or roomy, but it was messy: crinkled tissues, a tube of lipstick, a comb, several scraps of paper. Frustrated, Madison dumped the contents of the purse onto the floor and scoured through them.

On the third try, she unfolded a small receipt from the Waldorf-Astoria gift shop. It was marked with the date and time—08/16/08, 2:18 p.m.—and listed only two items: a bottle of water and a packet of Gas-X tablets.

Gotcha!

Madison's first thought was that the watercress salad had done a number on everyone's stomach. Her second was one of shock and excitement—this was proof that Poppy hadn't left the hotel when she said she had. Instead, she'd hung around. *And where did you go?* Madison wondered. *Did you hightail it up to the penthouse right after Coco left? Did you argue with Elijah? Did you and Ina plan everything beforehand?*

Her hands trembling, she slipped the receipt into the pocket of her jeans and then swiftly scooped up the items on the floor. She dumped them back into the purse and chucked it into the bin. As she stood up, turning around, her knee slammed against something she hadn't even noticed a few minutes ago: a small two-drawer file cabinet. The pain that shot through her right leg was intense, but Madison ignored it as she realized the first drawer had opened from the impact of her knee hitting the handle. She slid it toward her. Inside were several manila files, each one labeled in the right-hand corner with a name. *Ben Affleck, Kelly Clarkson, Tom Cruise, Jennifer Garner, Brad Pitt, Anna Wintour.* Name after name after name. Who would have guessed that Poppy kept files on her clients?

Madison yanked one out and flipped through it. She didn't find a handwritten account of a psychic reading.

Instead, she found magazine articles and newspaper clips and little torn gossip columns—anything that gave her an inkling into the life of the person she was going to meet with. It was research. Poppy obviously used her carefully gathered information and pretended, later on while sitting in the spirit room, that she was receiving little nuggets of truth from the spirit world.

"Unbelievable," Madison whispered. She pulled the drawer out farther, wondering if her instincts would prove correct.

They did.

She found the file labeled *Traymore, Elijah* and yanked it out. Inside were articles from *Vanity Fair, Art in America, GQ, Men's Vogue.* Pictures of Elijah and Tallula. Snapshots of his sculptures and of Tallula's abstract paintings. Then there was a series of articles that had clearly been printed from the Internet: Elijah visiting an art colony in California; a Q and A that featured Elijah discussing his paranormal beliefs; a gossip column from the *Post* in which Elijah had been quoted bashing the Republican party.

But it was the last article that caught Madison's attention.

Caught it, and held it until a chill shot through her bones.

She stared down at the grainy sheet of paper, her eyes locked on the small black-and-white image in the very middle of the page. She recognized Elijah on the left. And she recognized the good-looking young man standing beside him smiling broadly, holding both his thumbs up in a gesture of support. The caption read: *Elijah Traymore (left) with student Brooklyn DiMarco at Meet-the-Artist Day at LaGuardia High School.*

Madison heard herself gasp. For a long moment, she simply sat there, clutching the sheet of paper and listening to the heavy pounding of her heart. The noise coming from the spirit room—another round of clapping, Poppy screaming—did nothing to startle her.

Brooklyn DiMarco.

The list of suspects had just gotten longer.

16

An Unusual Suspect

For the tenth time in an hour, Madison waved the sheet of paper in the air and pointed to the picture of Elijah Traymore and Brooklyn DiMarco. "It's proof!" she said. "Right in front of us! You can't deny it!"

"You really can't," Park added gently.

"Maybe I just don't want to talk about it, okay?" Lex snapped. "Maybe I just want you both to leave me alone!"

They were standing in the living room of their penthouse. Lex, visibly upset but equally defiant, stood in the doorway with her arms crossed over her chest. She didn't want to face her sisters and their knowing stares. She didn't want to consider the possibility staring her squarely in the face. It was too painful to accept. She hadn't known Brooklyn DiMarco for more than a day, but the magic between them—the huge spark—was undeniable. Lex had seen it in his eyes this evening. She had even felt those butterfly tremors in her stomach when he'd kissed her. Now, however, she felt a heavy sadness in her heart, ebbed by a growing tide of anger.

"Honey, it isn't something we can just ignore," Park told her. "You know that. A suspect is a suspect."

"But why does Brooklyn have to be a suspect?" Lex shot back. "All that picture proves is that he and Elijah met back in March."

"But Brooklyn told us he had only met Elijah the other day," Madison pointed out, trying to keep her tone even. "Why lie about something like that?"

Lex huffed. She fanned herself with her hands as she stomped over to the terrace doors and threw them open. She was hot and annoyed and flustered. She had changed into shorts and a tank top, having torn off her sweat-soaked clothes the moment she stepped into the apartment. She and Park had gotten quite a workout in Poppy's spirit room: two sets of tangos, a round of the tarantella, and then a quick detour into a few hip-hop moves. When it came time to bounce and kick to one of Kanye's beats, Poppy had all but fainted. She'd been spooked by the flying books, by Lex's strange noises, by the look of mock possession Jeremy had assumed as Park batted him with the plastic rose. It had been a successful night, but it had also been a bad one.

A really, really bad one, Lex thought as she stared out at the shimmering skyline. She felt Park's hand on her left shoulder, Madison's hand on her right forearm. It was a tough couple of minutes, but Lex knew she couldn't stay silent for much longer. "I really like him," she finally said. "He's so different from anyone I've ever met."

"No one's saying Brooklyn is a killer," Park stated firmly. "But there *is* reason to talk about him—and, eventually, to talk *to* him."

Lex turned around. "Does he really have to jump onto the suspect list? I mean, can't we just concentrate on all the stuff we've already uncovered about Ina and Poppy?"

Park shook her head. "At this point in the investigation, Brooklyn has to be considered a suspect, honey. We'd be bad detectives if we just let this little fact slip by unexamined."

"I know it hurts," Madison said. "But that's a homicide investigation for you—one shock after another. And I *know* what it feels like to have the guy you like on the suspect list. Has anyone forgotten that my boyfriend was once wanted by the cops?" Images of that terrible time flashed through her mind—Theo's picture on every TV channel, everyone in the city calling him a killer. It had been hell. Madison had never experienced such gut-wrenching pain, and she hated seeing those same little flashes of hurt in Lex's eyes. Lex was, after all, the baby of the family, and as the firstborn, Madison couldn't help feeling overprotective of her.

"Lex, you're sure Brooklyn never mentioned meeting Elijah before he and Tallula and Ina checked into the hotel?" Park asked cautiously.

"No," Lex replied. "He told all of us that he met Elijah the other day."

."But we know that Brooklyn met Elijah a few months ago," Madison said. "And there's no way Brooklyn could have just forgotten about that. I mean, it's not like they met five years ago at some Starbucks on Columbus Avenue. They met right there at his high school. Even posed for a picture together."

"Right," Park agreed. "It isn't the kind of thing you forget. It's the kind of thing you don't want people to remember."

Lex scowled. "What's *that* supposed to mean?"

"When a person is murdered, it's very common for people who might have even a little bit of information to totally wimp out," Park explained. "No one wants to be questioned by the cops—or us, for that matter. That goes double for Brooklyn: he works at the hotel, and so does his father. The last thing he wants is for anyone to draw a link between him and Elijah Traymore."

"But even though we've drawn a link between them," Lex said, "what does it prove? It totally doesn't prove that Brooklyn's a killer. I mean, what's his motive? Hello?"

"Motive is usually the last thing that comes to light," Madison answered. "You know that."

Park started pacing the floor. "Come on, it's time to try and piece this together chronologically."

Madison and Lex walked over to the couch and sat down.

"We're going to start with Poppy," Park said, holding up a finger. "She comes up to us yesterday at the luncheon and tells us that something terrible is about to happen. She flat-out says that someone's about to be covered by the shawl of death, right? Then she leaves. But she doesn't leave the hotel as she claimed to—we know that now."

"Right." Madison nodded. "Then we spot Coco and Elijah talking, and we meet Elijah. Total sleaze."

"And *not* a well-dressed one," Lex tossed in.

Park shrugged. "I actually liked his boots."

"Oh, please." Madison made a sour face. "Biker boots and jeans at a society luncheon? That's called having no taste."

"Taste or not, Elijah left the room a few minutes later and went back up to the penthouse," Park continued. "Coco leaves—tells us she's going to the bathroom. In fact, she heads up to the suite at what's probably the exact time Tallula and Ina are leaving the suite."

"So Coco gets up there and Tallula and Ina get down to the luncheon," Lex said. "I leave to go look for Coco and bump into Brooklyn in the lobby. We talk for a few minutes, and then we go our separate ways."

"So at this point in the equation, we know three things." Park held up a finger every time she made a new point. "One, Coco is upstairs with Elijah. Two, Poppy's still in the gift shop buying medication for whatever gas problems she's experiencing. And three, Brooklyn Di-Marco has just gone somewhere. Maybe he has an alibi, maybe he doesn't."

"Fast-forward," Madison said. "The luncheon's over. We leave to start searching for Coco; Tallula and Ina go back upstairs. Tallula spots Poppy leaving the gift shop. Coco is already in the stairwell trying to make her way downstairs."

"We know what happens next," Lex said impatiently.

"Ina goes to take a shower and Tallula leaves and gets stuck in the elevator. So that leaves Ina in the suite with Elijah, but it also leaves Poppy unaccounted for . . . and at this point, it leaves Brooklyn unaccounted for too."

"And the only reason we're even considering that fact is because Brooklyn flat-out lied to us," Park added. "And, now that I'm thinking about it, Brooklyn would've totally been able to shove Elijah overboard."

Lex sighed, annoyed.

"Potential motives," Madison said. She reached for her purse and pulled out a nail file. She started with her left hand, filing along the edges. "Elijah had info Poppy wanted kept private. Ina's probably pregnant with Elijah's child and maybe he didn't like it. As in, maybe he didn't want her having the baby and started threatening her."

"Or maybe something else," Park said.

Lex looked at her hopefully. "Like what?"

"Like something that connects her to the art code I found in Elijah's wallet, and to that painting he was interested in," Park answered.

"So then, where the hell does Brooklyn come into all this?" Lex asked sharply.

"An accessory to the crime," Madison said. She made an ugly gesture with the nail file, pretending to draw it across her neck. "He knows something about the murder."

Lex stood up and walked back to the open doors. A soft breeze drifted into the living room. "Do you both have any idea how crazy this all sounds?" she snapped. "We have three suspects and only a couple of motives. And now we're thinking about linking all three of them together on this. I mean, why the hell would it take three people to kill Elijah? Or, better yet, why would any of them *want* to kill him?"

"Because he had some sort of info on each one of them," Park replied right away. "Maybe he was blackmailing them, or threatening to blackmail them. Do you know how many people get whacked every year because of what they know?"

"Whacked?" Madison's eyes widened. "You're starting to sound more and more like you belong on *The Sopranos.*"

"You know what I mean," Park said. "And when you look at Ina, Poppy, and Brooklyn, you have a very obvious link—they were all in the hotel when the crime occurred, and they're all somehow connected to Elijah from the past."

"Crazy," Lex muttered. "I know Brooklyn, and he isn't a killer!"

"You've only known Bensonhurst for like two days," Madison said, chuckling at her own joke.

"Well, that's enough time for me to know he has nothing to do with this." Lex plopped back onto the couch and folded her arms across her chest. "And excuse me for asking, but if Brooklyn *is* guilty of something, why would he try to be wooing me when he knows we're involved in this investigation?"

"He's acting like a pretty typical suspect," Madison explained, doing her best to sound nonchalant. "He's trying to get close to the investigation so that he can sabotage it. And maybe that's what Poppy wanted to do tonight with her little séance." A pause. "Park, I think it's time we call the police and fill them in on what we've uncovered."

"No way!" Park shot back. "If we don't have enough info, they'll make sure we don't get the chance to get any more—it will guarantee Coco goes to trial."

"So then, what are we doing?"

"Tomorrow morning, we'll pay Brooklyn a visit," Park said. "Then we'll have to find Ina, and maybe we'll get on Poppy's case again. One of them is going to break down under the pressure eventually. Just one more little clue. That's all we need."

Lex's eyes were unnaturally bright, but she didn't allow herself to cry. She felt like she'd been hit in the head with a wooden platform. "I guess I was just stupid," she whispered. "Stupid and caught up in the heat of the moment."

"Heat is very powerful," Park answered gently. "Especially when it shows up in the form of a tall muscle-god with sexy eyes and hands as big as baseball gloves." She looked up at the ceiling. "Is the air-conditioning on in here, or am I just getting a little hot myself?"

"Control yourself, will you?" Madison said, dropping the nail file onto the coffee table. "We need to remind Lex that Brooklyn's good looks don't matter. He lied to her."

"Girls?"

They jumped at the sound of Lupe's voice. She was standing on the threshold, her hands behind her back, a weird expression on her face.

"What is it?" Madison asked. "Did we wake you?"

"No. You no wake me. I been up." Lupe twitched her nose nervously.

"What's wrong?" Lex asked.

Lupe walked over to them. Her eyes flashed with a

sudden mixture of fear and rage. "I guess you no see the *People* magazine yet."

Park shook her head. "No, we haven't. Why?"

Lupe brought her arms out from behind her back. In her right hand was the newest issue of *People*. She twitched her nose again as she held the magazine up.

And in that instant, Madison experienced a dizzying rush of tunnel vision. She couldn't believe her eyes. She couldn't believe the stab of pain in her chest. She forgot all about tonight and flashed back to what Poppy van Lulu had told her yesterday afternoon—that dire prediction no one had wanted to talk about.

Someone close to you will reveal himself as a liar.

There was a big, grainy picture of Theo on the front page of the magazine; snapped from an angle, it showed him standing on a beach in Antigua, his shirt crumpled on the sand and his arms locked around a tall, thin girl.

Caught! the headline read. *Playboy Theo Cheats on Madison!*

Lex reached out and grabbed the magazine. "That little shit!" she screamed, baring her teeth like a wolf. "Oh! The nerve of him!"

"Madison? Are you okay?" Park asked worriedly.

But Madison was frozen, her eyes locked on the floor.

"I knew he was an asshole!" Lex ranted. "I'll tell every tabloid editor in America that he has a nasty case of herpes!"

"Lex . . . stop." Madison wiped away the first tear that trickled down her cheek. "I don't want anybody to do anything."

"It's too late," Lupe whispered. Her lip curled into a

sneer as she pulled her trusty dish towel from the front pocket of her apron. "Saturday, when Theo gets home, he's gonna meet my little friend." She unfurled the towel and whipped it against the side of the coffee table.

Park and Lex recoiled in fear.

Madison didn't seem to notice anything except the headline. She buried her face in her hands and ran from the room.

◇   ◇   ◇

It was nearly five a.m. Ordinarily, Poppy van Lulu would have been in bed, but sleep hadn't touched her all night. She had lain awake for several hours, tossing and turning, trying to dispel the aches and pains shooting through her legs and back. She hadn't done the tango in months, let alone the tarantella. And the last time she'd danced to hip-hop music, Lil' Kim had been sitting in the spirit room, asking Poppy how long her incarceration would last.

Now Poppy was walking around her bedroom. She slipped into her favorite Missoni jumpsuit and went to the mirror. She ran a hairbrush through her short locks. Her face looked fatigued, so she applied some blush to her cheeks and tied a colorful vintage Camerino scarf around her neck. She stepped back to inspect her appearance. Not as good as she'd like, but it would have to do. At five o'clock in the morning people generally don't look their best.

It felt strange moving around the apartment at this odd hour. But then again, she really didn't have much of a choice. The phone call had come just a half hour ago, rattling her nerves and shattering the silence of the apartment.

The voice on the other end of the line had sounded frantic: *I need to see you. It's a desperate situation. May I please come over?*

Poppy had agreed to the meeting immediately. She would never have done so under ordinary circumstances, but nothing about the past forty-eight hours was proving to be ordinary.

The doorbell rang.

Poppy ran out of the bedroom, through the living room, and into the foyer. She pulled open the door and smiled. "Hello—or should I say good morning? Please, come in."

"Thank you for seeing me." The figure walked past her and into the apartment, head bowed, blazer collar pulled up high around the ears.

"I'm actually very glad you called," Poppy said. She closed the door behind her and went around the sofa, turning on a lamp. "There's so much to tell you, dear. So much that's happened. Don't be scared. Elijah is here. He's ready to speak again."

Silence.

"Dear, are you all right?" Poppy turned around. "Can you hear me?"

The tall, powerful figure standing before her didn't respond.

Poppy's eyes widened in horror as she saw the steel barrel of the gun emerge from inside the blazer. She didn't have time to move. She didn't have time to scream. The shot came out in a quick spit of fire, and a few seconds later, Poppy van Lulu caught her first true glimpse of the Other Side.

17

On the Run

In the gritty blue of dawn, Ina Debrovitch slipped the key into the lock of her hotel room door and turned it. She realized that her fingers were trembling. In fact, her whole body felt as if it were running on nothing but adrenaline. That made perfect sense: she hadn't eaten in nearly twenty-four hours, nor had she slept. It would be a long time before her life returned to normal.

She stepped into the room and shut the door behind her. Sunlight bled through the musty curtains, illuminating the drab furnishings, the scarred wood floor, the yellowed walls. The little hotel on Houston Street in

Greenwich Village was flat-out ugly; it was dingy and small and smelled of cat pee, but here she had a tiny slice of peace, a space in which to gather her thoughts and make sense of her plans. She wouldn't have been able to do that in Connecticut. Ghost Ranch wasn't her home anymore. She would never again stare out of that second-floor bay window and glimpse deer sprinting through the trees. She would never again sit at the breakfast nook and share a pot of coffee with Tallula. Those days, while so achingly wonderful, were long gone.

She shrugged out of her linen blazer and tossed it onto the bed, glad to be rid of the sweaty material that had been clinging to her arms all night. She tore off her pants as well. She kicked off her shoes. Her feet were swollen from all the walking she'd done, but it had been neces-sary. All part of the plan. Had she taken a cab or bus, someone might have recognized her, and that would have created countless problems. She unclipped her hearing aid from her ear and tossed it onto the bed. In the blazer pocket was her airline ticket, and just seeing it made her feel a little calmer.

She stepped into the small bathroom. She flung on the light and winced when she saw the grimy tub with its brown rust stains around the drain. It didn't matter. She needed to stand under the hot jets of water. She needed to cleanse herself thoroughly. Pulling back the plastic cur-tain, she turned the knob and stood beneath the shower-head, letting the heat cut through her hair and cascade down the length of her body. Late last night she had wandered in disguise into one of the small local bodegas and bought soap, tissues, and bottled water. Now, as she reached for the scented bar and worked it into a thick lather, she couldn't help but smile. She was thinking of the disguise and of how easy it had been to walk into the Waldorf-Astoria; what made her angry, however, was how quickly she'd lost her nerve. She'd planned on riding that elevator back up to the penthouse suite, but at the last possible minute, she chickened out and busted out of the hotel. Her nerves had gotten the best of her. But she hadn't panicked. She'd gotten off on the twelfth floor, hung a sharp right, and taken another elevator right back down to the lobby.

She turned around and let the hot jets splash over her body a second time. She shampooed her hair, scrubbed the grit from under her nails. She even lashed the soap across the soles of her feet. Exhausted, she turned off the water and toweled herself dry. Back in the main room, the sunlight was streaming through the curtains. Dawn. A new day. Her last day here in the United States. Soon she would be boarding a plane for home, jetting across the ocean and away from the mess her life had become. She had no intention of returning to the little village where she'd been raised. Instead, she was going to head to the capital and get lost in the teeming mass of people. With a new name and a whole new identity, she would be able to start over. If the cops ever came looking for Ina De-brovitch, they would find little more than a crumpled blazer and a big turban.

She hadn't wanted to take such drastic actions. But she was young and intelligent and ambitious. She had a whole life ahead of her. And a new life growing inside of her.

Ina lowered herself onto the bed and gently stroked her belly. The baby wasn't due for another seven months, but already she could feel its energy coursing in her blood. She had spent the past several weeks wondering if it would be a boy or a girl, if it would sleep through the night, if it would eat all its vegetables. If it would look like its father.

Elijah, she thought, pulling up an image of him on the screen of her mind. She closed her eyes against it. She held back her tears as she mentally stroked his cheeks, his chin, his lips. She chided herself for still missing him, for still loving him. After all the heartache and the pain, why did she feel the need to mourn him?

Throughout their brief but passionate affair, Elijah hadn't once shown her the slightest bit of affection. He had seduced her on that chilly April night while Tallula worked in her studio. A warm touch, a long kiss, a sweet nothing whispered in her ear, and Ina had simply melted into his embrace.

She had known that Elijah was attracted to her. She had caught him staring her down on several occasions, his eyes squinted, his gaze almost predatory. There'd been times when he'd even shot her coy little winks right behind Tallula's back. At first, Ina was shocked and angered by his overt passes. But then, little by little, she found herself waiting for those startling little communications, for the steamy excitement that roiled in her stomach. It was wild. It was reckless. It was completely unlike anything she had ever done. All her life, she'd been the good girl, the proper pupil, watching from the perimeter as life happened to other people. But Elijah had ignited a secret circle of fire, and Ina willingly stepped into it and stoked the flames.

She asked herself all the pertinent questions—*Am I pretty enough for him? He doesn't mind that I wear a hearing aid? Does he like me more than Tallula?*—and realized that maybe she *did* possess the qualities a famous young man like Elijah looked for in a girl. Tallula was beautiful and talented, but Ina knew perhaps better than anyone how bitchy she could be, how superficial and cold she acted when things didn't go her way. It seemed to Ina that Elijah was slowly but surely falling out of love with Tallula. And that, of course, was no one's fault. People fell out of love all the time. Relationships cracked and crumbled and people went their separate ways no matter how long they'd known each other.

And in the beginning, following that first night of heated seduction, Ina had believed that simple equation to be true. She believed Elijah wanted *her* and not Tallula. That he was piecing together in his mind a plan that would one day allow them to live openly as lovers. Maybe even husband and wife. He had spoken of those things every time they ran off for one of those secret meetings. Telling Ina he loved her. That soon things would be different. That she had to keep quiet about their affair no matter what. And Ina had believed him. Like a stupid, mindless, inexperienced junior high girl, she had fallen into his deceptive hands and allowed herself to be betrayed.

Last month, when she told him she was pregnant, Elijah panicked. *You can't have that baby,* he'd said. *You can't do this. It's not the right time.* Days of anger and resentment and fear followed, the hardest days Ina had ever endured. Elijah didn't look at her, didn't so much as acknowledge her presence when she walked into a room. Ina worried every minute whether or not he was going to break down and confess his sins to Tallula. Ina would have lost everything in a single instant—her job, the roof over her head, her security. It had never occurred to her not to have this baby, but without Elijah and his support—his money—Ina couldn't imagine what her life would amount to. And when she finally confronted Elijah about it two weeks ago, telling him the baby was as much his responsibility as hers, he whirled around and glared at her coldly. *You're the slut who let it happen,* he said. *You're the stupid one. And if you want to have that baby, you'll do it without anyone knowing. As soon as you start to show, you quit this job and get the hell out of here. End of story.* Ina hadn't been able to protest his cruelty. Before she could say a word, Elijah threatened her in the worst way possible, reminding her that she was working in this country illegally and that one phone call would have her deported.

Initially, the thought of going back home frightened Ina. Such a bad economy. No chance of finding a job. And with a baby on the way, her life in Romania would have been nothing short of disastrous. So she swallowed her anger and kept quiet. Avoided Elijah completely. Started looking for housekeeping jobs when Tallula wasn't around. Ina had planned on quitting and leaving, just as Elijah had instructed her to do. But the rage in her blood grew stronger, and whenever she glimpsed him walking through the house, she gave herself over to the secret, silent fantasies. How quickly feelings of love turned to visions of murder.

She could never have imagined he would die by way of

the sky. But he had, and he had deserved every last second of that free-falling fear.

I hate you, Elijah, she thought now, letting the tears streak her face. *I hate you and I still miss you. And I know the guilt I'm feeling will kill me one day.*

But today wasn't that day. Today, Ina knew she had to continue with the next phase of her plan.

Wiping her face with a tissue, she got up and started reviewing her list. She didn't have much time. It would be difficult and dangerous, but her choices, at this point, were few.

She got dressed, making certain to put the gun in her purse.

18

A Secret at the Society

"You don't have to do this," Madison said for the tenth time in as many minutes. "I really am fine."

Coco sighed and shook her head vehemently. "I know I don't *have* to do it, but I want to. I don't care what you say—you need a friend right now."

They were sitting in the Hamilton limo, headed south. It was shortly after nine a.m. and the traffic had let up. Coco was in a light disguise: cowboy hat, sunglasses, a white polo shirt, and her favorite pair of Sass & Bide jeans. Despite the stress of the past two days, she looked good, if not a bit Western.

Madison, on the other hand, looked like a washed-up runway model. Her hair was thick and flowing as usual and she was dressed impeccably in an A.P.C. minidress and belt. But behind her sunglasses were red-rimmed eyes and an altogether tense expression. She had spent most of the night riding the roller coaster of emotions: crying, screaming, getting angry, getting depressed, punching the pillows on her bed, pretending to dance with a broom, pigging out on champagne and chocolate milk and a bowl of leftover spaghetti. She hadn't slept much. And when she woke up, the first thing she thought about was the headline: *Playboy Theo Cheats on Madison!*

Even now, it was enough to make her puke.

But she had showered and changed and decided, against everyone's better judgment, to keep her mind occupied. She, Park, and Lex were trying to clear their friend's name, and that deserved the utmost attention.

She took off her sunglasses and stared at Coco. "You really shouldn't be outside your apartment," she said. "I know you're out on bail, but it's best to stay behind closed doors."

"My lawyer is on the phone with the DA right now," Coco said confidently, tossing her head back. "And after the charges against me are dropped, we're going to sue the police department *and* the hotel."

"Why the hotel?"

"Are you kidding me?" Coco said. "I had to walk down a million stairs in heels because that elevator was broken— if that isn't emotional distress, I don't know what is. I could have died in that stairwell."

Madison frowned. "Well, I'm glad you're here, but I

just want you to know that I don't need a chaperone. I'm feeling fine."

"That's total bullshit, but I'll ignore it right now." Coco stared out the windows as the limo drove down Fifth Avenue. "The fact is, you *can't* feel fine. The science of that little thought just doesn't compute. You've just found out, along with the rest of the world, that your boyfriend is a cheap whore in a well-made suit. A snake with nice hair and a good stylist. An aardvark with a—"

"I get the picture, okay?" Madison snapped. She folded her arms over her chest and glanced out the opposite window. "You're as bad as Lex with this whole name-calling thing. I wish the both of you would just give it a rest."

"How can we give it a rest? We happen to care about you."

"I understand that, but calling Theo names doesn't make me feel any better."

Coco shrugged. "It makes *me* feel better. And just for the record, I agree with Lex."

Madison stayed quiet. Then she turned to Coco and said, "What gets me is that Theo didn't even have the decency to call me in the past two days. And standing on the beach with that model, throwing his arms around her like that when he *knew* someone would eventually snap a pic of him and sell it to the tabloids . . . that's what *really* pisses me off. That he didn't even try to hide it."

"Pigs will always be pigs," Coco answered. "They roll around in the mud all day and don't care. Incidentally, did you know that pigs eat and relieve themselves at the same time?"

"Thanks for the visual," Madison snapped. "I really needed to know that."

"It's a metaphor." Coco took off her sunglasses and looked at her friend earnestly. "I know it's still too new and everything, but as soon as Theo gets back, you need to dump him in a very public and humiliating way. Lex and I are going to coordinate that."

Madison stared down at her hands. "Nothing like that is going to make me feel better," she said quietly. "After it's all said and done, I'll still be the dumb girl who was cheated on by the stud."

"Has Theo even called you yet?"

"He left me three messages this morning," Madison replied. "Along with everyone else."

That was certainly true. Madison's cell had started ringing at dawn. First it was her father, Trevor, calling to tell her that he was sorry to have read the story, that she would be okay, and that she should never have gotten mixed up with a West. Trevor Hamilton was flying back to New York on Saturday night and promised to bring Madison a great big present to help make her feel better. But this time around, Madison knew that not even a five-million-dollar Picasso sketch—like the one he had bought her last year—would lift her spirits. And after Trevor, there had been messages from Angie, from Cate, from the other Kate, from Hayden and, shockingly enough, even from Paris. The consensus was all the same: guys totally sucked.

Madison had saved every message—except the ones Theo had left. She'd deleted them without even bothering to hear them completely. What was the point? Theo had no damn excuse. He was frolicking in the sand with seventeen-year-old French model Collette Deneuve and probably loving every freakin' minute of it. Holding her. Kissing her. Running his hands through her hair . . .

"Madison."

She blinked back to reality. "Yes, Donnie?"

"I can't make a left onto the street," Donnie told her. "Construction crews are blocking it off. Should I leave you girls at the corner?"

"That's fine." Madison reached for her purse.

Coco pushed the cowboy hat farther down on her head, tucking in a few loose strands of hair, then climbed out of the limo and followed Madison onto the street.

The Royal Crown Society of the Americas was located in a turn-of-the-century brownstone in Gramercy Park. Ivy wound up the front of the building, and the small plaque beside the door read: RCSA, SUPPORTING ART FOR OVER A CENTURY. Madison rang the bell and removed her sunglasses. Then she patted at the dampness under her eyes, hoping the swelling had gone down some.

"I suddenly feel totally underdressed," Coco said nervously.

"Don't worry about it," Madison assured her. "We're meeting with Gunilla O'Hara Miskin. She's totally old but very sweet and classy. She's been a member of the society for sixty-nine years, and she knows everything about art."

"I've heard of her. She's the one who owns those two islands near Capri?"

"That's her."

"And you think the society is going to solve this whole mystery? I still don't get it."

"I'll explain everything," Madison promised. "But I'm hoping to get some answers first."

The door opened and a man dressed in a tuxedo smiled down at her. "Ambassador Hamilton," he said with a respectful nod of his head. "Please come in." He moved to one side and ushered her into the spectacular two-story foyer. "My name is Geoffrey, and I'll be your guide for the duration of your visit. May I show you to the parlor?"

"Yes, thank you," Madison said. She gestured her head at Coco. "This is my friend—"

"Anne," Coco said quickly. She smiled up at Geoffrey, relieved to be hiding behind the sunglasses and cowboy hat. "And actually, if it's okay, would you mind if I just toured the grounds while Madison has her meeting? I'd totally love to check out all the art in here."

"If Madam Ambassador wishes." Geoffrey looked at Madison.

"Why?" Madison whispered. "You're more than welcome to sit in on my meeting."

"I just feel more comfortable not being there," Coco said honestly. "I don't want anyone recognizing me. I don't feel like having to explain myself. Really. I'll be out here waiting for you."

"Okay," Madison answered with a shrug. "I'll try not to be more than a half hour." She followed Geoffrey through the foyer and the two large front rooms. Though she had been here before, she couldn't help marveling at the extraordinary works of art hanging on the walls: paintings from the Renaissance, medieval, and neoclassical periods; Impressionist paintings, Baroque paintings, even

Pre-Raphaelites. It was like stepping into a vortex of art history.

"Right this way," Geoffrey said. He stopped on the threshold and extended his arm.

Madison walked into the parlor. Sitting in a chair in the center of the room was Gunilla O'Hara Miskin—New York socialite, international patroness of the arts, and self-avowed historian of all things elitist. Gunilla was nearly ninety and looked every bit her age. There were deep wrinkles in her small face and liver spots on her hands, but her brown hair was meticulously coiffed and her nails perfectly manicured. She was dressed in a colorful red and white patterned Chanel suit, signature magnolia pin and all. A multicarat diamond ring sat on the forefinger of her right hand like a pet.

"Oh, Madison, my sweet child!" Gunilla said dramatically. "Come here and let me take a look at you."

Madison leaned down and kissed Gunilla's cheek. Then she stepped back and modeled her outfit.

"Just extraoooordinary, you are, darling! Extraordinary."

"Thank you," Madison replied. She sat down across from Gunilla, resting her hands in her lap and assuming a proper, professional posture.

"What a lovely afternoon we had at the luncheon," Gunilla said. "You and your sisters looked delicious. But oh—I was so sorry to hear about that brilliant young man Elijah Traymore falling from that penthouse." She shook her head; her hair, of course, didn't move. "Just devilish how things happen! And what a shock, that Coco McKaid would be charged with the crime."

Madison fidgeted her thumbs in a nervous gesture and cleared her throat. "Coco McKaid is innocent," she said, gently but firmly. "My sisters and I have uncovered evidence that the district attorney is viewing right now. Please believe me, Mrs. Miskin. She's innocent." *And she happens to be walking around the first floor right now.*

Gunilla's lips curled up slowly in a smile. "Well! This *is* surprising! But I don't doubt you, darling—you and your sisters know about crime."

"We pretty much do, yes."

"Extraooooordinary, darling. A rare breed you three are. Intelligent. Beautiful. Knowledgeable about the world. Quite like myself when I was your age." Gunilla chuckled. Then her eyes fell to the round English coffee table and, realizing there was nothing on it, she gasped and quickly clapped her hands.

Geoffrey came striding into the room. "Madam?"

"Geoffrey," Gunilla said in a chiding tone, "when you are in the presence of ambassadors, you *must* remember to bring about refreshments *immediately.* We *don't* like to be kept waiting, dear."

"Yes, madam." He turned around and disappeared into another room. Less than a minute later, he came back holding a gleaming golden tray; on it were two gold espresso cups with matching spoons, and two delicately folded napkins.

Madison took a quiet sip of her espresso. She knew exactly what she had to ask Gunilla, but there was an appropriate way to do things here at the society. You didn't just blurt out questions or make demands. You never gave the impression that you were in a rush, or that the society's mission didn't come first and foremost in the world. What you *did* do was schmooze, and Madison had plenty of experience in that area. "How are your islands, Mrs. Miskin?" she asked pleasantly.

"Oh, my love, they're simply *paradise.*" Gunilla drank the last of her espresso, leaned forward, and set her cup down on the tray. "You must come and stay for a while. Your mother visited with me last year, and I've just finished building the new compound. Right on the Mediterranean. Sweeping views."

"How big is the new compound?"

"It's roughly twenty thousand square feet. Twenty-one bedrooms, love, so the whole family can vacation at the same time." Gunilla paused and studied Madison with a hard, practiced eye. "I'm extending an invitation to you, darling, because I suspect you need a bit of respite. It's always stressful when the tabloids start putting your name on the front page."

Madison held her breath. Inwardly, she felt a tremor of shock pass through her. She hadn't expected Gunilla to bring up Theo's cheating ways and the brewing scandal, but then, she and Theo had been a favorite of the tabloids for a few months now. Everyone knew their tumultuous story. She went rigid in the seat. She didn't say anything.

Gunilla kept her gaze steady. "You're no longer just another little rich girl," she said firmly. "You're a young woman of special breeding and uncommonly high social status. You must choose your private passions more judiciously."

Madison looked down again. "I understand, Mrs. Miskin. And you're very right. I haven't been very smart about this whole relationship. The truth is that I love Theo West, but I know now that he doesn't feel the same way about me. He doesn't take us seriously—maybe he never has. It's my own fault, I guess."

Gunilla leaned forward and put her gnarled hand over Madison's. "Most young women in this world say that you can't help who you fall in love with, but that cannot be true for you or your sisters, darling. Because of your wealth, your fame, your status, every action you take— every decision you make—the mind must lead the heart. The world will be watching you girls forever. You cannot afford to be slandered in public, especially by men."

"I understand, Mrs. Miskin," Madison said quietly, feeling better about the whole mess as the seconds ticked by. That was the funny thing about emotional pain—the more you confronted it, the less it hurt.

"I know you feel terrible right now," Gunilla said. "But remember this: if an artist doesn't recognize the beauty before him, he'll never be able to paint it. Theo West, my dear, is no artist."

Madison let the words sink in. *Really* sink in. She didn't know how to reply, but then again, there wasn't any need to reply—a true statement was final.

"Now, tell me, darling, to what do I owe the pleasure of this meeting?" Gunilla asked, her tone turning professional and curt.

Madison reached into her purse and grabbed the piece of paper on which she'd written the code. She handed it to Gunilla. "I'm correct in assuming that the code you see there belongs to the society, right?"

Gunilla squinted as she studied the code. "Oh,

indeed," she said. "It's one of ours. Every piece of art the society has ever acquired is given a code. Mind you, there are literally thousands of codes in our files by now. The society acquires all kinds of art, as you know—even art from up-and-coming artists whose names might never be well known." She looked at the piece of paper again. "Does this code refer to an object you wish to study, darling?"

"Yes, it does." Madison cleared her throat and fought to keep her composure. She wanted to get up and start tearing through the files until she found the very one that contained the mysterious work of art Elijah Traymore had been pursuing. But she had to remember her manners. She said, "I wanted to ask if maybe you remember the particular painting or object that code refers to, Mrs. Miskin. I believe it's a painting entitled *To the Penthouse*. Does that ring any bells?"

Gunilla's lips parted ever so slightly. She cocked her head to the left. Her expression started off as pensive, but it quickly changed to recognition. "Oh, why, yes. Yes, I *do* recall that painting. Yes indeed. Such a long time ago. Yes. Of course. *To the Penthouse*. Oh yes. Why, that must've been twenty years ago."

"So then you know the painting," Madison said excitedly. "And you think the society acquired it twenty years ago?"

"Yes," Gunilla replied with a firm nod. "A fairly small canvas, but quite a beautiful one. A landscape of Manhattan, interestingly enough. Yes, I remember it now. Strikingly beautiful. I never did know much about the artist. Typical recluse, from what I recall. And now . . . let me see . . . if my memory is correct, I think it was the only painting ever done by that particular artist."

Madison had inched to the very edge of her seat. "Where is the painting now? Do you remember the artist's name?"

"I'm afraid that's a blank, darling. But it's a small matter—a virtually unknown painting. Nothing ever came of it, as I recall. Twenty years ago, the society tried its best to promote emerging artists who showed great promise, and I'm sure that's what this acquisition was all about. Why are you interested in it, may I ask?"

Shit, Madison thought, *how the hell do I answer that?* She thought for a few seconds but didn't come up with anything good. "Well, actually . . . ," she began. "Well . . . it's because I . . . well . . ."

Gunilla smiled. "It doesn't really matter, love, does it? I'm sure a future art historian such as yourself has plenty of reasons."

"Yes. I do. Does that mean I can search the archives?"

"Records going this far back would have been sealed by now," Gunilla replied.

Madison's heart sank. "Sealed?"

"Yes, darling. You would need the approval of the executive board to riffle through them."

"Approval?" Madison repeated, her heart sinking lower.

"And that could take weeks, I'm afraid."

"Weeks?" Madison didn't care how childish she probably sounded, repeating Gunilla's words like a toddler. She was about to launch into an articulate protest when Geoffrey came back into the room and addressed Gunilla.

"Ambassador Miskin," he said quietly. "I'm sorry to interrupt. But the First Lady is on line one. She says she'd like to speak with you about the upcoming gala at the White House."

Gunilla sighed lightly. "Oh, yes. I'd forgotten she was going to call. Lovely woman, but I don't know what she ever saw in that husband of hers." She gave Madison a warm smile. "Darling, if you'll excuse me . . ."

"Of course." Madison stood up, kissed Gunilla's cheek, and then turned and strode out of the room. She picked up her pace as she reached the parlor. "Coco!" she called out in a harsh whisper. "Where the hell are you?"

Coco came out of one of the adjoining rooms. "This place rocks! Did you know they have a bunch of Warhols in there?"

Madison grabbed her friend by the wrist and together the girls raced up the grand staircase, winding around the massive crystal chandelier until they reached the third-floor library. "Just play along with me," Madison said quietly, gesturing toward the mousy-looking woman sitting at the reception desk a few paces ahead.

"What are you doing?" Coco asked.

"I can't explain right now. Just follow my lead, okay?"

Coco shrugged. "Okay."

Her head held high and her shoulders thrown back, Madison walked into the library. The walls were lined with books. The shelves behind the French doors were dusty and cluttered with paper. "Good morning," Madison said curtly to the receptionist.

The middle-aged woman stood up, dropping her pen onto the desk. "Oh, Ambassador Hamilton. Good morning. How may I help you?"

Madison retrieved the sheet of paper from her purse and handed it to the woman. "I'll need the file that corresponds with this code, please." She kept her voice sharp and businesslike to project a slight air of bitchiness—which she hated doing. But being sugary and polite wouldn't work in this case.

The older woman sat back down. She quickly typed the code into her computer. Then, as her eyes traced over the information that had appeared on her screen, she grimaced. "I'm so sorry. This is an archived file. You would need permission from the board to see—"

"I've already received the board's permission," Madison cut in sharply. "Don't you *know* that?"

"Well . . . no." The woman blinked and pushed her red-framed glasses farther up the bridge of her nose.

Madison sighed. She tossed her head back. "I don't have much time to spare, so please just get me the file right away."

"I can't do that. I'm sorry. Maybe I should call downstairs and ask Gunilla—"

"Don't you dare call her!" Madison snapped. "Gunilla's on the phone with the First Lady and can't be disturbed. And I'm late for a brunch with my publicist. Now, if you can't get me that file, I'll just have to voice my concerns to the board."

"A complaint from an ambassador," Coco said, inching closer to the desk. "That could be really *bad* for you."

Blinking rapidly, her lips twitching, the woman stood up again. She turned around and disappeared behind a door.

Madison ran a hand over her face. "Oh, God—did I sound totally horrible?"

"Welcome to Bitch City," Coco said. "You'd better hope she doesn't come out of there with a can of hair spray ready to fight."

But when the receptionist came out of the back room, she was smiling and holding a weathered brown folder. "Here it is," she said. "It's not a very big file." She held it out.

Her heart racing, Madison took the file with a curt smile and walked across the room to the small reading table beside a window. She unclipped the edges of the file, quickly opened it, and began to scour its contents. On the very top of the first page were the words *To the Penthouse, painting acquisition, 10 October 1988.* Following this was a description of the work: *A 3 x 4 canvas done in oil, magnificent use of space and color, highly original texture and execution; the painting is a landscape of the Manhattan skyline as seen from the penthouse of a high-rise apartment building. By first-time artist L. K. Corcoran.*

Corcoran.

Corky.

Madison heard herself gasp. She flipped to the next page, which was a copy of the contract the society had offered to the artist twenty years ago. *To the Penthouse* had been purchased for the modest sum of twenty-five hundred dollars. But who was L. K. Corcoran? Nowhere in the pages was there a biography of the artist, or even an address. Was L. K. a man or a woman? From her own research into the society's past, Madison knew that the small painting had been acquired because it had showed unique promise, and because the society's mission supported up-and-coming artists. But L. K. Corcoran was an unknown artist. Had L. K. established him- or herself over the years, there would have undoubtedly been more biographical information in the file. As far as Madison could tell, L. K. Corcoran had sold only one painting.

Corky.

But why had Elijah been trying to track this particular painting? Why had he become obsessed with the artist?

She flipped to the back of the file, her heart racing. That was when she found the wrinkled yellowed envelope. She opened it and three photographs fell out. Grasping the edges with trembling fingers, she stared down at the colorful images of *To the Penthouse* that had been taken twenty years ago. A gasp escaped her lips.

She knew instantly why the painting looked so familiar. She had seen it last night, held within a ring of candlelight, hanging on the wall of Poppy van Lulu's spirit room.

19

Brooklyn

The fury Lex had been feeling boiled over the moment she set eyes on Brooklyn DiMarco. He was standing by the front desk in uniform, waiting for her. She had called him an hour ago and told him that something was terribly wrong and that she sure as hell had to talk to him. He'd sounded scared. But he hadn't tried to brush her off as she had expected him to.

Now, as she and Park strolled across the lobby, Lex took a series of deep, cleansing breaths. There was no easy way to do this. She had to keep her suspicions in front of her while shoving away her attraction to Brooklyn, which was a lot like trying to scale the side of a building in heels: nearly impossible.

"Now, just remember to be cool," Park whispered in her ear. "And don't fight with him. The best way to get someone to talk is by staying quiet."

Lex shot her a tense glance. "Well, if I get loud and fling my purse at him, feel free to jump in and save the day, okay?"

"No swinging of purses," Park warned her. "That purse can very easily be a lethal weapon, and one murder is enough, thank you very much."

They approached the front desk.

"Hey," Brooklyn said brightly. He cracked a ghost of a smile. The look in his eyes was pensive, and his smile quickly turned down to a tight-lipped grimace. "Uh . . . what's up?"

Lex took off her sunglasses and hung them on the front of her shirt. "Is there somewhere we can talk in private?"

"Yeah, sure. Follow me." Brooklyn turned around and led them past the desk and through a closed door beside the concierge stand.

The room was small and cramped, with a single two-seat sofa and a scuffed table. The walls were bleak. The overhead light was dingy.

"This is kind of our little break room," Brooklyn explained. "It used to be a big closet, but they cleaned it out last year. Now we get to sneak in here when no one's watching and catch a few minutes' rest." He cleared his throat nervously. "Um, you want something to drink?"

"We're not here on a pleasure call," Park said quietly. "This is business."

"Business?" He raised an eyebrow and looked at Lex.

"Yes," she said. "Business. Because you lied to me."

Brooklyn started. "Lied to you? About what? What are you talking about?"

"Why don't you have a seat?" Park said, pointing to the sofa.

Brooklyn lowered himself slowly onto the musty pillows.

Lex sat down beside him but kept her body a good distance from his. If their knees so much as touched, she knew she would start thinking about the hot kiss they had shared last night.

Park leaned against the small table.

"Anyone wanna tell me what this is about?" Brooklyn asked sharply.

"Look," Lex began, staring down at her hands. "I know we've just met and we don't really know each other well, but I like you and—"

"I like you too, Lex," he cut in briskly. "You know that."

She sighed quietly. "Yeah, I do know that. But I don't like it when guys lie to me, especially when there's a crime involved."

"A crime?" Brooklyn's voice rose.

"Yeah," Park said. "Remember the body that fell from the penthouse?"

He made a stupid face. "Duh. Of course I do. But—wait—what are you saying? You think I lied about something?"

"You did," Lex said. "You told me that you had never met Elijah Traymore before he and Tallula and Ina checked in here. And that's not true."

Brooklyn was silent. Then he shrugged and shook his head. "It's . . . not?"

"No, Brock, it's not." Park stared at him. "You know exactly what we're talking about."

"I do?"

"Stop playing dumb!" Lex snapped. "You met Elijah Traymore a few months ago! He came to your school and gave some sort of talk!"

"And you probably didn't know this," Park chimed in, "but there's a picture on the school's Web site that proves it."

Brooklyn closed his eyes. He shifted uncomfortably in the sofa. He ran his fingers under the collar of his shirt. "Well . . . yeah . . . okay. That's true. Elijah did come to my school, and yeah, I met him. But—"

"Why did you lie about it?" Lex cut him off sharply.

He swallowed hard. "Because it was really no big deal. I shook his hand, we talked for a few minutes. Someone snapped a pic of us talking, but that was it."

"So why lie about it?" Park kept her tone even-keeled, her stare hard and unflinching.

"Why lie about it?" Brooklyn repeated. "Are you serious? Of course I don't want people knowing I met Elijah. You mention one thing like that when someone gets killed, and the cops start crawling all over you."

"But if you're innocent and have nothing to hide, why would you care if the cops start crawling all over you?" Lex asked.

"Because it's scary!" he replied, his voice rising. "Who the hell wants to get caught up in something like this? I was here when he got shoved off that balcony!

That's all the cops would've needed—to poke around and make me a suspect, even though it would've only lasted for like ten seconds. But ya know, it wasn't exactly easy for my dad to get me this job here. He had to pull a lot of strings and I complain about it and shit like that, but the truth is, I make good money here and I don't wanna lose it."

"But how well *did* you know Elijah?" Park asked. "Did you guys talk to each other after you met him at your school? Did he recognize you when he checked in here?"

"I didn't keep in touch with him, if that's what you're asking," Brooklyn answered quickly. "Why the hell would he have kept in touch with me? I'm nobody—he was a celebrity. I spoke to him for about three minutes that day at school, and that was it."

"And did he recognize you when he checked in?" Lex repeated.

Brooklyn sighed again. "I didn't kill him, okay? I mean—holy Jeez! You don't really think that! You're not serious about this!"

Lex and Park looked at each other as silence fell over the room. "Just answer the question," Lex said firmly. "Did he recognize you?"

"Yes." He closed his eyes again. "He recognized me."

Park was quick to catch the marked hesitation in Brooklyn's response. She didn't like it one bit. He was totally hiding something. Aware that it was time to up the ante on this interrogation, she stood up straight and began pacing the floor—back and forth, back and forth—her hands locked behind her back, her head held high—back and forth.

When Brooklyn opened his eyes again, he followed Park as she moved from left to right, then as she circled the small sofa. "Hey—what're you doing?"

"I'm just thinking," Park replied. "If you're totally innocent and have nothing at all to do with what happened, why do you look so scared?"

"I don't look scared," he said defensively, and unconvincingly.

"Oh, please." Lex clucked her tongue. "You totally look like you're about to piss in your pants."

"A little decorum, Lex," Park said quietly. "We don't say *piss,* we say *tinkle.*"

Brooklyn slipped his fingers underneath the collar of his shirt again. He had begun to sweat profusely. "I'm telling you the truth here, okay? I had nothing to do with Elijah's murder. I didn't push anybody off some balcony. Hell—I helped you try to figure stuff out, didn't I? I broke you into the penthouse!"

"We're not talking about us here," Lex shot back. "We're talking about you. If you're hiding something, spill it."

"The only thing I haven't told anybody is . . ." He grunted, annoyed and on edge.

Park stopped walking. She was standing directly in front of him. She trained her gaze on him and didn't so much as blink.

"Here's the thing," Brooklyn said. "When Elijah checked in, he recognized me, and I thought it was really cool and he said hi and asked me about school and all that stuff. I was really flattered. I mean, the guy was, like, famous. So anyway, the day before he got killed, I was walking through the lobby and he sees me and he goes, 'Hey, Brock. Can I talk to you?' And I was like, 'Yeah, sure.' But then he walked into the bathroom and told me to follow him. And I thought it was weird and all, and I knew it wasn't something cool because as soon as we got inside he looked under the stalls to make sure no one was there. And then he turns to me and he goes, 'Listen, I need a favor.' Then he took out this small yellow envelope and held it up. And he goes, 'Can you hold this for me for like two days?' And I told him that I could put it in a hotel safe for him, and he said he didn't want that. He just wanted someone to sort of . . . I don't know . . . hide it for him.

"So anyway, at first I said no because it seemed totally shady. I wasn't down with it. An envelope? Why not just put it in the hotel safe? Well, I knew why—because he didn't want to leave a paper trail. Weird. So I said no again, and then . . . well . . ." He sighed heavily and stared down at the floor.

"Then what?" Lex asked impatiently. "Finish the story."

"Then Elijah took out a wad of cash and he handed me five hundred bucks," Brooklyn said quietly, reluctantly. "And I know it was stupid of me and all, but, like, it was five hundred bucks. Clean cash. So I took the freaking envelope and held it for him. But listen—if anyone finds out about that, I'll totally get fired. And the cops will be all over me for something stupid. And my dad will get in trouble and—"

"Just forget that for a second," Park cut in quickly. "What was in the envelope?"

"I don't know," Brooklyn said. "I . . . I didn't look."

"Bullshit." Lex shook her head. "You so know you opened that envelope."

He sighed again. "Okay—I did. I couldn't help it. I carried it around in my pocket for a day and I got curious. There was a key in the envelope. That was it."

"A key? Where is it now? Do you have it?" Lex batted his arm.

"No, the morning of the luncheon, Elijah took the little envelope back from me," Brooklyn explained. "And I kept the cash. End of story."

Park hadn't really heard the last chunk of his answer. She was too busy scrambling for her purse, digging inside it. Her heart hammering, she found the key that she'd picked up a few feet from Elijah's body and held it up and out. "Is this it?" she asked, trying to keep her voice steady. "Does this look familiar?"

Brooklyn shot off the sofa and grabbed the key from Park's hand. "Holy Jeez!" he cried. "This is it—I mean, I'm pretty sure this is it." He stared down at it with wide, nervous eyes. "It's a multi-lock key."

"A what?" Park and Lex asked in unison.

"A multi-lock key," Brooklyn repeated. "See the blue top? It means you can't make a copy of it unless you have the card it comes with. You pay extra for that, ya know? Hey—wait a minute! Why do you have this key? I gave it back to Elijah!"

Park shifted her weight from one foot to the other, pondering her response. She looked at Lex, but Lex's face was as blank as hers.

"Hello?" Brooklyn snapped. "Like, *hel-lo?* Now who's got some explaining to do?"

"All right," Park said quickly. She whisked the key out of his fingers. "I found this next to Elijah's body. I had no proof it actually belonged to him—until now."

Brooklyn's jaw dropped. "You *stole* evidence from a crime scene?"

"I borrowed it," Park answered, shrugging. "I was planning to give it back."

"Oh really?" he said, raising his eyebrows. "What were you gonna do? Put it in an envelope and mail it to heaven?"

Lex got up and waved her hands. "Okay, people. Let's chill. Brooklyn, when did you give that key back to Elijah?"

"Wednesday, right before he came into the luncheon. He came up to me. He didn't say anything and neither did I. I knew what he wanted, so I just handed it over."

"Well, can you answer me another question?" Park asked. "Where were you when Elijah was shoved off the balcony?"

Brooklyn crossed his arms over his chest in a defensive manner. "You did not just ask me that."

"Oh, but I did." Park put her hands on her hips and struck a fearless pose.

Brooklyn stared at Lex. "You know, I'm totally offended here."

"Just answer the question," Lex said. "Where were you?"

"Running around the hotel, doing my job. Like always."

Park and Lex exchanged dubious glances.

"But," Brooklyn said, "I might as well tell you right now since you'll probably find out anyway. I *did* happen to get into the elevator with Tallula Kayson and her assistant when they left the luncheon. I got off on the sixth floor—and I have three witnesses who'll vouch for me on that." He smirked sarcastically. "So *there*."

"Did Tallula or Ina say anything to you? Did you guys speak?" Lex batted his arm again.

"No, nothing," Brooklyn replied.

"What were Tallula and Ina doing?"

He shrugged. "Talking, I guess. I don't know. Going through their bags, putting on makeup. Stuff girls do."

Lex felt a little lightbulb go on over her head. "Hey, did you see Ina put on any of that moisturizer we found in the room last night? Remember?"

Brooklyn thought about it for a while. "Actually, yeah. I think she did. She slathered stuff on her hands. I think that was right about the time I got off the elevator."

"Shit," Park whispered. "Brooklyn—you might totally have to tell that to the cops! That's like . . . major info."

"It is? Why?"

Park flashed back to the afternoon following the luncheon. Brooklyn hadn't seen Elijah's body up close; he didn't know about the semi-handprint on the white fabric of Elijah's shirt. "Forget about it for now," she said. "But don't forget about it altogether, okay?"

He stared at her, visibly spooked.

"Listen," Lex said, stepping in front of him. "I have another question. Is there any way to find out where that key belongs? Like, why Elijah had it?"

"I guess you can try and call the locksmith where he got it," Brooklyn answered. "Call the number on the key and see if they'll tell you."

"The number?" Park held the key up. "What number?"

"Right there on the body of the key, etched into the silver part, you should find a phone number," Brooklyn explained. "That's the locksmith."

Lex dug into her magic purse and pulled out her trusty magnifying glass. She handed it over to Park.

Resting the key in the palm of her left hand, Park studied it through the magnifying glass. And there, printed on one side of it in nearly microscopic print, was a seven-digit phone number. She reached for her cell, flipped it open. She punched in the number and waited as the line rang.

"Big John's Locksmiths," a male voice answered. "Can I help ya?"

"Um, yes," Park said. "Can you tell me where you're located?"

"We have seven stores in New York State," the man answered tersely. "You've reached our main store and office in Manhattan. Lower Manhattan, to be exact. You need a locksmith?"

"No, thanks." She closed the cell. A surge of adrenaline shooting through her, Park slipped the key into the pocket of her jeans and grabbed her purse. "Hey, Brock? You've been a big help." She patted his shoulder. "Thanks."

"Thanks?" he snapped. "You come here and practically accuse me of killing Elijah Traymore, and all you can say is *thanks*?"

Park grinned. "You explained yourself, so I pretty much don't think you're our killer."

"Pretty much?" Brooklyn asked, still incredulous. "How about saying you think I'm totally innocent? That would be nice."

"Park doesn't think anyone is totally innocent," Lex told him. "It's the detective mentality." She swung the magic purse over her shoulder and looked up at him. She felt relief floating through her body. She wasn't sure Brooklyn DiMarco would ever want to see her again, but at least he was the nice, cool guy she'd initially taken him for. Good news for him, and good news for her. She batted her eyes, gave his forearm a gentle squeeze, and then she followed Park out of the room.

"Hey, Lex?" he called after her.

She turned around.

"Can I still call you sometime?" he asked with a reluctant smile.

She nodded right away and shot him a wink. "I think so. And as it turns out, I'm free this weekend. . . ."

Park grabbed her by the wrist and yanked her into the lobby. "Amazing," she huffed. "On the hunt for a killer and you're making a date. Why doesn't that surprise me?"

◇　◇　◇

Big John's Locksmiths was located on Chambers Street in Lower Manhattan. The cab ride from Midtown had taken a full thirty minutes, and Park and Lex had used the time wisely, knotting silk scarves around their heads and tucking their hair in at all the right angles. Now, as the cab came to a full stop, they slipped on their sunglasses. Park paid the driver and popped open the door.

"Well," she said, standing on the sidewalk and glancing around the bustling, narrow street. "It's been a long time since I've been down here. It's . . . so busy."

"And kind of ugly," Lex replied. "I've never seen so many people wearing gray."

Park gestured at the large storefront window just ahead. The words BIG JOHN'S LOCKSMITHS, FAMILY OWNED AND OPERATED SINCE 1922 were stenciled on the grimy glass. She pushed through the front door, surprised to see such a big, wide floor. From somewhere in the back, a machine was clunking noisily.

"Maybe that's Big John," Lex whispered, referring to the short, thin, balding man at the front counter.

Park approached him and cleared her throat. "Hi," she said gently.

"How ya doin'?"

"Fine, thanks." Park reached into the pocket of her pants and pulled out the key. "I found this key in my father's old office, and I was just wondering if you could tell me anything about it?"

The little guy sucked a poppy seed out of the corner of his mouth and turned the key over in his hand. "Oh yeah," he said. "This key is one of ours. A standard multi-lock. Whataya wanna know about it?"

"Could you tell me who bought it?" Park asked. "Or what address it's registered to?"

"No," the guy said flatly. "I can't."

Lex stepped up to the counter. "Why not?"

He sucked at the corner of his mouth again. "Because that's private information."

"But it's kind of an emergency," Park pressed. "You

see, we think that key might open up a door in one of the other—"

"It doesn't matter," he cut in quickly. "Now, if you had the security card that came with this here key, I might be able to help you. But you walkin' in off the street just like that and askin' for private info—that's not something I can help you with."

Irritated, Lex decided to take matters into her own hands. Park dealt with problems one way, and *she* dealt with them another. She dug into the magic purse, pulled out three crisp one-hundred-dollar bills, and dropped them onto the counter. "And how about Benjamin Franklin?" she asked, her tone sweetly sarcastic. "Will you tell him stuff about that key?"

Park held her breath.

The little man eyed the bills, then scooped them up and slipped them into the pocket of his jeans. He walked over to the computer beside the cash register and, holding the key in his left hand, typed in some data. "This here key belongs to a . . . Tallula Kayson, at one-*tree*-nine Round Hill Road in Greenwich, Connect-the-dots." He slid the key back across the counter. "Pleasure doin' business with ya."

"What?" Lex snapped. "Are you sure?"

"Yep. Have a good day."

Park took the key, locked her fingers around Lex's arm, and together they raced out of the store. "Holy shit," Park said. "Tallula's house? Why? What's that all about?"

"I don't get it." Lex scratched her head through the scarf. "But it's obviously an important key. I mean, why pay Brooklyn five hundred bucks to hide it?"

Park was about to pose another theory when her cell rang. She opened it and held it to her ear. "Hey, Madison. What's the scoop?"

"Oh my God!" Madison screeched into the phone. "Park! Where are you guys? You're not going to believe this! Poppy van Lulu was shot in her apartment early this morning. *She's dead!*"

Park stumbled and nearly dropped the phone. She grabbed on to Lex's shoulder for support. *"What?"*

"What happened?" Lex asked.

Madison was sobbing into the phone. "The police are everywhere in front of the Dakota. Reporters everywhere! And listen to this—the doorman apparently gave a description of the person who visited Poppy this morning. There's a statewide manhunt going on for a girl with a star-shaped birthmark on her chin. . . ."

20

The Lost Artist

Heart pounding, tears still wet on her cheeks, Madison raced up the steps of the New York Public Library at Fortieth Street and Fifth Avenue. The beautiful, stately building was teeming with bodies. She shouldered her way through the crowd at a frantic pace, unconcerned with how she looked or who might recognize her. Her mind was focused on one goal.

After leaving the corner of West Seventy-second Street and Central Park West, she had dropped Coco off at home and then ordered Donnie to drive her here. The front of the Dakota had been a mass of police activity.

Madison had watched it briefly from the back of the limo before turning on the small TV beside the minibar. That was when she'd caught the breaking headlines. The murder of Poppy van Lulu was a major media event. Every channel was running stories about the eccentric New York socialite-turned-psychic. The initial clips had showed Poppy walking on the red carpet at last year's Academy Awards ceremony, sitting front row center at Fashion Week, entering Buckingham Palace for tea with the queen. A number of celebrities gave statements as well, speaking highly of Poppy's "intuitive nature and amazing abilities." The producers of *America's Next Top Model* and *American Idol* confirmed to Diane Sawyer on ABC News that Poppy van Lulu had, indeed, accurately predicted the winners of both shows every season—along with the chalky career paths of the runners-up.

The second biggest story of the day was the manhunt for twenty-four-year-old Ina Debrovitch. Her picture was being flashed across the screens, the unique star-shaped birthmark on her chin highlighted as a distinguishing characteristic. Ina had last been seen leaving the Howard Johnson's hotel on East Houston Street. It was confirmed that she matched the description the doorman at the Dakota had given to police.

Details about the murder were few. A detective told reporters that Poppy's apartment had been ransacked and a painting stolen from one of the walls, and *that* was the little nugget of information that had thrown Madison over the edge.

Even now, walking into the library and running up to the second floor, she couldn't stop trembling. She couldn't wrap her mind around the fact that just last night, she, Park, Lex, and Jeremy had been sitting in Poppy's apartment, unaware that Ina Debrovitch had already hatched a brutal plan. But that plan was fractured: as far as Madison was concerned, there *had* to be a link between Ina and the mysterious artist known as L. K. Corcoran. Why else would Ina have broken into Poppy's apartment, killed her, and then stolen the painting?

Madison was certain she already knew important facts; the first was that L. K. Corcoran was dead. Elijah had wanted Poppy to channel "Corky," which meant that he had to have known something about L. K.'s demise. The second was that *To the Penthouse,* the painting in question, was much more valuable than anyone could have thought. Including Poppy van Lulu. Twenty years ago, Poppy had been a young member of the society, and she had probably followed in the footsteps of several other members and acquired the painting from the society for a small fee, wanting to promote an up-and-coming artist. But for whatever reasons, the mysterious L. K. disappeared—or so the society had simply assumed. But Elijah Traymore had known something else, a missing link that had dominated his thoughts to a nearly obsessive degree. You didn't ask a psychic to channel a dead person unless you were totally fixated.

When she reached the second floor, Madison went directly to the information desk. An older, petite woman with ash blond hair looked up and smiled instantly. "Hi," Madison said, quietly but quickly. "I need to see articles from the *New York Times* for the week of October 10, 1988. Preferably arts-related." She opened her purse, found her wallet, and began flipping through it. She found her library card—more valuable than her AmEx, as far as she was concerned—and dropped it onto the desktop.

"Yes, thank you," the librarian replied softly. "Just give me a minute."

Madison watched her disappear into a back room. She crossed her arms over her chest and remained in the same rigid position, with her head facing the empty desk. She didn't want to look around and risk the possibility of making eye contact with someone who might recognize her and then ask for an autograph or picture. She didn't mind being approached by people, it was just that she didn't want to be disturbed when time was running out.

Ina, where are you hiding? she thought now. A chill snaked up her spine and made her shiver in fear. She couldn't help picturing it—the gun, the shot, the blood. She had a heart-wrenching image of Poppy van Lulu's waiflike body being blown back a foot just after the trigger was pulled. Had she been shot in the head, at close range? Madison knew it didn't matter, but she hoped Poppy had escaped a painful end. She had certainly died with a shocked look on her face. Why had she let Ina into her apartment?

"Here you are," the quiet voice said.

Madison broke out of her reverie. She looked down and saw the ream of microfiche the librarian had pulled for her. "Thank you," she replied. She picked it up and carried it over to one of the empty stations. She sat down, put her purse beside her, and slipped the microfiche into action.

The pages of documentation were numerous. She

scanned through the sections of the *New York Times* swiftly, bypassing the stories that had made headlines the week of October 10, 1988, and focused instead on all the smaller arts-and-culture-related articles. The society had long published its acquisitions, and Madison hoped against hope that she would find some biographical information on L. K. Corcoran that she hadn't been able to find in the thin file back at the society's library.

She scanned. She moved the images back and forth. She read the small print and scoured the captions until her eyes ached and her temples throbbed. Back and forth, one page after another, hundreds and hundreds of lines and names and captions.

Come on, she thought restlessly. *Something. I need something.*

She worked diligently, unaware that a full hour had passed, unaware that most of the people who had been sitting in the stations surrounding her had gotten up and left. She didn't care. She would stay here until the lights went out.

She got to the end of the ream, then turned it back to the beginning and started all over again. Back and forth.

There has to be something. L. K. and Ina—what's your little connection?

And then she saw it.

A small boldfaced headline at the very bottom of that week's Sunday Arts section. It was so minuscule, Madison wasn't surprised that she'd missed it the first time around.

**Prestigious Art Society Awards Grants
to Five Emerging Artists.**

Her heart started hammering again. She scanned the script. It ran onto the next page, so she had to break her concentration and refocus it after sliding the film forward. At the bottom of the article was a list of the five artist awardees. Madison started reading the minor blurb on L. K. Corcoran, and the hammering in her chest came to a shocking and painful stop.

. . . To the Penthouse, *an oil landscape of the panoramic Manhattan skyline as seen from the penthouse of a high-rise apartment building, is by first-time artist L. K. "Corky" Corcoran. It will be on display at the society's headquarters this week for members, patrons, and benefactors. L. K. (Lisa Kathleen), 25, is married to William Kayson. They reside in Redding, Connecticut, with their two-year-old daughter, Tallula.* . . .

◇　◇　◇

The two men from the Connecticut State Police Department sat down in the opulently furnished study of Ghost Ranch. Officers Robert Martinson and Eddie Kaller were both fair-skinned and portly, their big bellies straining over their waists. "We know this is a difficult time for you," Martinson said evenly. "But we're here on behalf of the NYPD."

Tallula didn't flinch as she sat on the edge of her chair. She didn't feel much like talking, and she knew anger and disinterest showed on her face. She only hoped the rest of her looked good. She was wearing vintage Halston flares and a silk Armani shirt—a shirt Elijah had bought for her last Christmas. The white Southern-style hat on her head was huge, its edges flopping down to her shoulders. "I understand completely why you guys are here," she answered quietly. "I hope I can help you, but apparently, I'm the moron in all of this."

"What do you mean?" Martinson asked.

"I mean that I didn't know either my boyfriend, Elijah Traymore, or my assistant and friend, Ina Debrovitch." Her voice cracked, and she cleared her throat. "At least I thought Ina was my friend. Now I know they were both liars."

"Okay, that's a start," Martinson said. "You know, obviously, that Ina Debrovitch is wanted for questioning in the murder of Poppy van Lulu, and that's why we're here. We need you to tell us anything and everything about Ina. She has disappeared, and she's armed, and we don't know what her next move is going to be."

Tallula narrowed her eyes at both men. "I can tell you about Ina—or what I thought I knew about her. But as for where she might be—I haven't the foggiest idea. Personally, I think she's on a plane right now, headed for home."

Eddie Kaller flipped open a notepad. "It's been confirmed that Ina bought a plane ticket," he said. "She was planning on boarding an Air India flight to Paris tonight, and then continuing to Romania from there. The airlines have already been notified, and she has to know by now that she's not going to get past security at JFK."

"And?" Tallula said.

"And . . . well . . ." Kaller fidgeted uncomfortably in his chair. "Where else do you think she might be? Did she have any family here in the States? Any friends?"

"She had no one," Tallula answered. "Just like me.

Alone in this big, wide world. All of her family is in Romania, but who knows whether or not that was even true."

"How about any friends?" Martinson asked.

Tallula shook her head. "Nothing like that. You have to understand that she lived a very structured life. She was my assistant, and we spent most of our time here, at Ghost Ranch. Whenever I traveled, she traveled. She didn't have friends. No one I ever knew about, at least. No calls on her cell, no letters or anything like that."

"How long had Ina known Poppy van Lulu?"

"To my knowledge, Ina had never met Poppy van Lulu," Tallula said. "I can't imagine why she went to her—the poor old woman—or why she killed her."

"So you never heard her mention Mrs. van Lulu's name?" Martinson's tone was laced with confusion. "That apartment in Manhattan was ransacked, and a painting is missing. Any thoughts on why Ina might've stolen it?"

"Your guess is as good as mine."

"Did you know Poppy van Lulu?"

"I know *of* her," Tallula said. "I'd never met her personally. If Ina was carrying on some sort of contact with Poppy, it was the secret kind."

"Is Ina a secretive person?"

Again, she gave them a narrow stare. "Obviously she is."

"What did Ina say when she left here?"

"Only that she was sorry, and that leaving was something she had to do. I kept asking her why, but she wouldn't answer me. She cried a lot. We both did." A pause, and Tallula cast her eyes downward. "But that was it. No real discussion about it. Like I said—it came out of nowhere."

Kaller looked at his notepad. "Did you know Ina owned a gun?"

"Of course not," she whispered. "I don't allow weapons in my house."

She stood up and walked over to the window. Stared out at the vast patch of green that spilled into acres of thick woodland. "Look, I know I seem disinterested and probably, frankly, weird to the both of you, but I've been through a lot, so you'll have to excuse me for seeming that way. But let me make this easy for you, okay? Ina Debrovitch had been harboring many secrets from me—and so had Elijah. I never in a million years would have suspected Ina had it in her to be so deceptive, and so evil. But obviously she does have that in her. Killing two people proves it, don't you think?"

Both Martinson and Kaller continued to stare at her silently.

"Up until this morning, I was still clinging to the belief that Coco McKaid was guilty of killing Elijah and that Ina had just been spooked by the whole thing," Tallula continued. "I even thought she was going to come back here and just resume her life with me. But now I know what really happened." She turned away from the window and fixed the two men with a furious gaze. "She and Elijah were obviously having an affair, and the other day, after I left the hotel room, they started fighting. Ina didn't get into the shower like I thought she did. She must've waited for me to leave, and when I did, she confronted Elijah. About what, I don't know. But the fight had obviously been nasty. And she just . . . did it." Tallula gulped down her tears. "She shoved him off that balcony, then raced back into her room, broke her hearing aid to make it look like Elijah had done it, and jumped into the shower."

Martinson and Kaller remained silent and stony.

"And Coco McKaid," Tallula whispered. "She obviously really had been attacked by Elijah—or something like that. The fact that her cell phone was found in the penthouse was just . . . bad luck for her. But very good luck for Ina. Until now, at least." She heaved a sigh, but this time, she allowed the tears to stream down her cheeks and over her chin.

Martinson stood up. "I'm sure the police in New York are exploring that possibility," he said. "But right now, we have to stay focused on finding Ina Debrovitch. Are you *absolutely sure* you don't know where she could be?"

"I don't know!" Tallula cried. She stomped away from the window and leaned against the small secretary's desk pressed up to the wall. "She's probably on her way to Canada, or Mexico! God knows what's going on in her mind right now!"

"Okay, Ms. Kayson. We understand." Officer Kaller nodded politely. "Why don't you sit down now? Is there anyone you can call? Anyone who can be here with you?"

"No, there's not," Tallula sobbed. "Don't you *know*? I'm alone! I have nobody! My whole life is cursed! I'm meant to be alone forever!"

Kaller, a man of about forty, looked at her with a fatherly concern. He was about to put a hand on her shoulder, but Martinson reached out and cut the gesture short.

"You have to find her!" Tallula shrieked. "You have to! She'll probably kill anyone who gets in her way now!"

"We understand, Ms. Kayson," Martinson said soothingly. "Please calm down and let us reassure you that we haven't any doubts that Ina Debrovitch will be apprehended within the next few hours."

"Hours!" Tallula glared at them, her eyes wide and rimmed with wet black mascara. "She could hijack a plane in *hours*. She could kill a bunch of people in *hours*. She could even show up here and kill me in *hours*."

Kaller stepped forward. "Do you have any reason to believe Ina might want to come back here?"

"Of course not," Tallula answered quietly, quickly regaining her composure. She straightened herself and wiped her cheeks again. "She's out there, somewhere. And I just hope you find her."

"We will. And we'll be in touch." Martinson dropped his card onto the table, and then he and Kaller started out of the study and through the rest of the house.

Tallula followed them. She opened the front door and watched as they went down the steps and into the police cruiser. She remained in that rigid position until the cruiser had disappeared behind a tangle of trees and bushes where the long driveway wound to the left. Then she stepped back into the house and closed the door behind her.

She stood for a few moments in the silence.

So much silence, in fact, that she heard the accelerated beating of her heart in her ears. She heard the blood rushing through her like a train. She took several deep breaths, but nothing would work against the angst she was feeling. No amount of booze or pills. No reassurances that everything would be okay. She would have to get through the next few hours on edge, and she would have to keep everything moving the way it had been moving up until this point. Had the cops sensed her true edginess? Her unwillingness to open up to them completely? No. She had succeeded in concealing her truths.

She climbed the stairs to the second floor. In her bedroom, she took off her clothes and changed into her paint-splattered jeans and a wrinkled white shirt. She pulled a thick sweater from one of her drawers and yanked it over her head. Never mind that it was ninety degrees outside and barely seventy in the house. Never mind the humidity either. The sweater was the best kind of flame-retardant material money could buy.

She took a pair of running sneakers from her closet and slipped into them. She tied her hair back into a ponytail.

All was in readiness.

She walked calmly to the window and stared out at the deepening twilight. She watched as a crow shot from the trees, its black wings flapping against the purple visage of the sky. It cawed three times.

Elijah would have called that an eerie omen of what was to come. And now, for the first time, Tallula agreed with him.

21

Hello, Mother

"Her mother," Park said for the hundredth time.

"Her mother," Lex repeated.

Madison looked up from the screen of her cell. "Yeah. Her mother."

They were sitting tensely in the back of the limo as it sped north on the Hutchinson River Parkway, cutting through the posh suburbs of Westchester County. In less than twenty minutes, they would be in Connecticut. At Ghost Ranch.

Madison cast her eyes down at her cell again. She hit Send and brought the phone to her ear. The call went directly to Tallula's voice mail. "Damn," she muttered. "Still nothing."

"Forget it," Lex said. "You've tried Tallula twelve times already—she's obviously not going to turn on her cell. And it doesn't really matter. It's not like she'll turn us away or anything."

"That's not the point." Madison glanced at her sisters. "I'd just like her to *know* that we're coming."

"And that we have a few questions," Park added, her voice taut.

Madison sighed. "Will you drop the suspicion, please? I've already explained it to both of you, and there's nothing to be scared of."

"Explain it to me again," Park said. "It's not clicking together in my mind, and that's a bad sign."

Moving her purse off her lap, Madison repositioned herself on the plush seat so that she was leaning against the door. "Elijah and Ina were having an affair," she began. "Ina got pregnant but that's still a secret, obviously. Somewhere in the very recent past, I think Elijah found out that Tallula's mother had sold a painting to the society twenty years ago, and I think he filled Ina in on that. And together, I think they were planning to blackmail Tallula."

"Blackmail her how?" Lex asked.

"The oldest trick in the book—extortion," Madison replied. "That painting, *To the Penthouse*, wouldn't be worth anything today—but it *is* worth something because it's directly linked to Tallula. She didn't paint it, but that doesn't really matter. She's a celebrity. There's a whole mother-daughter angle the public would love to sink its teeth into—*and* there's only one painting, making it more valuable. Basically, it would create a lot of unwanted publicity for Tallula—her whole story about her parents being strict and her painting in secret would be hard to believe, calling her past into question."

"But you think Tallula knows about *To the Penthouse*," Park stated flatly. "You think she knows her mother painted it."

Madison nodded. "Of course. She probably has the original contract from the society in her mother's papers. That's probably how Elijah found out about it, because I'm sure as hell Tallula never mentioned it to him. She's smarter than that."

"I'm not so sure." Park frowned.

"So basically," Lex chimed in, "that painting proves that her mother was more than just the strict parent Tallula has made her out to be."

"It could," Madison said. "But it's more than just that. It would open up a whole can of worms for Tallula."

"So then, fast-forward to Elijah's murder," Park urged her. "Paint me a picture."

"Very funny." Madison shot her a disapproving look. "I think Elijah and Ina planned to use that painting against Tallula, but then I think Elijah had a change of heart. He wasn't as successful as Tallula, you know. Didn't make as much money. But I think he told Ina he didn't want to go along with the plan, which made her angry, because there she was, pregnant and all, and the guy she'd probably fallen in love with pretty much dumped her. So on Wednesday afternoon, after Tallula left the penthouse suite, Ina and Elijah probably started arguing. *Boom*—she shoves him through the air, then breaks her hearing aid and jumps into the shower. And when Coco's cell is found at the scene, that's totally lucky for Ina."

Park remained silent as she weighed the possibilities. She uncapped a bottle of water and took a sip. "But Ina never really believed she'd get away with it. Because she left Tallula and planned to disappear."

"Right."

"But why not just board a plane and go home and resume your life there?" Park tossed out. "I mean, why would Ina go to all the trouble of killing Poppy and stealing the painting?"

"Because Ina has no money," Madison said. "She's pregnant with Elijah's baby and she's angry and she still needs to extort money from Tallula. So she stole the painting and went into hiding, and she'll use it to her advantage."

"But kill Poppy?" Lex protested. "Why couldn't she just have knocked her out or something? Why resort to murder a second time?"

Park held up her hand. "Technically speaking, Ina killing Elijah the way Madison described it is manslaughter. Poppy's murder was . . . well . . . murder."

"Oh, whatever!" Lex snapped. "You know what I mean."

"Ina went to that length because she was desperate," Madison said easily. "When people are desperate, they'll do anything. We've seen it before, haven't we? Most people commit drastic crimes because they're desperate about something."

"Ain't that the truth," Park agreed.

"Wait," Lex said impatiently. "If Elijah decided he

didn't want any part of the blackmail scheme, then what was the whole thing about him wanting to channel Corky—or Tallula's dead mother, as we know her now?"

"A very good question." Madison settled more deeply into the seat. "Elijah likely came across two sets of paperwork in whatever stuff Tallula keeps on her mom. The first is the contract the society issued to L. K. Corcoran for the acquisition of the painting and the grant she received. But, a few months later, when Poppy van Lulu bought the painting from the society, another set of papers went out to L. K., and *those* papers would have listed Poppy as the buyer. He needed to get into Poppy's apartment somehow, so he used his interest in the occult and his fame to do that. He probably even told her that he didn't believe in that whole experiment at St. Stephen's College. You know, he probably made her believe that he thought she was a real psychic."

"And you think that, in the beginning, when he and Ina first hatched this little journey, Elijah was planning to steal the painting off Poppy's wall?" Park asked, her tone tinged with disbelief.

"I think he just wanted to make sure it was there," Madison answered. "Once he had confirmation that the painting still existed, he knew he'd be able to blackmail Tallula."

Park frowned. "So now Elijah comes off as some sort of good guy? Like, he decided he still loved Tallula and didn't want to completely betray her?"

"You don't think Elijah having an affair with Ina was betraying Tallula enough?" Lex snapped.

"Of course it was," Park replied. "But, if Madison's

theory is right, then it looks like Elijah may have experienced a moment of . . . redemption."

"It would be nice to think that," Madison said quietly, almost romantically. Then her expression flashed into something dangerous. "Especially since men are nothing but complete mindless belly-scraping crap-eaters!"

Park and Lex remained silent, but they exchanged worried glances.

Madison quickly ran a hand over her face. "Sorry, Donnie," she called out. "I didn't mean you. You're the exception."

"That's okay," Donnie said from the driver's seat.

Park leaned over and gave Madison's hand a squeeze. "I just want you to know that I think it's totally brave and awesome the way you're handling this thing with Theo. You know—not letting it eat you up."

"Yeah . . . well . . ." Madison looked away. "I have no choice right now. I have a job to do. *We* have a job to do."

"Speaking of which," Lex said, sitting up straight. "How exactly are we going to explain all this to Tallula? I mean, why do we have to do this in person? Why do we even have to see her?"

"Oh, I guess I didn't completely explain that part." Madison cleared her throat. "I should have said this earlier, but I think Tallula knows where Ina's hiding."

"*What?*" Park screamed.

"Dude, you're totally fried!" Lex said.

But Madison nodded firmly. "Trust me—Tallula knows. Ina already contacted her today, probably right after she stole the painting, and the last thing Tallula wants is more scandal and bad stuff attached to her name. She's probably trying to figure out a way to meet Ina and buy back the painting."

"And then what?" Park asked, her tone overflowing with outrage. "What happens to Ina?"

"Nothing," Madison said. "Ina will take the cash and try to make an exit out of the States."

"And you think Tallula will accept that?" Lex stared at her incredulously. "You think she'd forget that her boyfriend and Poppy were murdered just to get that painting back and avoid a scandal?"

Madison gave a long, weary sigh. "This is a case about desperation, and what people will do when they're desperate. Tallula's not a killer, but right now I think she's in her own desperate place. And *we're* going over there to convince her to give Ina up and face whatever's coming."

"And what if she doesn't want to do it?" Lex asked.

"Then we have no choice but to turn what we know over to the police," Madison stated flatly. "And they'll be the ones to shake Tallula down and flush out Ina from wherever she's hiding."

"Oh, great!" Park slugged the seat. "We do all the work, but the cops get to take down the perp? That sucks!"

"Hey, girls?" Donnie called out over his shoulder. "We're almost there."

They stared out the window at the gathering darkness as the highway curved into a narrow-lane exit. It was all trees and shadows and black sky. Three minutes later, the limo was slowing down and turning into the entrance of Ghost Ranch. Madison opened her window, prepared to ring the buzzer and politely ask Tallula to open the front gates. But there wasn't any need for that. Madison saw even through the darkness that the gates were propped open just enough to allow a car entrance.

"That's totally bizarre," she said, alarmed. "Why on earth would those gates be open? Donnie, drive up to the house."

The limo started moving again.

Madison leaned over the front seat to get a better look at the property. All she saw were skittering shadows as deer fled through the woods.

"You know, that's not really a good sign," Park said. "Those gates should've totally been closed."

Up ahead, the main house of Ghost Ranch came into view—but only hardly. It was completely dark. Not a single light burned in the windows. The limo came to a stop at the end of the gravel drive, and Madison pushed open the door. She, Park, and Lex climbed out into the balmy night. Together, they scanned the blackness, seeing nothing but patches of fissured sky and grass trampled by deer.

Then Madison walked several paces to the far end of the property and saw, in the distance, the little white clapboard house that was Tallula's studio. It was lit up like a ballroom, light blazing from the tall, wide windows. She went back to the limo and looked at Donnie. "Wait here for us," she said. "Tallula must be working in her studio. I'm going to try to convince her to come back to the city with us tonight, so you might have one more of us in the car."

"Okay," Donnie replied, nonplussed.

Madison looked at Park and Lex. "Come on. Let's head over to the studio."

"This ground is totally unsteady," Lex complained as

they walked past the main house. "My heels are wobbling." She clutched the magic purse to her chest and held on to Park's arm for support.

A minute later, they reached the front door of the studio, shoes intact. Madison knocked loudly on the scarred wood paneling. "Tallula!" she called out. "It's me, Madison. Can you open the door?" Her voice echoed like thunder through the wood.

Seconds passed in silence.

Finally, Park reached out, grasped the knob, and turned it.

The door opened.

"That's weird," Madison whispered. "Tallula said she never lets anyone into her studio. I'd figured she kept it locked."

They stepped over the threshold.

The main room was ablaze with lights, illuminating Tallula's work space, with its easels and canvases and palettes. Paint-splattered rags were bunched in the corners. Pieces of plywood were piled against the back wall. The hardwood floors were gleaming; dust caked the big windows.

"Tallula!" Park called. "Hello?" She looked up and saw the small loft space above. Not much more than a rectangular storage area, it was entirely visible from the first floor. And it was empty.

"Tallula!" Lex shouted.

"Where could she be?" Madison asked.

Park followed the floor around a sharp bend just past the easels, coming to a stop where the wall met the staircase. Yet another odd nook. Nothing here but three feet of space and several tubes of paint. She was about to turn around when her eye caught something.

A keyhole in the wall.

Blinking, Park ran her hand over the keyhole. It wasn't until she pressed her face nearly to the wall that she saw the thin indentations in the wood cutting out a perfect square: a door. But no knob. She eyed the keyhole again. *Could it be?* she thought.

"I just don't get it," Madison was saying. "Where could she be?"

Park reached into her purse and retrieved the multi-lock key. She slipped it into the keyhole and turned it.

The lock clicked.

Her heart pounding, Park pulled on the key, making certain it didn't slip out of the hole. Shockingly enough, the door was lightweight, sliding out of the wood wall like a partition. "Madison! Lex! Come here!" When they got to her side, Park yanked the door open completely and found herself staring into blackness.

"What the hell is that?" Lex asked.

Park stepped into the inky void, raking her hands over the nearest wall. She found a switch and flipped it.

The single overhead bulb illuminated a narrow, dingy staircase that led straight down to a cellar.

"That's totally creepy," Lex whispered.

Park ignored the very true statement and began the descent. The wooden stairs creaked beneath her feet. She took them slowly, leading the way down as Madison and Lex followed.

The cellar was a wide, square space with a scarred concrete floor and a low ceiling. It smelled of wet soil, of earth. Though dim, the light cast a glare over the brown paneled walls and what lay pushed neatly against them.

Canvases. No—paintings. Beautiful, colorful abstract paintings held in place by wood slats. One after another, at least twenty or thirty of them. A virtual library of art.

"Oh my God," Madison whispered. "Look at these! They're amazing!" She bent down and ran her finger over the edge of the first one she saw.

"I don't get it," Park said, looking around. She held up the multi-lock key. "This was the big deal? Why would Elijah be hoarding this key? We're standing in a storage cellar."

"An ugly storage cellar," Lex added. She shivered, as though chilled.

"But it's amazing," Park said. "I mean, Tallula's a total workaholic. I've never seen so many paintings."

"Me either. I think—"

"Park? Lex?" Madison's voice was low and strained.

They both whirled around to see her facing the corner of the farthest wall. "What is it?" Park asked.

"We have to get out of here," Madison said nervously. She took a step back, but her eyes were frozen on something.

"What is it?" Lex asked, going to her side.

Madison stared, unblinking, at the small framed canvas on the floor. Her lips were ashen. She held her right arm out and pointed. "That's *To the Penthouse*," she said gravely.

"W-what?" Lex stammered.

Park squatted down slowly and studied the painting before her.

The familiar Manhattan skyline, looking south. The bridges lit up. The skyscrapers twinkling. The East River and Roosevelt Island. The painting was dramatic and beautiful—and very clearly a portrait of New York as seen from up high.

"Madison?" Park said. "Are you sure?"

"I'm sure," Madison replied in a whisper. Her throat was dry. She couldn't tear her eyes from the painting; she stared at it, transfixed by fear. "It's the one that was hanging in Poppy's apartment, and the one I saw in the photos at the society today."

"Excuse me," Lex said. "Hello? Why the hell are we standing here? If that painting is here, then that means—"

"That Ina must be here," Park said, finishing the chilling sentence. She rose to her feet slowly, looking up at the ceiling.

"You think she did anything to Tallula?" Lex cupped a trembling hand over her mouth. "Shit. Come on. We have to get out of here."

"Wait a minute." Madison's voice was firm, her gaze suddenly intrigued. She bent down and picked up the framed painting. She held it up close and studied it.

"Madison! We have to go!" Lex tugged at her arm.

But in that moment, Madison was lost in place, utterly transfixed by what she was seeing. "God's eyes," she whispered.

Park stared at the painting. "What?"

"God's eyes," Madison said again. "Look. You can see them right there, in the sky above the East River. *God's eyes.*"

"So what?" Lex snapped. "Let's just get out of here!"

"No, don't you get it?" Madison held the painting farther out. "Tallula's mother, L. K. Corcoran, painted this twenty years ago. And she used God's eyes—she was the first to use them. And I think the only one to use them." She handed the painting to Park and turned around. Her eyes darted around the cellar, back and forth over the rows of paintings. She bent down and picked one up. Held it out against *To the Penthouse*. "My God," she whispered.

"Madison, what is *wrong* with you?" Lex said harshly.

Madison repeated the process with another painting she'd whisked from the cellar floor. She held it up, examined the unique style, the brushstrokes, the use of color and light and shadowing. "Don't you understand?" she asked them.

"Tallula copied her mother's idea for God's eyes?" Park replied. "Is that what you're saying?"

"No." Madison pointed to the rows of canvases on the floor. "I'm saying that Tallula's been using her mother's paintings all along. The ones she sold. The ones that she claimed she painted when she was a teenager—those aren't Tallula's paintings. They were painted by her mother."

"*What?*" Lex nearly screamed. "Are you freakin' kidding me?"

"Madison, are you sure?" Park asked.

"Of course I'm sure—look at all these paintings and then compare any one of them with *To the Penthouse*," Madison said. "It's different. *To the Penthouse* is an actual landscape—probably the only landscape L. K. Corcoran ever painted." She raked a hand through her hair. "I don't believe it."

Park picked up another canvas. "You mean the paintings Tallula's been selling, the ones she's been passing off as her own—they aren't hers? She didn't paint them?"

"She couldn't have," Madison said. "And *To the Penthouse* proves it. Her mother painted that when Tallula was two. And her mother must've gone on painting throughout her life, but she never sold or exhibited another thing." She pointed to the bottom right corner of *To the Penthouse,* to the small scripted name: *Corky.* Then she picked up one of the other paintings and found the same faint signature.

"No shit," Park whispered. "So then Tallula's . . ."

"Forging work that isn't hers," Lex said.

The full weight of the discovery hit Madison. "And if *she* has *To the Penthouse,* then that means she had to have been in Poppy's apartment. . . ."

Footsteps sounded on the staircase.

Madison and Park dropped the paintings they had been holding. Lex grabbed their arms. They stood frozen in the center of the floor, watching as a shadow spread across the wall and a figure appeared on the landing.

Holding a gun.

22

Smoke and Mirrors

Tallula stepped into the cellar. She looked at each of them, then tightened her grip around the handle of the gun. "Well," she said quietly, "I knew you'd come. And you're right, Madison. You did it. You figured me out."

Madison licked her lips nervously. She was standing slightly in front of Park and Lex, and her body went rigid as they both dug their fingers into her arms. She couldn't think of anything pithy or profound to say. She couldn't figure a way out of the confined space they were standing in—and if there *was* a way out, she had a feeling that gleaming silver gun would stop her.

"You were all so talkative a second ago," Tallula said. "Why the sudden silence?"

"You did a good job of fooling me," Madison blurted out, her anger flaring. "You . . . you did a good job of fooling everyone. Of fooling the whole world."

Tallula smirked. "And what does that tell you about the world?" She took a step toward them. "The world is a shallow place. People want to be fooled."

"But why?" Park asked. "You've painted your own things, haven't you? Why did you take your mother's paintings instead of your own?"

"Because my mother was a brilliant artist," Tallula answered quietly. "You can see that. Everyone saw that. She was much better than I am. Oh, I paint—but not like her. She's . . . the genius."

"Why did she stop?" Madison asked. "I don't understand."

"She painted all her life," Tallula began. "*To the Penthouse* was her first real sale. That brilliant and snooty society had brains, and they awarded her a small grant to continue working. She was twenty-five, she and my father had been married for two years. My mother would have gone on painting and probably had a brilliant career if it hadn't been for my father. He was a beast. He's the reason she stopped pursuing her art. He became a religious fanatic just after she sold *To the Penthouse*. He thought painting was sinful and dirty and evil. Seriously, he did. So my mother—everyone called her Corky—did what a good little wife is supposed to do, and she severed her ties with the society and the art world in general."

"But she obviously continued painting," Lex said,

gesturing her head at the canvases on the floor. "She didn't stop."

"No, she didn't. She couldn't. A true artist can never be taken away from her art." Tallula waved the gun at the paintings. "She worked in secret, while my father was out all day, and that was when she got into abstract art. She hid most of the canvases. I knew about them, and I loved them. I begged her to pursue art, to leave my father. But it was no good. I was only a teenager, and she didn't want to listen."

"You were a teenager when she did most of these paintings," Madison said. "Right? That would make your own story seem true. You claimed that you painted all your works while you were a teen, so even if the paintings that made you famous were ever carbon-dated, the truth wouldn't come out."

A smile spread across Tallula's face. "Such a smart girl you are. But yes, that's exactly right. It's funny—I started doing it as a joke. When I dropped out of college and had my first show, I exhibited eight of my mother's paintings and two of my own. Just to see what would happen. And boy, did shit happen. All those critics and art collectors— they took one look at my mother's paintings and saw the brilliance in them. They didn't even glance at the two that were really mine. And that's when I knew. It happened so fast—overnight, as they say. And I just went along with it. The money. The fame. The power. I just . . . went along with it."

Park leaned into Madison, keeping her eye on the gun. "Until Elijah found out," she said. "That's why you killed him. He was going to expose you, right?"

Tallula sighed. "Oh, Elijah. My cheating, scheming,

incredibly smart boyfriend. He went snooping around, did exactly what you girls just did, and found everything out. This was about a month ago. He—"

"He found the paperwork from the society," Madison cut in. "Right? That was how he knew about *To the Penthouse,* and how Poppy van Lulu had it."

"Yes, that's how. I did a stupid thing and got sentimental when my parents died," Tallula explained. "I kept all my mother's things, including the paperwork from the society. She was always so proud of it. She was a good woman. Weak and feeble, but good. I never threw the documents out, I only filed them away. *I* knew Poppy van Lulu had *To the Penthouse,* but it didn't matter to me, because L. K. Corcoran was nearly impossible to trace."

"Not so impossible," Madison countered. "I found the connection in an old article in the *New York Times.* Anyone can access that article."

"And if none of this had happened, why on earth would anyone other than Poppy van Lulu have even cared to look for it?" Tallula asked. "Everything was fine until Elijah walked in on me one day. I was upstairs, painting over my mother's signature on one of the paintings. He couldn't believe his eyes." She chuckled. "He made the connection pretty quickly. And the past month had been nothing but threats from him. Threats and screaming and fighting. He even stole my spare key, which I believe is in your hand, Park. It was either me or him, girls." A pause. "I didn't want to do it. I'm not a killer that way you're thinking. I just had no other choice."

"But how?" Lex asked. "You were in the elevator, weren't you?"

"Ina and I went back up to the penthouse," Tallula

said matter-of-factly. "She really did go into her room and start showering, and she saw me start to walk out the door. But Elijah and I started fighting. I came back in. He went on and on, accusing me of being a fraud, and I just knew right then and there that it wasn't going to end nicely. I knew I couldn't go on living peacefully now that he knew my little secret. He went out onto the balcony. He kept talking as he stood there, facing me. And then . . ." She glanced away for a moment, and her eyes clouded over. She swallowed hard. "I went up to him and gave him a shove. A hard one."

Madison gasped and covered her mouth with her hand.

"It was horrible," Tallula said flatly. "But it all happened in the space of a minute—the whole fight, his walk onto the balcony, everything. A minute. Maybe five seconds more than that. I only panicked for a split second. Honestly, I did. I can't explain how that happened. And after I pushed him, I ran into Ina's room to make sure she was still in the shower, and I saw her hearing aid on the nightstand, and I just . . . broke it."

Madison shook her head, disgusted. "Why?"

"I knew I needed to make it look like Ina was involved somehow," Tallula replied. "And initially, that's how I thought it would play out. I thought Ina would get the blame for it. After all, she and Elijah had been having an affair."

"So you knew about that," Park whispered.

"Of course I did. I'm not *that* naïve. I was angry at both of them, but I had to play it cool—I didn't want Elijah turning Ina on me too, so I had to pretend I didn't know about the affair. I figured I would throw it onto the table after the cops accused Ina of pushing him. But I didn't have to—your little friend Coco dug her own grave."

"The elevator," Lex said. "You mean to tell us that after all this time, you weren't stuck in that elevator?"

"Of course I was." Tallula smiled thinly. "And *that* was the greatest stroke of luck, my little munchkins. After leaving Ina's room, I dashed out of the suite and jumped right into the elevator. I figured I'd make it down to the lobby and let myself be seen while Elijah was splatting all over the avenue. But an even better thing happened—the elevator got stuck, and I had an instant alibi. I kept ringing the front desk, talking with them, repeating my name so that they'd know I was trapped in there. Elijah hadn't been on the ground more than thirty seconds by the time I made it into that elevator. It was perfect."

Madison swayed, hit by a spell of dizziness.

Park caught her and gave her a shake. "Stay strong," she whispered. "We need you."

"And Poppy?" Lex blurted out. "You killed her too?"

"I knew I had to," Tallula said. "Madison, don't you remember? When you came here to talk to me, you asked me if Elijah had known anyone named Corky. That was when I knew that you'd made some sort of connection. I knew I had to get that painting out of Poppy's hands, so very early this morning, at around three a.m., I drove into Manhattan, parked my car five blocks from the Dakota, and gave Poppy a call from a phone booth on Columbus Avenue. I told her I needed to see her immediately, that Elijah had been haunting me relentlessly. That was all I needed to say. She was such a candy bar. She told me to come right over."

"And you put on a cute disguise and drew a fake

star-shaped birthmark on your chin," Lex said. "Which is what the doorman saw. Thinking it was Ina."

Tallula nodded. "Left the building easily with the painting hidden in my big blazer. Walked to my car, and drove home slowly. I was back here before dawn."

"And what happened to Ina?" Madison's voice broke. "She's the innocent one here, and she's missing."

"Who the hell cares where she is?" Tallula made a sour face. "Probably running for her life like a little dog. The cops will get her soon enough. And when that old doorman sees her, he'll peg her as Poppy's killer. I've done a very good job of leading the police in her direction. Everyone thinks she's guilty. She'll never get away with it."

"But the handprint," Lex said. "Ina put moisturizer on in the elevator on the way up to the penthouse. She was using that oil-based—"

"Oh, yes," Tallula said. "That homemade stretch-mark cream. Raw shea butter and oil and other shit. It's actually very good for dry skin. I put it on in the elevator after her. But until now I wasn't aware of any handprint."

"It doesn't matter," Madison said firmly. She met Tallula's stare. "What do you think you're going to do here? You think you can just kill us and run away? You think you'll disappear into the woods?"

Tallula kept the gun level with her right hand and, with her left, reached into the deep pocket of her heavy, oversized sweater. She pulled out a can of turpentine and popped the lid. "You all just don't know how to mind your own beeswax," she said, walking around, splashing the acrid liquid onto the floor. "I mean, do you realize that if you hadn't poked your noses into this, things would have been completely different?"

Madison stared down at the floor, at the puddles forming everywhere around them. "Please, Tallula," she whispered. "Think about what you're doing."

Splash. Drip. The odor seared the air.

"I *have* thought about it," Tallula said. "I don't want to do it. But I have to. And later, when the smoke clears and people find your bodies, they'll say, 'You see? Those nosy Hamilton triplets got themselves caught in a fire. Boo-hoo.'"

"You'll never get away with this," Park said. "You'll never make it out of the country in time."

"And what about all these paintings?" Lex cried. "You're going to ruin them?"

"There's plenty for me without these," Tallula replied. "I have others." She flung her hand out, and another arc of turpentine sputtered across the floor. She gestured at them with the gun. "Now be pretty little doves and step back against the wall."

Madison shook her head, nearly overcome by the fumes. "Tallula, please—"

"Now!" Tallula shrieked, holding out the gun.

Park and Lex huddled against Madison as they shrank against the wall. "I don't believe this," Park whispered. "She's gonna light us up!"

Tallula walked backward to the staircase landing. She ran to the very top of the stairs, then dropped the can of turpentine onto the floor, where it spilled the rest of its contents.

"Bitch!" Lex shrieked. "Don't!"

Tallula raised the gun, aimed it at the can of turpentine, and fired.

The shot exploded into a wall of flames. The deafening roar seemed to shake the whole cellar, but not before Tallula leaped over the threshold and disappeared.

Madison had been holding on to both Park and Lex. In the sudden, stunning aftermath of the conflagration, she felt herself being thrown to the floor, her hands slipping from theirs. When she looked up and tried to right herself, she saw nothing but bright orange flames and a growing curtain of black smoke.

"Oh my God!" Lex screamed. "Help!"

"Lex! Where are you?" Park yelled.

Madison heard their desperation through the crackling of the flames. She forced herself onto her feet. She drew in breath to scream, but the clots of black smoke caught in her throat, and she began coughing violently. She stumbled and slammed into a wall.

"Madison!"

"Park!"

"Where are you?" Madison managed to choke out. She steadied herself against the wall, trying to peer through the smoke and flames, but the air was thick, burning her eyes. She finally caught a glimpse of movement on her left—the unmistakable sheen of Lex's magic purse bobbing wildly in the air. Madison lurched forward and grabbed on to it.

With a cry of shock, Lex stumbled into her and together they crashed back onto the floor. "Madison!" Lex cried. "Oh my God!"

"I can't breathe!" Madison screamed.

Squirming onto her side, Lex shoved her hand into the purse and pulled out a scarf. "Put it around your nose and mouth!" she said frantically. "Hurry!"

Madison took the scarf in her hands and quickly knotted it around her head, bunching the front of it over her face. Her breaths grew steadier, but the smell and the thickness of the air made her want to gag.

"Park! Where are you!" Lex hoisted herself onto one elbow. She winced as a flame licked her arm. The heat was unbearable. Sweat pooled over her face and neck. She cupped a hand over her eyes and tried to peer through pulsing darkness.

The ring of fire was growing. Bright orange spikes hit the ceiling, quickly eating away the beams.

"Park!" she screamed again.

"Lex! I'm over here!" Park called out from somewhere.

Madison struggled to her feet, pulling Lex up with her. "Come on! Hurry!"

"I can't move!" Lex said. "I can't breathe!"

"Yes you can!" Madison tore the scarf from around her face and held it over Lex's nose and mouth. "Come on!"

But even as Lex got up, the small path before them disappeared as the canvases began to ignite. One by one they fell into the swirling smoke, dozens of colorful images shriveling in the intense heat, wood splintering and popping along the floor.

It sounded as though a freight train were hurtling toward them, rattling the walls.

Madison kicked at the mess on the floor, but her shoe

hit a patch of turpentine, and flames burst around her leg. She recoiled in horror.

Then something flashed through the air—a heavy tarp unfurling, spinning, cutting through the flames and fanning them at the same time.

Park had torn the tarp from one of the easels. Now she was forcing it down onto the floor, stomping on the flames. "Over here!" she yelled. She reached her hands out, grabbed on to Madison and Lex, and yanked them toward her.

A moment later, a tearing sound rumbled from above. A chunk of the ceiling came crashing down, narrowly missing Lex as she slammed into Park. Bits of plaster and wood spun against the fire and into the smoke, blinding them.

The tarp created a path across the floor. They dashed across it just before its edges went up in flames. Then another small explosion rocked the cellar, throwing Madison onto her knees. She slipped and tumbled onto her side. She looked down and saw that the end of her shirt was on fire. She started screaming as searing pain stabbed in her back.

"Roll!" Park screamed, forcing her onto her stomach. "Go! Now!"

"Hurry!" Lex shouted.

Madison gritted her teeth and rolled twice. The stabbing pain in her back intensified, but the flames died away, leaving the end of her shirt charred. Before she could even take a breath, she felt herself being pulled up.

A wave of black smoke assailed them. Gasping and coughing, they formed a human chain, Park leading them across the hot floor, through the tiny pockets where the fire hadn't yet reached. Visibility tunneled to a pinprick. Then a flame knifed the darkness in a flash, illuminating the staircase.

"There!" Park screamed. Feeling as though she were being held underwater, her lungs bursting, she pushed forward until she reached the landing. Half the banister was on fire. She thrust Lex and Madison ahead of her, shoving them up the stairs. Black smoke blurred her vision. She caught sight of Lex kicking through the door.

"Hurry up!" Madison cried, trailing closely behind Lex.

Park rushed forward, but just before she reached the last two steps, the boards beneath her feet started trembling violently. She slammed into the wall. She fell forward, grasping at the landing just as the staircase gave way beneath her feet.

"Park!" Madison screeched, whirling around.

Dangling over the hellfire of the cellar, the flames licking at her legs, Park held on to the edge of the landing. She felt the muscles in her arms constrict. She moved her head from side to side, trying desperately to find a pocket of fresh air. Sweat poured over her eyes. She didn't dare look down. "Madison! Go—get out of here!" she screamed.

"No!" Madison was kneeling above her, a precarious weight on what was left of the landing. She laced her fingers around Park's wrists.

Park strained to lift herself up. Another tearing sound boomed through the smoke, and one of the wooden ceiling beams came hurtling toward her. With all her might, she swung her body to the left.

The beam crashed into the wall above her head, missing her by not much more than an inch.

Instead of shrinking away in fear, Park remembered the stunts she'd performed on the set of *Short Fuse*. She closed her eyes and pretended a camera was rolling somewhere behind her. Even if she fell, it would be okay—there was a harness around her waist and a big mattress-type device beneath her. She wouldn't fall. She could take the risk of using the beam as a stepping stool. The landing wouldn't give way. . . .

With a grunt, she swung her body to the right. Her left foot found the beam, and she pushed up. She felt her sweaty fingers slipping from Madison's grasp, but then the magic purse popped in front of her eyes and Park grabbed on to the firm strap. "Leather," she said, sighing with relief. She hoisted herself up onto the landing. Then she was on her knees. She struggled to her feet and lurched out the door after Madison and Lex.

The first floor of the studio was swirling with smoke.

"This way!" Lex screamed. "To the left!"

They burst out of the front door and into the balmy night air. They tripped and stumbled and went sliding on their stomachs into the grass.

Coughing violently, Park looked up and scanned the darkness. She caught a glimpse of headlights and saw the limo turning around and screeching down the gravel drive.

And in its wake, lying motionless on the ground, was Donnie Halstrom.

No, Park thought, forcing herself to her feet. Renewed by a fresh burst of adrenaline, she charged across the grass and to the front of the house.

"Donnie!" Lex called, running toward him.

Madison, in pain and moving slowly, started sobbing.

Park dropped to her knees beside Donnie. She wrapped her hands around his face just as she saw the red stain spreading across the front of his shirt. "Oh my God!"

"She shot me," he gasped. "The bitch shot me and took the limo!"

"You'll be okay," Lex cried, reaching into the magic purse and grabbing her cell. She flipped it open and punched in 911.

Madison threw a last glance over her shoulder. The white clapboard house was entirely ablaze. She knew it was only a matter of time before the remaining cans of turpentine and aerosol paint heated up. "Guys! Get up! We're too close!" she screamed.

Together, they pulled Donnie to his feet and rushed across the lawn. They dove for safety as the studio exploded and debris rained down around them.

23

Pressed for a Conference

On Saturday afternoon, Madison, Park, and Lex were officially released from Lenox Hill Hospital following twelve hours of observation and a battery of rather disgusting tests. They had been pinched, poked, prodded. They had been x-rayed and photographed. As Lex would later recount to Whoopi Goldberg on *The View*, every nurse in Manhattan had seen her butt and her boobs. In the end, they each had nothing more than minor smoke inhalation and first-degree burns.

But it was impossible to explain something in a small way when dozens of reporters and cameramen were waiting for you. And so, after undergoing extensive hair-and-makeup treatments, Madison, Park, and Lex did exactly what they knew was expected of them: they held a press conference.

It was nearly nine-thirty on Saturday night when they stepped into the lobby of their building. Madison was wearing her favorite leopard-print Triple Threat skirt and white silk shirt. Park had followed her usual boyish fashion tastes and opted for a Triple Threat pinstriped suit with a matching top hat. Lex, unable to leave her inner wild child behind, had selected her highest pair of heels and her tightest black cocktail dress; she had the magic purse slung over her right arm as she cradled Champagne in the crook of her left.

"Oh, wow," Coco said when she saw them. "You all look totally sweet."

"You're not looking so bad there yourself!" Lex commented, noting Coco's choice of outfit: a white fifties-Hollywoodesque dress that wrapped her trim figure and tapered down to her calves; it was complete with white gloves and a matching handbag.

"Diane von Furstenberg sent it to me," Coco explained. "Isn't it amazing? She said the dress was quiet but strong and pure. You know—innocent."

Madison gave her a thumbs-up. "I'd say so."

"Oh, me too," Park agreed. "And now that everyone knows it, you should flaunt it."

Late yesterday afternoon, Manhattan District Attorney Peter Shoren had officially dismissed all charges against Coco McKaid.

"How is it out there?" Lex asked, trying to sneak a peek through the front windows of the building.

"A madhouse," Coco replied. "I had to use the side

349

entrance to get in. I swear, there must be a hundred reporters outside!"

"Now, remember," Park said, popping open her compact and giving her face a quick once-over. "Let's not reveal every last detail of our plight. A lady never tells it all. Keep some mystery in the air."

Just then, Lupe came bounding across the lobby. "Hey," she said. "I just take care of reporters outside who I no like. You wan' me to keep them quiet a little more?" She gave the customary sneer.

"No," Madison said. "I think we're ready."

Lupe disappeared into the small conference room just off the lobby, where she grabbed her knitting needles and turned on a rerun of *The Sopranos*.

Madison led the way around the next corner, and then came to an instant and jarring halt as her eyes met the three boys standing beside the fluffy chintz sofa.

Jeremy Bleu.

Brooklyn DiMarco.

And behind them, separate from the picture but still part of the image, Theo West.

"Talk about a stud train," Coco whispered.

Park immediately walked up to Jeremy, kissed his cheek, and accepted the bouquet of roses he offered her.

Lex, blushing ever so slightly, pranced over to Brooklyn and gave his arm a playful pat.

"Holy Jeez!" he said. "I thought you'd be in bandages! But you look totally hot."

"Thanks," Lex said, snuggling up to him. She gratefully accepted the tote bag he was holding, which included a bottle of champagne, a simple heart-shaped box of chocolates, and a glass jar of his mother's homemade tomato sauce.

Madison didn't quite move. Her heart hammering, she stared past the sofa and locked her eyes on Theo. She had known this moment would come; she had imagined it repeatedly over the past two days and always just assumed that she would bust out crying when she saw him. But that didn't happen. Instead, her stomach closed and her body went tense. She felt overcome by a remarkable sense of anger that quickly corkscrewed into courage.

It was an awkward moment. Madison knew that Park and Lex, Jeremy and Brooklyn and Coco, were watching the scene unfold with bated breath. The air grew thick with anticipation.

Madison cleared her throat and slipped her purse under her arm. "Theo," she said curtly.

"Hi," he answered. He slipped his hands into the pockets of his jeans, clearly uncomfortable. He didn't know whether to approach her or run from her.

Like well-trained guard dogs, Park and Lex assumed their positions exactly three feet in front of Madison. They stood rigidly, shoulders squared, lips set in straight lines, eyes narrowed.

"Why don't you follow me, Theo?" Madison said calmly.

He came forward. But he stopped when he reached Park. He waited for her to move out of his way or, at the very least, to say something. But she stared at him, angry and unblinking, until he stepped to one side and walked around her. That was when he nearly bumped into Lex. She, too, had that soldier-going-into-battle look on her face. Her eyes were gleaming with rage, and as Theo stared at her, waiting for her to move out of his way, he felt a chill pass through him. Lex gave Champagne a little tap; the dog started and launched into a barrage of violent barks aimed directly at Theo.

"Jesus," he whispered, jumping back a foot. Then he sighed and walked around Lex as well, having to press himself uncomfortably against the wall to get past her. He didn't look at Coco, but he heard her wolfish growl.

Madison led the way back around the corner. She didn't dare step into the conference room. Instead, she walked to the elevator banks, stopping just in front of the table adorned with a fresh bouquet of flowers. She turned around and looked at him.

Theo was standing three feet away, his hands still in his pockets. He was sun-kissed and looking customarily gorgeous.

That fact didn't escape Madison. It didn't make her weak in the knees either. "So," she said quietly. "Go ahead. Speak."

"Here?" Theo said, glancing around. "Can't we go someplace and sit down and talk?"

"No." Madison shook her head. "I don't have that much to say to you. At first, when I saw the tabloids, I thought I'd have a whole lot to say. But now that you're standing in front of me, I just . . ."

"You just what?"

She shrugged slowly. "I just don't think I'm going to upset myself over you any more."

"Madison," he said quickly. "Listen—it didn't happen the way the reporters said it did. It wasn't like that."

"Then what was it?"

"I . . . I didn't . . ." He struggled to find the words.

But there aren't any right words when you're admitting that you're a liar, a cheater, and a skank, Madison thought, staring him down.

"I didn't mean to do any of that stuff," he finally said. "It was just a stupid mistake. I don't like that girl at all—I was drunk, I was working really hard with my dad and I—"

"I know what it's like to work hard, Theo," she cut in briskly. "I do it every single day. And you know what? I never had problems staying faithful to you." She swallowed over the lump that had sprouted in her throat.

Theo stared down at the floor.

"I gave you everything," Madison whispered, letting her hurt show. "And I trusted you. Deep down, I really did. That's what totally sucks. I thought you were my friend before you were my boyfriend."

"I am," he said right away, looking up and meeting her eyes. "I'm both of those things."

"No, you're not."

"Madison," he said tensely, reaching out and grabbing her hand. "I love *you.* I'm an idiot for doing what I did, but I know one thing—*you're* the one that matters to me. I wouldn't have come here if that weren't true. We've been through too much together. Please—just hear me out. Because I love you."

Emotions washed over Madison in a hot, spinning wave. She saw it all flash before her—their first kiss, their long walks in Central Park, the future she had always envisioned for them in striking, romantic detail. She held on to those images for several seconds, then let them settle into that strange, powerful place in her heart she didn't quite understand yet: it was a room she would always cherish but not one she would ever return to.

She took a long, final look at Theo West. She gently pulled her hand out of his. "I think you should go now," she said quietly.

Theo looked as though he had been blown back a foot. He smiled nervously, let out an incredulous chuckle . . . and then he caught the look in Madison's eyes, a look he had never seen before. His own eyes glassed over. He turned around and quickly walked away.

Madison waited a good minute before moving. The wave of emotions hit the shore and broke, but the current didn't drag her out to sea. She was okay. And she would be from now on. She knew it. She took a deep breath and strolled back out into the lobby.

Park and Lex were waiting for her just around the corner. "Well?" Park asked, touching her arm. "Are you . . . ?"

"I'm a strong single girl," Madison said, finishing the sentence. "I'm fine."

Lex smiled. "Good. You look really amazing."

"And just think of the fun we'll have in a few weeks," Park added, flicking the edge of her top hat. "When we officially declare war on the West family and take over their little empire."

The thought made Madison smile just a little. "Anyway," she said. "Let's head outside and give the press what they want."

"There's a lot to tell," Park reminded them. "But I'll leave that up to you."

Madison nodded gratefully as she reviewed the facts in her mind.

Donnie Halstrom, shot twice in the abdomen, had been whisked into surgery at Greenwich Hospital late last night. Both bullets had drilled through him completely—and both, thankfully, had missed severing his arteries. At Park's request, he had been transported back to Manhattan via helicopter and was now resting fitfully at Lenox Hill Hospital. It would be a couple of weeks before he returned to his chauffeur duties.

Tallula Kayson's flight from the maelstrom she had created ended with quite a bang: after stealing the Hamilton limo and driving out of Ghost Ranch, she led police on a two-hour high-speed chase through the wooded regions of upstate New York. In the pitch black of night, she crashed the limo and then tried to escape on foot. Bloodhounds found her an hour later crouched in a ditch, bleeding heavily. A full confession followed her arrest. Charged with two counts of murder and four counts of attempted murder, Tallula Kayson would be painting nothing but steel bars for a very long time.

In a stunning—and sad—twist of fate, Ina Debrovitch had also been arrested. Following her depature from the hotel on Houston Street yesterday morning, she had descended into the subways and, using a disguise and a series of twisting routes, made it to the outskirts of John F. Kennedy Airport. There, she'd carried out the last stage of her carefully executed plan and held up a small deli. Armed with a gun and a knapsack and a desperate need for cash, she'd almost succeeded. But an undercover New York City police officer who had been in the deli buying doughnuts wrestled Ina to the floor and handcuffed her. She'd been brought to the nearest precinct declaring her innocence.

"Hey," Coco called out, waving her hand in front of Madison. "You okay?"

Madison nodded. She got between Park and Lex, led the way around the corner, and stared at the front doors.

Cameras flashed. Reporters were already calling out questions.

"Looks like we're going to be front-page news again," Park said with a smirk.

"We're certainly dressed for it." Lex struck a fashionable pose.

Madison smiled happily. "Yeah, that's true. I have a feeling we're going to make headlines for the rest of our lives."

They linked hands and walked outside, where the familiar whirlwind welcomed them.

ACKNOWLEDGMENTS

Talk about having fun: I get to spend large amounts of time dreaming up cool characters and cool stories. I get to do it alongside so many wonderful people, and that's what makes it really fun.

My editor, Krista Marino, continues to surpass herself, lending her smarts and her style to my books. She's never met a sentence she can't improve or an idea she can't strengthen. I am grateful for her guidance and friendship.

My agent, Michael Bourret, still has the difficult job of dealing with me on a daily basis, but he manages to do this with great care and professionalism. A thousand thanks, Mike. You rock.

Beverly Horowitz continues to provide me (and so many wonderful writers!) with a home at Random House Children's Books. I am honored to have a place on the greatest list in the biz. Thank you, Beverly, for being the very best.

May the stars shine brightly on my publicist, Noreen Marchisi, who does a masterful job of getting the word out. She is gracious and enthusiastic and so darned good at what she does!

Angela Carlino once again worked her creative magic and designed a truly beautiful cover. There isn't a design feat that she can't accomplish. I am so thankful for her talent and good cheer.

For getting the Celebutantes series published in various corners of the globe, I thank Jocelyn Lange, Ashley Hinkle, Pam White, and Kim Wrubel. They do, indeed, make a world of difference! Their hard work is greatly appreciated.

Books wouldn't make it to readers if it wasn't for the sales teams and the booksellers, and for all they do, I am incredibly grateful.

My family is, quite simply, the best. I couldn't do any of this without their steadfast support, encouragement, and love. I am blessed to have them.

A native New Yorker, *Antonio Pagliarulo* has a special fondness for the Metropolitan Museum of Art, Bloomingdales SoHo, and penthouse views (looking west). He has friends who are Celebutantes, but he isn't dropping any names . . . yet.

Don't miss Madison,
Park, and Lexington's other
million-dollar mysteries.

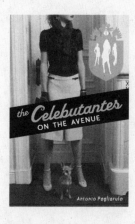